THE SECRET

WINSLOW BROTHERS BOOK THREE

max
monroe

New York Times & USA Today Bestselling Author

AUTHOR'S NOTE

The Secret is a full-length romantic comedy stand-alone novel in the *Winslow Brothers Collection*. This book is full of fun-loving laughs, but it's also got a steam factor level of 5000—or whatever number you consider *smokin' hot, need-to-fan-yourself* high on your scale.

We're talking *loads of spice.*

Now that you know, don't contact the authorities on us because *The Secret* starts a small fire at your place of residence. Anyway, we're pretty sure you can't report a case of arson in your pants.

Also, due to the hilarious and addictive nature of this book's content, the following things are *not* recommended: *reading in public places, reading in bed next to a light-sleeping spouse and/or pet and/or child, reading on a date, reading on your wedding day, reading during the birth of your child, reading while eating and/or drinking, reading at work, reading this book to your boss, and/or reading while operating heavy machinery. Also, if suffering from bladder incontinence due to age/pregnancy/childbirth/etc., we recommend wearing sanitary products and/or reading while sitting directly on a toilet. It might seem like a long list of places not to read, but we assure you, if you do it in the right setting, it'll be worth it.*

Happy Reading!

All our love,

Max & Monroe

DEDICATION

For the people who played capture the flag as a kid—thanks for inspiring the idea for the very *adult* version of that game in this book.

To the makers of chocolate-covered donuts—thank you
for sustaining us.

To desks—thanks for maintaining the weight of our absolutely messy chaos until we finished this book. We promise we'll clean you now.

INTRO

Monday, April 22nd

Ty

I can't believe I'm in Staten Island to seek out a fortune-teller.

Who would have thought that the land of the former world's biggest dump is also the home to long-sought-after answers?

Gravel crunches beneath the tires of my Range Rover, and I pull to a stop in front of an old, worn-out brick building.

I've officially left my normal haven of skyscrapers and busy sidewalks and entered the place that birthed famous mobsters and Angelina from *Jersey Shore.*

Personally, I have no doubts the charlatan I'm here to find fits right in.

The early afternoon sun pushes through my windshield, and I have to squint as I cut the engine and look up at the shabby pile of bricks that took me nearly three months to find.

Two familiar words glow in red above the front door—***Fortune Teller.***

I've seen this sign before. About fourteen years ago, to be exact. Even with so much time passed, the feeling in my gut is eerily similar. Although, its location was far more convenient back then—smack-dab in the center of New York City and on the same street as the strip club where we took my eldest brother Remy to celebrate his upcoming—and ill-fated—nuptials.

"This is fucking nuts," I mutter to myself one last time as I hop out of the driver's side door. I shut it behind me and beep the locks, my boots crunching audibly in the rough parking lot, but before I can head toward the entrance, my phone vibrates with an incoming text message. It only takes a quick glance to see it's in a group chat with my siblings.

Winnie: Dinner is at 7:30 p.m. You all better not be late tonight, or I'll start donating my time to cooking for a family who deserves it.

Winnie is the baby of our Winslow crew. Though, she's not exactly a baby anymore. She's married, a successful physician for the famous professional football team the New York Mavericks, and the mother to my one and only niece, Lexi.

Win isn't the type to take any bullshit, and that probably comes from years of dealing with four rowdy older brothers and working in an environment with men who are all twice her size.

Flynn: Got it.

Remy: I'll be there.

Another text populates on the screen, and I'm not surprised by the sender or the response.

Jude: Tonight? What's tonight?

Jude is the youngest out of Remy, Flynn, and me. Between the two of us, we have the laid-back, jokester role covered. Flynn is much more serious and straight to the point. And Remy is a healthy mix of everyone, along with the kind of dramatic past they write books about.

Winnie: JUDE.

Jude: Relax, Win. Sophie and I will be there.

As you can see, Jude is no longer a single bachelor like the rest of us Winslow men. He's an "us." And it's *fucking weird.* Trust me, if you knew Jude before Sophie, the radical change would make your head explode too.

About a year ago, my soon-to-be sister-in-law Sophie ensnared him in her web, and the bastard has been a goner ever since. My baby brother went from the world's biggest player to committed fiancé in the span of a year. Not to mention, in less than six weeks, he'll officially be a *husband.* And that, right there, is a big part of the reason why I've spent the last several months tracking down a fortune-teller by the name of Cleo.

Sounds crazy, I know, but trust me, I haven't even scratched the surface of it yet.

Nearly a decade and a half ago, when we were just twentysomething assholes looking for a good time, this woman predicted our fortunes on the night of Remy's bachelor party. It was all supposed to be a joke. Just something ridiculous to do to make Rem's big night memorable.

But now, it's starting to feel as if the joke was on you.

A week after we let some stranger predict our futures? The first of Cleo's prophecies rang true. Rem was left at the altar with nothing but a canceled wedding and his heart ripped out of his chest.

Thirteen years after that? Jude went from being a frequent diner at the all-you-can-eat pussy buffet to a fucking monk who wants to commit himself to one woman for the rest of his life.

I didn't realize the magnitude of that until a few weeks ago, when we were in Vegas for Jude's bachelor party, and he drunkenly revealed to me just how right Miss Cleo was—*she'd predicted a bet would change his life, and that's exactly how he met Sophie.*

Needless to say, my head's been upside down and tucked inside my ass ever since.

And now, you feel like the only way to un-fuck your head is to go straight to the source…

I inhale a deep breath, shove my phone into my back pocket, and close the distance between me and the tattered building. The instant I step over the threshold, a large bell rings above the door, and I'm hit with the smell of dust and candles and incense. The same dark burgundy curtains adorned with gold ropes from almost a decade and a half ago highlight the room, and clichéd knickknacks I saw only once before through bachelor-party-buzzed eyes fill my vision.

It's as if I've been teleported back in time.

What the fuck am I doing? I shouldn't have come here.

I start to turn back for the door, hell-bent on scrubbing Staten Island from my memory entirely, but four words stop me in my tracks.

"I've been expecting you."

That voice. Holy shit, I remember that voice.

I look around the room with wide eyes that would rival Bugs Bunny when he spots Wile E. Coyote, looking for Cleo and her frighteningly green gaze, but she's nowhere in sight.

"Take a seat, Ty." The raspy female voice fills my ears again, and this time, I can pinpoint its location. Behind a set of velvet curtains that lead toward a mysterious back room, the woman I'm looking for taunts my stomach into tying itself in a few more knots.

After several long moments, Cleo, the infamous fortune-teller, appears. Her distinct green eyes meet mine immediately and without timidity, and I swear on everything, my balls just about jump inside my stomach.

Fuck, this is weird.

"Don't worry, I won't bite," she teases, and it's disconcerting how this woman hasn't aged a day since I last saw her. Beneath a velvet hood, the same mane of thick black hair hangs past her shoulders. Her eyes feel too wise. And her mouth showcases the familiar dark lipstick that my twenty-year-old self remembers. This isn't the work of Botox or fillers or any of that shit. This is something biological—something creepy as fuck.

She gestures with her hand toward two chairs that sit in front of a table with a silk tablecloth, and for as much as I came here of my own volition, I still hesitate to follow her command.

"Oh, my favorite professor." A confident smile that just barely lifts the corners of her lips accompanies her words. "I think you and I both know you didn't come all this way to not ask me all those questions that are floating around inside that handsome head of yours."

It's unnerving as hell that this woman knows my name. *Remembers* my name. And somehow holds the knowledge of my profession.

But she's right. I didn't drive over an hour to Staten Island just to be a chickenshit.

On a sigh, I take a seat across from her. The room is quiet besides some kind of fortune-teller-themed soundtrack of wind chimes, and the floor almost seems as though it's vibrating. That might be because my knee is bouncing much, *much* more than normal, but I don't fucking know. All this feels supernatural.

Whenever Crazy Cleo holds eye contact, I can't help but avert my gaze. I don't know what it is about this woman, but I feel like she can see too much—like she's inside my head.

"It's okay." She smiles again. "Your internal thoughts are sacred, my child. I don't judge what I hear, and I only listen when I feel it's necessary to help you."

I shut my eyes for a brief moment, mentally questioning how I managed to get myself here.

Easy, bro. You paid over ten dollars in tolls. Time to man up.

I meet Cleo's eyes again. Her hands now rest gently on the table.

"You don't disappoint, my dear," she says with a little grin. "I knew you'd only get better with age."

Is she flirting with me?

If that's the case, I can't blame her. I *am* one good-looking motherfucker, but it's a little strange, considering all the circumstances.

"How are you and your brothers?"

"Well, they haven't aged as well as me, but you and I both know, this face right here sets the bar pretty high."

A soft laugh escapes her throat. "Your confidence is something to be admired, my dear."

It's also probably a coping mechanism, but hey, no need to get into the details of that.

Her eyes glow with wisdom, and her mouth crests up in a knowing smile. "Remington, Flynn, and Jude are lucky to have someone as invested in their lives as you are."

Fuck me. How does she remember all this shit? Does she keep note cards and pictures of past clients? Does she have some kind of photographic memory? Or maybe she's secretly in the CIA and is currently wearing an earpiece that has intel streaming inside her ear?

Bro, the odds of this woman being CIA are about as likely as you following in Jude's footsteps and wanting to commit to one woman for the rest of your life.

"Go on," she encourages. "Ask away."

"How?" I eventually blurt out. "How did you know about...?" But I stop before I give her too much information.

"My connection to the cosmos allows me to see things that no one else can see."

Connection to the cosmos? What a crap answer. Not only that, but it's also vague as fuck. If her connections to the cosmos are so great, then she should know *who* I'm asking about and *why* I'm asking and dive right into that shit.

Cleo gestures for me to give her my hand, and I falter for a moment before eventually giving in to the madness. When in Rome and all that bullshit, you know? I shouldn't have come here if I'm not going to commit to doing whatever's necessary.

Her long, red-tipped fingers wrap around my palm, and she stares down at where we're connected and then closes her eyes for ten seconds. I wait impatiently for her to open them again, staring a hole right through her face until she does.

She smirks as soon as she sees the intensity of my stare. "Jude's fate has proved to bring him great happiness, wouldn't you agree?"

Her question is an earthquake, shaking the shit out of my equilibrium, and all I can do is nod.

"I know you think I was only partially right about Remy, but my dear, you left before I finished giving his fortune," she continues. "His time will come. An unexpected second chance will enter into his life and change everything."

"You realize it's been fourteen years, right? I mean, fate sure seems to be taking her sweet-ass time to make all your kooky predictions come true." I laugh at the absurdity of it all. "Have you ever thought that you're just not very good at your job?"

"Fate works on her own timeline." She runs her index finger over the creases etched in my palm. "You four men are stubborn mules when it comes to finding love. You fight it. Refuse it. Ignore it. Over *and over* again. But it's understandable, with how you've seen things go with your father and Remington."

My father? Ha. That asshole hasn't been in the picture since we were kids. He's a nonexistent factor—and as far from a dad as you can get.

"I know you're here because, deep down, you're worried. Maybe even a little scared."

I roll my eyes. "I'm not scared."

Cleo grins. "Of course you're not scared. Ty is never scared of anything, right? He's the adventure-seeker, the lover of action, and the most fun any woman can have."

Finally, she's saying shit that makes sense.

"That sounds like me."

"Don't worry, you still have time, my child."

Time? I question silently to myself. *Time for what exactly?*

I'm thirty-nine years old, and I fucking love my life. I love the way I live my life, and I love my job as a professor at NYU. I don't need time for anything besides more of my kind of fun.

"You still have time to keep living in your comfort zone," she expands. "Time to avoid commitment. Time to keep having the kind of fun you think you want."

"I *think* I want?" I narrow my eyes. "Cleo, doll, I have the fun *I want*. Period. End of story."

"Of course you do," she responds, her voice placating. "And you can relax into the truth of knowing you still have time to play your games. You still have time to keep finding brief companionship with women who catch your eye. You still have time to leave a trail of broken hearts in the wake of your fun."

"A trail of broken hearts? Let's not be so dramatic. These women know the deal."

Sure, I have strong tendencies to date around and to stick with one woman for only a short amount of time, but that's just who I am. And I sure as hell am not purposely leaving a trail of broken hearts behind me. Considering I rarely date one woman for more than a few weeks, the mere idea of that is ridiculous. I mean, no one can fall in love that quickly.

Trail of broken hearts, my ass.

"One day, you'll see the truth," Cleo states. "But you can hold steadfast in the knowledge that there's still time before fate decides she's ready for you."

I snort. "What's that supposed to mean?"

"You're not next. Fate is too busy with someone else at the moment."

Her words make me burst into laughter.

"Yeah, okay," I say and tug my hand out of her grasp. "Whatever you say."

"Fate will find you soon enough. But right now, there's someone else whose life is changing as we speak."

I quirk a challenging brow, and Cleo's steady eyes never waver from mine.

"You'll know what I mean soon enough. Just give it time, my dear."

"Give it time? Like I said, it's already been fourteen years, Cleo. And frankly, the only one you sort of got right was Jude."

"All of Jude's predictions came true. It's the whole reason you came here. Because it scared you to think that I held all the answers."

"Yeah, well, you say give it time, and I say it's already been a lot of fucking time."

"Well, my handsome professor, you're about to see fate work her magic with another one of your brothers. And then, she'll move to you."

"Is that right?" I question with narrowed eyes. "And what exactly is fate going to do with me? Maybe you should give me a reminder?"

Truthfully, I don't need a reminder, but there's no way this woman even remembers what she said to me all those years ago.

Her responding smile is unsettling. "There's a kinship between you and Eve that's unmistakable. The forbidden fruit will prove irresistible for you, and I'm afraid you'll take more than a bite. The secret of this indiscretion will bring turmoil and pain. The journey will be rife with unrest, but the end will bring you great joy and relief."

Word for word, she tells me *exactly* what she told me on the night of Rem's bachelor party, and it closes my throat, robbing me of a comeback.

I wish I could say my contributions to the MTA were worth it. But I'll be fucked if I'm not more messed up now than I was when I decided to come here.

I glance at my watch and then back up at Miss Cleo, whose smile is the kind that makes you want to shove your middle finger in someone's face.

I'm not quick enough, though, and instead, she gifts me with her own version of saying those words to me.

"Go, my child. You don't want to be late to family dinner."

Son of a bitch. I have to get out of here.

I jump up quickly and head for the entrance, not bothering with pleasantries for the woman of my nightmares. I shove out the door and fast-walk to my Range Rover, climb inside, and press the button to secure the locks immediately.

It's a valiant effort, to run away from everything she said to me in there. *Only problem is, locking that shit isn't going to protect you from what's already inside.*

"Ty! Earth to Ty!" my mom calls, trying to grab my attention from across the island in the center of Wes and Winnie's kitchen. When I finally look up, I'm met with a motherly glare so familiar, it's nostalgic.

"What?"

She rolls her eyes. "Would you make yourself useful and get the door?"

"I know you've got a lot on your plate, standing there drinking a beer and all," Winnie chimes in with sarcasm in her voice. "But as you can see, some of us are actually getting dinner ready."

I look around her kitchen to find that, besides my mom, Aunt Paula, Winnie, and Jude's fiancée Sophie, I'm the only other person in the room. Everyone else—Jude, Remy, Uncle Brad, Winnie's husband Wes, and my niece Lexi—is outside on the back terrace.

"You okay?" Sophie asks, her lips cresting up into a soft smile as she searches my eyes. She seems serious enough, but I can barely find my tongue inside my mouth, let alone use it.

Truthfully, I can't even make sense of the concept of time. It was daylight when I went in to see Crazy Cleo and dark when I left, and the time I remember spending inside doesn't add up. It's as if I got momentarily lost in another dimension.

So, no, I'm not okay, but I refuse to tell anyone in my family about my little day-trip. No doubt, my brothers would have a field day with that information. Plus, the four of us have an unspoken rule to never talk about the green-eyed witch-teller ever again.

Although Jude didn't exactly live by the rule, did he? The bastard. If it weren't for him being all boozed up in Vegas and confiding in me like we were two chicks on Gossip Girl, *I wouldn't even have been busy with this crap.*

When I realize Sophie is still looking at me curiously, more so now that I've detoured to a fucked-up filmstrip of memories in my head, I quickly brush off her question.

"I'm always good, Soph," I say with a half smile, hopping off the barstool to answer the door at the same time. At this point, whoever it is has probably started to wonder if they're ever going to be let inside.

I can't help it, though. Nothing about me seems to be functioning as normal—except my ears. Judging by how clearly I can hear the conversation that continues in the kitchen following my absence, I'd say they're working just fine.

"Is it just me, or is Ty acting really weird?" Winnie whispers as I walk down the hallway to the front foyer.

"He does seem out of sorts," Sophie agrees quietly.

"And he didn't even bring some random woman to dinner," Winnie adds. "He came alone. He *never* comes alone."

Her words make me pause in the middle of the hall and change gears from overhearing by happenstance to eavesdropping with purpose.

"I'm sure he's fine."

"*Mom,*" Winnie continues to blather. "Think back to all of our family dinners and get-togethers over the past ten freaking years. Can you think of a single time when Ty didn't have some random chick on his arm?"

"Winnie, stop it," our mother chastises. "I'm sure he's fine."

"Dude, what are you doing?" Remy asks from right next to me, startling me so much with his presence that my back bumps into the hallway wall. He doesn't dally, instead bypassing me completely and heading straight for the door I was supposed to answer.

I sigh. Lord knows that bastard will tell all the Winslow women about this, and I'll have to deal with more whispered worry. *Great.* With a shake of my head, I start walking again, just as Remy opens the door.

"Uh, hey… Can I help you?" Rem asks, and I step up behind him just as the door swings the rest of the way open in the wind.

Standing at the threshold is a beautiful woman with a wild mane of light-brown curls. Her gaze moves from Rem to me as I study her, and then our eyes meet. And I don't miss the instant recognition that appears on her pretty face.

Shit. Did I invite her here tonight? And if I did, when the fuck did I secure this date? I know I haven't been on my A game mentally, but this is—

"Oh. She's with you." Rem glances back at me. "I should have fucking known."

Without another word or even a hello, my eldest brother retreats back down the hallway, smacking me on the shoulder as he goes.

I look back at the gorgeous woman on the threshold, studying her closer, and eventually, I decide to just go with it. I mean, it's pretty damn obvious she knows who I am. It's written all over her face. And there's something about her that seems familiar to me too. Fuck it. "Well, you certainly *are* my type. Did I ask you to come here tonight?"

Dude. Way to make her feel awkward.

She mutters something I can't hear or understand, nerves obviously getting the better of her, and I know I have to right the situation and try to make her feel less like a woman who was invited to dinner by a man who doesn't remember and more like a woman who came to family dinner with a man she barely knows. I'm not sure either of those is a great option, but the latter has to be better than the first. "Come on. Let's head to the kitchen and get a drink. We're about to start dinner soon."

Upon my return to the kitchen, I note that everyone is back in the house, chatting and laughing around the center island.

"Well, dang!" Jude shouts with a slap to the quartz counter, wrapping his arm around Sophie. "I thought that was gonna be Flynn at the door. For once, I can actually attend family dinner because we're not working around Winnie's schedule and doing it on nights I'm at work. I'm ready to enjoy this feast!"

"Stop whining, Jude," Sophie retorts with a wry grin. "You know Flynn will be here any minute. He's reliable."

That makes me laugh. "Unlike the rest of us, right, Sophie?"

She shrugs. "You said it. Not me."

Everyone in my family moves their eyes toward me and the woman I've nearly forgotten about again who is standing beside me. They move their gazes in other directions quickly, just like they always do, and I take a minute to evaluate how their prolonged indifference to all my dates makes me feel.

I come to a conclusion pretty easily. If I had any moral high ground to stand on, I should be offended. But I'm the man who completely forgot he invited her to dinner, so…yeah…it's safe to say I have no room to feel snubbed from my place in the center of this metaphorical crater.

Oh well.

A few minutes later, my mom announces we're ready to eat, and I gently guide my date to the table. We've not spoken in all that time, and it occurs to me that I don't know even the first thing about her.

You think you should try to figure out her name, you douchebag, and stop being such a dick?

I pull out her chair, helping her into the seat beside mine, and try to find an opening to figure out who the hell she is, but my brother Flynn's arrival pulls my attention toward the other end of the room. Everyone greets him as he steps inside the dining room, and my mind struggles to remind me of the priority at hand—*get it together, man, and try to figure out your date's name.*

I attempt to meet her eyes, but she's too busy looking at something else.

And it only takes one tap to my shoulder to realize she was watching Flynn walk toward us.

"You mind moving so I can sit beside my wife?" he says without preamble, and I blink what must be one thousand times.

Did he just say wife? As in, bless the bride, lady in white, till death do us part, husband and fucking wife? I can be kind of a scumbag, but how the hell did I manage this one?

Flynn is going to kill me.

"I'm sorry…" Winnie speaks up over the audible silence that has taken over the whole room. "Did you just say *wife?*"

It's only then that it registers that I'm not the only one surprised, and the fact that I'm accidentally trying to date her is the least of my concerns. *When in the fuck did Flynn get married?*

I turn to look at the woman in question again. Her cheeks are now flushed, and her mouth is parted in shock. "You're here with *Flynn?*" I ask, trying to make sense of a shred of something.

"I-I… Well, I tried to…um…say something, but—" Her voice shakes, and Flynn puts a steady hand to her shoulder and meets my confused eyes.

"Ty, it's your own fault that the whole family, including *you*, automatically assumes any new woman at family dinner is here with you."

"That's because he's a manwhore."

"Jude!" our mom snaps. "Language! There are little ears at the table!"

More commotion fills the room, more chatter and laughter from my family, but my brain is too busy trying to understand the fact that Flynn has a wife.

My heart pounds erratically inside my chest, and my mind races with Cleo's stupid words. *"Well, my handsome professor, you're about to see fate work her magic with another one of your brothers. And then, she'll move to you."*

Sweet mother of mercy, I thought those fuckers would have the courtesy to haunt me for a year or two. You know, burrow inside my brain like little parasites. But proving themselves true *tonight?* Without even giving me time to take a breath? That's pure evil.

"You know you've got problems when you don't even know which woman at the family function is yours." My uncle Brad's voice breaks through the ringing inside my ears. "Now, Ty, please remember, this woman right here is your aunt Paula. My wife."

Frankly, I don't even know what I respond to that. It's as if my mouth is currently on autopilot while my brain tries to make sense of the bomb Flynn just dropped in my sister's dining room.

The room erupts into obnoxious laughter, most likely on my account, but I couldn't care less. I mean, Flynn is *married* and Cleo's not a sham?

If there was one Winslow brother whom I was certain Cleo's predictions wouldn't come true for, it was Flynn, more so than even myself. He's a broody, reserved bastard who never dates, never brings women around, and acts completely fine with being alone.

If he's not safe, what does that mean for Remy?

And more importantly, *me?*

ONE

Nearly nine months later…

Friday, January 4th

Rachel

A New York winter night is the kind of *cold* that makes men's balls disappear and women's nipples freeze right off. It's as if the massive concrete structures and pavement have given up all their heat in some sort of ritual sacrifice, leaving them—and us—with only ice.

My knees shiver and shake as we head down the sidewalk toward a nightclub with velvet ropes and a long line of people waiting outside, surely turning any piece of sexiness in my walk into the likes of a newborn filly.

"Yep." My sister, Lydia, flashes a giddy grin at me. "It's going to be a good night," she says, brushing her long brown hair over her shoulder. "I can feel it in my bones."

"That's interesting. Because the only thing I can feel in my bones is the expansion of ice."

Lydia snorts in a way that's contagious and manages to put a smile on my lips.

Halfway toward our destination, my phone vibrates inside my purse, and I shimmy the zipper to check the screen like the psychopathic technology addict I am. I'd like to say I could live without my phone—with only the books and brilliance of the olden days—but my entire adult skill set is a little too wrapped up in Google searches.

Dad: Despite it being last minute, I managed to get a dorm secured for you on campus.

I sigh, knowing the *last minute* remark is meant to be a dig at my time management and planning. Still, tonight's meant to be fun, unclouded by drama with my dad, so I try to respond in a pleasant manner.

Me: Dad, I appreciate that, but as I already told you, I have an apartment.

Dad: I think it would be easier for you to focus on your studies if you were on campus. The commute alone would save you a lot of time.

Always pushing. Always prodding. No admission that I've told him what's going on and it's *he* who has neglected to listen. That's my father, all right. At least, that's how he's been since I was old enough to communicate.

"Who are you texting with?" Lydia asks, and I pointedly shove my phone back into my purse.

"No one of importance."

Harsh, sure. But for tonight, at least, true. Our history is complicated—in a way that could never come close to getting solved with one text exchange. Basically, figuring out how to come to a truce with my father will require an extensive examination of all my life's choices, including, but not limited to, how I ended up back here, exactly where he wants me.

And that's not what tonight is about. It's about having a good time with my sister Lydia and her wife Lou.

After eight long years of being on the West Coast, I am officially back in New York. The city where I grew up. The city that holds all the memories of my youth. The one place that still has the power to make me think of my mother.

Somehow, I feel lost and found at the same time.

The three of us walk arm in arm past the long line of people behind the velvet rope, through a cloud of cigarette smoke and visible puffs of air that only come from your breath when it's cold enough to be considered a crime, and straight toward the front of the new nightclub that's apparently all the rage in this city.

A bouncer in a black puffer jacket and a beanie stands at the front of Orchid's entrance, holding a clipboard. He notes our arrival with a quirk of his brow, and Lydia is quick to hold up her gold-embossed invitation that led us here.

He offers one curt nod and unclips the velvet rope standing between us and the entrance.

My sister's smile consumes her whole face. "Is it just me, or is this the perfect way to celebrate the fact that Rachel is finally back home?"

I'll be honest, my one and only older sister is the best. There's something about her that always makes me feel good. She's the glass half-full, positive, happy person who brightens everything and everyone around her.

"I agree, hun," my sister-in-law Lou responds and turns her head to grin at me. "I'm really glad you're back in New York, Rae."

"You two act like I never came home to visit," I retort on a laugh. "I was here nearly every Thanksgiving and Christmas. Even managed several summer trips, too."

"Yeah, but occasional trips are not the same as you *living* here," Lydia interjects as the three of us walk past the bouncer.

Lou holds open the door for Lydia and me, scooting us inside and into the kind of warmth that makes my body shiver from the abrupt shift from the frigid outside temperature.

"I can't deny," I say with a knowing quirk of my brow as Lou steps inside and the door falls closed behind her, "if there's one thing that's better about LA, it's the weather. There's no snow. No cold winter nights that make me feel like my boobs are about to vibrate right off my body."

Lou laughs. Lydia rolls her eyes and pointedly glances at my attire.

"I told you heels and a dress weren't a good idea."

"In my defense, I'm wearing a jacket." I glance down at my shiny black stilettos, bare legs, electric-blue shift dress, and cream fake-fur shrug. "And you told me to dress for a nightclub. This is certified nightclub attire. Saying a dress and heels aren't a good idea while also saying nightclub attire creates a glitch in the matrix."

"That is a joke of a jacket, and you know it. Fifteen degrees doesn't care about the matrix or Keanu Reeves. Fifteen degrees cares about no one."

I laugh. "I'm not talking about *The Matrix* with Keanu."

"As far as I'm concerned, there is no matrix without Keanu."

I shake my head with a defeated grin. "Next time, I'll make sure I have a parka on hand for the nightlife tundra that is New York in the winter. Maybe I can dress it up with some gold hoops or something."

"Stop being so grouchy." Lydia laughs and nudges me playfully with her shoulder. "And don't even try to act like you're not happy to finally be back home. I can see it in your eyes, Rae."

"I would've been happier to stay in tonight and, you know, be all warm and cozy in my new apartment while I unpack all the boxes that have swallowed my living room."

Despite what my father so obviously wants, all thanks to Lydia and Lou, my new home is located on top of their bakery, Little Rose Bakeshop. A quaint one-bedroom apartment in Nolita that showcases the kinds of hardwood floors and big windows New York landlords would charge a fortune to rent.

But not Lydia and Lou. They insist the only rent I pay comes in the form of helping out at their bakery part time. And even that comes with the knowledge that my bakery hours will be second priority to my grad school classes at NYU.

"Does LA only allow boring types? Just to make the celebrities feel more interesting or something?" Lydia teases. "You've never been the type of girl who passes up a night out at a VIP club to unpack some stupid boxes."

She's not wrong. I've *always* put fun above everything else, *especially respon-sibilities*. But this year, I'm making a concerted effort to get my shit together. I'm twenty-six, and now that I've taken four years off after graduating with my bachelor's degree from Stanford, it's time for me to grow up a little and focus on my future and my career.

You can only fly by the seat of your impulsive pants for so long, you know?

And while I would've loved to stay on the West Coast and finish my master's degree at Stanford, the fact that my dad's position as head of the English Department at NYU comes with free tuition for his daughter was a little too good of a reality to deny.

No one wants to be stuck under the crushing weight of student loan debt. Although, no one wants to be stuck under their pushy father's thumb either.

Professor Nathaniel Rose's overbearing tendencies and high expectations are heavy as hell.

Don't go there, Rachel.

"So…why are we here again?" I question, forcing myself to focus on the present. I hand my coat to the check station from which Lou's already taken a number for us, pointing my thawing body in the direction of the massive club.

Lydia and Lou turn, arms linked in front of me, but Lydia looks back over her shoulder to talk as she walks. It's hard to hear her over the growing noise from inside, but I can still make out everything she says…I think.

"Because our friend Sophie invited us. It's a big night for her and her hus-band Jude. The official launch party for The Secret Club."

"And who is Sophie, and what is The Secret Club?"

"Sophie is an event planner…" Her voice fades out as she turns to glance at where she's going and then back to me. "…known for years," Lydia ex-plains. "One of our favorite clients."

"And The Secret Club is a new brand that's about to be all the rage for couples," Lou adds, twisting back to smile at me briefly.

Music vibrates the floor, making my feet jostle a little in my stilettos, and I follow my sister and her wife as we make our way into the club's official entrance.

The place is packed to the gills. People are pretty much *everywhere*—on the dance floor at the center of the room where a DJ booth holds court above them, at the large bar in the front begging for drinks, and all around the dimly lit edges where private booths and tables are positioned.

LA has its share of nightclubs, but nothing compares to what New York brings to the table.

The mere thought makes me smile. No matter how many years I resided on the West Coast, I'll always be a New York girl at heart. A little rough around the edges and rebellious in a way that isn't always in my best interest, this city is in my bones. LA is too…uptight. And pretentious. At least, the part of it I knew.

It doesn't take long before we've grabbed some drinks from the bar and Lydia and Lou spot a few friendly faces in the form of a hipster-looking guy with a thick beard and wire-rimmed glasses and a petite woman with a jet-black bob.

As they catch up, I politely remove myself from their conversation about an art gallery in SoHo and walk over to see what all the fuss is about at the main table that's drawn an impressive crowd.

It's a promotional table that focuses on explaining the meaning of The Secret Club, and I quickly find out this brand is all about couples exploring *pleasure*.

I'm talking *sexual* pleasure.

Honestly, I kind of dig it. It's a fresh take on a way for couples to safely *and playfully* explore their fantasies and desires together, and it all revolves around earning badges that remind me of being in a Girl Scout troop when I was a little girl.

I quickly realize that a stack of cards sits in the center of the table, and they're meant to be used as a fun game for everyone to play. **Challenge yourself tonight**, the framed instructions read.

You should do it, my inner wild child nudges.

My body rocks as someone bumps into me from the side. I look up, ready to rumble, but it's just my sister.

She reads the same instructions at the center of the table and shakes me excitedly, smiling. "Ohh, that looks fun."

I nod calmly in agreement.

"If you do one, I'll do one," Lydia adds, jerking her head toward the stack of cards that I've seen at least twenty people take from over the past five minutes.

"Why the hell not, huh? When in New York, right?" I wink at her, and we both reach forward to grab a card.

She takes it upon herself to go first, turning her card over and silently reading the words.

"What's it say, Lyd?"

"Surprise someone with a sexy kiss." She grins at me, and I snort.

"Well, that's an easy one, considering you're here with your wife."

Lydia just giggles but then turns around to close the distance between herself and Lou, who is still chatting with the bearded hipster and the black bob. *Yes, I'm sure they have names, but I'm not sure I'm invested in learning them.*

Their conversation quickly comes to a halt—*Lou is literally midsentence*—when Lydia steps up and places both hands on her wife's pretty face and tugs her closer for a slow, exploratory kiss.

It lasts long enough for the bearded man to make amused eye contact with me and for Lou to fall into the kiss, threading her fingers into Lydia's hair.

It's taken me a while to weave my way through the mingling crowd to get over to them, but when I do, I tease, "Get a room, you two!"

Lydia ends the kiss at my callout, giggling as she pulls away, while Lou looks half dazed, quirking a brow as if to ask, *What was that for?*

My sister holds up her card, and Lou reads it, smiling the entire time.

"Mission accomplished, hun."

Lydia places one last smacking, playful kiss to her wife's lips before turning to me and tapping the card that's still in my hand with one nosy index finger. "Okay, Rae. Your turn."

I lift it closer to my face and read the challenge silently to myself.

"Ah, ah, read it aloud."

I roll my eyes but concede to Lydia's demands. "*Make the hottest guy in the room remember you for the rest of his life.*"

Lydia bursts into laughter immediately, and I glare.

"Pretty sure your challenge was way easier than mine."

"Yeah, but this one is right up your alley."

I scrunch up my nose. "What's that supposed to mean? That I'm a floozy?"

Lydia laughs. "You know exactly what it means, Rae. You've always been the girl who thrives off a challenge. Especially, when it comes to two things…"

"And what would those two things be?"

"Men and rebelling against our father."

"The rebelling against our father, I get, but men? I don't see the connection."

"Get real," she retorts through a snort. "You are the OG love 'em and leave 'em party girl from back in the day."

"I wasn't *that* bad."

"I watched our father drag a boy out of your room at three in the morning, and then, for two weeks straight, that boy called our house non-fucking-stop. Dragged out of our house, shoeless and by the waistband of his boxer shorts, and he still couldn't walk away from you. Trust me, Rae, you *are* that girl. And I absolutely adore you for it."

"You do realize I was only seventeen, right? It's been a long time since I was that much trouble."

"Not *that* long."

I roll my eyes. "The only reason you never had to sneak people into your room was because Dad didn't realize you were into girls."

"That was definitely an advantage for me." Lydia giggles and nods. "But this isn't about me. It's about *you*. And that card in your hand."

"You know, I came back to New York to be the professional, responsible adult our father has always wanted me to be."

"Bo-ring," she teases, letting her mouth pop on each syllable. "Now, who's the lucky guy?"

"You're a bad influence."

"Says the girl who talked me into lying for her for two months straight so our father thought she was at some kind of library-themed summer camp, when in reality, she was touring the country with her rocker boyfriend in a beat-up van that probably shouldn't have been allowed on the road."

Well, *shit*. If I keep giving her openings, she's really going to make her point. Yes, I, Rachel Rose, used to be known for making some questionable judgments. But I'm trying to be different now. I'm trying to be *good*.

"Get out there and be the badass goddess I know you to be," Lydia orders with a little grin as she leans closer to Lou to wrap her arms around her wife's waist.

"Fine." *As if I could ever back down from a challenge.*

"That's my girl!"

"But you have to give me a minute to find the right guy," I add. "This club is huge, there are a ton of people here, and I refuse to do this shit half-assed."

"Don't worry, Rae," Lou chimes in. "We're both well aware that you're an all-in kind of gal."

Lydia nods in agreement, and I wink at both of them.

Now…to find the hottest guy in the room…

"The night isn't as young as it was an hour ago, Rae." Lydia takes a sip of her wine and smirks at me over the glass.

"The card said the *hottest* guy in the room. A girl needs some time to survey the potential."

Truthfully, I've known who my unsuspecting victim would be since about thirty seconds after I started scouting. And after a quick trip to the bathroom, I've been ready to live up to that stupid card's task—***Make the hottest guy in the room remember you for the rest of his life.***

"After Rachel does the damn thing, we're leaving, right?" Lou questions, and I nod, even if the question wasn't intended for me.

"Yes."

"What? Why would we leave?" Lydia squints her eyes in a rebuttal. "This party is fantastic."

"Because we own a bakery," Lou retorts on a snort. "Four in the morning comes way too soon."

"You have a point." Lydia laughs and then looks at me. "Okay, Rae. Make us proud, and then we're out."

"Fine." I shrug, take one last sip from my wine, and hop off my barstool. "I only need fifteen minutes, tops."

"Wait...you picked the guy?" my sister asks, setting her drink on the table and leaning forward dramatically.

"I've known the guy since I picked the damn card, honey." I reach out to playfully flip the ends of my sister's hair. Lou laughs.

"Who is it?" Lydia glances around the massive room. Her eyes search over the people waiting for drinks at the large bar, then skim over the patrons grooving on the dance floor, until finally, they meet mine again.

"Dance floor. Five o'clock."

Both Lydia's and Lou's gazes move quickly.

"The insanely tall dude with the goatee?"

I snort. "Get real."

"Wait...the guy with the sexy brown hair?"

"Yes."

"Black suit? White shirt?" Lou questions, confirming she's looking at the right one. "Top three buttons undone?"

"Uh-huh."

"A crowd of women around him?" Lydia moves her eyes back to me.

"Yes," I emphasize. "Enough description already. You've found him."

Lydia and Lou share a look. It's quick, almost imperceptible to the naked eye, but it makes me feel like I'm not on the inside of something.

"What am I missing?" I rest my elbows on the cocktail table and glance back and forth between them. "You don't think he's the right guy?"

"Oh no," Lydia responds. "He's definitely the right guy."

"Yep," Lou agrees with a steady nod. "If I liked dick, he'd be the guy I'd choose, for sure."

Lydia cackles. "Same, babe. Same."

"So, it's settled, then? I'll go make this guy remember me for the rest of his life, and then we'll blow this popsicle stand and grab some street tacos on the way home."

Lydia gives me a thumbs-up.

"Go get him, girl," Lou chimes in and lifts one hand to give me a high five.

I smirk, make a show of fluffing up my boobs enough to make them both laugh, and turn on my favorite Prada heels—a birthday gift from Lydia on my twenty-first birthday from a secondhand shop on the Upper East Side.

It doesn't take long before I'm jockeying through the crowd of dancers and heading straight for the action, where my challenge and his harem of female fans reside.

Coiffed brown hair, a devil-may-care smile, and the brightest blue eyes I've ever seen in my life, this guy has the goods. The closer I get to him, the more I realize just how right I was.

He is, hands down, the most attractive man in this club.

Just the right kind of tall, just the right amount of muscles, and that perfect playful, charismatic smile, combined with the fact that he can actually dance, all explain why so many women are vying for his attention.

I discreetly sidle up to him, positioning my body in a way that he can't avoid me. I know I'm pissing off a few women, but my presence will only be momentary. They can have him back soon.

I move my body with the music, shaking my hips and lifting my arms in sync with the seductive bass coming from the DJ's speakers. It's a heady remix of Stromae's *"Alors On Danse,"* a French song I know all too well. The track is so good that it could make even the most anti-dance people bob their heads.

Purposefully, I let my head fall back, elongating my neck and pushing out my breasts in a way most men can't deny. With a thick ass and prominent hips, I've always been a curvy girl. Though, it took me years to find confidence in my body. The outside pressures of society making impressionable teenage girls think skinny was the only way to be sexy was a hard obstacle to overcome.

Obviously, now, I know that to be an outright lie. Sex appeal and confidence come in all shapes and sizes. It's skinny. It's curvy. And it stems from how you feel about yourself.

I feel the moment he notices me. His eyes flit across my face and then take a slow, seductive once-over of my body.

Game on.

"Hi," he mouths, and that devil-may-care smile is back. It's so damn good, *so appealing*, I swear it urges goose bumps to roll up my arms and neck.

But I know this isn't the type of guy you immediately show you're interested. *No way.* You have to slow roll him. Make him feel like there's a test he has to pass to win your attention.

I keep dancing, only letting the hint of a smile show on my face.

He moves closer to me then, the distance between us now mere inches rather than feet, and I look up at him purposefully with big, curious eyes.

"Wanna dance?" he asks, his voice a seductive whisper that somehow finds its way over the music and into my ears.

I shrug. "That depends."

"On what?"

"Are you married?" I question, and he smirks at the forwardness of it.

"No."

"Girlfriend?"

"Also no." That smirk of his morphs into an amused smile. "You?"

I make a show of looking at the space around me. "As you can see, I'm here by myself."

A raspy chuckle jumps from his throat. "You know what I meant."

"And there's no husband or boyfriend waiting for me at home either."

"So…now that we have that out of the way…how about that dance?"

"A dance?" I tilt my head to the side and let my gaze wash over him. "With you?"

He steps closer. "Well, doll, I am the one who's asking."

"But are you fun?"

His responding smile could melt panties off a mannequin. "I'm the most fun a girl could ever have."

That cocky confidence of his should probably be off-putting, but somehow, it makes him more appealing. You have to be one cool motherfucker to sell yourself that well.

"Okay." I shrug one shoulder with nonchalance. "Sure. Why not."

He's not eager like I expect. Instead, he drags it out, slows it down, and that shows me he's a man who knows what he's doing.

Gently, he reaches out and takes my hand into his. All the while, his blue eyes never leave mine.

His thumb caresses the top of my hand, my fingers, and doesn't stop until it hits the ring I always wear on my right ring finger.

He looks down at my hand, focuses, and smiles. "Is that a mood ring?"

I nod as his steady gaze comes up to search mine.

"What's your mood tonight?"

I don't hesitate. Because the truth is, back in the day, Rachel Rose could be one cool motherfucker too. "A little wild. A little reckless."

The hint of a smirk kisses his full lips. He moves closer then, closing the distance to mere millimeters now, and before I know it, my hands are around his neck and his arms are around my waist, tugging me closer to his body.

I can feel the warmth of his skin through the material of my dress, and the sensation goes straight to my head.

Damn. He feels good.

We are as close as two people can physically be, and his body knows exactly how to move. His hips guide mine, and his hands put just the right amount of pressure on my waist.

Somehow, he manages to keep us close but make me feel like we're not close enough.

This guy is smooth with a capital S.

The smell of his soft but masculine cologne consumes me, and I have to blink a few times to remind myself of why I'm even here, dancing with him.

Five years ago, I would've thrown caution to the wind and endeavored to let this moment go wherever it took me—which, undoubtedly, would have been to a place without clothes.

I wouldn't have cared that he might as well be one giant walking, talking red flag. I wouldn't have minded that all these women were so obviously vying for his attention. And I wouldn't have cared that he was clearly the type of guy you didn't bring home to meet the parents.

But I'm not interested in being that girl anymore, and even if I were, that's not what this is about.

This is just a short-lived game that will end *very* soon.

"What's your name?" he whispers into my ear and leans back to meet my eyes.

"Whatever you want it to be."

He lifts one eyebrow. "You're really not going to tell me your name?"

"No." I shake my head. "But I do want to give you something."

"Give me something?"

"Uh-huh. Close your eyes."

The corners of his lips curve up in amusement, but confusion has him tilting his head ever so slightly to the side.

"Just trust me," I say confidently.

"Trust the girl who won't give me her name?"

I bite my bottom lip and nod. "Sometimes you have to live a little dangerously, you know?"

He chuckles then, but also, to my surprise, he listens. Eyes closed, he stops dancing and stands there, waiting for my next move.

I lean forward and position my lips so that they are right beside his ear. "Hold out your hand," I whisper and just barely brush my mouth against his neck as I pull away.

And he does. Hand out, eyes still closed, he follows my instructions.

Discreetly, I pull the sheer pink panties I took off in the bathroom over an hour ago out of the only place I could hide them—my cleavage—place them in his hand, and close his fingers around the delicate material.

"You can open your eyes now."

The gorgeous blue of his eyes is back in view, and he looks down at his hand for a long moment before eventually opening his palm to reveal my panties.

Intrigue, amusement, and a whole bunch of emotions flash across his face as he lifts his eyes to meet mine. "I take it these are yours?"

I nod.

He looks down at his hand again and then back up at me, but this time, he steps forward and grips my elbow gently with his free hand. "And what are these supposed to mean?" he asks, his voice a delicious rasp against my skin.

Fuck, he's tempting. I'd be lying to myself if I didn't admit that fact.

But that's why I know it's time for me to go.

"For memories," I say and gently place my lips against his cheek, but when I take a visible step back and start to turn away from him, he calls out to me.

"Wait…are you leaving?"

"I am."

His expression is made up of a furrowed brow and confused eyes, and I only offer four final words over my shoulder.

"Thanks for the dance."

And then, I move my ass through the crowd and right off that dance floor, far away from Mr. Temptation before I do something stupid like change my mind.

TWO

Ty

A gust of icy air slaps me across the face, and I pick up the pace as I head toward the English building on Greene Street. Thankfully, we're still in the middle of winter break at NYU, and I don't have to jockey through crowds of students to get to my destination.

Though, in about a week's time, that will all change. The campus will be bursting with energy again, the lecture rooms will be filled, and I'll be back to spending the majority of my days teaching English Lit to college kids.

Damn, who would've thought Ty Winslow would be a tenured English professor at the age of thirty-nine? Ha. Sure as hell not me *or* my family.

If I'm being honest, when I was eighteen and just starting my first semester at Harvard, I had no idea I'd end up here. I had more interest in the social clubs—which is just a fancy way of hiding the fact that they were fraternities—and women. And boy oh boy, did I have *a lot* of interest in women. Truthfully, I fucked around for the majority of my freshman year and barely learned a thing.

It took me nearly a year into my undergrad before I declared my major and a year into graduate classes at NYU to actually call it a passion. A pivotal master's-level class about nineteenth-century American literature with a professor by the name of Nathaniel Rose is what lit a fire under my ass.

He helped me realize my connection with literature and hone it into something I could craft a career out of. He guided me, verbally kicked me in the ass more than a few times when I needed it most, and ended up being one of my biggest mentors.

He's also the reason I'm here before ten on a Monday morning during winter break. *The early bird bastard.*

As soon as I set foot inside, wiping the icy slush from the soles of my boots on the entry rug, I'm greeted by Alison, the department's main receptionist. She's otherwise known as "the Gatekeeper" and once had dinner with Tony Soprano. Or so I've heard. I always thought James Gandolfini was an alias to protect his true identity of Tony by wrapping it in a TV show and calling it made-up, so as far as I'm concerned, it could be true.

Here at NYU, she keeps track of all of the staff's appointments and class schedules and, I'm sure, a whole bunch of other important shit that comes with the territory. A lot less exciting, sure, but pretty important if you ask me. Because of that, I try to stay on her good side. And if you're me, the easiest tactic for doing that is flirting.

"Good morning, Professor Winslow," she all but purrs from her spot behind the main desk, and I offer a friendly smile.

Alison never hesitates to shower me with attention, and I don't mind it. It's an innocent little exchange that helps both of us get through our days. I'm a man of few rules when it comes to life, but not fraternizing with my fellow NYU staff or my students is one of the only things I've managed to keep as a hard limit.

"Mornin', Alison."

I walk behind the reception desk to check my mailbox, and I can hear the metal of her chair squeak as she spins around to face me. "I missed you at the staff Christmas party."

I glance up from the stack of mail in my hands to find her looking at me with a coquettish lift of one eyebrow. "C'mon, Alison, you know I never go to those things."

"Well, you should. I would've loved to have a drink with you."

It's not that I don't like parties, because, yeah, I do. I would just rather party with people of my choosing, rather than at a work-sanctioned event where the only reason for an invitation is your paycheck.

I slide the stack of mail from my inbox into the front pocket of my leather briefcase and walk back around the reception desk. Alison and her spinny chair follow me the entire way.

"Speaking of drinks…when are you going to take me out for one?"

I almost want to laugh at the forwardness of it, but I shouldn't be surprised. We've been dancing around the subject for the last two years—since the moment she started working here.

Obviously, I can relate to the thrill of the chase, but as much as I'm for keeping *the Gatekeeper* on my good side, an actual dalliance is never going to happen.

"Have a good day, Alison." I grin and lift my Starbucks cup in the air toward her, and I don't wait around to see her reaction or response. Instead, I head toward the long hallway and the stairs at its very end. Staff offices and the faculty breakroom area are on the second floor.

Halfway toward my first stop of the morning, my phone chimes in my suit pocket. I pause at the top of the landing in the stairwell and jockey my leather briefcase and coffee in one hand to pull my cell out of my pocket and check the screen.

Jude: Is it just me, or was Friday night the best fucking party you've ever attended?

Stroking Jude's ego isn't a priority, but since that's not the only option for a response, I'm more than happy to type out a quick text.

Me: Just you, man. That party sucked ass.

Jude: Screw you, dancing queen. You can't hide those lying eyes. You enjoyed yourself. All night long, like you were Lionel fucking Richie. And so did everyone else in attendance.

His message spurs a rush of memories, and a vision of the woman of mystery is the one I stall my brain on.

Perfect curves. Jade- and gold-flecked green eyes. Full lips. And the kind of hips that'd make any man's head spin. PS: You'll also never see her again.

I squash that shit down and fire off another text in our group chat.

Me: Well, I can't help it if my magnetism made your party look better than it actually was. Keeping busy was the only way for me to tolerate the boredom, but you're welcome for providing the entertainment you obviously forgot.

Jude: Fuck your mom. You're so full of shit.

Overcome with annoyance, Jude obviously forgot who he's talking to.

Jude: Fuck, I'm disturbed. Scratch that. Don't fuck your mom. Go fuck yourself.

I burst out laughing, and the sound echoes in the empty stairwell.

He's right, though. I am full of shit. Friday night was one hell of a good time.

But no one should've been surprised by that. Sophie has been in the event planning business for years, and Jude has been in the nightclub promotion business even longer. Put the two of them together, and they're a party-planning, good-time-encouraging machine. Their launch of their new company, The Secret Club, really had nowhere to go but Awesomeville.

Remy: Don't listen to Patrick fucking Swayze, Jude. He was too busy dry humping every woman in attendance at your launch party to notice that it was fun.

Dry humping? *Pfft.* He's just jealous he can't move like I can.

Me: Really, Rem? You're complimenting Jude?

Remy: It's the one thing he's managed not to screw up lately, so...yeah.

Jude: You sure know how to backhand me after a compliment, Rem. Fuck you very much.

Flynn: Jury's still out on the party's success, Jude. Daisy and I never got out of our seats.

My sister-in-law Daisy, Flynn's wife, is *very* pregnant. With twins. It's safe to say, her reasoning for staying seated for the duration of Friday night's events was more than warranted. Still, Flynn's dig makes me laugh.

Jude: Come on! That's because Dais is, like, two years pregnant. It's not my fault she wasn't moving, Flynn. It's yours.

Flynn: Nearly 8 months, you fuck.

Remy: The scariest part of this whole conversation is that there are about to be two more Winslow boys in the world.

Did I mention she's having boys? Watch out, world, because Remy's right…more Winslows are coming.

Me: I can't wait to meet my nephews, especially little Ty Junior.

Jude: Hey, asshat, Flynn is not naming one of his kids after you.

Me: How the fuck would you know?

Jude: Because I know you, and I know that you're a dick. People don't name their kids after dicks.

Me: A dick who helped keep your party from being a boring disaster. Honestly, I should've been on your payroll as the MC or some shit.

Jude: Who do I make the check out to? John fucking Travolta?

Remy: Greased Lightning!

Me: Make it out to Ty Winslow Junior so I can put it in my future nephew's trust fund.

Flynn: Not happening.

Jude: Anyway, I just wanted to tell everyone but Ty thanks for coming out Friday night. You made the launch a success.

Me: So, you and Soph sold a lot of sex badges?

Jude: The Secret Club doesn't sell sex badges, but I wouldn't expect you to understand anything about sex and intimacy. Don't worry, I'll dumb it down for you one day.

Me: Only if you promise to do it at another boring-ass party with an open bar.

Jude: Fuck you.

I laugh and put my phone away, shaking my head as I jog the rest of the way up the stairs to the second floor. I swear, life is fucking weird sometimes.

My brother and his wife are probably going to become rich from selling T-shirts and sex badges, and Friday night, a random woman left her panties behind—*literally put them in my hand*—like she was Cinderella at the ball.

And you kept them like some kind of pervert.

In my defense, I've never had a beautiful woman give me her panties and just…walk away…before.

I've had a woman take her panties off so I would fuck her. I've taken a woman's panties off her body so I could taste her. I've even had a woman box herself up in nothing but panties and deliver herself to my apartment. But I've never experienced a panty-gift-and-dash.

She didn't give her number or her name; all she left was an impression.

Hot, sexy, and completely entrancing, she's popped into my brain one too many times since she left me standing alone on the dance floor with her sheer pink panties in my hand.

It might be one of the hottest mindfucks I've ever experienced.

Truthfully, the only thing that stopped me from chasing after her was my goddamn brothers bum-rushing me on the dance floor mere seconds after she walked away.

So, I slipped them into my pocket and tried to convince myself it was no big deal. Just a random, crazy encounter that meant nothing.

Problem is, it's that very encounter that's been screwing with your head all weekend.

Glancing down at my watch as I'm about to step inside my office, I realize I've fucked away so much time shit-talking with my brothers that I now only have about thirty seconds to make it to my appointment with Professor Rose on time. I abandon the idea of dropping off my stuff before I go and power walk to the other end of the hall.

Three raps to the thick wood of his door and his voice fills my ears, "Come on in!"

I open the door to the vision of him on his metaphorical throne—the current literary king of the NYU English Department, behind the massive desk in his office.

"Ty, son, it's good to see you," he greets, and I don't hesitate to close the distance between us and shake his hand across the desk. Signs of respect for this man aren't hard, though. Professor Nathaniel Rose has been a mentor of mine for the past decade. He's a man I admire. Look up to. He's the man I worked under as a TA, and he's the man who helped guide me into a career as a successful, tenured English professor at NYU. *He's like the father I never had.*

"Good to see you too, Nate."

If I help one student the way Professor Rose helped me, my career will be made.

"Make yourself comfortable, please," he says, gesturing toward a leather chair across from his desk.

I sit down, but I also flash him a wry grin. "Should I be worried? I mean, it's not every day you ask me to come into your office with an appointment scheduled through Alison."

He chuckles and leans forward, resting both of his elbows on the desk. "You have tenure, son. You'd have to commit a murder for me to get rid of you."

I laugh at that. "That's true, Professor."

"Not to mention, you're the only professor I have on staff who can actually invigorate our undergrads," he adds with a raise of his brow.

"But you could always see if Kip could handle the job," I tease, and Nate guffaws.

"We'd lose enrollment."

"Or what about Adele? She's aces with the Renaissance."

He shakes his head on another laugh and runs his fingers along the edges of his beard. "Again, we'd lose enrollment. And I'd probably end up with several freshmen sobbing in my office."

He's not lying. Both Kip and Adele are *hard-asses*. I should know; I experienced both of them when I was finishing my PhD.

"So…if you're not going to try to fire me, what's the big occasion? Want to bring some freshmen in here and listen to them sob together?"

He chuckles, shaking his head. "I want to ask a favor of you." He steeples his elbows on his desk and rests his chin on top of his hands. "My youngest daughter Rachel has finally decided to move back to New York and get serious about her career, but she needs guidance. She needs someone who can show her the ropes and inspire her to follow through with what she's meant to do."

"And what would that be?"

"Well, deep down, she's a writer. And she's brilliant. She had no issues maintaining a 4.0 GPA at Stanford during her undergrad because, simply put, literature is in her blood. Honestly, she reminds me a lot of Nadine."

Nadine, as in Nadine Rose, his late wife. A brilliant professor and writer, and there is no doubt she was taken from this world too soon. I never had the pleasure of knowing her, and it's a sad realization that she was only able to publish one book under her name before she became ill with brain cancer.

But anyone who is anyone in the literary world knows the name Nadine Rose.

"So, what's your daughter's plan here at NYU?"

"Well, son, she's finally buckling down and has come back here to finish her master's degree. Something she should have completed about four years ago," he muses with a sigh. "Because of that, I'd like you to take her under your wing and let her be your TA over the next few semesters."

"Of course," I agree because I'd never not agree to a favor for Nate. I owe him so much that I don't think I could repay him in ten lifetimes. Honestly, if the man committed murder and needed me to help hide the body, I wouldn't report him to the cops or the tenure board. I'd bring the damn shovel.

"Now, you should know, she can be a bit stubborn. A lot of these gray hairs I have are proof of the hell she put me through during her teenage years. But I'm thinking your brand of teaching—caring about students having fun and all that," he says with a fake roll of his eyes, "might be the ticket to getting her in the mind-set of tackling responsibility head on."

A soft laugh jumps from my throat. "I'm pretty sure we all gave our parents hell during our teenage years. And it's no problem. Consider the favor done."

"Really appreciate this, Ty, and—" He pauses midsentence, his ringing desk phone grabbing his attention. He holds up one finger and answers it with a curt, "Professor Rose."

While he chats about an upcoming department meeting, I spot a picture on his desk, one I know that's been there for a long time, but I've never paid much attention to.

It's two young girls, both brunettes, and they look to be in their early teens. One is smaller than the other and showcases a mouth full of braces. And since I know that Nate has two daughters, I quickly assume that the smaller of the two girls is his youngest, Rachel, the one who will be my new TA.

Though she's older now, midtwenties from what I understand, I try to get an idea of what she might look like these days. It's pretty tough, as I highly doubt she's still sporting a mouth full of metal.

Nate chuckles loudly at something, and I know him well enough to understand this call won't be short and sweet. Up from my chair, I stand and offer him a knowing wave, silently saying, "I'll see you later," and he quickly places his hand over the receiver.

"Thanks again, Ty. I really appreciate you taking Rachel under your wing." His smile is equal parts amused and concerned. "I just hope she doesn't give you as much trouble as she gives her father."

I grin. "I'm sure it'll be fine, Nate."

A sometimes-stubborn, twentysomething, studious bookworm? I mean, how hard could it be?

THREE

Monday, January 14th

Rachel

I step off the subway, moving with the crowd that encompasses the Monday morning rush. It's not easy staying on your feet when you're wearing heels and sandwiched between what feels like half of New York, but I manage to walk up the steps that lead out of the underground tunnel and to the outside world without falling on my face.

Sunlight brushes across my cheeks just as a burst of cold air blows my coat open and tries to become besties with my bones.

Damn, it's cold.

It's like New York is trying to punish me for being away for so long. Either that, or she wants me to haul ass back to LA, where I know it's sunny and seventy-five degrees.

Keeping my head down, I grip the edges of my khaki wool pea coat and pull it tighter to my body as I pick up the pace to finish the short walk to NYU's campus.

Today, I'm here to meet someone. As of tomorrow, the official start of the spring semester, I get the pleasure of being a random professor's teaching assistant. All thanks to my dad's convenient position as head of the English Department at NYU, he took it upon himself to set this up—*without* talking to me about it first—with a professor he deemed worthy.

That's typical Nathaniel Rose. If he thinks you should do something, he'll find a way to make you do it. Your thoughts and feelings on the matter be damned.

Honestly, since this is my first semester back at school, I would have preferred just to focus on my grad school classes and work at Lydia and Lou's bakery part time, but that wasn't what my dear old, very bullheaded dad had in mind.

And while the urge to skip this little meet-and-greet and tell my dad he can fuck right off with his plans is strong, I didn't come back to New York to have tension with my father.

I came here because I want to get serious about my career.

Sure, I'm still not certain what it is I want to do with a master's in English, but I know, with time, I'll figure it out. If you asked my father, he'd probably have a different opinion. Say something along the lines of me following in my late mother's footsteps and becoming a professor who will later publish her first novel.

But it's those expectations that had me running off to the West Coast as soon as I was a legal adult.

My mother, Nadine Rose, was a force to be reckoned with—one I could talk about with pride until I'm blue in the face. But living up to her achievements is a cross I'm not sure I'm ready to bear.

My father didn't get the memo—he never does.

At least you were able to stand strong on the apartment thing…silver lining?

I sigh and pull my phone out of my pocket just as I'm pushing through the entrance doors of the English Department building and check the email my dad sent last week one more time.

Rachel,

Professor Ty Winslow has agreed for you to be his TA. He's a brilliant, astute man who has built an incredible career for himself here at NYU.

Brilliant, astute man? No offense, but he sounds kind of boring.

He primarily teaches undergrad classes at NYU, and I think that is the best place for you to start this year.

He thinks that will be the best place for me to start. What I think, evidently, doesn't matter.

I roll my eyes and scan the email again, looking for Professor Winslow's office number, but a female voice grabs my attention.

"Can I help you with something?" a pretty blonde with soft coral lipstick asks, looking at me from behind a massive reception desk. I drop my phone and put it in my pocket. *Yeah, that seems easier.*

"Yes, actually. I need to find Professor Winslow's office."

"Professor Winslow?" she questions in a way that both confuses me and makes me want to glance at my phone again to make sure I'm saying his name right. I don't need to look, though. I've read it enough times to know that's right.

"Yes. Professor Winslow. That's who I'm looking for."

She purses her lips, picking up the receiver of the phone on her desk. "And what business do you have with him?" When I feel my eyes narrowing on the phone and then the woman who apparently ate piss-Cheerios for breakfast this morning, she tries on a fake smile. "Just want to let him know what to expect."

"I'm his new TA," I say. "And he knows to expect me because we have an appointment for this meeting."

She slams the receiver back down, lets out a little scoff, and points toward the stairs with one French-tipped index finger. Apparently, she's the only one allowed to get salty. "Second floor. Room 213."

"Okayyy. Thanks." I turn for the stairs, but her voice has me turning around once more.

"I'm Alison, by the way," she states, but her words drip with cattiness and pent-up angst. "I handle Professor Winslow's class schedules and appointments and other *very important* things."

"Great," I remark. I could give a single shit what this woman's job is if it doesn't have anything to do with mine.

"I work *very closely* with him."

I have no idea what the story is behind Little Miss Coral Lips and the professor I'm supposed to be TA'ing for, but I'm finding it hard to believe it's anything besides sharing a Google Drive. I mean, any man my father describes as astute and brilliant generally ends up being a fiftysomething dude with a beard, glasses, and a penchant for sweater vests.

And Alison doesn't look like the type of woman who gets horny for Mr. Belvedere.

Maybe she's just having a bad day?

"Well, that's good to know," I answer, offering a friendly wave to end the interaction despite the bitchy vibes rolling my way. "Thanks for the help."

I don't waste any time on Alison after that. Quickly, I head to the long staircase and walk up the two flights to the second floor.

I glance at my phone to check the time and see it's 7:58 a.m. Even with the weird conversation with the chick at the reception desk, I've still managed to get to the appointment my dad set up on time.

Consider it a Monday miracle.

The hallway is eerily empty, most likely because it's an in-service day for staff only, and every time my heels engage with the Travertine tile, a *click-clack* echo bounces off the walls.

Heels that I'm already rethinking, by the way. But walking several blocks and standing on a sardine-packed subway train for fifteen minutes will do that to you.

My eyes take in the numbers on each big wooden door, and I quickly calculate that Professor Winslow's office is at the opposite end of the hall from my father's. And since there's only one office with lights on and a door opened, I have a pretty good sense that I've found where I need to be.

I stop at the threshold, knocking lightly. A man dressed in black slacks and a crisp white shirt that's tucked in beneath his belt is rummaging through something on one of the shelves behind his desk, but I can't be sure yet that it's him.

From behind, he has broad shoulders, a narrow waist, and a ridiculously firm ass. Basically, this guy is the exact opposite of what I pictured by my father's description. There's not a bald head or sweater vest in sight.

"Um…" I clear my throat. "Professor Winslow?"

"That's me," he responds, but he doesn't turn around, his hands still busy with whatever is on the shelf. "Can I help you with something?"

"I'm Rachel…*Rachel Rose*…your new TA."

"Oh shit, sorry," he mutters, promptly turning around to face me while juggling a large book in one of his hands.

When his eyes meet mine, a rush of memories fills my head and recognition sets in. Instantly, I want to drop to the floor and take cover like a street-smart gang leader on the bloody end of a drive-by shooting.

Oh, holy irony.

My heart picks up a hard and fast rhythm inside my chest and the urge to let my jaw fall open is strong, but I overcompensate and end up smashing my teeth together so tight it makes the muscles in my neck ache.

Is this some kind of sick joke?

Blue eyes, full lips, and the kind of insanely gorgeous face a girl could never forget. This isn't the first time I've met Professor Winslow. *Oh no,* we've been acquainted before. About two weeks ago, on a dance floor, when Lydia and Lou dragged me to Orchid.

He's *the* guy. Mr. Tempting. My *challenge.* The one I gave my freaking panties to!

This is not good, Rach. Not good. At all.

His face morphs into a mixture of bewilderment and recognition and a whole lot of other shit that comes with the awkward territory, and there's no doubt I'm not the only one who's put the pieces of the panty puzzle together.

"*You're* Rachel Rose?" he questions, and all I can do is nod. My throat is too clogged by shock to speak actual words. "Professor Rose's daughter? That's *you*?"

I nod again. He scans my face closer.

Don't just stand there, you idiot. You have to do something.

"You're—" he starts to continue.

"And you're Professor Winslow, correct?" I blurt out in a rush, cutting him off before he can say anything else.

Seemingly, my knee-jerk reaction, when I'm confronted by the consequences of giving my underwear to a complete stranger and then having to face that stranger again in a professional setting, is to ignore the giant pair of pink panties in the room.

"Yes…" He nods and narrows his eyes. "That's me."

"Well, it's really great to meet you." *Again.*

"You look *familiar.*"

Ha-ha-ha…fuuuuuuck.

"*Really?*" I retort a little too loudly and have to fake a soft cough into my hand to hide my nerves. "You know, I get that a lot. I think I just have one of those faces."

I circle my head with my hand, *a la isn't-Rachel-so-casual-and-collected.*

"No. I don't think it's that." An amused, all-too-knowing smirk lifts one corner of his mouth. "We've met before."

"No," I lie, shaking my head three too many times. "I don't think so."

"It was two Friday nights ago," he states. "At Orchid."

Are you really just going to act like it never freaking happened? Is that what you're doing right now?!

"Orchid? What's that?" I question, completely ignoring logical thought and settling, instead, for a fake bout of amnesia.

"A nightclub."

"*Oh,*" I respond and shrug. "Never heard of it. But that's probably because I just moved back from the West Coast."

"You've never been to Orchid?"

"Nope. Can't say I have."

He furrows his brow and stares at me for so long that I feel compelled to break the silence and distract him.

"Is it fun?"

"Is what fun?"

"Orchid. The nightclub you're talking about."

"Yes," he says suspiciously. "It is."

I nod and force a laugh from my throat. "I guess I'll have to go sometime, huh?"

He's not convinced, but who could blame him? I'm talking from so deep in my ass, a proctologist wouldn't even know what I'm saying.

"So…it looks like I'll be your TA for spring semester," I muse, in an attempt to change the subject.

"What did you do Friday night, two weeks ago?" he asks, calling my bluff.

"Huh?" I question, so far down this rabbit hole, there's no coming out. I might as well change my name to Alice and do some networking in Wonderland. Hopefully, it's easy to get a job there, because I'm well on my way to tanking this one at NYU.

"Friday. Night. Two weeks ago."

"Friday night? Two weeks ago?" I tap my chin. "Um…I…uh…spent the night in. Unpacking boxes. You know, because I just moved back here, and I had a lot of boxes to unpack. I probably had, like, twenty boxes to unpack. Lots of unpacking—" *Oh my God, stop rambling! Only a liar would feel the need to keep giving information!*

He stares at me, and I decide to shut my mouth. Opening it isn't getting me anywhere good.

Seemingly dropping the subject, he steps around his desk, holding out his hand toward me. "It's great to meet you."

Hesitantly, I place my hand in his, only to startle when he rubs his thumb against the mood ring on my right ring finger. It was my late mother's ring and one I pretty much never take off. Not when I sleep or take a shower or, you know, go to freaking nightclubs.

Facepalm.

Professor Winslow smirks down at me, his eyes telling me all I need to know—*he knows exactly who I am, no matter how much shit I sling.*

I could easily give in to the truth, but I'm just stubborn enough not to. The nightclub was dark and the drinks were flowing and, goddammit, I'm not admitting defeat yet.

Holy hell, Rach. This is a mess.

But what other option do I have? How can I tell the professor my father waxed poetic about, the one I'm supposed to assist for the next two semesters, that *yes, I am the girl who gave him my underwear in the middle of a nightclub?*

Nice to fucking meet you.

FOUR

Ty

I glance pointedly down at the ring—*a mood ring*—on her right ring finger, and she lets go of my hand like it's morphed into a scorching hot plate.

Rachel Rose *is* her. The woman from Orchid.

"What's your mood tonight?" I asked her.

And she answered with a seductive, "A little wild. A little reckless."

The conversation I had with her that night replays in my mind, and I know there's no way in hell I'd get those big green eyes and entrancing lips of hers confused with someone else.

And fuck me, this woman, she's even more of a goddess than my brain allowed me to remember.

Her skirt, coat, and blouse are classic and professional, but even they can't hide the mind-blowing curves that lie beneath the material. Her breasts are full, her hips and thighs perfectly rounded, and her legs shapely in a way that reminds me of paintings from the Renaissance.

She is the exact type of curvy that turns me into a fool.

And her face is undeniably beautiful too. More so than the dim lights of Orchid allowed me to see.

"Rachel," I repeat her name, letting it fall slowly off my tongue. "It's always good to be able to put a name to a face."

Her laugh is awkward, but that's probably because she's been lying through her pretty little lips ever since we made eye contact. "Well, it's nice to meet you too, Professor Winslow."

"Please, Rachel, just call me Ty."

"O-okay," she answers and swallows hard against a nervous titter in her throat. "So…uh…what would you like for me to accomplish today?"

How about you acknowledge that you gave me your panties? is the very first thought to come to mind. *Is that something you do often?* and *Or was it just something you did for me?* are the second and third.

Thankfully, my brain-to-mouth filter seems to be connected today because no matter what my dick has prepared in its PowerPoint presentation, this is Nate's *daughter*.

I can't go there.

"We'll keep it laid-back today. I have a folder of information for you. My class schedules, some teaching plans for the semester, that kind of stuff," I answer, even though everything inside me wants to press her more about that Friday night. I swear, this woman has some balls to just outright deny something we both know is true.

To be honest, in a weird way, I think I might admire her for it.

"Okay, cool," she answers calmly, but I don't miss the way her fingers fidget with her coat.

I walk back over to my desk and shuffle through the mess of papers and files to find the stack that's for her. "I went ahead and compared our schedules. The only class of mine that you'll be able to attend consistently is my afternoon English 101 class with the freshmen. Though, I'd love to see you fit in a few of my other courses throughout this semester, but not to the detriment of your master's workload."

I hand her the thick file, and she takes it with hesitant hands, her eyes acting like my face is the sun and avoiding direct contact for long periods of time is needed for survival.

"This is probably not everything, but it will give you a good start," I instruct, and for some insane reason, I can't swipe the smile off my face. There is just something about her and the way she is avoiding the reality of our initial introduction that, the more I think about it, is amusing as hell. "Log-ins for my online drive, my class schedule for the spring semester, some of my teaching plans for English 101, and a few other odds and ends I know will be of use."

She stares down at the file in her hands. Which I'm guessing has more to do with avoidance than interest, seeing as it's a plain manila folder. "Great. Thanks."

"I also think it would be a good idea for us to get to know each other a little better," I say and lean back against my desk, crossing my arms at my chest. I know I'm putting her on the spot, but I'm so fucking curious if she's ever going to break from the façade of acting like Orchid never happened, it feels like I have to push. "So, tell me a little bit about yourself, Rachel."

Her green eyes flicker up and hold, and I know immediately that something has changed. She's formed a backbone or found her courage or is gearing up to tell me to go fuck myself. Whatever it is, it's beautiful. "What do you want to know exactly?"

"Just a little about you. What are your greatest passions in literature? Your likes? Dislikes?" *And how often do you go to nightclubs and give men your underwear?*

She shrugs. Toys with the file in her hands. "Well, I got my bachelor's at Stanford. Took a few years off to…I don't know…not focus on my career." Her laugh is self-deprecating. "And literature, devouring books, writing…I love all of it. Though I'm not certain what I want to do with my master's, I know it will lead me to where I should be."

"And what do you do for fun outside of NYU's campus?"

You bastard. You just can't help yourself, can you?

"For fun? Off campus?" she questions. "I don't know. I mean, I just got back to New York, so I'd say that answer is pending." The hint of a fire blazes behind her eyes, and what leaves her gorgeous mouth doesn't disappoint. "And personally, I don't think what I do for fun off campus should be any of your concern."

I love it. She knows when to put her foot down. Strong, curvaceous, beautiful women are my fucking weakness.

Though, because this is Nate's daughter, *you're going to be strong. Right?*

"Knock, knock," a familiar male voice calls out from the doorway, and the timing couldn't be any worse. *Speak of the fucking devil.*

When Rachel spots her dad, her brow furrows and her lips morph into a thin line. I don't have the time nor the inclination to consider why. I've got a half-chub to hide.

"Hey, Nate. Good to see you," I greet easily, doing all the speaking for myself and my panty-partner-in-crime.

"I'm glad to see the two of you have met." His responding smile is big. "Rachel, darling, how is it going? You feel ready to buckle down and focus this semester?"

Her back goes stiff and her shoulders look like they're carrying the weight of the world, but I don't insert myself. It's none of my business.

"Oh yeah, Dad. So ready," she forces out.

"That's great to hear. Do you think—" Nate starts to question, but Rachel cuts him off. Knowing everything I know about Nathaniel Rose, I'm surprised he lets her.

"Speaking of buckling down…" She holds up the file I gave her mere minutes ago. "I better get home and start preparing for my first day. Lots of reading and information to digest."

Something odd is afoot here, that's for sure.

She grabs her purse off the surface of my desk, tucks the file to her chest, and turns in the direction of my door, ready for departure.

"Now that's the spirit," Nate responds, ignoring the thick tension pulsing between them. I don't know if he's doing it on purpose or if he's playing at naïve, but there's no way this intelligent man I've known for a decade isn't picking up on the things his daughter is broadcasting.

Rachel offers a halfhearted wave and smile, and then she's gone. "See you tomorrow" are the last and only words she offers before she hauls ass out of my office.

"Looks like you two have started off on the right foot, yeah?" Nate offers, pulling me from my blind stare at the door.

Ha. Oh yeah. Really started off with a bang.

If this were a romantic comedy movie, all this shit would be hilarity gold. But it's not a romantic comedy. It's my actual fucking life.

"Yep. So far, so good," I say, forcing a neutral smile to my lips. "I think Rachel will be a great TA."

As long as you can remember TA stands for Teaching Assistant…not tits and ass.

Oh yeah, this semester should be interesting.

FIVE

Rachel

Duh, DUH, duh-duh, duh, DUH…

Tom Cruise's badass agent theme song plays in my mind as I go on the run because I'm a woman on a mission of my own…to get as far away from NYU's campus, my father, *and* Professor Ty Winslow as I can, as fast as I can. I don't recommend running ten blocks in heels, but under these circumstances, it's the only damn viable option. And Ethan Hunt would definitely do it if he had to, too.

Once I'm off the subway, I shove my way through the crowd to speed walk up the stairs, two steps at a time, as quickly as possible. I'm pissing people off left and right, but I can't bring myself to care.

"Hey!" and *"What the fuck!"* they shout over the squeal of trains below and street noise above.

I don't dare stop, I don't turn back, I don't apologize. All I can do is run like the wind. Can't stop, won't stop until I reach my sister's bakeshop.

I swing open the doors of Little Rose and burst inside so chaotically that Maude, the friendly lady who is one of the bakers on Lydia and Lou's staff, startles behind the register.

"Rachel?" she asks, her eyes wide with shock and confusion as she puts a hand to her chest. "Are you okay?"

"Where's Lydia?"

"In the back," she answers and closes the register drawer, surveying me closely. Her face turns pitying, as though she can see the word hysteria written on my forehead. "Honey, can I get you something?"

"Yeah." A hyena-like laugh bursts from my lungs. "A time machine."

"Does that…does that have sprinkles?" she asks, ever controlled by the mind of a baker.

"I'm just joking," I offer, trying to calm my ragged breath.

She's looking at me like I'm crazy, and right now, I can't blame her. I *am* a lunatic.

A lunatic who needs a powwow with her sister, ASAP. *Sorry, Maude, but I don't have time to explain.*

Around the glass shelves at the front showcasing today's goodies, I push through the swinging door that leads to the back and find my sister and Lou working on a three-tiered wedding cake.

"I'm so fucked!" I shout so loud that a soufflé on the back table collapses. I wince. *Shit. Shouting was not designed to be done in confectionery sugar havens, Rachel!* Lydia stops piping icing along the edges of the cake to look up at me. She has no verbal question, but I don't make her wait; I dive right into my word-vomit explanation.

"I met the professor I'm TA'ing for today."

"You're going to be a teaching assistant?" she questions, scrunching up her nose.

"*Oh yeah*, I forgot to tell you. Dad took it upon himself to offer up my TA services to a professor he deemed worthy to help guide me in the career he's apparently got all planned out for me."

"Okay…" She pauses and looks over at Lou, who has also stopped working on the cake and is throwing the now-ruined soufflé in the garbage. "I can see how that might be frustrating. Maybe not worthy of the screaming banshee entrance, but hey, what do I know."

"That's because that's not even the tip of the story, sis," I counter and let my head fall back for a brief moment. "Inches and inches of penetration are still pending in the story of my fucking."

Lou's laugh fills my ears, and she leans her elbows into the metal prep table. "Okay, this I have to hear. Give us the full stroke, honey. Let her rip."

"The professor I'll be TA'ing for? The guy Dad arranged for me to work with without my permission?"

They both nod, Lydia vocalizing, "Yeah?"

"He's the guy from Friday night."

Lydia furrows her brow, trying to remember what Friday night I'm referring to.

"Lydia!" I mean, she has been working all day, but I'm going to need her to look alive. "The guy I gave my panties to!"

Lydia blinks several times, looking at Lou like she's a contestant on *Who Wants to Be a Millionaire* using a lifeline. "Should I know what you're talking about?"

"The card, Lyd! That stupid card with the challenge about making the hottest guy in the room remember me for the rest of his life!"

"Wait a minute," Lou chimes in. "You gave that guy your underwear?"

"You're serious?" Lydia questions, her voice rising with each syllable. "You gave him your underwear?!"

"The card said to make him remember me for the rest of his life!" I remind them. "What are you two not understanding about this?"

"So…you took off your underwear in the middle of the dance floor and gave them to him? How the hell did I miss that?"

"I'm not a super sleuth." I roll my eyes. "I took them off in the bathroom *before* I approached him. I only *handed them to him* on the dance floor."

"Holy shit," Lydia mutters through a shocked laugh and glances at Lou with big, amused eyes.

"What?" I question, looking back and forth between them. "What's that look for?"

"Well, sweetheart," Lou says through a cringe. "I think you're going to be seeing a lot more of that man."

"You think? I'm supposed to be his TA! Are you listening at all?"

"I'm not talking about that." Lou shakes her head. "You'll probably be seeing him around here too."

I narrow my eyes. "What do you mean?"

"Ty Winslow, right? That's his name?"

I nod.

"Well…he's a regular," Lydia adds. "I'm pretty sure he lives in this neighborhood. Stops by the bakery weekly."

My jaw drops. "And you didn't think this was good information to have before I gave him my underwear?"

"In my defense," Lou responds, holding up both hands in neutrality, "I just thought you were going to flirt and dance with him a little. I had no idea you had plans to make your panties disappear into his pocket."

"So, what you're telling me is that not only is he the professor I'm TA'ing for, but he's also a regular at the bakery I live upstairs from and work at part time?"

Lou winces through a smile I'd like to wipe off her normally lovely face. "That is correct."

"This is so messed up." I let my head fall back again, emitting a whine that the most vocal of pigs would envy.

"These kinds of things always seem worse than they really are," Lou attempts to soothe, reaching out to put a comforting hand on my shoulder.

Snapping my head forward, I eye my sister-in-law with a pointed stare, lifting one eyebrow.

"Relax, Rae," she responds with a small smile. "You obviously talked to him today without spontaneously combusting. It should only get better from here."

"Maybe it would have…if I hadn't pretended to have never met him before."

"*What?*" Lydia snorts. "You acted like you weren't you from Friday night?"

"What else was I supposed to do?" I retort, holding out both hands. "He works with *our father*, Lydia. You know how much Dad is on my ass as it is. The last thing I need is for him to know I gave one of his professors my freaking underwear. My goal is to make him realize I can handle my own life and he doesn't need to meddle, not make him concerned for my mental sanity so he gets even more overbearing."

"But you eventually told him, right?" Lou asks, and I shake my head.

"No freaking way. That's a secret I'm taking to the grave."

Lydia narrows her eyes. "But it's not a secret…"

"Fine." I shrug. "It's a *truth* I'm taking to the grave."

"So…" Lou pauses. "You're just going to act like it never happened?"

I mull over the reality, and even though it's probably completely irrational, I've made my bed full of lies, and I'm going to cuddle up under the comforter of avoidance like that Kim Kardashian GIF—the one under the gray blanket. "You bet your cake-baking ass that's what I'm going to do."

Lou laughs outright, and Lydia mutters, "You're crazy."

"Yeah, probably." I nod. "Now, if you don't mind, I'm going to go upstairs to my apartment and bask in my misery and loathing in a hot bath. Because I have to prepare myself to face the professor who's seen my underwear tomorrow. Again."

Matilda, otherwise known as the bakery cat, chooses that time to walk over and rub her fur against my bare legs.

Yes, a cat in a bakery could come with some pretty expensive health code violations. That is, unless you manage to get said cat qualified as a personal "service animal" to help with something like anxiety or depression—which is exactly what Lydia and Lou did.

It's a boon, really. Because right now? It sure feels like I could use a personal anxiety service animal of my own.

I reach down and pick up Matilda, feeling compelled to have some sort of companionship during this momentary mental breakdown of mine.

"Girlfriend, shit is a mess," I mutter to her as I rub my fingers through her soft fur.

She just purrs in response and snuggles closer into my arms.

"I'm stealing her," I declare easily, walking past Lydia and Lou with Matilda in my arms.

As I head toward the back hallway, where the stairs to my upstairs apartment are located, Lou holds out a generous hand containing a small box of their signature snickerdoodles.

"Here, take some cookies," she offers, her eyes soft with sympathy. "They might not be able to solve problems, but they certainly have the power to take the edge off."

I don't hesitate to snag it from her hand. "Thank you."

Pretty sure anyone who accidentally gave their new boss their underwear needs cookies. Especially since said person—*me*—is going to have to face him again…*tomorrow*, on the first official day of classes.

At this point, I don't know what's worse—my dad and his constant need to press me on everything, or the fact that I have to face Professor Ty Winslow every Monday through Friday for an entire semester.

Is it possible to go back in time and just…stay on the West Coast?

SIX

Ty

While my American Lit class exits my lecture hall, I kick up my feet on the desk and check my phone until it's time for my next class. I have a few missed texts, which is nothing new when you have as many yappers in your family as I do. Someone is almost always saying something, and for the most part, I don't even bother checking messages until several have accrued.

One is from my sister Winnie about an upcoming Mathletes fundraiser for my niece Lexi. She's the smartest person I know, and I'd put money on her winning even if it was my last dollar. Not that that's the point of Mathletes for kids, but you know, if it were, she'd kick all those kids' asses. Regardless, I let my sister know I'm game to donate a hundred bucks and move on to the next unread.

This one is from Tiffany, a woman I dated for about two weeks last month, wondering if I'd like to meet up for drinks later. I groan. I might've brought her along for some of the Winslow Christmas festivities, but our relationship ran its course, and I sure as shit don't want to lead her on. As politely but succinctly as possible, I decline.

And then there's a text from my mom, Wendy. The two of us are something of buddies, but we've done a decent job of keeping it a secret that I'm the favorite child—wouldn't want everyone else getting a complex.

Mama Winslow: Have you ever used Match.com?

Texts between my mom and me are normal, but the subject matter today? That's a whole new venture. I sit up, sliding my feet from the heavy wood surface of my desktop down to the floor, and type out a response.

Me: Um, no.

Mama Winslow: What about Tinder?

I nearly laugh at the absurdity.

Me: Mom, I don't need to use Tinder to find women.

If there's one thing my mother would like to see happen, it's for me to find a nice woman to settle down with and, eventually, give her some grandbabies. It's what she wants for all her sons, and while Jude and Flynn have managed to find the women of their dreams, and Flynn is getting started with the bambinos, I'm happy living life the way I am. I'm not lonely—I'm content.

Mama Winslow: Ty, honey, I think you and I both know you don't need help finding women. If anything, you need help NOT finding women. I always make extra food, just in case you drag one in off the street.

Me: You have a lot of bachelorettes just lurking outside your house, Ma?

Mama Winslow: You wish, son. What about TapNext? I hear that's one of the better sites.

Me: TapNext is good, I guess. You know Kline Brooks runs that, right? Anyway, like I said, I'm not getting online. I don't need another place for people to find me.

Kline Brooks is a family friend. He's best friends with my brother-in-law, Wes, and his wife Georgia is one of Winnie's gal pals.

Mama Winslow: I'm talking about online dating for me, not for you.

Hold the fucking phone.

Me: WHAT? You're getting on Tinder?

Mama Winslow: I'm considering it.

Me: Mom, I fully support your dating, but for the love of God, do not start a Tinder profile.

Mama Winslow: What's wrong with Tinder?

Me: Because it's for hookups. Booty calls. Not date nights.

Mama Winslow: But what if that's what I'm looking for?

Is she high?

Me: WHAT?

Mama Winslow: LOL. I swear, you boys are so easy to mess with. Anyway, Aunt Paula is here. I gotta go. It's a girls' shopping day.

Me: Wait a minute, crazy lady, so you were joking about the whole online dating thing? Or just Tinder booty calls?

Mama Winslow: I know it's hard for you boys to believe, but all women, even your mother, want to find companionship.

Me: You act like all of our monthly date nights don't even exist. Are you trying to tell me I'm not enough for you, Mom?

I'm the only one out of the five of us who takes Wendy Winslow out on monthly date nights to fancy restaurants, the opera, and her favorite Broadway shows. I pull out all the stops, and what? Now it's not enough?

Mama Winslow: Very funny, Ty. You know I love our little date nights, but I'm looking for something it'd be illegal for a son to give me.

Me: MA!

Mama Winslow: LOL Relax. I'm teasing you…mostly.

My mom has been a single woman, *a single mother of five kids,* for most of my life. My father fucked off when we were young, and she made raising us her only priority. Honestly, she gave us the world.

All five of her kids are well-adjusted, successful adults, and even though Jude is still kind of a lunatic, it's safe to say she did one hell of a job.

Truthfully, it's about time she started dating and focusing on herself.

Me: I fully support you in this endeavor, but no Tinder, okay? It's not like

Kline needs money from another membership, but that's the best option of them all.

Mama Winslow: Deal. TapNext, it is. Love you, honey.

Me: Love you too, crazy lady. Have fun with Aunt P.

The clock on the wall behind me ticks loudly to the beat of the second hand, and all the crap on my overloaded smartphone suddenly seems boring as hell. I have twenty minutes to kill before my next class and absolutely no motivation to get up and move.

An idea hits me, and instead, I make a FaceTime call to my brother Remy. He answers by the second ring, and his big head consumes the screen of my phone within seconds. I wouldn't normally spread my mom's shit around, but if anyone can keep it to himself, it's my brood-tastic eldest sibling.

"Yo."

"Mom is going to start dating," I say by way of greeting and note that he's currently eating a banana.

"What?" he questions around a mouthful.

"Mom was just texting me about Tinder and Match.com and shit. She wants to start dating."

"No shit?" He looks at me with the banana half in his mouth, and I feel like I'm watching my brother suck on a dick.

"Rem, for the love of God, do you not understand anything about banana-eating etiquette? I'm talking about Mom wanting to play the tickle tango, and you're doing your damnedest to show me exactly what it's going to look like."

"What the fuck are you talking about?"

"There's a right way and a wrong way to eat a banana in public, and you're definitely doing it all fucking wrong."

He stares at me and continues to take big, slow-as-hell bites of the phallic-shaped fruit. The whole time, his eyes staying locked with mine.

"You're deranged."

He grins and goes even more X-rated by closing his eyes and moaning like the fruit tastes so good it's orgasmic.

"You're fucked in the head."

"Is that the only reason you were calling me? To tell me about Mom's big dating plans and criticize the way I snack?"

"No, actually, I wanted to talk to my financial adviser about my investments. I just thought, I don't know, you might be more interested in what's going on with your family."

He rolls his eyes. "Ma can do what she wants. She deserves to be happy. Who the fuck am I to judge how she wants to achieve that? Also, I'm not your financial adviser."

He's right about my mom. I knew it was none of my business before I even started the call, so I move on to the other subject at hand. "But you handle my investments."

"I give you advice," he corrects, and I grin.

"Same difference."

"What do you want to know?"

"Do I need to pull out of Tesla?"

"No."

"And your reasoning?"

"Because you asked me, and I'm telling you not to."

"Okay. And your reasoning that's not pretentious and actually explains things would be?"

"Because if you hold, Tesla is going to make you an obscene amount of money over the next few years."

"How sure are you?"

"Dude. I'm not a fucking fortune-teller. I can only tell you what I see is a statistical probability. I can't predict black swan events that will rock the market. But if nothing insane happens, then yes, I'm certain. Tesla is highly undervalued and will become a big asset in the EV market."

The only words my brain registers are fortune-teller, but I quickly squash that shit down.

Rem is an investing genius. He knows shit it feels like God doesn't know sometimes. I'd be a prick and a half not to listen to him, as he's made me and all my brothers more than financially stable. We're all pretty much set for our lifetimes. Winnie's husband is rich as fuck, so I don't know that she really needs Rem, but before that, he made sure to take care of her too.

The truth is, Remy's been the father figure of our family practically all his life.

"So, I need to hold, then?"

"Yes, sweetheart, like I said, *hold.* Don't sell. And if you're smart, you'll keep adding to your investment monthly."

"I don't know, man. I feel like you might be losing your edge—"

Rem chuckles, but I'm not listening anymore. Suddenly, all I can see are curves, topped with long dark hair and the sexiest soft green eyes on the planet.

Rachel Rose. In the flesh.

She walks into my lecture hall, ready for the first official class of ENG 101, and I'd be a liar if I said I haven't been anticipating this part of the day since the instant I got out of bed this morning—hell, since she left my office yesterday.

Instead of greeting me directly, she keeps her head down and shuffles on her heels toward the far-right side of the room. She's dressed in similar attire to yesterday—skirt, heels, and silk blouse—and my gaze doesn't miss the way her perfectly rounded hips and ass move with each step she takes.

"Ty?" Remy's voice grabs my attention, and I realize I'm still on the phone with him. "What are you doing?"

"Nothing, man. My class is about to start."

"What are you looking at?" he questions, his brow furrowed as he searches my face. "Or should I say *who* are you—"

"I have to go," I say and quickly end the call, tucking my phone into my pocket and jumping to my feet.

Rachel seems oblivious to my presence as she chooses the last seat in the front row and drops her belongings beside it. I look at my desk, push the book sitting by the edge with my fingers, and look back at Rachel as it hits the floor with a loud, unavoidable thud.

Rachel still doesn't look up. *Definitely avoiding me.*

I probably shouldn't find it so amusing that my teaching assistant won't look me in the eye, but fuck if I'm not entertained.

"Hello, Rachel," I greet, closing some of the distance between us. She offers a half smile as she sets up her laptop on the table in front of her seat and not much else.

I waggle my eyebrows, and she fakes an attempt at turning her half smile into a full one before verbally acknowledging me.

"Hello, Professor Winslow." She's all business, formal and professional, and her body language is as impenetrable as one of those shark-dive cages. For a guy like me, though, that does nothing but chum the waters.

I can't let it go. I can't move on. I can't give her the distance and space I should. I have to chip away at the frostiness because I don't do tense work environments—to be honest, Ty Winslow doesn't do tense environments, period.

Besides two or three students who have managed to get to class early but choose to sit in the far back of the room, there's no one else in the lecture hall besides us. I still have plenty of time and space to do my shark work.

"First day of classes going well for you?" I ask, getting close enough that our conversation is just between the two of us. I put a foot up to the small rise under the front row of stadium seats and box out the rest of the room.

She doesn't even look up at me, her eyes staying fixated on the screen of her laptop as she offers a quiet, "Mm-hmm."

Spotting the ring on her finger again, I try a different tack.

"What's your mood today?"

Her fingers pause over the keyboard, and her eyes are full of attitude when she looks up at me. She knows what I'm working at, and instead of being embarrassed, she's annoyed.

God, her strong sense of self is such a turn-on.

Rachel meets my eyes and then pointedly glances down at the ring on her hand, the one we are both acutely aware of. "Apparently, today, I'm green."

"And green means?"

"Mixed emotions."

I'll be damned if I can't relate to that. The emotions of my dick are in a very different place from the emotions of my brain. They can't seem to agree on what to do with the strong, undeniable fantasies that involve my cock inside Nate's daughter.

"Hmm…interesting," I say and rub at my jawline with one hand. "You know, I haven't seen a lot of women wearing mood rings before."

"Really? Mood rings are pretty common," she advises calmly, nearly making me laugh. Even with effort against it, a smile still makes its way on to my face.

More students start to file into the lecture hall, and Rachel goes back to whatever it is she's doing on her laptop, pointedly evading me and my curious mouth. A large part of me wants to stay right where I am, but when I glance at my watch and see it's time to start class, I decide to back off… *for now.*

"Welcome to English 101. I'm Professor Winslow," I announce as I spin away from Rachel, jog toward my desk, and jump up onto the raised platform at the front of the room. "This class is incredibly easy if you do the following three things. Number one, attend the class. Number two, read what I tell you to read. And number three, engage in the discussions," I decree with a smile, grabbing the clipboard roster and immediately diving into roll call.

It's a lengthy process I won't do every class, instead, doing it at random. I like to keep them on their toes and, occasionally, give them the chance to get lucky.

"Winter break reading," I announce after finishing with the roster and tossing it back onto my desk. I look up into the massive crowd of students. "Who successfully completed all 1000 pages of *Anna Karenina?*"

About half of the class raises their hands, while the other half looks around bashfully. This is nothing new, truthfully. If anything, it seems like we might be starting with a higher percentage of completion this year.

"Okay. And who avoided the reading?"

More uncertain looks. As if they're not sure if they should tell the truth or avoid it, though a few brave hearts raise their hands without guilt. The overwhelming majority was bold enough to skip the assignment but scared to admit to their actions.

Kind of like Rachel. I glance over at her to see she's watching me—or she was, jerking her eyes away as soon as I make contact. I smile and turn back to the class.

"And who in this class is so disorganized they didn't even know they were supposed to read something?"

Laughter overtakes the crowd, and about three hands go up, one belonging to a freshman with a headful of unbrushed blond hair who is currently eating from a pack of Twinkies in the second row.

A lot of the older professors I work with hate teaching freshmen. But I find an insane amount of enjoyment in it. They are still figuring it all out and haven't quite broken all their high school habits yet. They're used to being led around on a leash, and college is about learning to blaze a trail of your own. I love being witness to the shift in mind-set—and you really only ever get that in large proportions with freshmen.

"Have you ever read Tolstoy?" I ask the Twinkie-eating blond kid, and he shakes his head.

"Nope. Never heard of him."

That makes me chuckle. "Looks like you're about to learn today, son."

The kid just shrugs and takes another bite of his Twinkie as the rest of the class laughs.

"May I suggest you put down the snack cakes and take some notes?" I offer with a sly grin. "Or, you know, just keep eating and remain unprepared for the exam this Friday."

"What?" He groans around a mouthful of cake and cream. "There's going to be an exam?"

"It's Landon, right?" I question and he nods.

"That's me."

"There isn't going to be an exam for the rest of the class. But for you? There's a possibility of an exam."

"What's that supposed to mean?"

"It means, you have a choice. Either you come to my class ready to engage in discussion, *or* you can stuff your face with Twinkies, act too cool for school, keep not-so-secretly checking social media shit, and definitely end up with an exam on Friday."

"Okay. Okay." Landon smirks and sits up straighter in his seat. "I can dig that."

"Look," I state and move my attention to the entire class. "I know, for most of you, this class is just some dumb prerequisite you have to complete.

And I know this because I was you once. Actually, I was an asshole like Landon once."

"What the hell, Prof?" Landon scoffs above the laughter of everyone else.

I just grin at him. "But I know for a fact that if you go through life looking at things like they're a to-do item on a checklist, you're setting yourself up for some real misery." I turn toward the giant whiteboard behind me and grab a black marker. "Life isn't a checklist. Life is something to experience. It's something to *feel*. It's something to marvel at. So, with that mind-set, let's talk Tolstoy and *Anna Karenina*. I know it's a long book. I know, at times, it can feel boring AF, as the kids say these days. But why is this book a timeless masterpiece? Why is Tolstoy revered as one of the best because of it?"

I write out the words **What makes Anna Karenina so fucking great?** on the whiteboard.

A titter rolls through the room, and kids look back and forth at one another excitedly.

I glance at Rachel to find her sporting just a hint of a smile, and I can't stop myself from drawing her into the conversation.

"Everyone, I would like to introduce you to my TA this semester," I announce and point the now-capped black marker in my hand toward Rachel. "This is Rachel Rose. You'll be seeing a lot more of her this year. Also, it should be noted, she will be tasked with grading some of your papers, so I'd be nice to her if I were you. Maybe woo her with chocolates and friendly smiles every once in a while—get in her good graces."

The class laughs.

"Hi, everyone." Rachel smiles and offers a little wave. "I'm here as a resource when you need me, and no, chocolates and wooing are not required."

The class dissolves into a fit of giggles again, and a couple of young, strapping boy-men sit up in their seats a little bit taller. Rachel Rose is going to be something of a regular in quite a few spank banks, I'm afraid.

"So, Rachel, what do you think?"

"What do I think about what?"

I point toward the whiteboard over my shoulder. "What makes the book so great?"

One would assume that the daughter of the great Nathaniel Rose would know a book like *Anna Karenina* like the back of her hand, but one would also assume that a woman who gave you her panties in the middle of a nightclub wouldn't try to pretend it didn't happen.

So, I'm done being an ass by assuming. Instead, I'm all ears for her response.

"Because it transcends time," she answers with something that's been said a million times before.

"That is what all the critics say about it, yes, But why do *you* think it transcends time?"

Her eyes narrow ever so slightly, the pressure of being put on the spot placing a weight on her eyelids. I can't wait to see what she does with it. *Fight or flee, Rachel, fight or flee.*

"Because at the core of the book, no matter the time period in which it was written, are the fundamentals of human nature," she expands confidently. "Tolstoy was a master of showing things that every human can relate to, no matter the era. Things like jealousy and boredom and insecurity *and* the double standards we create in society because of various factors like wealth and class and gender."

"Double standards," I muse, nodding in agreement before continuing to test her knowledge. "And what double standard struck you the most in the book?"

"Well, I'd say Anna's brother sleeping with the nanny and finding forgiveness from his wife and everyone else is a serious double standard when you compare it to how Anna was treated in the theatre. I mean, that scene is my least favorite scene in the book."

"Wait…there's sex in this book?" Landon questions, and I waggle my eyebrows dramatically.

"Ahh, this is exactly why you shouldn't act like you're too cool for school, bro."

Landon is still confused, glancing around the room and undoubtedly wondering if *Anna Karenina* is an undercover porno book he should've been wanking off to over winter break, but the rest of the class, thanks to Landon's question and Rachel's description, is now seriously invested.

As for me, I'm left wondering how Rachel's shapely thighs, smooth skin, full breasts, and sultry eyes are now playing second fiddle to her mind in terms of my attention.

She's as brilliant as Nate said she was and then some, I have a feeling. But he's not the only one who's underestimated her.

Rachel Rose is proving to be a lot more trouble than I bargained for.

SEVEN

Rachel

I've only observed fifty-five minutes of Professor Winslow in action, and even though it pains me to admit this because I don't like to agree with my father on pretty much anything, I can see why he considers Ty Winslow a brilliant teacher.

Ty commands his class's attention without aggression or fear tactics. He doesn't *dictate* them into paying attention. He simply *convinces* his students to engage in the discussion in a way that makes them feel like they're choosing to do it. And he also gets them to have fun in the process.

That's a hard thing to do when a book like *Anna Karenina* is the topic.

At least, it is if you're not teaching pupils like me. I, personally, happen to love that book—have always loved that book—but for most people, it is a painful endeavor to actually finish. It's long and can feel tedious at times. And the way in which it is written can feel difficult to interpret and navigate.

Sure, this first class didn't come without putting me to the test, but annoyed or not, I understood why he did it.

By bringing me into the discussion, he took *Anna Karenina* and all its complexity and made it seem conversational. Students who arrived feeling nervous and uncertain left feeling interested and confident in Tolstoy, of all things.

He made them feel like they could relate to the book, and he did it without knocking even a single notch of his charming smile out of place.

I wish I could say I haven't noticed how insanely good-looking Ty Winslow is, but even without our *real* first introduction, admitting that he is a different brand of handsome would be unavoidable.

He's walking sex, and it shows in the fluttered eyelashes, coy smiles, and giggles of every female student in the classroom. He could have any of them if he wanted, but so far, he hasn't given any of the attention a second glance.

Ty glances at his watch briefly, and with a quick look to the clock above him, I know what's coming.

"All right. Get out of here, kids. Your first brush with *Anna Karenina* is officially dismissed."

Chatter fills the massive space as students shove their laptops into their bags and snag their notebooks off the long lecture hall tables and start heading to their next class.

I follow in kind, gathering my things as quickly as possible. I'd like to get out of here without talk of mood rings or Orchid or anything else if I can help it.

Ty stands by the exit door, gabbing with students and answering any questions they might have before they leave his lecture hall, and that puts a bit of a kink in my plan for a clean getaway.

I try to wait him out, hoping that maybe a student will pull him into a long conversation, or he'll head back to his desk, but I can't stay here forever, as much as the power of my will compels me to. I have places to be.

Resigned to womaning up and making my exit, I'm surprised when Professor Winslow calls out to me as I'm slinging my messenger bag over my shoulder.

"Hey, Rachel, can you do me a favor?" he asks from the door, garnering a nod from me in response. "Before you leave, I have a file with a few changes to next week's teaching plans for you in my office. It's in my desk, the second drawer on the right. Would you mind grabbing that before you go?"

Okay, that's a reasonable request. One that even sends me somewhere other than where he is. I'm relieved.

"Sure thing," I agree eagerly.

My shoulders sag as he heads back to the desk in the lecture hall, and I head out the door. *Maybe denying the truth of the panties doggedly was the way to go after all.*

Since the lecture hall is on the first floor, I make my way down the hall and up the stairs to the second and then all the way to his office. Staff and students linger around in discussions, some of whom I'm at least familiar with because of my dad, but I keep to myself in an effort to be in and out in no time.

Ty's door is open, and I head straight for the other side of his desk. Years of age and use have made the second drawer on the right a little snug, but I manage it open with a few rough tugs.

And then nearly piss my pants.

Oh, what the hell is this?

My sheer pink La Perla panties lie across the top of a manila folder with my name on it, staring me in the face. *This motherfucker kept my freaking panties—which, admittedly, was the intended consequence of giving them prior to all the complications—and now he's haunting me with them like Cas-Perla, the underwear ghost.*

God, I wish I had the capacity to be embarrassed, but I don't. I'm angry— and I'm really fucking impressed. *I can't believe he lulled me into complacency this easily.*

I grab the yellow Post-it note that sits on top and read it.

You and I both know these belong to you.

That bastard thinks he's going to win this game? *Screw that.* Rachel Rose never says die.

I snag the file out of the drawer and slam it shut so hard that a few pieces of paper shimmy off his desk and onto the floor, leaving the underwear and the Post-it right where I found them.

If I took them, I'd be admitting the truth, admitting *defeat*, and I'm no quitter. No matter how many lies I have to continue to tell, I'll ride this lying train until the cows come home or until it goes down in a blazing fire—whichever comes last.

This is war.

I head out of his office and into the hallway, and it comes as no surprise that I only get halfway to the stairwell before the devil himself smiles through his stride in my direction.

He's coming to see the spoils of his efforts, but he's going to be sadly disappointed.

I'm not admitting shit. At this point, he could strangle me with the panties themselves, and I'd pretend I wasn't choking.

Sheer pink La Perla panties I bought with three years of birthday money? Never fucking heard of them.

Without hesitation or uncertainty, I walk toward him with a defiant chin, steady eye contact, and a throbbing gut full of anger and excitement. He's a bastard, but I haven't felt this alive in years.

"Find *everything* you need, Rachel?" he questions, and I don't miss the ways his eyes flash with amusement.

"Sure did." I wave the file in the air. "You said the file folder in the second drawer on the right, correct?"

His brow furrows ever so slightly and I know he's wondering where my stupid panties are, but he recovers quickly. Ty Winslow isn't a novice either. "Correct."

"Well then, I'd say I got everything I need, *Professor.*"

He searches my eyes for a moment longer, but eventually, he takes a step back, opening a path for me. "Well then, I guess I'll let you on your way."

"Great." I start to walk past him, but his voice makes me stop in my tracks.

"Oh, and Rachel?"

"Yeah?" I look up to meet his steadfast gaze.

"In the future, never hesitate to grab anything out of my desk or office, okay?" he states with a coy smile I want to smack right off his face. "My things are your things."

Oh, hardy-har-har. Very funny, asshole.

"Duly noted." My responding smile is so fake it could be a sugar substitute. "See you tomorrow."

And then, I walk around the smug bastard and head right for the stairwell.

He might think he can make me break, but he hasn't experienced the stubbornness that is Rachel Rose.

Game on, Professor. I hope you came to play.

EIGHT

Ty

"Have a great weekend. See you, Monday," I announce with a grin and watch as my four o'clock Advanced Creative Writing class packs up their bags.

If there's one guarantee on a Friday, it's that every student in the class will make a beeline for the door. There will be no questions or concerns to be had. The priority is the weekend, and anything class-related can wait until Monday.

Frankly, I don't mind, and I stay put at my lecture hall desk, scrolling through some missed notifications on my phone while my mostly junior and senior students exit the room.

First, I hit my text inbox and find a message from an unknown number. The anticipation makes my heart rate kick up a few notches, but when I open it, the excitement comes to a screeching halt.

Unknown: Hi, Ty. It's Clara.

Who is Clara? That name isn't ringing any fucking bells.

Thankfully, she's provided an explanation via two additional messages.

Unknown: *We met at Orchid a few Fridays ago. Danced a bit. Had a drink at the bar.*

Unknown: *I ended up getting your number from your brother Jude. He's an old friend. And since I had such a good time with you, I wanted to reach*

out and see if you'd be interested in meeting up for a drink this weekend. I'd love to continue what we started. ;)

I can appreciate the sentiment, but without sounding like a dick, I still don't remember her.

That's because there's only one woman you remember from Orchid.

While I decide whether I need to kick Jude's ass for giving out my number to random women, I move my focus to a text from my mom.

Mama Winslow: Ty, what time are you picking me up?

Tonight is one of our monthly mother-son date nights, and the plans include surprising her with a fun dinner at Tavern on the Green. It's one of her favorite restaurants, and it's been over a year since we've gone.

I also plan to do a little reconnaissance on Wendy Winslow's online dating adventures.

Apparently, she's already started an account on TapNext, and while it's no booty-call Tinder buffet, it's not exactly Christian Mingle either.

Me: Your handsome, wonderful, fantastic, and most favorite child will pick you up at 7:00.

Mama Winslow: You know I don't play favorites, Ty.

Me: Oh, I know, Mom. ;) Your secret is safe with me.

Mama Winslow: You're incorrigible.

Me: See you at 7.

Emails are the next item on my to-do list, and while most of the shit in my inbox can wait until Monday, there's one email in particular that stands out above all the rest.

I click it open without hesitation.

To: Professor Winslow

From: Rachel Rose

Subject: ENG 101 Short Essays & Grading Rubric

Good afternoon, Professor Winslow,

I'd like to get a head start on grading the short essays for your ENG 101 class. Can I get them from you before I leave campus today?

Also, a grading rubric would be helpful. It's one item I haven't managed to locate in the Google Drive or the files you've already given me.

Thanks,

Rachel Rose

Graduate Student, NYU English Department

TA to Professor Winslow

Yesterday, I told her she would be tasked with grading the short, handwritten essays I assigned to my ENG 101 students and gave them until three p.m. today to turn in. In this digital age of Microsoft Word and Google Drives, there was a lot of grumbling over the handwritten part, but it was a fairly easy assignment—a two-thousand-word review of *Anna Karenina*—and one I thought would be a good start in getting Rachel's grading feet wet.

As I scan her email, I don't know why seeing the words *TA to Professor Winslow* urges a smile to my lips, but it does.

Silently, I add *Curvaceous Goddess* and *Sexy Panty-Giver* to her list of attributes.

Bro, you have got to stop it.

In my defense, for the past few days, I've been good. I've kept any conversations with her to class discussions and her TA-related duties and abandoned my wily ways from the first day of class. And trust me, that's taken some real fucking effort. The whole panty coup is the kind of thing dreams are made of for a guy like me. Not messing with her again after she left the panties in my drawer and silently—*and with extreme confidence*—pressed play on this little game? Nearly impossible.

Because mentally? I'm obsessed.

Rachel Rose and her panties are quite literally one of the only things I think about.

Fingers to the keys, I shoot her a quick response.

To: Rachel Rose

From: Professor Winslow

Rachel,

Since I'm not the easiest to get ahold of by email, here's my cell: 555-134-6879.

I have the short essays and grading rubric for you. If you're still on campus, shoot me a text.

Professor Ty Winslow

English Department NYU

Frankly, I'm just as easy to get ahold of by email, and I know I already gave her my cell, but a nudge to use it proves too hard to resist. All of my willpower has apparently been triangulated to a very specific area—my dick.

A few minutes later, my phone pings with another text message from an unknown number.

Unknown: It's Rachel Rose. I'm still on campus. Meet you in the lecture hall?

This time, however, it's a number I'm happy to program into my phone *and* respond to the sender. I know she's avoiding my office for a reason, and I'm just enough of an asshole to push the limit. It'd be easier for both of us if she came here—to the lecture hall—where I already am. But some things aren't meant to be easy.

Me: My office work for you?

Rachel: I can be there in about 10 minutes.

Her response is quick and accommodating, and I find myself impressed with her once again. She's in a whole other league than any other game player I've ever met.

Me: Great. See you there.

Without hesitation, I toss my laptop into my leather bag and shut off the lights of the lecture hall.

In a matter of minutes, I'm jogging up the last few steps of the stairwell and heading down the hallway of the second floor. I unlock my office door with ease, flip on the lights, and step inside.

The small box of files I have for her sits in the corner of the room, and I pick it up and set it on my desk, my gaze flicking down to my desk drawer, where those infamous pink panties still remain.

I open the drawer with the intention of just taking a look, but before I know it, her panties and the note I left her the other day are sitting at the top of the box of files.

Fuck, Ty, my more responsible inner voice chastises. *What are you doing?*

Attempting to return these panties to their rightful owner, I argue back instantly. *I'm trying to do a good deed.*

Every working brain cell inside me knows that's horseshit. But the blood supply for those cells is currently headed elsewhere, and yeah…I'm a kind of a fucking douchebag, but I can't seem to help myself. The woman challenges me beyond my greatest fantasies, and I'm becoming an addict to her reactions.

After a moment of hesitation, I leave the panties where they are, still snug in the box of files, and brace for impact.

"Knock, knock." An all-too-familiar female voice fills my ears, and I look up to find Rachel standing in the doorway. *Oh shit. It's time.*

She's far more casual today, dressed in jeans and a cream sweater and a pair of brown boots. However, the fit of the sweater and the jeans is so perfectly snug that my gaze can't help but home in on the way her clothes show off her delicious curves.

This shit is becoming painful.

But it's as if God himself sculpted this woman with only my desires in mind, and the kind of arousal that produces is unavoidable. It's literally heaven-sent. Which, considering the fact that she's Nathaniel Rose's daughter and I'm not supposed to touch her, makes me wonder if this is some form of punishment for all the bullshit I put my mom through when I was an asshole teenager. Penance, I suppose you could call it.

Her eyes steal a quick once-over of my face and then my body, and my suffering grows even deeper.

I *know* that look in a woman. I've seen it hundreds of times. It's *the* look. The subconscious one that can't be controlled and tells me she likes what she sees.

It's the same look I've been giving her for days—the one I have no business acting on, considering the circumstances.

"So…the essays?" she prompts, straightening her spine and crossing her arms over her chest.

"Yes," I answer, clearing my throat. "I have them right here." I nod toward the box on my desk and busy myself with a whole bunch of nothing on the bookshelf behind me. Normally, I would be a gentleman and hand them to her, but giving her a little privacy during the moment she discovers what's inside the small box is a higher priority. I am definitely an asshole—but I'm not trying to upset her. I just *have* to see how long she's willing to play it this way.

"Grading rubric is in there, too, by the way," I add and silently count to ten in my head, hoping that's more than enough time for Rachel to realize she can finally wave the white flag on her lies without any drama or a witness if she'll just take them now.

Five.

Six.

Seven.

Eight.

Nine.

Ten.

When I turn back around, though, the panties are still in play. Frankly, they're in play in a *big* way.

With one hand, Rachel takes a pen off my desk, lifts her underwear out of the box, and drops them on top of a stack of papers beside my conference phone. The Post-it stays stuck to the delicate material until they reach their destination.

The entire time, she keeps her beautiful green eyes locked with mine.

The rush of adrenaline that floods my veins is nearly enough to knock me off my feet.

Goddamn, she is something else.

"Thank you, Professor," she says, her voice confident and her chin raised high. "I appreciate you getting this together for me."

"You're welcome, Rachel," I answer, not even trying to stop my smile. "Anything else you need? From me? From the office? Anything at all?"

"Nope." She shakes her head, and a little tsk leaves her lips. "Pretty sure I have everything I need right here." She lifts the box in her arms and smirks, one eyebrow climbing pointedly up her forehead.

"See you Monday, Professor," she calls over her shoulder as she turns and exits the way she came, leaving me standing there with her panties on my desk and the kind of hard-on usually seen on pubescent boys or produced by little blue pills.

I grab it through my pants, squeezing at the base to cut off the blood supply and remind it of the rules.

This is a game—one I'll let run its course because she's a worthy opponent and a fascinating adversary.

But at the end of the day, that's where it stops. Rachel Rose is off-limits, and when the panty tug-of-war ends, so will the rest of it.

I nod to myself.

Ty Winslow has finally found a line he won't cross.

Right?

NINE

Friday, January 25th

Rachel

I've almost survived another full week of classes at NYU.

My master's workload is certainly challenging, but it's manageable. I feel like I'm fitting in enough shifts at Lydia and Lou's bakery that I'm actually helping them out, and I'm not exactly minding sitting through Professor Winslow's classes.

He is an entertaining guy. Kind of an asshole at times, but I think that's what makes it interesting.

And I've only had to experience my panties appearing once this week. Before Tuesday's ENG 101 class, he asked me to run out to his car and grab something he needed for class, and when I got there, *surprise, surprise,* my underwear was nicely folded up in his back seat, the Post-it note still present.

However, even that little note is starting to show the wear of this silent game we're playing. Its edges are wrinkled, and the sticky adhesive is hanging on for dear life. The physical display of my persistence made me smile.

Obviously, I didn't take them. If he wants to drive around with women's underwear in his back seat, that's his problem. Not mine.

While the ENG 101 students finish getting settled into their seats, I steal a quick glance at my phone. First, my calendar, noting what grad work I need to get done tonight after pulling a few hours at the bakery.

Next, I move to my messages, where one from my overprotective sister sits front and center.

Lydia: Are you sure you want to pick up a shift this evening?

She's *always* asking me this question.

Me: Positive. I'll pull the 6-9 shift so you and Lou can go grab dinner or something.

Lydia: That's really sweet of you, Rae. Are you sure?

Me: Yes. And I won't take no for an answer.

Truthfully, I could use those three hours to get grad schoolwork done, but Lydia and Lou are doing so much for me. I want to make sure I'm showing my thanks in some way, even if it means I have to occasionally burn the midnight oil. They've put so much effort into keeping their bakery open for after-office hours, working sixteen hours most days for years, I'm glad to be able to take away some of the burden.

"Yesterday, we discussed the role of infidelity and sexual desires in *Anna Karenina*," Ty begins to address the class, and I promptly lock the screen of my phone and slide it back into my bag. "Today, we're going to delve deeper into the roles that gender and societal norms played in the book."

He turns toward the whiteboard and writes, **Is Tolstoy a misogynist or a champion of women's rights?**

"If you search anything about *Anna Karenina* on Google, you will undoubtedly see this question within the first couple pages of search results. It's a common debate—factor in Tolstoy's complicated personal life with his wife Sophia, and it's something a lot of people have very fierce opinions on," Ty continues and turns back toward the class. "But I want to know what *you* think the answer to that question is. Not what some literary scholar has told you to think, but what *you* think Tolstoy's opinion of women was after reading the book. Did he have compassion for women? Or did he have a prejudice against them?"

Ty walks around the front of his desk and rests a hip against it, keeping his eyes toward the students in the lecture hall.

No one is eager to offer their opinion, but Ty waits patiently, watching as his students waver between avoiding his eyes and grabbing their copies of *Anna Karenina* and scrolling through the pages.

"Is it just me, or has this classroom grown eerily quiet?" he teases, flashing everyone one of his fanciest smiles. It's the one that makes his eyes shine like mirror balls and his tiny dimple settle into his cheek. It's the one that's the most playful by a mile, and it's one of several I hate to admit that I know this well.

But watching him is like breathing, his personality is so magnetic.

"It's okay. I know it's not an easy question to answer for yourself. So, let's break it down together."

He turns back toward his desk and reaches over it to pull a small box out of his top desk drawer. "We can all agree there are very simple things that our minds think of when it comes to the differences between men and women, right?"

Most of the class nods in agreement.

"Okay, so if we look at the differences on a very superficial level, we'd probably do something like this…" He pauses, reaches into the box, and proceeds to hold up a pair of men's black boxer briefs and a pair of women's underwear—*my* underwear.

You've got to be kidding me. I've changed my mind. All of his smiles are stupid, and so is his personality.

"So, these boring black underwear are considered the standard for men," Ty continues. "Can we all agree on that?"

One female student raises her hand. Ty calls on her immediately. "Um… are those yours, Professor?"

"Katie, I think we can both agree that's an inappropriate question, yeah?"

She blushes a little, but Ty doesn't drag out her embarrassment. *Oh no. That's something he reserves only for you.* He raises the pink panties into the air now, spreading them out and holding them by the fabric at the hips.

"And when we see these beautiful, delicate underwear, we instantly associate them with women."

"Yeah, Prof. Hot women. Damn, those are sexy," Landon croons, running a hand through his shaggy blond hair.

A lot of students laugh, but Ty shakes his head. Just when I think he might look over at me, he doesn't. Perhaps, in an effort not to bring that kind of attention to me. Of course, if he really wanted to be a hero, he probably wouldn't have flashed my panties at the class in the first place.

"Again, *inappropriate*," Ty rebukes Landon, setting both the boxer briefs and panties back in the box on his desk. "So, these are simple superficial things we view as differences between men and women, right? And we can keep breaking things down like that. We can say men and women tend to have different expectations related to facial hair. Men and women have different hygiene habits. Men and women have different perspectives related to clothing and shoes. It's an endless list. But it's not those things that we need to look at when it comes to Tolstoy."

Ty looks up at the class and points to a female student with her hand held in the air.

"Yes, Amanda."

"I think Tolstoy had a certain view about women because of the time period in which he lived," she said. "I don't necessarily think he thought women were powerful or strong, but I also felt that he had compassion for them."

"You're on the right track, Amanda," Ty says, bolstering her confidence with a proud smile. "But it's not because I think you have the right answer, or that any of us can have the right answer when it comes to how Tolstoy really viewed women because we're not him. I asked you to explore the answer for yourself, and that's what you've done. Can anyone else expand on what Amanda said? Or maybe even disagree?"

Another female student raises her hand. "I don't think he liked women. It felt like he viewed them in only two categories, either the Madonna or the Whore. With nothing in between."

"Interesting, Jessica," Ty says with a nod. "So, you think, in Tolstoy's eyes, Anna was the whore?"

"Well, yeah," she agrees. "Anna was the one who committed adultery."

"Okay," he says and turns back toward his desk. And before I know it, the underwear, *my* underwear, are back up in the air again. "So, we know that Anna committed adultery. And let's just pretend that Anna fancied herself wearing this type of underwear beneath her clothes."

"I'm down with that imagery!" Landon shouts between cupped hands.

"And there is no one in this class who is surprised by that, dude," Ty counters. "But if these underwear stand for Anna, the one who found herself in a passionate affair with a man who wasn't her husband," he states and pauses to grab the boxer briefs. "And these underwear stand for Anna's brother Stiva, the one who had an affair with his children's governess. Why did society only get worked up over these?" He shakes the panties in the air. "Why was she shunned, outcasted, and put through so much pain it ended up being her downfall?"

When I glance behind me, I note that a large majority of the students are riveted by what Ty is saying. He has their *full* attention. In fucking undergraduate college English.

Even though he's used my damn panties as a prop in his discussion, I have to admit it's been effective.

I hate to say it, but I'm impressed. Somehow, he managed to make my stupid panties appear…*again*. And this time, he even succeeded in making a small part of me admire him for it.

The bastard is clever as hell and, I'm convinced, has some kind of voodoo juju.

When no one in the class speaks up, he turns his attention to me.

"Rachel, do you have anything to add to the discussion?"

Now, he's testing me. But honestly, I don't mind. Talking about Tolstoy is one of my comfort zones.

"Sure. I'd love to."

"By all means, then, come on up," he answers, setting my panties back down on his desk, taking a seat next to them, and waving a magnanimous arm to indicate the floor is mine.

Up and out of my seat, I walk across the lecture hall, my heels clicking on the hardwood floor with every step, and head to the whiteboard.

Ty watches as I walk by, but I focus on the task at hand, grabbing the black marker to write a few things on the board.

Was Anna intelligent?

Was Anna bound by consequences and societal constructs?

Was Anna in a happy marriage or a loveless marriage?

When it came to her affair, did you feel that she was completely wrong, or did you find yourself having understanding for why she did it?

Did Anna have compassion for others?

Did Anna prioritize her own needs over what society wanted her to do? And, if yes, was that selfish?

I turn back around and find Ty smiling at me. "Interesting choice of questions."

"For me, these are the questions that help me decide the answer to *your* question," I state, and with the marker, I tap the place on the board where his initial question sits. "Sure, I could attempt to dissect Tolstoy's personal life and his marriage to Sophia, but I think the fairest assessment of his view on women can only come from the words he was willing to give to the masses."

"I couldn't agree more," Ty says and turns back to the class.

"If you look at Rachel's questions, and really try to sort through them, where does it leave you on your view of Tolstoy and his opinion of women?" Ty questions the class, and I head back toward my seat. "I know you guys are going to hate me for this, but I'm officially assigning you another essay.

No fewer than five pages, and I want your final answer to my question with sound and logical reasons backing you up and showing me how you came to that conclusion."

Audible, annoyed sighs are heard in the class, but Ty is undeterred.

"I was going to offer giving you the rest of this class and all of Monday's class to work on said essay, but if you're going to be like that…I could just as easily assign it as weekend homework…"

"No! No! We're all so happy about it!" Landon chimes in, standing up and looking around at his fellow students. "We can't wait to write it, Prof. *Right?*"

The entire class nods and offers verbal—*albeit, fake*—responses of wanting to start on the essay right now.

"I had a feeling you guys would say that." Ty chuckles. "All right. Well, I'll let you guys get to work. We'll finish this discussion on Tuesday, once everyone has come to their final conclusions and turned in their essays."

"Wait, Prof!" Landon interjects. "Can we at least…uh…do this essay in the digital age of computers?"

Ty smirks. "Considering I've seen your shit handwriting, and I'm sure it was no easy feat for Rachel to grade your last essay, yes. Turn this one in via the Google Drive."

Landon isn't offended at all. "Thank you!" he exclaims and plops back down in his seat.

The sounds of fingers tapping across laptop keys fill the room, and I start to use the time to get a little grad work done, but Ty's quiet voice grabs my attention.

"Hey, Rachel, you mind stepping out for a quick chat?"

I shrug and get up from my seat, following his lead into the hallway.

"All right," he says and leans against the now-shut door of his lecture hall. "What's your final answer?"

"My final answer?" I question with a tilt of my head. "On what?"

"On Tolstoy."

"Are you assigning me a verbal essay right now?"

His stupid smile is contagious. "Something like that."

"Okay, well, I think it's pretty obvious what I think." I snort. "Tolstoy was ahead of his time in how he viewed women. Although he wasn't exactly a leader in the feminist movement, he certainly showed the kind of compassion for women that wasn't common during that time. Especially in Russia."

"Hmm." Ty rubs his fingers over his chin. "Interesting."

"Wait…you don't agree?"

He stares at me for a long moment, searching my eyes, but then his face morphs from serious to amused. "I'm just messing with you. Of course I agree."

"Geez." I roll my eyes, and it's as if my hand has a mind of its own, reaching out to nudge him playfully in the shoulder. "Does everything have to be a game with you?"

"But aren't games so much fun, Rachel?" he teases back and waggles his brow. "I certainly love games."

"I'm aware," I say, and for the first time, it's almost as if I'm silently acknowledging what we both already know.

"Oh, Rachel. I *know*."

I find myself playfully nudging him again, this time with my elbow, and Ty smiles at me. This is his sexy smile, the one that makes most women turn giddy and flirty and all the other things he probably loves so much.

Hello, kettle. Meet pot.

When I realize I'm smiling back at him like an idiot, I roll my eyes and glance over my shoulder, trying to collect myself. But in my search for equilibrium, it seems I've found something else—a familiar set of scrutinizing eyes, studying my every movement.

My father strides down the hallway, heading right for us, and in a knee-jerk reaction that pisses me off, I step away from Ty a bit. A twenty-six-year-old woman shouldn't feel like she needs to hide something from her dad, especially when, in all reality, she's not even doing anything wrong. I mean, we're discussing Tolstoy, for shit's sake.

"Rachel, Professor Winslow," he greets us, his voice more firm than friendly. "Everything going okay today?"

"Just a healthy debate on *Anna Karenina*," Ty offers easily, his voice every bit as relaxed as it was moments ago. If he can feel the tension vibrating off my father, he's doing one hell of a job pretending he can't.

"One of Rachel's favorite books," my dad answers for me with a smile that doesn't meet his eyes. He turns to me then, expression dropping the façade entirely. "Rachel, do you mind stopping by my office later today?"

"I would, but I have a class at three," I say, doing my best to avoid the coming confrontation. Normally, I have a lot of fight in me, but today, I'm really not in the mood.

"Not a problem, sweetheart. I'll still be there when you're done."

I could try to refute again, but I know it's a useless endeavor where Nathaniel Rose is concerned. He's holding the line, and I'm expected to tow it.

Pigeonholed, I agree with a "Great. See you then" and excuse myself from what feels like an awkward powwow to head back into the lecture hall.

For a woman who came back to New York to live her own life and figure out her career path without worrying about her father's expectations, I sure seem to be doing just the opposite.

At a little after five in the evening, I walk out of my Literature and Philosophy class and start on the march of death.

Maybe that's a little dramatic for a visit to your own dad's office at a prestigious university, but I have enough receipts from over the years to prove my point in a full-page spread on Page Six.

I shuffle down the hallway, jockeying through the last of the students who remain on a Friday evening, and head up the stairwell to the second floor.

I have no idea what stuffy Professor Rose wants to talk about now, but I'm sure he has a point, a presentation, and notes for me to take home for studying. If there's anything he loves to do, it's listen to himself breathe hot air in my direction.

Upon arrival at his office, I step through the open door with a truncated knock to its surface and find my father sitting behind his massive mahogany desk. It's one he's had for a long time, one that came from his office in the old Greenwich Village brownstone we lived in for many years—one my mother had made for him.

"Hi, sweetheart." He greets me warmly enough. Nathaniel Rose is not the type of guy to raise his voice or fly off the handle or address anyone with outright disrespect. He's old-school—classy. But all that means shit when he's talking down to you the way he's done to me since I can remember. He knows best, and I never know enough. Always.

"Hey, Dad," I respond, taking a tentative seat on the edge of the big leather armchair that faces his desk. "What's up?"

"Well, I want to talk to you about a few things," he says, sliding off his reading glasses. "Remind you of a few things, I guess you could say."

I furrow my brow, envisioning a direction this could go that would not end well. "Remind me of what exactly?"

"Well, Rachel," he starts and stands up from his chair to walk around the massive desk and perch his hip on the side closest to me. He crosses his arms over his chest, and his face turns from warm and soft to firm and serious. "I want to remind you that you're here for your career. Not for distractions."

"I know," I rebuke immediately. I'm carrying a full load of graduate classes and TA'ing for another professor because of him. I don't need a reminder of what I'm swamped by every day.

He studies me closely, uncrossing his arms and letting his hands settle onto the surface of his corduroy-covered thighs. "When I made the arrangement for you to be Professor Winslow's TA, I did that with the expectation that you would keep it strictly professional. And from what I saw of you two in the hall earlier today, I think it's possible that some lines are getting close to being crossed."

Is he serious with this shit?

This is *none* of his fucking business, and yet, here he is, having the nerve to think it is.

"You can't seriously be saying this to me right now."

"A relationship between a professor and his subordinate at this university—at *my* university—is not appropriate, Rachel, and I won't condone it."

"There is no relationship, *Dad.* I'm his TA, just like *you* assigned me to be."

I want to tell him to fuck off with his expectations and give him my official resignation from NYU, but a photo just beside him on his desk stops me.

My *mother.* That photo is my father's favorite picture of her, and it always pulls at my heartstrings. She looks so young, so happy, and I see so much of Lydia and myself in her eyes.

If my mother were still alive, I know my relationship with my father wouldn't be like this. She was the glue of our family, and without her, it's all falling apart.

In her absence, he seeks control over me. Together, they read voraciously, they challenged each other, and our dinner table conversations often revolved around debating books like *War and Peace* and the reasons why Nabokov's prose was so brilliant.

He wants *me* to be the next Nadine Rose because then, it would feel like he still has a part of her in the literary world—and his. And maybe, just maybe, that would make her loss more bearable.

But I don't want to fill Nadine Rose's shoes. She was beautiful and bold and interesting—but she wore a size nine. My size seven foot just doesn't fit.

"Things like this have huge consequences, Rachel. You're here for your career, and now is not the time to lose focus," he continues, unfazed by my denial. It's not a surprise. He never hears a word I have to say.

This is why I was on the West Coast for so long. I needed space away from this. Away from him.

He doesn't own me and my actions. He doesn't decide what is a distraction for me and what is not. He doesn't get to dictate my life.

I decide what my career path is. *I* make my own choices. And he might be my father, but I'm an adult woman. He doesn't get a say in *any* of this.

I stand from my chair suddenly, surprising my dad and, if I'm honest, even myself a little.

"I'm focused, Dad. As focused as I've ever been. So, either take me off Professor Winslow's service, or leave me alone. You pick. But I'm not living the entire semester under a shadow."

My heart beats a million miles a minute, and my stomach churns with anxiety. Never in my life, even with all our issues, have I spoken to my father like this.

Never have I faced down the confrontation and stood up for myself like this.

And never have I ever felt so close to puking without a gastrointestinal reason.

He stares me down for several seconds and then silently rounds the desk, takes his seat, and places his glasses back atop his nose. And just like that, I'm dismissed without the courtesy of a response.

Instantly, I feel half an inch tall. Humiliated. Belittled. *Un-fucking-seen.*

Aggravation stirs in my gut, and a wave of rebellion washes over me so strong, I don't know if I'll ever come up for air. No one, not even my father, gets to make me feel this way.

No one gets to choose for me.

No one tells me what to do.

A plan is already swirling in my mind, setting up shop, and making notes on my next move. One conversation with my father and I've regressed ten years emotionally. Not only am I not going to stay away from Ty Winslow, I'm going to stir the motherfucking pot.

Rebellious old habits die hard, huh?

Evidently, with a father like Nathaniel Rose, they don't die at all.

TEN

Monday, January 28th

Ty

"Everyone, make sure you turn in your essay via the link in the Google Drive, and I will see you tomorrow afternoon," I announce to my ENG 101 class. "Oh, and Rachel, don't forget to stop by my office to grab the paperwork I told you about."

It's boring paperwork that every TA in the English Department needs to fill out and turn in on a biweekly basis. Just a bunch of admin bullshit if you ask me.

She offers a little nod of acknowledgment, but that's it, and I try to busy myself on my laptop, checking emails, while my students pack up their stuff and head out of the lecture hall.

I can't deny, though, the entire time, my gaze flickers toward the dark-haired, green-eyed goddess in the beige silk dress and heels. Sometimes, I even tilt my head a little to the right to see her past the line of college kids exiting the room.

Time moves at a snail's pace, but eventually, my lecture hall is empty, and Rachel is on her feet.

I'm on my feet too, and I walk briskly behind her, the anticipation of another round of our little panty war almost enough to make me rub my hands together like an evil overlord.

I'm honestly not sure why I still find it so fun after nearly two weeks of playing at it, but I can't deny that I do. Finding ways to tussle with Rachel

Rose has nearly become the number one item on my list of priorities. Honestly, it reads something like this:

1. *Mess with Rachel.*

2. *Breathe.*

3. *Eat.*

4. *Sleep.*

Generally, my interest in a woman runs its course pretty quickly, but Rachel still feels fresh. I don't know what it is about her, but damn, she's a fucking enigma. An exception to my normally short-attention-span tendencies.

Maybe it's the ripe shine of forbidden fruit, but there's something about this woman that makes me want to keep playing. If the frequency of my masturbation over the weekend is anything to go by, getting schooled by someone on Tolstoy is evidently on my top five list of turn-ons.

I'll have to be careful with that, though—some of the other professors in the department are experts themselves. And I just can't picture myself getting a hard-on for ol' Kip or Adele.

Anticipation builds as she clears the threshold of my office and strides toward the shelf that I instructed her to check for the paperwork. It's there, of course, I'm not completely sadistic, but so are the panties, almost garishly displayed like a flag. She has a tremendous ability to ignore and avoid, though—almost as good as my eldest brother, Remy. Her track record proves it.

She walks to the shelf easily, and I lean into the jamb of the door, waiting for our normal banter. I'm almost salivating like one of Pavlov's pathetic pups, but she shocks me completely by bringing my drool up short.

"Oh, here they are," she states so matter-of-factly as she snatches the most perfect delicate, sheer pink panties I've ever held in my hands.

After a weekend of anticipation—of planning and waiting—my brain short-circuits. Those are not the words I expected, nor is the expression on her face. We've never actually gotten to the point where she admits to being the owner of the underwear, and to be honest, I was starting to suspect we never would.

The game would either be laboriously infinite, or they would just disappear one day, no explanation given. Those were the only two possibilities I had even considered.

The ease with which she's claiming them now almost makes me think I'm hallucinating.

"Huh? Here what are?"

"My underwear," she says nonchalantly. "I've been looking for them."

Wait, what? She's been looking for those panties as much as I've been looking for a farmer to milk me from the teat. All she's done for the last month is pretend underwear in general don't exist. The president of the United States? As far as Rachel is concerned, he goes commando. And now she's acting like she's Lewis or Clark on the Great American Panty Expedition.

"You have?" I can feel my eyes narrow in challenge, but she doesn't flinch. Her face is a stalwart admiral in the Royal Panty Navy.

"Yeah. I'm really glad you found them. I forgot to put any on this morning, so I could really use them."

"You...f-f-f-or...got underwear?" I slur practically drunkenly, surprising myself. I don't usually sound like that. I don't think I have *ever* sounded like that. I'm confident. Self-assured. And I can handle people slinging shit because I've slung enough to beat out everyone else for five lifetimes.

I clear my throat and tilt my head from one side to the other, glancing down to the hem of Rachel's dress involuntarily. *Relax, Ty. She's fucking with you.* I speak again, this time steadying my voice to something a lot closer to normal. "You forgot your underwear?"

"Mm-hmm," she hums, licking at her bottom lip with just the tip of her tongue. I can almost feel my eyes dilate like a cartoon character, every ounce of cool, calm, and collected evacuating the building as though it's been declared condemned. She nods then, to affirm all the things her hum only hinted at, and I almost can't believe how sexually enticing the simple movement is.

I want to say something to taunt her back, to regain some of my control, but she's relentless in her actions, holding out the panties in front of herself by the dangle of just one finger. Her eyes are warm and inviting, and the corner of her mouth is turned up in a seductive smirk. "You want to help me put them on?"

Excu-fuck-what? I open my mouth to answer and will my mind to signal my head to nod, but all I manage is the wooden gulp of a man frozen by mere surprise. She watches me closely, her head tilting just enough to make the bright green of her eyes turn dark and all the air from my lungs to get trapped in my throat.

What the hell is she playing at?

When I don't say anything, she moves on to do the talking for me. And by the assumption she makes, she's either the most torturous woman on the planet, or she doesn't know me at all. Based on how vocal a college campus can be with salacious fodder, I'm betting on the first.

"No?" she says with a pout. "Okay. Some other time, then." With a quick flick of her wrist, she postures her ankle out in front of herself and slips her pink panties on one foot at a time, shimmying them up her legs and into position under her dress.

I watch the hem flutter down like a sheet on a clothesline billowing in the wind. It takes everything within me to stop myself from stooping down to try to get a view of the promised land underneath.

She rounds the desk, grabbing the paperwork she needed off the shelf on the way, and I'm left standing there, my mouth gulping like a big, dumb fish. I wish I could remember all the types and species and shit from all the years fishing with Uncle Brad so I could at least come up with something to liken myself to, but I'll be fucked if my brain can tap into anything other than hormones right now.

Our chests almost touch as she stops in front of me, her eyes traveling up the line of my throat until they capture mine. There's a sparkle in hers. Playful, mischievous, challenging.

The normal Ty Winslow would lean toward her, push her back into her space. But I'm so out of equilibrium right now, I doubt I could say my own name aloud if someone asked me.

"Excuse me," she says, her voice a sultry whisper. One eye closes in a teasing wink, and my chest swings back of its own accord. She fills the space I've vacated, stepping around me and heading out the door without looking back.

However, I watch the swing of her curvy hips with avid interest the entire way. I love a woman with the body of a woman. Voluptuous, sultry, inviting. I like a body I can get lost in for a while.

And now, I'll have the memory of watching that exact description walk away, leaving me behind with slurred speech, a missed opportunity, and a half-hard dick for the rest of my life.

I'm starting to think Rachel Rose is a whole lot of things her dad doesn't know about—and a couple I'm not ready for myself.

But the thing that worries me the most, is not knowing what the hell changed so significantly in three days' time...and what that means is to come from here.

I think I might be in trouble.

ELEVEN

Ty

Blue Oyster Bar is largely abandoned on Monday nights, and after the day I've had, I'm glad for it. Rachel hasn't exactly left me ready for bright lights and the main stage, so low-key is what I need.

And thankfully, Blue Oyster is just that. The noise level never goes above a dull roar, a game is always on, and the seafood is always fresh. Frankly, that's why Remy refuses to branch out and go anywhere else.

It's habit, and it's evidently the good kind, according to him. I'm pretty sure he's bullshitting so he won't have to answer for the rut he's let his life fall into, but I'm in no position to play counselor tonight.

After Rachel's little show in my office, it's a miracle I've managed to prevent the swallowing of my own tongue for this many hours. I'm on the edge of a precipice—one that just happens to feel like fucking garbage on both sides. I don't like the idea of letting all this playful buildup lead to nowhere, but I also hate the idea of breaking the trust of a man who's been the kind of mentor I was missing my whole life. And ever since Rachel left my office this afternoon after taking our taunting up about a million notches, I've been a walking case of frazzled nerves and mental confusion.

A blast of fresh cold air hits me as I open the door—a startingly odd feeling at the end of January in New York. Normally, the heat is on max, hitting you like a wave of hot tub water the moment you lift your foot across the threshold of indoors, but not this place. It's practically one of those ice resorts, and I usually never take off my coat. But hey, sacrifices have to be made to keep the seafood fresh and a grumpy older brother happy.

The hostess smiles and waves me forward as I approach, knowing I'm there to meet my brother and knowing I'm running late to meet him as usual.

She has her best smile in place, one she reserves for me when I come in, and one I normally at least acknowledge.

But I can't. Not tonight. Tonight, I'm struggling just to put one foot in front of the other without giving myself a flat tire like a bully on the grade-school playground.

"How's it going, Ty?" the hostess asks with a bright smile as we pass a table of other regulars, attempting to bring the robot version of me to life.

I try to put words together, something to the effect of, "Going well," and end up choking on my tongue and tripping on the toe of my boot. Two stumbling steps and a set of flailing arms carry me directly into the table behind the male regulars—empty, thank God—but the resting glasses and dishware clink and clonk, and the table rocks up onto the far side of its bear-claw leg.

"Oh my goodness! Are you okay?" she practically shrieks, horrified. And I can relate. I've managed to transform into a ninety's rom-com heroine in the span of half a day. Lord only knows what I'm going to be like tomorrow.

Silently, I wave her off and pull myself up with sheer will so I can stumble over to Remy's regular table in the back. When he comes into view, his eyes are up and alert, having heard the commotion.

"What the hell's happening up there?" he asks, trying to get a peek at the moron who can't keep himself on his own two feet. Little does he know, he has a front-row seat to the clown show. I slide into the leather booth opposite him and unbutton the front of my coat. I'm suddenly feeling a little overheated.

"Nothing," I dismiss quickly, opening my menu and pretending I don't get the same damn food every time I come here. "Something with the hostess, I think." My eyes flick from the menu to him several times, scoping the situation manically. Remy looks to the front another couple times, taking a swig of his beer in between, but finally settles in to perusing the menu himself.

I'm thankful Remy's dropped his investigation into my fuckup in the front, but I still have to find a way to make it through an entire dinner without falling into any other tables. Thanks to Rachel fucking Rose, I'm on an alert level even Homeland Security isn't familiar with.

"How's class going this semester?" His tone is purely conversational, but I'm instantly suspicious. I don't know how, but Remy always has a way of *knowing* shit.

"What do you mean?"

His eyebrows draw together, and he puts his menu down on the table. Unlike me, he has reason to read—he actually changes his order every now and then—and I've somehow acted weird enough already to interrupt his routine. Truth be told, I haven't felt like this since I went to see Cleo in Staten Island.

"I mean, how is your job going? You are still teaching, right? You haven't joined an all-male revue, have you? The fuck?" he rails, his eyebrows making a mountain peak in the middle of his forehead.

I knew I was a little off-kilter, but apparently it's worse than I thought. *Fuck, man, get it together.*

"Work is good. Good group of students this year. Even a couple who aren't taking my class just to get the course credit."

"They'll get over that by the end of the semester."

A soft chuckle jumps from my throat. "Screw you."

"I'm just saying…I can't believe you somehow conned your way into a tenured position at a prestigious university. *You.* The guy who dipped his cock in green paint for Saint Patrick's Day when he was thirty-five years old."

"Hey, that was a one-time deal, and it wasn't paint. It was edible candy coating, and if you'd experienced what I had as a result, you sure as fuck wouldn't be making fun of me." To an outsider, it might sound like we're having a squabble. But for me, falling into the easy rhythm of shit-talking each other is oddly comforting. For the first time tonight, I'm feeling a little bit like myself.

"You really are disturbing on so many levels. No wonder you haven't set-tled down with a woman. They're generally looking for men at this age."

"You haven't settled down either, you bastard."

"Yeah. By choice. You hold America's Next Girlfriend auditions every mo-ment of your waking life."

"I keep the company of women because it's better than not keeping the company of women. I'm not auditioning anyone for shit."

Though, technically, you haven't kept any company for over a month…

My brain wants to pause on that thought, really fixate on the fucker, but Rem's next question brings me back to the present.

"You don't want to find someone like Jude and Flynn?"

An image of Rachel slipping into her panties in front of me this afternoon flashes through my memory, singeing my brain at the edges and allowing the discomfort of a few minutes ago right back in. My stomach turns and my pulse elevates, and I have to wipe a nonexistent bead of sweat off my brow just to give my shaky hand something to do.

Rachel's panty tease was hot as hell, sure, but why am I thinking of it right now? When Remy's asking me about settling down, for fuck's sake. It's not like it meant anything. It was just taking our game to the next level. That's it.

"Helloooo…earth to Ty."

I blink to glance over at Remy, and he's looking at me funny.

"What?"

"What is with you tonight? When's the last time you got laid, bro? Don't tell me you've already managed to run your dick through all five boroughs."

I open my mouth to answer with any number of pithy comebacks I know are waiting to be used in the back of my mind, and none of them step for-ward. All I can think about is how much I don't want a random girl from the rolodex. Or any random woman, for that matter. All I can think about is how badly I want to get laid—by one specific person.

Remy's forearms release completely, laying the menu on the table and crossing his arms over his chest. He knows something is up, and I'll be damned if I get out of here without at least pretending to get a problem off my chest.

Shit. How am I supposed to come up with something to play this off when I'm barely even functioning on a basic level? Would I be better off just giving him a glimpse?

I could just skim over the details, give Rem a little insight into the scrambled eggs in my head. Maybe it'd actually help to get some of it out there. To word vomit some of the sexual tension just to evacuate it from the confines of my body.

"I don't need to get laid," I murmur easily enough, adding, "I think it's the opposite problem, actually."

He laughs. "What? You're getting laid too much? Surely that can't be right."

"No." I chuckle a little and shake my head. "Wanting to get laid with the wrong person, is all."

The waiter approaches the table then, interrupting at quite possibly the most inopportune time. Remy's chuckle is annoying, and I can't tell him to go fuck himself with a knife in front of a stranger. I mean, even brotherly shit-talking has its boundaries. Namely, not getting the police called on one or both of us.

Remy orders first, his laughter continuing to roll around in his throat the whole time, and I glare at him with rays as powerful as the sun. He's immune to their strength, though, as I suppose any eldest sibling of five would be.

The waiter turns his attention to me, and I rattle off my standing order out of pure habit. "An order of shrimp cocktail to start, and a ten-ounce rib eye, medium, crab cake combo, with mixed vegetables and risotto on the side. Oh, and a Guinness."

The waiter nods and scribbles, smiling briefly before walking away and leaving Remy and me to fuck with each other again.

"I didn't know a wrong person to lay existed for Ty Winslow," Remy muses, falling right back into the conversation as though we weren't interrupted.

"I'm not an animal. I have boundaries."

Remy scoffs, blowing a mist of his half-drink of beer all over the table in front of me. "Since when?"

"Since forever," I reply with a scowl.

"Ty, you fucked one of the bridesmaids in the hall at my non-wedding."

"You know about that?"

"Of course." He rolls his eyes. "I know all the shit you and Jude get into. Flynn's the only one who manages to keep his dick's activity off the tri-county blotter."

"The fuck you say. I'm not that bad."

"Ty, I could open up the New York City phone book, point to a random spot on a random page, and probably still land on someone who had no more than two degrees of separation from a woman you've slept with. You alone have elevated the national average of sexual partners from six to seven."

"Whatever," I grumble, rubbing at the condensation on my water glass as the waiter interrupts once again. Remy, just like before, is laughing.

"Your shrimp cocktail and your Guinness, sir."

I nod, afraid if I open my mouth to say something to the poor guy who just works here and is very obviously just doing his job, I'll threaten him with the "family."

I don't have actual ties to the mafia that I know of, but when I was a young kid and people would ask about our dad, I always found it easier to pretend he'd been whacked for his role in the mob. I guess that sounds a lot cooler to most ten-year-olds than, *yeah, he didn't want to be around me anymore.*

"Thanks."

He nods and steps away again, and I chug a mouthful of beer before sighing at Remy. "Look, you might be right. *Normally.* But this is different. This is someone who's really off-limits."

He shrugs, the bastard. "So, leave her alone, then."

If only it was that easy…

"I want to. I do. But the more time goes on, the deeper and deeper I seem to get." His eyebrows rise, and I get defensive. "It's not just me. She's a willing party too. I just… I can't figure out how to put an end to it without making us both miserable."

"Ahh, I see. Your whole befuddled fuckboy thing you have going on tonight is starting to make more sense."

I flip him off, and he laughs. "I just mean this is new territory for you. Very grown-up, in fact."

"I'm almost forty, blowhard. I've been grown up for a while."

"In age, sure. In maturity? Not so much."

I narrow my eyes. "Do you have any actual, I don't know, advice to contribute? Or were you just going to use this as an excuse to insult me all night?"

"Look, there's not much I can say, bro," he says, and his voice is calm and serious. "If she's *really* off-limits, Ty, then I think you already know what to do. You just don't want to do it. It's up to you to figure out where to go from here."

I know he's right. Remy is almost always right, as much as I hate to admit it.

I need to find a way to distance myself from Rachel. To take things back to a professional level. And to keep them there.

Period.

TWELVE

Tuesday, January 29th

Rachel

Thanks to too much cake and gossip at the bakery last night, combined with staying up until five a.m. doing research for my thesis, I'm running late to my first class of the day. It's my ENG 101 class with Ty, and because of some sort of convention that's taken all my graduate-level professors to Cabo of all places for the rest of the week, it's all I have on the docket at the university before going to the bakery for a shift later.

The lecture's already started, I know it, and I'm just hoping I can sneak in and grab a seat without throwing Ty off too much—a goal in complete opposition to the wild woman I was yesterday. The one who shamelessly took back her panties and even asked for a little help putting them on.

Call it frustration or fun or whatever you want, but even I can't explain my actions. My sister Lydia would probably say it's totally something I would do—I'm not a wallflower—but it's not a set of actions I would normally entertain exchanging with my boss.

Because that's essentially what Ty is—an authority figure. I don't have to agree with my dad to adopt and acknowledge that. As long as I'm in charge of my own destiny, I'm willing to recognize that and respect it. I *think*.

Today's topic is usually a student favorite—sexual desires of women in early literature, a direct transition from their essays on Tolstoy's level of misogyny—and I've heard legend of how unabashedly rowdy Ty lets them get. He's popular for a lot of reasons, not the least of which being how hot the female undergrad population thinks he is while talking about early sexualization and the prominence of promiscuity.

I creep on my high heels to the edge of the door and push my ear to the wood briefly. Surprisingly, I don't hear any carousing or yelps or laughter. *Maybe I'm not running quite as late as I thought?*

Softly and with ease, I push the door open into the classroom and peek around the edge. Ty's at the front with his back to the room, scribbling on the board, so I move quickly, tiptoeing toward the seats in the front as fast as I can.

The class titters slightly at the intrusion, just enough that Ty turns to see what's going on. I bolt up straight and wave in apology, but Ty jumps as though I've shot an ice missile from my hand, like I'm fucking Elsa of the Northeast. He bumps his back into the board on retreat and jumps forward with a yelp of pain that could cut through glass.

Shoot.

"Sorry, sorry, sorry. I'm late, I know," I apologize quietly as I walk toward my normal spot in the front row on the far-right side of the lecture hall. Ty stares at me the entire time, so hard I feel like he's reading the dialogue on my soul, and I become overwhelmingly self-conscious. *What is he doing? Why isn't he teaching?*

"Anything I can do for you, Professor Winslow?" I ask softly, hoping to jar him back into action. But it's not until the words leave my lips and Ty's pupils dilate to saucers that I realize just how dirty it sounds. His eyes flick from my face to just below my belly and then quickly back to my face again. That's when it hits me.

Is he…still freaking out about the panty thing I did yesterday?

Holy shit. I think he is. I, Rachel Rose, simple TA, have rendered the biggest player at the university speechless. I wonder when I'm going to get my award.

An angel and a devil sit on my shoulders, willing me to choose my path. *Come on, Rachel, he's in the middle of class,* the angel says. *But think of how fun it'll be to watch him stumble,* the devil challenges easily. *He would definitely mess with you if the roles were reversed.* I never imagined he wouldn't be over my little stunt by now. He's the point guard of games. He's not supposed to be this easy to mess with.

"Again, sorry for the intrusion. I'll just take my seat," I say, choosing a neutral position until I have a little more time to consider. I mean, I'd love to feel the rush of adrenaline I felt yesterday, but is that really the right thing to do?

I take one of two empty seats in the front row and fold my notebook to my current page. I have a lot of jobs as his TA, but one of the easiest is picking out some test questions while listening to his lectures. The students don't know that, of course. They think I'm just taking notes. Otherwise, I imagine they'd be swarming me as if I were their queen bee.

But I love listening to the interpretations of a writer's intent and then funneling that into questions based on where Ty takes the discussion.

Two girls next to me wear low-cut blouses without bras and puff their chests into the cool air of the lecture hall. Normally, I wouldn't pay it any mind. Ty certainly doesn't. Evidently, staff *and* students are a hard no, even for a guy like him. I'm sure Alison at the English Department reception desk isn't a fan of that fact, but it is the reality of how Ty handles his professional life. A kind of shocking reality for Professor Casanova, if I'm honest.

But today, the overtly flirtatious freshman girls give me an idea. One I can't pass up. I have only a thin camisole under my sweater, and I, too, have nipples to show through my lace bra. And those nipples can certainly serve as a reminder to the professor in the front of the room. The one who thought he was leading our silent game, but sadly, he underestimated his opponent. This will be the second time in a row that I hold the upper hand. And, I can't be sure, but it sounds a lot like an outright victory to me.

Looks like the devil won out, sister.

Yes, I know, I'm a shit-stirrer. It's one of my dad's least favorite qualities in me and, ironically, something my mother always championed. *She's annoying you now, but she's going to grow up to be a woman who knows her worth and knows when to stand up for herself, Nathaniel,* she always used to say.

Sometimes I miss her so much it hurts. And hell, I don't know, a psychologist might have some things to say about the reasons I am the way I am. But at the end of the day, it's the only way I know how to be.

I unbutton my cardigan slowly, listening as Ty talks about how differently women were viewed in classic literature than they are now.

"The softness and curves of a woman were seen as desirable and unique during these times. There wasn't a diet culture in place—in fact, it was the opposite. Food, and the weight it contributed to, were seen as luxuries—as evidence of class and wealth. Look at any period art, and you'll see the same thing. Voluptuous women, secure and sexy in their curves."

I know the words aren't meant directly for me, but as I pull off my sweater, folding it over the back of my seat, and turn around to find Ty's hard eyes locked on my chest, it still feels like it. The hold of his stare, the weight of his words… Together, they feel like an actual touch of his warm hand, sliding across the focus of his gaze—my breasts.

And it's sexy as hell.

My abdomen feels heavy with arousal—a physical line in the sand that should very well indicate we're approaching a point of no return here. But its effect is just the opposite. It fuels me further. It drives me to drive him as close to the edge of the cliff as I can get him. It makes me crave the power of watching him stumble—to see the evidence firsthand, that I'm the kind of woman who can bring even a man like him to his knees.

It's a whole kick in the ass to the insecurities of my childhood.

"A little part of our assignment today involves a demonstration." He glances at me again, but this time, it feels different. It feels calculated, like a move to regain some power is coming.

I brace myself.

"But I'm going to need a female volunteer. Someone who is confident and not shy," he explains. "Someone who is willing to stand up here and let a few people give body-positive descriptors."

He glances around the classroom, and both of the girls beside me have their hands raised up high in the air. A few other girls raise their hands too, but Ty's gaze is on me again. "Ms. Rose?"

I glance around the classroom as every set of eyes comes to me, and I bite my lip. Suddenly, taking off my sweater isn't seeming like such a good idea…

You made your bed, Rachel. Now you get to lie in it, nipples out and all.

Shit. I almost say no, but when I feel like he wants me to say no, like he did this to prove some kind of "don't flash your nipples at me" point, I end up agreeing.

"Sure." I shrug one shoulder. "Why not."

Ty smirks, crooking a finger at me and announcing to the class, "Looks like we have a volunteer. Ms. Rose, why don't you put your sweater back on and come up here."

Ohhhhh. Put my sweater back on? Ha. That's cute.

And what if I don't want to put my sweater back on? No one told Jennifer Aniston to put a sweater on when she was on the set of *Friends*. Hell, you could see her nipples on every freaking episode.

I might not be Rachel Green, but I am *Rachel* Rose. And you know what Rachel Rose doesn't like? She doesn't like when men try to tell her what to do.

Anger starts to roll around in my belly when I let his words marinate inside my brain. *The nerve of this man to try to cover me up.* What if I don't want to be covered up? I'm a grown-ass woman, and I can wear whatever the hell I want, *show* whatever I want.

Patriarchy rules be damned.

"Do you guys think I should put my sweater back on?" I ask the class, damn near blurting out the question before I realize what I'm saying. I almost feel shame over my audacity and apparent temporary insanity of forgetting that I'm in a class filled with college-aged boys, but when Ty's jaw practically hits the top of his fancy shoes and said college boys in the class offer their enthusiastic opinion of *No*, I can't stop myself from taking the proverbial ball and volleying it right back to Ty.

"Looks like you're in the minority, Professor," I say and climb from my seat, smoothing my skirt down my legs and pointedly leaving my sweater behind.

He clenches his jaw, and the look in his eyes is a mixture of shock and anger, but I don't let it falter my steps. I strut right toward him while holding his eyes in challenge. I intend to stop within only a couple of inches of him, but as soon as I get within a couple of feet, he stumbles back in a hurry and rounds the room to the other side, pointing to indicate that I should stand in the spot he's vacated.

I smother a smile.

"Okay, guys. I want you to look at Ms. Rose and give me some body-positive descriptors that you think might be found in classic literature." The class titters and several hands shoot up, but Ty doesn't call on anyone right away. Instead, he adds a warning. "Remember to keep it respectful. Anyone who chooses not to listen to that will get one hundred points removed from their final semester grade."

A couple of hands go down immediately, and it's all I can do not to roll my eyes as some of the class laughs.

"Yeah, David," Ty says, pointing at one of the more innocent freshmen in the front row who still has his hand up.

"Glowing. Healthy," David offers, and I smile. Okay, that's a nice start.

"Good. How about you, Amber?" Ty asks, calling on one of the girls who already had her nipples out before me.

"The sun," Amber says, honestly shocking me by being kind. I half expected her to be angry she wasn't the one getting the attention from the professor.

"Ah, yes," Ty crows with a smile. "I see someone paid attention while we were reading Tolstoy. Good job, Amber, you get a kiss." He grabs a Hershey's kiss from the shelf at the side of the room and tosses it her way, and she practically drowns herself in the compliments.

That's when it makes sense why she didn't go for mean.

"Henry," Ty calls, picking a guy who always sits in the middle of the back row. "Impress me."

Henry looks me up and down, to the point that I wish I could reach out and steady myself with a hand to a hard surface to prepare for whatever is about to come out of his mouth.

Please don't make it inappropriate. Please. Please. Please.

"Smokeshow," he proudly proclaims.

Oh boy. Suddenly, the room *is* feeling cold, and I'm acutely aware of just how many eyes are on me. *You're also feeling a lot like you never should have taken off your sweater.*

"Ah, man." Ty lets out a low wolf whistle. "There goes one hundred points right out the window!"

"What? Wait!" Henry looks around with big, shocked eyes. "That's respectful, Professor! It means she's beautiful. Attractive. How is that bad?"

The whole class dissolves into laughter at poor Henry's expense, and Ty shakes his head with a smirk, glancing at me briefly. "Okay, fine. I'm letting you go with a warning. This is your one free pass, my man."

Henry breathes out a sigh of relief and sags back into his chair.

And I fidget my fingers against my skirt as my palms start to grow oddly sweaty.

"And while I think we can all agree with your assessment of Ms. Rose's beauty, Henry," Ty continues, "I have my doubts that we'd find any uses of the word 'smokeshow' in classic literature. Frankly, if that's how you choose to describe women you're interested in, prepare yourself for years of rejection."

The whole class erupts again, and Ty takes that opportunity to offer me the chance to take my seat. His extended arm is all the invitation I need, and I head back to my spot, ready to put my cardigan back on.

Mentally, I feel like I've been knocked down a peg or two from where I started my seduction scene in this lecture.

"All right, settle down, guys. And let's give Ms. Rose a round of applause for fearlessly volunteering." The class claps and a few rogue students let out some piercing whistles, and I throw up a hand from my spot in my chair in recognition.

Yeah, yeah, thanks. Let's move on now.

Ty smirks in my direction when he notes my cardigan is back on, silently basking in his successful diversion of my attention, and my eyes narrow in response.

Look who has the upper hand now, my mind whispers.

Son of a bitch. I wish I could let it go, but there is just something inside me that can't let him get away with robbing the power from me. I *won't.* I came into this class with the advantage, and I'm going to leave with it too, so help me God.

"For homework, I want you to go back to *Anna Karenina* and pick out some other vocabulary Tolstoy used. Focus in particular on terms that might seem out of place in modern literature. We'll go over it first thing on Thursday, and I'll have a new bag of candy. You'll want to impress me."

The class laughs once again, and he waves a dramatic hand in dismissal.

I monitor their exit carefully, waiting patiently for the opportunity to talk to Ty privately, after they've all left. It takes them a little longer than I want, but I somehow manage to make it look like I'm busy packing up my belongings the whole time, scooting toward Ty's desk just as the last student heads out the door.

I swing my bag up onto my shoulder, my sweater still on but left open with a large percentage of my bust on display. His eyes flick to the showing on my approach but divert relatively quickly as he goes back to putting papers in his briefcase.

"Sorry for the tardiness today, Professor," I say smartly, raising just one eyebrow in a way that I know he'll understand.

He chuckles briefly before remarking, "That's okay. I'd say we're even now."

"Oh yeah. We are," I agree easily. "Interesting use of props for today's Tolstoy discussion."

"Definitely was interesting," he says, and his smile deepens. But it's more than just a smile; it's a nonverbal cue. It's his way of telling me he thinks he's won our little game.

That smile gets in my craw and turns my focus laser sharp. Instead of simply accepting the situation for what it is, there's nothing more important to me in this moment than leaving with me on top again.

I step forward then, pushing my body into the side of his arm and placing my lips to his ear. He shivers at the unexpected contact, his eyes widening slightly.

"There's just one thing no one managed to catch on to when they were describing me today," I whisper, grabbing Ty's chin and turning it so he'll face me. He swallows hard, and I grin.

"And w-what's that?"

"*Hot for teacher.*" I wink and push myself up on my tippy-toes to just barely brush my lips over his.

He jumps at the contact, and my stomach flips over on itself.

With one last bout of eye contact, I finally turn on my heel and head for the door without looking back.

Have I mentioned that I'll do anything to win?

Take that, Professor. Who's in charge now?

THIRTEEN

Saturday, February 2nd

Ty

I tuck my shirt into my jeans and roll up the sleeves to my forearms before grabbing my phone from its spot on the nightstand and checking for messages from my family.

There are a couple from my sister Winnie, primarily reminding me not to forget to show up for Daisy's baby shower today—as if I would flake out on something that important—and one from my mom, asking that I not mention the fact that she's trying out online dating to the rest of the family.

Don't worry, Wendy, that's exactly the last conversation I want to get into with Flynn, one of the most aggressively protective assholes alive, while I'm supposed to be celebrating Daisy's twins.

I mentioned it to Remy already, but honestly, he seemed more interested in blowing a banana than talking about our mom's love life. I don't think she has anything to worry about.

I shoot her a text back, promising to keep her sexual reawakening on the down-low, and then bop over to my contacts to scroll through my list of eligible women. After spending far too much time out of sorts, I'm ready to get back on my game. Obviously, I need a reminder of exactly who Ty Winslow is, and I'm going to give it to him—me...whatever.

I only have a little bit of time to secure a date, but I'm confident I can pull through.

After a random scroll, I land on a number and get ready to hit call, but another text message buzzes in my hand and sends a banner down from the top of the screen. I'm expecting another family member, but it's not.

It's the woman I've been avoiding for the last several days like a pussy. I couldn't help it, though. Every time she blinked at me with those big, sexy green eyes, I lost another ounce of cool. If I would've kept it up all week, there wouldn't have been anything left of me by today, and then I would have been a no-show for Daisy's shower.

And I'd also have to deal with Flynn resurrecting me from the dead just to kill me again. Honestly, it'd just be a whole messy thing.

Avoiding her was the way to go. Especially after she whispered *hot for teacher* in my ear. It had taken me a good twenty minutes to compose myself after she'd said those words and sashayed her curvy ass out of my lecture hall.

But surely a text message is safe enough. She can't get me flustered with words, right?

Rachel: Sorry to bother you on the weekend, but I need the finalized questions for the Classic Lit exam so I can get them ready for Tuesday. I'd do it tomorrow or Monday, but I have a paper of my own due. I tried to catch you after class the last few days, but we never seemed to cross paths.

That's…well…true. Because for the last few days, I've been putting more energy into avoiding Rachel than anything else in my life. Work, the gym, food—none of it has mattered, as long as I can get out of the building before Rachel every day.

Irony is at its finest, though, since she's actually the person I want to see most. It's just that I turn into a flaming fucking mess every time I come into contact with her, and that shit's not me. Ty Winslow doesn't let people mind-meld him. If anything, he does the mind-melding.

But Rachel Rose has some kind of power I've never encountered before. Something that makes me crazy. Something that makes thirty-nine years of learning to function seem obsolete.

In addition to that, I didn't do anything with the test questions yet. In fact, I didn't even remember them until now.

Me: Right. I can email them over later tonight. I'd do it now, but I have to head out for a baby shower soon.

Her response comes in a minute later.

Rachel: Let's be honest, did you actually make any changes? Because if not, I can do one last proof and then just get the test ready.

How the hell does she know that?

Me: What makes you say that?

Rachel: Because you haven't made any changes on the last two tests I've prepared.

Me: Haha. Okay. Wow, Sherlock Holmes. I guess I'm busted. Go ahead and use the questions you have.

Rachel: LOL. I'm just trying to make this easier on you.

Me: No, you're right. You write good questions, so I've been doing fuck all to them since you started.

Rachel: Well, thanks. I try. You make it pretty easy to pick them with the way you lecture.

Are we…having a compliment war right now? Because it sure as hell feels like it. *You're also doing a really good—more like, terrible—job of avoiding her, dude. Top-notch. Good enough to join the CIA.*

I tell my inner voice to take a hike. I mean, she was texting about work, and it's not exactly like I can cut her off completely. She's my TA.

Which is paradoxically also a good explanation for why I shouldn't be thinking about her. I'm pretty sure you're not supposed to whack off to thoughts of your TA on a nightly basis, and if you are, you should ask the department head for a change.

Of course, the department head is her father, and I promised I'd take Rachel on as a specific favor to him, so I guess I'm in a real pickle.

Life is really wild right now, honestly.

Rachel: Also, my mind just processed that you said you're going to a baby shower, and that is an incredibly hard thing for me to picture.

I snort. *Yeah. Tell me about it.*

Me: It's for my brother Flynn. His wife Daisy is pregnant with twin boys.

Rachel: Twins? That's a lot of babies.

I chuckle.

Me: Lol. Yeah. It is.

Rachel: Well, have fun partying it up today.

Me: Ha. Yeah. It's about to get real wild.

Rachel: Okay, I'm too curious not to ask. What kind of gift does a single guy bring to a baby shower?

What? A gift? Isn't my presence gift enough?

Me: Why would I bring a gift?

Rachel: Because that's what you do at baby showers. You bring the mom gifts.

Me: For real?

Rachel: OMG. LOL. You are such a guy.

Is she telling the truth? I'm supposed to bring a fucking gift?

Me: Seriously, Rachel? What kinds of gifts are you talking about here?

Rachel: Baby kinds of gifts. Diapers. Onesies. Bottles. She should have a registry.

Me: A registry???

Rachel: Oh my God. Forget the registry. Just go get some baby stuff. Two onesies. Pack of diapers. Some baby wipes. It's really that simple.

Me: What the fuck's a onesie?

Rachel: LOL. This just keeps getting better and better.

Me: For you, maybe. For me? It's getting worse and worse. Seriously, Rachel, what's a onesie?

Obviously, when it comes to babies, I don't know shit. My niece Lexi could cogitate before she was a year old, so she basically skipped the infant thing altogether. Plus, I wasn't exactly the first person in line when Winnie was looking to leave her in someone's care. Remy and Flynn have always been a *touch* more responsible than me.

Rachel: Baby clothes. If you go to any store that has baby clothes and find the nearest woman and ask her to show you the onesies, you'll find them.

I chuckle to myself, but then I realize I'm still texting with her like we're old pals. Like there is nothing in the world to be concerned about. Just… texting it up like two peas in a sexual-tension-filled pod that I'm trying to pretend doesn't exist.

And then I also check the time and see that I have exactly two hours to find a damn gift and get to Daisy's shower.

Overwhelmed, I immediately tuck my phone back into my pocket, walk down the hall to my kitchen, grab my wallet and shit from the counter, and head right out the door.

I'm not bothering with driving today because parking in the city is a pain in the ass and my head's not ready to dance with raging taxi drivers. Surely I can find a shop in my neighborhood that sells baby shit and take the subway to Daisy's shower.

Daisy's baby-themed party is hopping. What feels like everyone in the damn city is here, inside one of the lavish reception rooms at the Beekman Hotel, ready to celebrate the upcoming arrival of two more Winslow boys.

I have a feeling my sister-in-law Sophie was behind the planning of this event. That much is probably evident by the way she's scurrying around the room, making sure the caterers are keeping the buffet of appetizers stocked.

I grab a beer from the open bar and look across the room to find Flynn and Daisy greeting their guests as they arrive. They stand by the table that's covered in gifts, hugging and shaking hands with everyone. Every few moments, Flynn leans down and presses a kiss to his wife's forehead or rubs his hand over her round belly, and Daisy always gives him the same sweet smile in return.

Love sure is a motherfucker, isn't it? It can take down even the most stubborn of men.

Well, besides me. *Obviously.*

My phone vibrates in my pocket, and I pull it out to find a text that makes me grin.

Rachel: I have to know. Did you manage a gift?

Thankfully, with the help of a lovely woman named Susan at a little baby boutique shop thingy in Nolita, I managed to spend about two hundred dollars more than I probably should've on fancy fucking baby clothes and blankets and shit.

Susan was a real sleeper of a saleswoman. A little old lady with a soft smile but total shark instincts. She knew exactly what to say and how to get me to hand over my credit card before I even understood what was happening.

Me: Yes. I did. Lots of baby shit was purchased.

Rachel: Good.

I raise my fingers to type out another text, to tell her thanks for making me aware of the gift requirements, but my youngest brother's loud-as-hell voice pulls my focus.

"So, where is she?" Jude asks, drinking from a bottle of beer and settling his hips into a table covered with more baby stuff than I've ever seen in my life.

"Huh?" My stomach flips, and my chest zaps immediately, thoughts of Rachel popping into my head uninvited. How does he know about her? Did he see me texting her just now?

Holy hell, you're a fucking mess today.

Truthfully, I've felt out of sorts since I arrived at this shower. A little out of place, even.

All the happiness, all the couples, all the women talking about family stuff and planning vacations and musing about how happy they are with the state of their lives—it made me feel a bit like I wasn't ready to be there. Like I couldn't relate to my family. Like there's been a shift in the universe, and maybe we're going to start to grow apart.

It's stupid mostly, I know that, but the basic principle of the feelings isn't all that off-kilter. Two of my brothers and my sister, by and large, are entering a new phase of their lives. Hell, even my mom's looking for long-term love after all these years of going it alone.

And I'm…well, I'm the same as always. Sure, I've been messing around with Rachel, but it's all just a big game. She's not seriously into me. She just likes messing with me. At least, I think. *She couldn't have really meant that "hot for teacher" shit, right?* That was just to get under my skin.

"Yo, Ty!" Jude narrows his eyes at me. "Where is she?" he repeats slowly and like he's speaking to a child.

"She? She who?" I scan the room for more approaching siblings in the form of an ambush.

"Amy? Meghan? Lucy? Melanie? Adriana?" Jude scoffs. "How should I know. Whatever the fuck your random chick's name is. Where is she?"

I shake my head, waving him off. "I didn't bring anyone today."

"What? Are you serious? You, Ty Winslow, came to a family function without a woman?"

Initially, that was the plan, but then…I forgot. Well, I got *distracted* by the whole needing a gift debacle.

No, actually, you forgot because you got distracted by Rachel.

I roll my eyes, more at myself than at my brother, but I also quickly find a reason. "You don't bring your own beer to an open bar, dude," I tell him. "Baby showers are an all-you-can-eat buffet of women, if you haven't noticed."

And yet, you haven't attempted to chat up even one of the women here…

What is going on with me? Have I become some kind of monk? A masochist?

A fucking *masochistic monk?*

"Apparently, Daisy already knows every woman in the city," Jude says through a laugh. "She has no idea how lovable she is. Thought she'd have a few friends show up and that's it, according to Flynn."

Thankfully, I only have to halfway force the smile on my face. When it comes down to it, both of my sisters-in-law are the kind of women I'd want my brothers to end up with.

"You both found good ones. Of course, Flynn I understand because he has that whole tall, dark, and mysterious thing happening, but it's unbelievable that Sophie settled for a bastard like you. But hey, I guess you've always been lucky."

Jude nods, unperturbed. If there's anything that doesn't bruise his ego, it's suggesting that he married up when it comes to Sophie. He knows it, he admits it, he's proud of it. Which, having known the cocky bastard for nearly forty fucking years, is wild to me.

"I know," he answers smugly. "Now I just need to knock her up."

I choke on the swig of beer I was taking and eye him curiously. I knew the whole party was on a spawn kick, considering the reason for it, but I didn't know Jude was ready too. "You really think you're ready for kids? Isn't the whole commitment to one woman thing enough for now?"

Jude shakes his head tauntingly, a look of power and knowledge in his eyes. "You just don't get it yet, dude. Once you have the kind of thing I have with Sophie, you want to do all the stuff. The house, the babies, the growing old… It's a weird feeling but a seriously good one."

"Bull-shit," I squawk, loudly enough that it gets the attention of both Flynn and Remy from across the room. They head our way immediately, after exchanging a painfully annoying "older brother" look. The fucks started rubbing in their geriatric age the moment I could talk and haven't stopped since. I imagine they both think they're coming over here to school me somehow.

"What's bullshit?" Remy asks, crossing his arms over his chest in his favorite power pose, his feet planted shoulder-width apart.

"Nothing," I say with a roll of my eyes and a swig of my beer.

Jude laughs, the traitor. "Ty here doesn't believe me. I told him that when you find the right person, you like the idea of babies and shit. Want it, even."

"Okay, *like the idea*, sure," I correct with a wag of my finger and beer bottle. "But you're fucking rooting for it. And that, I don't believe."

"It's true. When you feel content, you want all that shit," Rem says, totally throwing me off. Of all the guys in this group, I thought he'd at least be on my side.

"You can't be serious, Mr. Hermit. For fuck's sake, I don't even think I've seen you learn a woman's name since Charlotte left you at the altar a decade and a half ago."

Jude's eyes round, and Flynn sighs. *I know, I know.* The whole left at the altar thing is something we don't ever talk about. But I'm sick of it. We're two fortunes down at this point, and there's no way everyone can ignore it forever. I know I can't. Not after I found Cleo last spring.

Remy glances from Flynn to Jude and then, finally, over to me. His eyes are hard, but in a completely unexpected twist, they're also shining with respect.

"You're right, Ty. I haven't settled down. I haven't found the one. And to be frank, I haven't even tried. But that doesn't mean I don't want those things.

That I can't see that Jude and Flynn are happy and what they have with Sophie and Daisy is real."

"What the hell? They must be pumping something through the vents here," I croon. "You've all lost your minds."

Flynn rolls his eyes and walks away without comment. It's not all that surprising since he doesn't say much ever, but I at least expected him to tell me to fuck off or something. Somehow, his silent exit is even scarier.

Remy and Jude share a look before shrugging.

"Think what you want, man," Jude says, unbothered. "You'll get it one day."

My eyes narrow at their dropping the topic so easily, and then I jump as arms loop through both of mine at the elbows. On one side, my sister Winnie. On the other, my mother.

I glance to the side to see Flynn standing there smirking, the bastard. I should have known he'd try to teach me a lesson, even if it wasn't with words. He's sicced the biggest romantics of the group on me.

"Ty!" Winnie cries excitedly, leaning into me and tugging on my arm. "Flynn said the shower's got you thinking about having babies!"

My gaze jerks to the dirty, backhanded bastard again, and Jude and Remy are smiling like a bunch of amused idiots.

"No, Win. I'm not. Kind of have to settle down with a woman first, you know?"

"And when are you planning to do that, Ty?" my mom chimes in, trapping me between a rock and a hard place.

"I don't know, Mom."

"Oh, Ty Alexander. I swear. I'm going to be dead before you give me grandbabies, huh?" she asks on a sigh, sarcasm in her voice.

"You have four other kids, Mom, and they seem pretty fucking busy—"

She points one stern index finger at me. "Ty, language!"

"I'm just saying…you don't need grandkids from me. You're going to have plenty."

"You don't get it yet, but one day you will, sweetie," my mother says with a gentle pat to my chest. "Grandkids are different from each and every child. Getting to see the person you've raised shape the mind of a little human is special."

"What if I don't want kids, though? Some people never want kids."

Winnie scoffs. "You're right, Ty. Some people. But you're not those people. You were built to be a dad. A good one. You just don't know it yet."

I don't know where she's getting that from, but I'm beginning to think they've both been hitting the booze a little too hard.

"You didn't even bring someone today," Winnie continues to argue. "You don't see it, but that means something."

"Why is everyone so focused on who I did or didn't bring? What the fu—dge does that have to do with anything?" I ask, improvising a "fuck" substitute when my mom gives me a hard glare somewhere in the middle.

The two of them share a look, and then my mom pats me on the arm. "You're right, honey. It doesn't matter. Don't listen to us, okay? You just make yourself happy."

The quick backpedaling is suspicious, but it's way better than continuing to sweat through their interrogation, so I don't question it.

I take a swig of my beer and look around at the blissful baby chaos around me.

What is it, exactly, that would make me happy?

I always thought I was good with the status quo—to keep things the way I have them. But now that I find myself in the situation I'm in with Rachel, I'm starting to wonder if I really know anything at all.

FOURTEEN

Sunday, February 3rd

Rachel

I tuck the blueberry muffin into the cute pink-and-white baggies Lydia designed and close it with a heart sticker from the roll beside the cash register. Little Rose Bakeshop is always busy on Sundays, but today feels like it's on another level. Maybe I'm feeling the effects of the rush a little more because I stayed up late finishing the tests for Ty's class and studying for my own, but then again, I'm not the only one acting crazy.

"That'll be five dollars," I tell an older lady in a yellow T-shirt and hand her the already prepared cup of coffee sitting on the back counter and her muffin of choice in the bag I've just sealed.

She hands me a five-dollar bill, thankfully making the transaction easily closed with nothing more than a smile. "Thanks for coming in," I say quickly as she pushes through the crowded space, headed for the door.

I'm about to call on the next customer in line when Lydia waves down my attention from the other end of the counter. I wipe my hands on my pink apron and scoot over to her as quickly as possible.

"Rachel, can you run in the back and get the other batch of red velvet muffins?" my sister asks, smiling at the customer in front of her like she has it all together. Of course, I know this is the sixth tray of red velvet muffins we've been through this morning—some kind of freak surge in demand— and truthfully, both she and Lou are on the brink of a breakdown. Years of customer service experience and a sunny personality are the only things keeping her from snapping.

"You bet." I jump into action, shoving through the swinging door into the back kitchen, and upon sight of me, Lou's eyes immediately round.

"Don't tell me. More red velvet?"

I nod cautiously. I don't want to be responsible for ruining all of the delicious, sweet treats with Lou's salty tears.

"What's going on in the city today? Is it a red velvet moon or something?"

I laugh, leaning into the metal bake table Lou's not using currently. "You know, I bet that's it. Or a red velvet tide. It's always the moon or the tide. Or maybe there's some sort of cultlike thing going on at all the churches in the city. Maybe—"

Lou shoots me a look of desperation so frank, I think it's going to change the cute little pixie lines of her face permanently. Immediately, I stop what I'm saying and try to redirect my next words toward something more helpful.

"You can do it, Lou. Just keep cranking them out. You're doing fantastic."

"Sure. It seems simple." She blows out a breath. "But with my luck, tomorrow, the moon will probably rotate or something, and I'll be drowning in something else. Probably more difficult. Like soufflés."

I shrug helplessly, easing the blow with a smile. "At least death will be tasty?"

She laughs, jerks her head at the tray of muffins in front of me, and then adds, "Take the cookies with you too."

I agree silently, grabbing both the muffin and cookie trays and shoving the swinging door with my foot to head back out front. My sister is fielding even more rabid red velvet customers, so I set the tray right in front of her and then head to the other end of the glass counter to put the chocolate chip almond cookies in their spot. I'm just settling them into place when a deep, playful voice weaves its way from the other side of the counter to my ears.

"I believe those are for me."

I look up, a smart answer just on the tip of my tongue—something Lydia has repeatedly asked me to curtail, by the way—but stop short when I see a very specific set of blue eyes staring back at me.

"Ty?"

He looks startled too, his smile jumping off his face, only to be replaced by shock and disbelief. But ultimately, he pulls it together and slides the easy grin back into place. "Hey, Rachel."

"How was the baby shower?" I ask, and he just keeps grinning, like he's not the least bit affected by me.

"It was good."

Sure, we texted off and on yesterday, mostly about test questions and a baby shower gift, but now that he's here in person, it's almost a disappointment to watch him pull it together so effortlessly after having a literal front-row seat to seeing him so flustered at school.

The power I felt with that kind of control was…*invigorating.*

But it seems his effort to avoid me for the rest of the week, only allowing a text exchange yesterday, didn't go without benefits for him. *He's had time to recover.*

This is the Ty Winslow of old. The Ty Winslow of legend. The Ty Winslow of cocky confidence.

Immediately, I have the urge to break all those men into a thousand tiny, scattered, floundering pieces.

So much so that before I even know what I'm doing, I tease, "That's good to hear. And, wow. I'm flattered…I guess."

He furrows his brow. "Flattered?"

"Yeah. That you missed me so much, you felt you had to track me down at my sister's bakery."

I know it kind of makes me an asshole to want to watch him suffer, but I know, without a doubt, he feels the same way about me. And if I'm not the first to strike, he'll have me pinned before I know it. That's how wrestling works.

And we all know how much Rachel Rose hates to find herself pinned under the weight of a man's thumb, even if it's all in good fun.

"What?" he snaps, a modicum of panic creeping into the edges of his otherwise powerful smile. "No, no. I…I didn't track you down. I come to Little Rose every Sunday. I live in the neighborhood."

I laugh, waving it off as I spin around to grab an empty box from the back shelf. "Listen, it's fine. It's not, like, full-blown stalking."

"No, no," he bumbles, his poised façade slipping even more. "No stalking at all. If I'm stalking anything, it's cookies. A dozen chocolate chip almond cookies, in fact. I have an account all set up and everything."

"Stalking chocolate chip almond cookies?" I say with a fair amount of suspicion—geared toward making him uncomfortable, of course. "That sounds like a cop-out, but I guess, if you need it that much, I'll let you have it."

"I don't need a cop-out," he says defensively, his back going straight.

"So, you *did* come here for me?" I assert with a lift of just one eyebrow.

"That's not what I said." The corners of his mouth are somehow completely straight. No smile, no frown, he's in the middle of an emotional onslaught he can't make sense of yet.

"Listen, it's okay. Really. I understand."

"Rachel, I didn't come here for you," he says without room for error or creative interpretation. It's a challenge to my original plan, but I'm not new to the game. I'm a wild child. I know how to pivot.

"Aw, that's a pity. I figured maybe, if you really wanted to see me that bad, that it'd be the least I could do to show some effort too."

"Effort?" He jerks his head back. "What kind of effort?"

"Oh, I don't know." I purposely lean over the counter and whisper, "Maybe I could show you what my underwear looks like today? Let you try to put them on again?" I shake my head and laugh. "But that's okay. Hell, I don't even know that I remembered to put any on today. It's just been so busy," I murmur seductively, before leaving him standing there with a slack jaw to gather his cookie order.

I stack a dozen chocolate chip almond cookies inside one of the hot-pink boxes my sister and Lou had custom made with their logo on the side and turn back around to face him.

He's still just standing there, trying to make sense of the situation.

And I feel fucking galvanized.

"Rachel, I don't… We shouldn't… I mean…" He tries to explain himself with a tied tongue. I get what he's saying, regardless, but I'm not about to let up right when I finally have him where I want him.

"I know. I do. I mean, we shouldn't, right?" I whisper for his ears only. "But I've just been thinking about you and me, and…well, I probably shouldn't say the things I've been thinking about, you know?"

I set Ty's box of cookies on the counter, and he picks them up quickly, stumbling backward into the table behind him as soon as he does. He looks back, as if it's just been placed there for the sole purpose of tripping him up, and I smother a laugh as I round the counter and head toward him.

He retreats in kind, backing up competently, but only with the help of an almost manic tic of his neck to look behind himself.

"Rachel…"

"Yes, Ty?" I coo, my voice a low grit of sex and promises.

"I-I have to go," he mumbles, practically running for the door and shoving his way through it. "I'll see you in class Monday."

I lean out the door and wave, a tiny pout on my lips to fuck with him a little more—sealing the deal. Rachel Rose *officially* has the upper hand.

When he finally makes it down the block enough to disappear into the Sunday morning crowd and a new customer walks past me, I step back inside and head back to work as though none of it happened. Although, there's an evil laugh cooling its heels inside me, waiting for there to be no patrons to scare off.

Lydia stares at me suspiciously, and I don't blame her. Running customers out the door isn't exactly protocol from the employee handbook. I don't know if she actually got a look at who it was either, with the crush of people in front of her. For all I know, she thinks I'm randomly sabotaging her business.

When she clears the customer in front of me, she pulls me to the side and whispers in my ear. "What in the hell was that? Was that Ty Winslow?"

Okay, so she did at least see who it was. That's actually helpful—less explaining on my end.

"Oh, that?" I say with a sassy smile I can't seem to help. "*That* was the sight of your sister taking back her advantage."

"What do you mean?"

I shake my head, feeling a little guilty at the crease of worry between her eyebrows. Lydia has enough to stress about without help from me.

"Don't worry. It's all in good fun, I promise. Ty Winslow knows the score."

She frowns a little but then grabs my hand and gives it a squeeze. "I sure hope you know what you're doing."

Me too, sis. Me too. Because I'm smart enough to realize…it might feel good now, but if I'm not careful, I might find myself in a whole lot of trouble.

FIFTEEN

Ty

It's been a full week since I ran out of my favorite bakery in the city to the sound of Rachel's supposed secret fantasies, and sadly, it only took me about a day or two to conclude that she was doing it just to get a reaction out of me.

Sure, I've fantasized about her—a lot—but the more I thought about what she said, the pictures she was painting, the more it sounded as if they were designed to elicit a reaction from a man rather than play into the strongest desires of a wanton woman.

I've read romance novels before—mostly because Winnie went through a phase in high school and I was really fucking curious what all the fuss was about, but partly because, after that, I really enjoyed some of them. Plus, our brother-in-law Wes's good friend Thatcher Kelly really has a way of sucking people into his shit, and his wife Cassie is trying her hand in the romance author world. All it took were two emails and a threatening but complimenting letter to find myself on one of her beta reading teams, Cassie's Carebears.

Yeah, I know. But it was like a fever dream, really. I can barely even tell you how it happened.

Regardless, I finally started to calm down when I realized what Rachel was trying to pull. But my hormones haven't gotten the same memo. In fact, they've been raging every time I see her. Since we work together, you can imagine my dick's been a bit of a loose cannon.

Let's just say, I've done a lot of standing behind things during lectures for the last week or so.

Otherwise, I've used a pointed tactic of avoidance. Rachel hasn't given up, though, trying harder and harder every day to make me crack. I didn't even go to the bakery yesterday to get my weekly cookies for fear she'd end up pushing my face in between her boobs for a motorboat or something. She's made a habit of upping the ante, and as an avid fan of watersports, there's no way I would have been able to turn something like that down.

But now it's a new week of classes—and for Rachel, a new level of determination. I've barely been able to concentrate to speak during this class today, and as the minutes tick by, she isn't letting up.

From the front row, Rachel spreads her legs lasciviously, licking at her lips as she makes a note on the page in front of her. She's nonchalant, unbothered even, and at this point, I'm convinced she's doing it on purpose. I just wish I knew what her endgame was. Like, what's the breaking point of it all?

I shake my head to clear it and continue with my lecture. "These words are powerful. These words are tragic. These words are romantic. But back when they were written, they weren't well received. In fact, they were heavily criticized."

My gaze flicks to Rachel's sexy legs, and she rubs them together, crossing them and uncrossing them, once again leaving me with a view of her perfect, sheer-pink-mesh-covered cunt.

I spin around to the board, even if I don't know what I'm going to do there, and grab a black marker, just to get a moment of solace.

I scribble on the board as I talk, and I'm pretty sure all I'm doing is writing exactly what I'm saying. "Writing is personal *and* subjective."

I put the marker down and turn back to the class, gathering my thoughts as I walk toward my desk and lean a hip into the side. My students' eyes might as well be ping-pong balls this morning, following me around the room as I bounce from one spot to another. If I had ADHD, I imagine this might be how I'd teach all the time.

"Even rejection isn't finite. Perhaps, in fact, rejection is just an indication that you're ahead of your time."

Craving a change of pace, Rachel's burning eyes and open legs calling me to look upon them once again, I jump up on the corner of my desk and crack open *Wuthering Heights*. After this many years of teaching this class, I know the novel backward and forward, though. I know what pages to look for, where the climax of the story happens, how many characters there are in each chapter. I know the rhythm and cadence of Emily Brontë's writing, and I know the parts that resonate most with an undergrad class of freshmen.

They like sex. They like scandal. They like the occasional use of "bad words" by their teacher. And I'm okay with that. If my putting a "cool" twist on classic literature makes this generation care about it, I'll give my lecture on a fucking hoverboard on TikTok while singing a song of swearwords.

Because hell, I like sex and scandal too. I've built a whole personal life based on sex. But the mixture of active sexual arousal and class time? Safe to say, I've never done it before.

I look back at the front row momentarily to see Rachel removing her sweater. She's wearing a silk shirt underneath, and I can see her pert nipples through the fabric as though there's no fabric at all. All I can think about is tracing them with my tongue.

Damn, Rachel, what are you trying to do to me?

I'm used to class. What I'm altogether not used to is one of the sexiest women alive, sitting in my front row of seats, taking notes and spreading her legs open so I can see up her skirt.

And those panties—I know those panties. They're *the* panties. *Sweet God Almighty.*

"So, if you'll turn to page…to page…" I clear my throat and will myself to look away from the space between Rachel's legs and back to the fucking book. *Come on, Ty, get it together.*

"If you'll turn to Chapter Nine, you'll see Catherine's first moral dilemma. To love or to do what's expected by society."

I look to Rachel and the sex rolling off her, despite her relation to a man I've respected and admired for years, and then bow my head back to the book.

Sometimes it's scary how much literature applies to life—especially classic literature to modern life.

"We can all relate to facing a moral dilemma at least once in our lives. Should you sleep with your best friend's girlfriend, even if she's willing and you think she's one of the hottest chicks on the planet?"

The class goes up in a roar, and I bite my lip and smile. That one always seems to get them stirred up. Eighteen-year-olds, by and large, are still trying to calibrate their moral compass. They're the perfect case study in would versus should.

"Or should you use a part of your body that isn't an appendage and maintain loyalty to your friend?"

I scoot off my desk and pace the floor at the bottom of the classroom's stadium seating, keeping my eyes pointedly away from the front row in an effort to concentrate.

"The decision seems easy now, here, in the light of this classroom with the weight of your peers' thoughts next to you. But does it feel the same in a dark room, with the smell of sex and the ache of arousal in every part of your being? Brontë captures this distinction poetically, and even still, maintains Catherine's moral compass."

I spin around to glance at the clock and catch a glimpse of Rachel's open legs once more on the journey. I've never wanted a class to end and continue on into infinity simultaneously before, but the clock picks for me. The protection of Great Barrier Students is about to end, and I'll be faced with the open waters of self-control.

"Time's up for today. But I want you to consider everything I've said, and I want you to reread Emily's prose with that in mind. If you were writing Catherine in modern times, would she have followed the same path? If you were writing her in the Victorian era, what then?"

The class murmurs and fidgets, their hurry to pack up their things and be on their way to someone else who's trying to shape their minds self-evident.

"All right. Don't get into too much trouble. Class dismissed."

Students practically jump from their seats, grabbing their backpacks and shoving notebooks inside. I turn back to the desk at the front of the room and start organizing too, readying myself to pack up because this was my last class of the day.

I don't look back at Rachel, and I don't take a full breath either. I swear I've somehow converted to something that doesn't need air—something amphibious or some shit—since the moment Rachel started messing with me an hour ago.

A fire burns inside me, both of desire and anger, and I'm faced with a dilemma. Let it go or confront her.

The rational part of me knows that letting it go is the better of the two options, but the flaming emotions inside me mean that's never going to happen.

I keep one eye to the door and wait for my moment.

The last student floods into the hallway, and Rachel is quick on her heels. She knows what she's been doing; she intends not to face it, and because of that, I intend to make her.

I follow immediately, leaving all my stuff behind on the desk without a thought.

I move swiftly, my legs working double time to both keep up but hang back enough that I can time my approach to just inside the door of my office—away from prying eyes. I know she has assignments to collect for grading and has run out of time to put it off. She has no choice but to stop by my office, and she has to do it now.

I keep step with her all the way down the hall, her legs churning and her head down and determined. If she has anything to say about it, she's going to get the hell out of Dodge, but this time, I'm going to be the one with the last word.

She ducks into my office and tries to shut the door, but I'm there, just in time to smack it back open, step inside and close and lock it behind me. She swallows deeply as she meets my eyes and lifts her chin.

"Just what the hell do you think you're doing?" I ask, dispensing with any kind of pretense that one or both of us doesn't know what's going on.

"I'm getting my stuff so I can—"

"No," I interrupt with a shake of my head. "Not that. In class, Rachel. The panties. What in the hell are you trying to pull?"

"I don't know what you're talking about," she tries to refute, turning to my desk to gather her belongings but coming up way short when I grab her elbow and spin her back around.

"Bullshit. You know what you were doing. What I want to know is what you expected to come of it? Do you want me to fuck you right here? Is that what you want?"

Her chest swells with the escalation of her breath, but she works diligently to maintain her innocence otherwise. "I was just messing around."

"Fuck that, messing around. The hidden panties? That was messing around. You taking your jacket off and tilting your tits toward me every time I breathe? Messing around. Even taking back the underwear and stepping into them while you were standing right here in front of me? Messing around. But that shit you pulled in class today was more than messing around, Rach. And a man like me? If you're not careful? I'll take it as a challenge. Is that what you want?"

I step toward her one, two, three paces, until our chests rub together with panting breaths. She has fire in her eyes—the kind that screams in opposition to everything I've just said, just so she can be right on principle.

But she's not saying shit because she knows I'm right. She wants me just as badly as I want her, and she *knows* playing with the bull this closely always gets you the horns. She knows it because she's an expert in hundreds of years of literature, just like me.

It's human nature. Eventually, the band of tension breaks. Always. She pushed me so I would be the one to snap it faster.

I look from her eyes to her lips, and right then, in that very moment, I know it's going to happen. Despite all the shit that says I shouldn't, despite very nearly hating each other as much as we like each other, I'm going to feel the flesh of her lips under mine if it kills me.

I *have* to. I have to know what she tastes like.

"I'm not kissing you," she whispers.

"I'm not kissing you either," I murmur back, the edge of my lips grazing the skin of hers. It's a bald-faced lie, and I know it. That's what makes it so fun.

"I'm not," she says again, a last-ditch attempt to hold the line, but her face moves closer to mine.

I don't bother with another leg of denial on my end. Instead, I push my lips to hers, an action that ignites an inferno that even Dante isn't prepared to handle.

Pushing and pulling and breathing and squeezing, the two of us are like animals, grasping for every piece of flesh we can find and fighting for dominance over the kiss. Her tongue toys with mine to shove them both back into my mouth, but I take control, tasting the corners of her pretty little mouth and committing them to memory.

I reach down and grab the slinky fabric of her skirt, scooting it up the flesh of her thigh and putting my fingers to the sweet heat between her legs. She's on fire, completely soaked, her whole engine burning with arousal from her game.

"You want me," I say, pulling back from her mouth just enough to make sure she hears me and then nipping at her throat. She moans; what she doesn't do is contest my assertion.

I stroke the thin fabric with two soft, teasing fingers, and my cock hardens as she pushes herself into my hand to get more pressure. I give it to her. One strong stoke, followed by another, until her back arches against my hand and her weight falls into me.

I rub the line of the panties' edge and crook just one finger to find my way under. Soft, warm flesh and a small dusting of hair are smothered in arousal. Immediately, my finger is coated, and I have to add another.

She feels so good, so fucking warm and wet, and my hands shake with the urge to rip her fucking panties off, but everything comes to a screeching halt when a loud pop sounds in the hallway. It startles us enough that a foot-wide space opens up between us. There's a laugh and a scuffle as the student moves on, likely having dropped their book and picked it up, but the sweet, mesmerizing fog of moments ago is gone.

In its place? The undeniable realization that we're about to dance over a mark in the sand that can't be put back. An actual sexual relationship between us might be prohibited by the university; however, if not, it would certainly be frowned upon by her father.

We shouldn't be doing this—I, personally, shouldn't be considering it at all.

"I should go," Rachel whispers, her breathing still ragged and her lipstick noticeably smeared across her face.

I nod and back away—the only two actions I can manage at this moment. Our it's-just-fun-and-games secret has taken a sharp turn toward dirty and forbidden. My heart is still pounding, and the sound of it whooshes in my ears. I want her so bad, I can hardly see straight.

She grabs her belongings from the desk, and the stack of papers for grading she came to my office to get in the first place, and scoots around me without a word.

I sink into the chair behind my desk and drop my head into my hands.

Only two piercing questions come to mind in the silence of this space—in the smell of aging books and years of hard work and the feel of an antique wooden desk chair gifted to me by my weakness's father.

What in the holy *fuck* am I doing? And how the hell do I stop?

SIXTEEN

Rachel

I sink down in the tub until every part of my body but my nose and mouth are under water. I breathe in air and wallow in the feeling of drowning at the same time.

What in the hell is wrong with me? Why, when it comes to Ty Winslow, do I not know when to stop?

I mean, sure, I've always been a bit of a limit pusher or a ball buster or a stubborn biotch who has to cut her own path in life no matter how much easier the one already cut would be, but this is the kind of behavior that gets you a padded room and daily meetings. Nearly fucking the professor you're TA'ing for when your very serious dad is the head of the department and specifically warned you against it? It's damn near self-sabotage.

And yet, I can't seem to stop myself. The push and the pull, the thickness of tension between us—they drive an ache between my legs that threatens to never end.

I push myself up and out of the water with a whoosh, slicking my hair back out of my eyes and blinking the droplets away.

Matilda sits on the bath rug next to the tub, staring at me with kitty judgment in her eyes. Apparently, even a cat can sense when a person is in the rock-bottom spiral of using no sense at all.

"I know, Matilda. I know," I tell her, sinking back into the water until my chin rests at its surface. "But you don't know what it's like. You don't know how it's been!" I argue with the silent feline, sealing my mental health diagnosis even further.

"He's…he's like a rash. You know you're not supposed to scratch it, know it'll probably leave you with all sorts of scars if you do. But it feels so good in the moment, you know? Just to get that little bit of relief to the unbelievable nagging itch."

I shift in the water as the ache between my legs flares again. "Nagging, clawing, relentless itch," I breathe, sliding my hand between my legs and just barely stroking myself. It feels good, so fucking good that I know the possibility of stopping my little trip to fantasy town zoomed by two train stops ago, but Matilda is still sitting at the side of the tub, watching me.

"I don't need an audience for this," I plead with her. "Trust me, my shame is potent enough without witnesses."

She pauses briefly, before plopping down on the rug and lifting her leg to lick herself. Perhaps it's a showing of solidarity, or perhaps she just likes the sandpapery tongue on her sensitive bits, but I decide *to hell with it*. If the cat wants to watch, she can. Considering just mere hours ago, I was flashing my underwear toward Ty in the middle of his lecture, it'll be the least questionable thing I've done all day.

And that's not even counting the whole, you-almost-fucked-him-in-his-office thing either.

It's true. I was seconds away from telling Ty to take my panties off and slide inside me.

Visuals of his face, the way he looked the moment before he kissed me, start to fill my head. And then I'm remembering how it felt to have his hand up my skirt, his fingers touching me, sliding inside me.

A moan escapes my lips, and with one hand clenched around the rounded tub edge to stabilize myself, I put my fingers back to my clit and start to make them dance. I close my eyes and imagine this is the encore to Ty's scant, brief touch. His hands, the warmth of his body, the feel of his lips at my throat—every detail from his office this afternoon consumes me.

"Oh God," I moan again, my head falling back over the rim and my legs opening salaciously. *So what if I'm throwing my life into a tailspin,* my imagination screams. *Have you seen the fucking ass on this guy?*

No question, Ty Winslow is one of the sexiest men I've ever seen walking this planet. His easy smile, his toned body, his unapologetic embrace of his personality. It's all an incredible turn-on, and if he weren't also the world's most annoying human and my direct *boss*, I probably would have already slept with him at this point.

There's a reason he's the guy I chose at Orchid. There's a reason I let him play with my panties for a month without reporting him to HR. There's a reason I'm here now, trying to rationalize masturbating to the thought of him.

And there's a reason I feel like I could be on the brink of coming, just after a touch or two.

He's the epitome of everything I could have built in a man if I'd picked out all his pieces in the MAN Store catalog.

I add a second finger to my stroking and circle them around my clit softly. I imagine, though, that Ty might be more aggressive—might shove two fingers inside me just to stuff me full. Eyes closed and lost in the fantasy, I do just that, gasping at the intrusion. It feels good—too good if you consider all the consequences. *Dangerously* good.

I shake my head to clear it because touching-yourself-in-the-tub time shouldn't align with finding-your-moral-compass time. No, quite the opposite, in fact. The two shall never meet. I refuse to let that lesson on *Wuthering Heights* mess with my self-pleasure-focused head.

I glance over to Matilda's spot briefly to find she's moved on and left the room, and the last tension in my body finally leaves. I sink deeper, throw both of my ankles up and over the edges of the tub to give myself room to work, and put my fingers back to my sweet spot.

With just a little coaxing, I slide them both inside again and pump in and out. Slowly at first, then faster and faster, a low moan starting in the base of my throat and expanding through my entire chest.

I can picture Ty in this very tub with me, stooped between my legs, his jeans still on his body because he couldn't even wait long enough to take them off before climbing in after me.

I reach out to brace myself as the water sloshes around me. My back arches, and my teeth dig into the flesh of my bottom lip. I hook my fingers to graze over my G-spot, knowing Ty wouldn't have any trouble finding it. He's been around the block a time or two, and he'd undoubtedly use that knowledge to impress me.

My tongue lashes out to lick my lips, and my eyes squeeze tighter as I tug at my own nipple with my free hand, imagining Ty's lips sucking the pert tip into his mouth. I can see the visual perfectly, and the rosy flesh paired with my mauve nipples is a sight to see. *Like it was meant to be.*

The odd, uninvited thought elicits a brief opening of my eyes and a hiatus from my climb to the top of Pleasure Mountain, but I shake it off and get back to business before it can derail me too far.

I *need* this release. More than anything else.

One, two, three more strokes of the tips of my fingers and a quick stroke of my clit and I'm falling over the edge and spiraling into an abyss of orgasmic pleasure I haven't seen in…well, in years.

Maybe it's the power of fantasy, or maybe it's the memory of Ty's touch from this afternoon, but I haven't felt that violent of a culmination maybe ever.

I feel almost ragged as I pull my now-shaky legs back into the warm water of the tub and once again sink to a level that only allows breathing. The water is soothing on my tingling, nerve-fired skin, and the noiselessness of underwater is the only way I can calm my racing heart.

Because as much as I thought I would, I don't feel satisfied. I don't feel like I've had my fill *at all.*

In fact, when it comes to fantasies of Ty Winslow, I'm even hungrier than before. But I know it has to stop. The teasing, the taunting, the flirting, the touching, all of it.

It *has* to stop here.

Tomorrow, Rachel Rose is going to be on her best behavior. Even if it kills me.

SEVENTEEN

Ty

The gentle squeal of hinges sounds from my left, pulling my attention from what I'm doing and bringing it to the door. I've been here, in my lecture hall, for half an hour, and the next students aren't due for another forty-five minutes. Needless to say, the visitor is unexpected, and my stomach jumps at the sight of Rachel as she walks into the empty classroom.

Her head jolts when her eyes meet mine. "Oh. Sorry, Professor Winslow," she murmurs, clutching her books even tighter than they already were to her turtleneck-covered chest. "I didn't realize you'd be here yet."

I'm only halfway through my lecture plans for today, and at the sight of her, I doubt I'm going to get much further. It goes without saying that she is the very last person I need to be left alone in a room with.

It appears we both had the same idea—get here early to get most of our stuff done, so when class is over, all we have to do is leave. No office encounters. No sexy kisses. No situations that include my hand up her skirt. Put simply: neither one of us wants a repeat of yesterday.

She's also dressed demurely, a change from her normal outfits and a failed attempt at keeping my mind off her body. Her curves are burned into my permanent memory, where I have a bevy of images that won't be stopped by fabric on her neck.

Still, I can appreciate the effort.

"No problem, Ms. Rose," I reply, the oddly stilted formalities between us creating a nearly visible cloud of weirdness. But we're both trying, and I'll give us credit for that. It's not easy putting someone else's wants and needs or rules above your own. It's not easy pulling back from someone who's basically become your obsession.

At some point, I've risen from my desk chair without noticing, and we both stand in silence for several long moments, our eyes locked while we try desperately not to look at each other.

"I can just take my work to the library if that—"

"That won't be necessary," I interrupt with a shake of my head. We're adults. Surely we can occupy the same space without launching our bodies into a clothesless state of wanton abandonment.

Right?

I'd at least like to think I can.

"Okay," she says hesitantly, perhaps the first time I've ever heard her speak with anything but confidence, and she searches for a spot to plant herself that's somehow within the walls of this lecture hall but also on another planet at the same time.

I put my head back down to my partially finished lesson plan, just to give her the space to find somewhere to be, but I don't see any of the words in front of me. Instead, a film reel of her skin and the catch of her breath in the back of her throat and the way her back arched at my touch plays relentlessly.

Rachel Rose is a core memory kind of woman. Not the one you forget or pass by or ignore pointedly like I'm doing now, that's for sure.

But she's also the head of the department's daughter and, more than that, the daughter of a mentor and a friend. I don't have many lines I don't cross, but going behind a friend's back and sleeping with his daughter is not exactly the man I want people to talk about at my funeral.

Over and over again in my head, I repeat a chant to remind myself of what's at stake. "Dead pariah, dead pariah, dead pariah."

Rachel jerks her head up from her spot in one of the stadium seats and asks, "What was that?"

Okay, so maybe I didn't just say it in my head.

"Nothing." I wave her off with a chuck of my chin and swat of my hand. "It was nothing."

She nods cautiously and then puts her head back down to her work, and I try to do the same. I write two words and then glance up to see what she's doing.

Amazingly, she's actually focused, and just as I put my head down again and try to do the same, her eyes flutter upward, barely snagging on the gaze of mine in passing.

I deliberately ignore it, clearing my throat and waiting for my eyes to adjust to the words on my paper. *What am I even saying at this point? Does this lesson even make sense?*

Breathing in through my nose and out through my mouth, I force a deep circulation of air through my lungs and try to reset. It's going to be a long day—and a truly long-ass semester—if I can't find some way to make peace with being in Rachel's presence without wanting to rip her clothes off.

Just focus on the job, Ty.

After a couple more deep breaths, I forget that Rachel is there and get back into the lesson. It's about *Love in the Time of Cholera*, a book I've always found interesting. It's complicated and messy and real. It's not a happily ever after wrapped up in a bow, and also, I'm a fucking liar because I've been thinking about Rachel and Rachel's eyes and Rachel's legs and Rachel's sheer-panty-covered pussy this entire time.

Fuck.

I shift my pen under the word *complicated* and underline it five times. It's a heavy theme today in more than just this book, that's for sure.

I close my notebook, placing my pen inside, and pick it up to carry to my office. Rachel's head comes up at my movement, and I try on a friendly smile. Which I'm pretty sure looks more like The Joker's signature grin than anything remotely normal.

"I have a couple of notes I left in the office that I need," I tell her.

Bullshit, bullshit, bullshit.

"I'm going to run and grab them." I keep lying through my teeth. "And then, I'll probably just finish up in there until it's time for class."

She nods carefully again, and I return the gesture with a little more fervor. Too much, if I'm honest.

"Okay, well…see you in half an hour."

"See you then, Professor Winslow."

I don't dally after that. On quick legs, I head straight for the door. The sooner I get the hell out of here and gather myself, the better for both of us.

Out in the hallway, I take long strides, jockeying around students, and swing open the stairwell door to jog up the steps to the second floor in a hurry. I barely look at anything other than my feet. Which is why when I crest the top of the flight and bump immediately into someone, I'm not all that surprised.

"Ty!" Professor Rose greets excitedly, laughing off the physical contact. "Where's the fire, son?"

My head jerks side to side quickly, and I force a smile onto my face. It's not that it's not good to see him—it's just that the timing could definitely be better. Generally, I try not to be thinking about a man's daughter's pussy when I look him in the eye. A small rule of thumb, if you will.

"No fire, sir. I just need to do a couple of things in my office before class starts shortly."

"Running your own errands when you have a TA?" He shakes his head. "I hope you're not going too easy on Rachel on my account."

The mere mention of her name makes me choke on my own saliva, and his eyes widen at the grotesque sound while I hack into a fist to gather myself. "No, sir. Definitely not."

"Good, good. She needs the structure."

I suck my lips into my mouth. I don't think there's anything safe to say here, so the best practice is to say nothing at all.

"Oh!" he says, almost startling himself and holding up a singular finger. "I almost forgot! I have something for you."

"Something for me, sir?"

He nods, swings his leather briefcase in front of himself, and roots around in the front pocket, eventually coming out with a single page of poetry. He hands it to me, and I study it quickly. It's Walt Whitman, and it looks really old—like it could be out of a first edition. *Holy shit.*

"Nate? Is this…is this what I think it is?"

He smiles proudly. "First edition. Brutalized, obviously, evidenced by the fact that I'm handing you a single piece of paper, but I found it in a pawn shop many, many years ago with Nadine, and it just resurfaced in my attic cleanout. I've been meaning to give it to you. I know what a fan you are of his work."

Not to be dramatic, but this whole exchange feels like a collection of all the understatements of the century.

"I don't know what to say."

He just chuckles. "A simple *Thank you* is all that's needed."

"Wow." I nod. "Thank you, Nate."

He slaps my shoulder with a hearty grin and steps around me to head down the stairs on his original trajectory. "You bet."

I stand there for several long seconds, poring over the details of the paper—the markings, the weight of it, the words I've read thousands and thousands of times. I cannot believe I'm holding an actual single sheet of paper from a first edition of *Leaves of Grass.*

Engrossed, I stare at it as I move down the rest of the hallway to my office and step inside. Lesson plans forgotten, I drop my notebook on the surface of my desk and round it to the standing shelves behind. I have several newer versions of Whitman's collection of works on the fifth shelf up. The placement is intentional. I wanted my most prized treasures to sit at exactly eye level.

Carefully, I move one of my book stands to the front of that shelf and unfurl the folds in the paper—I can't believe this extremely valuable paper is folded and Professor Rose was just carrying it around in his briefcase like a pack of fucking gum—and set it out as gently as possible. It's not exactly stable, but I do manage to get it to stay enough to be able to see what it is. Long-term, I'll probably frame it and hang it on the wall just to ensure nothing happens to it, but for now, this will have to work.

When things are finally settled, I glance at the clock on the wall to see I've wasted just about all the time leading up to class. I have a little bit of a game plan, but at some point, I'll have to wing it.

Luckily for me and my class, I'm something of an improvisational specialist.

Time to give them hell.

Oh, and you know, keep shit between Rachel and me completely PG.

No, actually, G. Starting from this day forward, if our relationship is made into a movie, Disney would own the rights and we'd be two fucking cartoon characters.

Strictly professional. I got this…I *hope*.

I jump up on top of my desk and croon to the rafters, and the class bursts into a cacophony of laughter and chatter. I knew they would, given my antics, but I also know this is the kind of shit that keeps them remembering a lesson forever.

Not many undergrad students get excited about reading a book like *Love in the Time of Cholera* on their own. But throw in a little drama? Add a little bit of spice, as this generation of TikTokers is saying?

And they go wild for it.

"What I'm doing now, howling at the wind and making a big show of myself? That's the volume of the symbolism that Marquez manages in this book, but it's done elegantly."

I climb down off the desk and find Rachel's eyes in the front row. She's watching me avidly enough that I swiftly move my gaze to something else. This lesson doesn't need any more distractions than it's already had today.

"Florentino is a man of big talk, but his follow-through could stand some work. I think we can all relate to having the best of intentions sometimes without exactly having the best of execution."

I glance to Rachel once more. "I sure as hell know I can."

The big red clock in the back of the room ticks over to dismissal time, and I jump down off the platform on which my desk sits and approach the class.

"I want you to write a five-hundred-word personal experience essay about a time you had good intentions but less than optimal follow-through." The class gets restless, and I laugh. "Relax. They're not for grades other than participation. On Thursday, I'll read through them anonymously. Now, get out of here."

They all jump up and pack their belongings, and I head straight to the front row—to Rachel. If the past couple of hours are any indication, she's going to blow this popsicle stand as quickly as possible without looking back, and to be honest, I don't blame her.

But that's not how I want it to be between us. That's not the kind of environment I want to foster for months on end. And it's certainly not the kind of working relationship that's sustainable.

The right thing to do is to talk it out. Come to a truce. Figure out a way to work together without so much mental anguish for either of us.

"Rachel," I call, grabbing her attention as she packs her laptop into her bag. Her head jerks up, and her pretty sage eyes round. "Can I talk to you in my office for a couple minutes after this?"

She glances around the room hesitantly, students still milling about as they make their way down the stadium steps and out the door, and then, finally, nods.

"Okay."

"Just talk," I assure her, reaching out to squeeze her elbow. It's a rookie mistake, touching her when I have this tight a tether on my control, but I suck in a gulp of air to keep it together and step away.

She glances down to the spot I've just touched as though I've branded her, and I back away another couple of steps. *Distance.* Distance is good.

"I'll meet you in there," I say, still backing away, and she agrees with a quiet, "Okay" again.

I can do this.

I can have a conversation with Rachel and keep things professional.

We can address the sexual-tension, constantly-challenging-each-other elephant in the room without it being awkward, or, you know, turning into a repeat where her tongue ends up in my mouth while my hand is up her skirt.

It's those thoughts right there that aren't helping you, dude.

Fuck. I mentally shake myself out of it and head to my office.

I can do this. *We* can do this.

EIGHTEEN

Rachel

Hesitantly, I step into Ty's office, and when I shut the door behind me, the quiet click makes my heart kick up at a nervous pace. I have no idea what's about to happen, but I feel like I've just walked into the lion's den.

Truthfully, it's odd, but everything between us has been anything but straight-forward and simple.

"Uh…hi." I swallow past my discomfort. "You wanted to talk to me?"

"Yeah. I did," he says, getting up from his chair to round his desk and lean back into the front of it.

All I can do is stand there and wait, barely able to meet his eyes.

This whole day has been awkward as hell, and I have no idea what he's going to do or say, but every part of my body feels like it's trying to head back toward the door. My nerves. My organs. My arms and legs. Somehow, though, I force myself to stay rooted to my spot, still staying close enough to the door that if I need to make a quick exit, it won't be a hard task.

"So…things are pretty weird between us." He finally says something, and for some insane reason, a laugh bubbles up from my throat. Call it embarrassment or nerves, I don't know, but it's the only reaction my body is willing to give.

Ty furrows his brow, but he also smiles. "I take that as you agreeing?"

"Yeah." I glance down at my heels and then back up into his searching gaze. "Things are definitely strange."

"We…uh…maybe let things get a little out of control, huh?"

Instantly, I appreciate that he's considering this problem a "we" problem.

"Yes." My smile is tentative. "We have."

"That's why I wanted to talk to you," he continues and uses his hands to stabilize himself on his desk. "I was hoping we could find some sort of truce. An agreement that would make our working relationship a hell of a lot easier than it is right now."

The push and pull, the constant playing and challenging, well, it's taken a nose dive ever since I found out what it felt like to kiss him.

Sitting through a root canal without being numbed would feel simpler than how it felt to sit in an empty room with him before his ENG 101 class. Hell, getting a Brazilian wax done by someone who doesn't know what they're doing would be easier than this.

A truce is probably necessary.

"Okay." My lungs let out the half breath I've kept locked up inside my chest since I stepped foot inside his office. "I can get behind that."

I don't miss the fact that we're both tiptoeing around the reality of our situation. It's like we're cautiously avoiding mentioning anything that might spur some kind of visceral reaction. Though, after the scene that played out in this very office, where I was basically two moans away from asking him to fuck me, avoidance of the specifics is probably the best option.

"Good." A sigh of relief follows his words. "I think it's safe to say we're attracted to each other, but it's not something either one of us should pursue."

Attracted to each other feels like he's putting it mildly, but I go with it.

"Probably wouldn't work out too well." I bite my bottom lip and grimace, and he scrubs a hand down his face, shaking his head.

"No, I'm pretty sure it's against university policy."

And my dad wouldn't be all that thrilled, I think, but I keep that to myself.

I know he wouldn't appreciate anything that's been going on between Ty and me, but that's not something I feel is necessary to get into. We're both trying to alter the route of this crazy train, and that should be what counts the most.

"So…a truce?" I question and meet his eyes. "No more games? No more panties appearing out of thin air?"

"No more challenging each other?" He flashes a knowing smirk and stands to his feet. "And no more erotic displays in the middle of my lectures?"

That last one almost makes me blush, but I swallow past the discomfort and focus on the solution. "If you can get behind that, I can get behind that."

He nods. "If you can, I can."

But he also steps closer to me, his body eating up some of my personal space, even though I don't think that's his intention. And we both just kind of stand there, in the middle of his office, unsure of where to go from here.

"So…it's settled, then?" I eventually ask, and he examines my eyes.

"Yeah. I think so, right? It's settled."

"Right. It's for the best."

He nods again. "Definitely for the best."

"For sure."

It's not lost on me how idiotic we both sound. Like two newly built AI robots trying to have a conversation that's based on software that only holds about ten flipping phrases and lots of fucking head nods.

"It's eventually not going to be this awkward, right?"

His question makes a soft laugh pop from my throat. "Goodness, I hope not."

But then I look up into his steady gaze again, and the way his blue eyes smile down at me urges a flash of memories to flood my mind—*dancing with him at Orchid, talking to him about Tolstoy in the hallway, the way his eyes would light up mischievously when he'd hide my panties somewhere he'd know I'd find them.*

So many visuals float around inside my head, and there's a teeny-tiny part of me that thinks it's a damn shame that I'll never *really* get to experience all the things I've been constantly fantasizing about when it comes to him.

You'll never get to see what Ty looks like without his clothes on.

Or what it feels like to have his weight above you and his cock filling you to the hilt.

You'll never know what he looks and feels like when he comes.

"So…" He pauses. "Do we make it official?"

I blink. "Official?"

"Shake on it?" he asks. But when it's apparent I'm a little slow on the uptake, he adds, "You know, a good old-fashioned handshake to really certify this agreement."

"Oh." My teeth dig into my bottom lip, and I watch as he holds out his hand toward me, signaling that we are, in fact, about to *shake on it.*

But something happens.

I don't know how exactly, but the only way I can explain it is to describe what must be an out-of-body experience. You know, when you're in the room, but you're not physically in your body? You're just kind of hovering above it, watching yourself do things that you definitely don't think you intended to do?

Needless to say, *that's* the something that happens.

From above my body, I watch myself lift my hand, but instead of grabbing Ty's hand, my hand somehow ends up somewhere else…*much lower than his hand.*

And directly on his black-dress-pant-covered crotch.

Holy shit. His penis is in my hand.

I'm shaking his penis.

I'm touching Ty Winslow's dick right now, and even through his clothes, I can tell he's big. Like, *really* big.

And you're still shaking his really big dick…

"R-Rachel?" he stutters, and I look up to meet his eyes, and that's when I notice that his hand is still held out, waiting for mine. "Uh…"

"This isn't your hand, huh?"

"N-no." He shakes his head manically.

And still, I'm touching his cock.

Why am I still doing that?

Great question. Oh, and FYI, the longer you hold it, the harder he's getting…

NINETEEN

Ty

I thought I'd gotten control—thought *we'd* gotten control. That we'd both come to a truce and found a reason and a motivation to move on.

I thought I was finally putting my professional foot forward instead of my dick.

And yet, here I am, Rachel's hand on my crotch and my cock ready to rodeo.

I take deep breaths, I think about old ladies and baseball, I think about my brothers and my mom and my scumbag dad who left us as kids. I try all the mental tricks to get my dick to retreat, and none of it works. None of it even touches how horny I feel or how stubborn my dick's being about getting touched.

He wants action and he wants it now, and Rachel's perfect hand is still right there, holding my cock between the warmth of her fingers.

"Rachel…" I pause, unsure of what the fuck to do. My brain is telling me to step away from her, but yeah, my other brain is putting on his cowboy hat and yelling out "*Yippee-ki-yay, motherfuckers!*"

"You're hard," she whispers, and her big green eyes stare up into mine. "Like, really hard."

"Fuck, Rachel," I say through a groan. "Don't look at me like that. I'm not a fucking saint."

She doesn't say anything; instead, she ever so gently rubs her hand against me.

It's not helping. She's not helping. Fuck me, why is she still touching my dick?

Because you're letting her. Because you want this. And apparently, she wants this too.

Fuck. Fuck. Fuck.

Something snaps inside me, and I grab Rachel by her shoulders, pulling her body close to mine with a yank and pressing my mouth to hers.

My kiss is greedy and erratic, and somehow her lips follow along like they know exactly what to do. She tastes so good and her breasts bump against my chest and her hand is still on my cock and I've completely forgotten about anything that happened prior to this.

On a growl, I reach down and lift her up by her perfect ass, and she wraps her legs around my waist. Our kiss gets greedier, and her moans fall into my mouth as I dance my tongue with hers. It feels like we were connected by a rubber band, the only thing that was preventing us from getting back here, and that fucker just up and snapped.

She rocks her hips against me, and I kiss her deeper as I move us to somewhere behind my desk. I sit her ass on the surface, paying no mind to anything that's beneath her, and lean back to tug open the buttons of her blouse, leaving her breasts only covered by a thin lace bra.

Fuuuuck.

I tug the delicate cups down and wrap my mouth around one of her nipples before I can even process what I'm doing. Her skin is sweet, and her nipple is pert against my tongue, and each time I circle it, Rachel whimpers.

I start to move to her other perfect breast, but she stops my progress by grabbing both sides of my face and pulling my mouth back to hers. I groan, and she pushes her hips toward me, the apex of her thighs pressing and rubbing against my cock.

I am hard. *So fucking hard* I feel like I could saw my goddamn desk in half, and she is so beautiful, so unbelievably tempting, that I wonder how I managed to keep myself from her for this long.

Her mouth moves to my neck, and her lips and tongue suck at my skin in a way that makes my cock think he should be next. She pumps her hips toward me, rubbing herself hard against me, and my head falls back while my hand latches on to the edge of my desk. Images of Rachel grabbing on to my bare cock with a rough grip and running her tongue over the tip dance vividly behind my closed eyes.

I know that would feel incredible. So much so that a groan starts at the base of my throat, and I can't stop it, no matter how hard I try.

"Ty," she whispers, and I feel her move to her knees now, but I am powerless to say anything, do anything, besides stand there and let whatever happens happen.

The sound of my zipper echoes in my office, and then her mouth is on me.

On my cock.

I gasp when her perfect lips slide down my length. Holy shit, this is not good, but it's oh-so fucking good at the same time.

And when I jerk open my eyes and see Rachel's dark hair below me, I'm stuck between feeling like this is the best thing that's ever happened to me and wondering if God is about to strike me dead right now.

She moans around the head of my dick.

"Fuck," I mutter, and my hands have a mind of their own, reaching out to gently slide into her hair.

This…this wasn't my intention. But just like I told my class, I've completely flubbed the execution.

A voice in the very back of my mind—a messenger sent by my cock, no doubt—poses the question of *how much could something be going wrong if it's ended with a mouth on your dick,* but I know better.

I…*think* I know better.

I know…something.

Holy shit, this feels beyond incredible.

I sink my hand deeper into her hair as she sucks me harder, and I nearly choke on my own tongue when she swirls hers around my shaft.

She's good at this. Like, really, really good at this. Taking a deep breath in an effort not to come immediately, I look up from her head and mindlessly toward the wall where one of my bookshelves sits.

And right there, at perfect eye level, is the priceless work of Walt Whitman that Professor Rose gave me as a gift of respect. In retrospect, maybe that wasn't the best place to put it after all.

Guilt niggles and nags at me, and I shift my weight from foot to foot, trying desperately to let it go and concentrate on how good Rachel's mouth feels.

I can't, though, and before I know it, the feeling of wrongdoing is so strong, I can't escape it. Put bluntly, it's smothering me. Choking, cloying, all-encompassing, for the first time in my life, I feel as if I'm following in my birth father's scummy footsteps. Selfish, want-centered abandonment of responsibility.

We can't do this—I *cannot* do this.

I reach down to Rachel's shoulders gently and pull her back to release myself from her mouth. She looks up immediately, her eyes rounding in question. She and I both know she was seconds away from getting to the best part. I shake my head, willing my mouth to convey the words I have to say compassionately. "I'm sorry…I shouldn't be doing this. I *can't* do this."

The tone is so much rougher than intended, grittiness brought on by arousal lacing my words with an edge.

"But I thought…"

I nod, trying like hell with a heavy swallow to make my delivery softer. "I know. I know. I just…this is wrong. What we're doing is wrong."

She gulps thickly and climbs to her feet, her eyes shimmering slightly before she turns her back to me and rounds the desk toward the door.

"Rachel, wait," I call, buttoning my pants and shoving my still-hard dick inside as she moves so quickly out the door, she doesn't even bother to take her stuff. "Fuck!" I snap to myself, hating the look I just put in her eyes so much that I feel nauseated. That wasn't how it was supposed to go. This isn't how it's supposed to end.

It's not right, and it's not fair, and I *hate* the idea that she thinks she did something wrong. Out of the two of us, I'm the most responsible for bringing us here. I'm the one who started the panty war instead of letting it go. I'm the one who's done her wrong.

She hasn't done anything other than play along with the environment I created. I'm the problem—the one who can't seem to make up his mind and land on a side of the fence.

I mean, fuck, I know I owe Professor Rose a lot, but why in the hell did I think I owed him more in that moment than I did her?

Hurting one person as a sacrifice to save another? That's bullshit.

I have to make this right.

Quickly, I move to the door and out it, running down the hall after her. She's gotten a head start, but I'll be damned if I'm going to let things end the way they just did between us. I'll be *damned* if I'm going to sit by and let her think she's not worth the risk.

She is. Rachel Rose is once in a lifetime.

And sometimes, lines get crossed.

TWENTY

Rachel

My legs churn through a wild walk, faster and faster until I'm jogging down the hallway and down the stairs to the first floor. I can feel his presence behind me, closing in, but he isn't saying anything, and I don't have the voice to tell him not to follow me even if I wanted to.

I'm moving past the lecture halls, the midafternoon hallway devoid of crowds because most students and professors are in the middle of classes.

A ball of anxiety and rejection sits heavy in the back of my throat, and I feel almost sick that I let myself get wrapped up so deeply in this stupid game.

Did I honestly think it was going to end well? That we'd find some way to have hot sex without complicating our jobs or lives or ambitions? That Ty doesn't think I'm some stupid escapade in the first place? That he even really wanted me?

My legs speed up in a race with my mind, and I'm nearly around the corner when a hand latches on to my elbow and pulls me to a stop. I don't have to turn around to know who it is, so I jerk at my arm without even looking back.

"Rachel, stop," Ty whispers sternly, grabbing it again and directing me into a supply closet across the hall and closing the door. My anger burns like a smoldering ember.

"Let me leave, Ty."

"No," he denies, backing away from me bodily but leaning his against the door and effectively blocking me in. "Not until we talk."

"What's there to talk about? Just let me go, and let's finally put this behind us, for shit's sake."

"Rachel, do you really think that's what I want? To put this behind us? You think I don't fucking want you? Is that what you think?" he challenges, stepping toward me with every question. "You think I don't think about my cock between your legs and the face you'll make when you come and sucking on your tits until you scream every fucking waking moment of the day?"

My breathing shallows, and it's suddenly hard to take a full gulp of air into my lungs. The walls of this small closet almost feel like they're closing in.

"You think I don't want to fuck you until we both pass out, our hearts beating so hard we're close to going into cardiac arrest?"

I swallow thickly, and he smacks the door at his back with an open-palmed hand.

"Wake up, sweetheart. You're all I fucking think about. When I'm supposed to be working, when I'm in the shower with my hand wrapped around my aching cock, when I'm teaching a lecture with your sweet little cunt and those hot-as-fuck panties teasing me in the front row. You. Are. All. I. Fucking. Think. About."

"Ty," I whisper, the throb of every word he's said finding a home between my legs. *Sweet land of the living, he's sexy*

"Before, I was trying to do the right thing. But right now, I don't give a fuck about anyone but you and me. And I'm going to show you just how badly I want you."

Ty spins us, pushing me gently against the door and sinking to his knees in front of me. I don't have time to open my mouth, and I don't want to. The only mouth I'm thinking about right now is Ty's.

He scoots my skirt up my legs with ease and grabs the side of my sheer pink panties with his teeth, pulling them gently down my legs until they're low enough for his hands to take over. I step out of them easily, and he tucks them directly into his pocket with a smirk. Once again, the infamous panties are in his possession as a souvenir. I'm not entirely sure I'll be getting them back this time. *But that was the point, wasn't it? I knew what I was doing when I put them on this morning, even if I pretended to come here to be on good behavior.*

At the end of it all, I knew this was what I wanted—*needed*—to happen.

"Put your leg over my shoulder," Ty orders, his voice coarser than normal. I do as he asks, stretching my leg up and over and hooking my knee on his shoulder so my calf runs down his back.

The air in the closet feels like a cool breeze against my newly exposed flesh—especially with how overheated it is right now.

Ty blows warm air over me, almost as though he can sense my thoughts, and my head falls back against the door with an audible thud.

Dear God, he hasn't even touched me yet, and I feel like I'm going to climb out of my skin. Call Hollywood to come pick up their extensively detailed bodysuit; I'm ready to shed a layer.

"Oh, Rachel, you have no idea how fun this is going to be," Ty muses, the sight of his shock of brown hair between my legs making them start to shake.

I swallow hard and grab a chunk of his hair, unable to stop myself from seeing what my fingers look like tangled up in it while he puts his tongue between my legs.

Sweet merciful pleasure, it's even better than I thought it would be. The soft tresses, his sizzling blue eyes holding contact, and the warm imprint of his hand on my lifted thigh—*heaven.*

"Ty, touch me, please."

He leans in, my hand still firmly holding his hair, and licks a long line up the center of my pussy. If it weren't for my position, effectively trapped between him and the door, I'm certain I would have collapsed. I'm also certain that if Ty's tongue on me didn't feel this good, I wouldn't be referring to it with the word "pussy."

But the wanton, horny version of myself evidently has the kind of mind that goes to the dirtiest place possible. Put me on the set of a porno; I'm ready to perform.

Just…you know…privately.

"Mm," he hums, destroying any and all ability to question myself. This is definitely good. Very, *very* good, and it should *absolutely* be happening. I can't even think of anything else that could be happening, other than Ty's mouth spending a languid amount of time doing just this. "You taste so good," he adds, licking another path through me and then stopping at the top to flick his tongue with the perfect amount of pressure.

My head falls back and hits the door with a much bigger thud this time, and Ty pulls me closer to his mouth. His face is right there, on me, doing the exact things I've been fantasizing about for the past month.

This is…hot and should be forbidden, but fuck, it's…indescribable how good it feels. Like his tongue has trained for months for a cunnilingus marathon.

I teeter a little on my heels, and Ty digs his hand into the outer meat of my thigh, steadying me, his tongue never stopping its work. Around the clit, down the sides, and then ending with his tongue inside me.

"Ty," I breathe, unable to come up with any other words. I know there are a lot of them—I'm a graduate-level student in literature, for shit's sake— but in this moment, I don't know any of them but his name.

He smooths his hand softly away from my thigh and crooks it in the crease of my panty line twice. My whole body shudders.

"I can't wait to fill you up," he says huskily, his fingers working from the side to the center and just softly teasing entry. "Do you want that, Rachel? Do you want to feel me inside you?"

Fucking desperately, the voice in my head remarks, but all I can manage is a stunted, "Y-yes."

He pushes the tip of one finger inside and swirls it in a soft circle.

"Now, Ty. *Please,*" I beg just as he pushes another finger inside along with the first.

It's an intrusion—considering I haven't had sex with anyone in a hot minute—but it's not at all overzealous. I'm soft and limber and completely ready for action.

"Oh yeah, you're ready," he agrees, pumping both fingers in once, twice, and then a third, languid stroke with a hook at the top. My back arches off the door, and my mouth opens in a gasp. He stands abruptly, knocking my thigh off his shoulder, and closes his lips over mine, swallowing the surprised puff of air and then sliding the warm tip of his tongue across my bottom lip. I lick it immediately after, tasting myself there.

"God, you're so sexy," he whispers against my lips, and a shiver runs down my spine and out the tips of my toes.

The words are so simple, but the power I feel from them is invigorating. I've been a curvy girl my entire life. Confidence is something found in the space between society's opposition to it for women like me. At this age, I've curated my don't-give-a-fuck-about-other-people attitude pretty well, but that doesn't mean hearing it from the lips of a man as good-looking and sensual as Ty isn't flattering as hell.

"So are you," I reply, running my hands across his solid chest and down the center line of his rigid abdomen. He really does have the body of a Greek god. It's crazy.

"No, Rachel. I mean you're sexy in the way that I can't eat, can't sleep, can't fucking function another day without sliding my cock as deep inside you as it'll go and staying there until I get to see you come."

Okay, I'm so for that. Like, totally in favor.

"Yes," I say aloud and then add another "*Yes*" for good measure. I add a nod too, nearly knocking our foreheads together, thanks to an unlikely mix of extremely close proximity and overzealous enthusiasm.

He smiles all the way to his eyes, and I count the wrinkle-laugh lines on each side. Three on the corner of his left eye, but only two on the right. Clearly, even though it seems perfect in every way, his smile is uneven.

I don't know why but realizing that puts me somewhat at ease.

He slides his hands up the backs of my thighs until they get to my ass, and then he lifts with incredible effortlessness and pushes my back up against the door once again. My pussy is directly against his cock; I can feel its hard outline through the material of his stylish work pants.

A moan escapes my throat of its own accord, and Ty puts a period on its sentence by grinding himself more solidly against me.

"I can feel the heat of you through my fucking pants," he growls, closing his lips over mine again and sucking at my tongue in a way that makes my belly flip over on itself.

"I want to feel you in me," I counter, proud of myself for finally coming up with something good to say. My brain's been on AEL—Arousal Emergency Leave—and it finally punched back in on the clock.

Ty doesn't mince words or time, expertly unbuckling the belt at his waist and shoving his pants down to his thighs without even so much as bobbling me. *Holy hell, he's strong.*

I glance down at his rock-hard, seriously big cock. I don't exactly have the best view from this position, but traumatized or not by the rejection, it's burned into my brain from before.

He pulls a condom from his pants pocket and hands it to me, instructing, "Here. Put it on."

For all my stubbornness with authority, it's never translated to school. As ever, I'm an excellent student, taking the package, ripping it open with the tips of my teeth, taking out the rubbery circle, and reaching down to unfurl it along his length.

When I look back up into his face, there's a flare in his eyes that I hope I'm ready for. Quite frankly, he looks like he could eat me alive, and it makes my breaths come out in erratic pants as my body tries to anticipate his next move.

Slowly, he swirls a finger around my entrance, pulling some of my moisture and rubbing it across the tip of his dick before aligning himself with me. I inhale deeply as the head of his cock seats itself perfectly inside me, and he freezes.

Our eyes meet, holding tightly, and my irregular breath swirls in the tight space between us. I'm expecting him to be rough—to seat himself in one smooth stroke—but instead, he moves almost painfully slowly.

Languid, measured, millimeter by millimeter, he pushes himself to the hilt and then squeezes his hands on my ass.

It's safe to say, I've never been this full in my life. I've had guys, I've had vibrators, I've even had a dildo that I got as a joke from some sex toy company, and let me tell you, none of them measure up to the feeling of Ty Winslow inside me.

We stay there for a long moment, just barely even existing past the connection of our bodies. When my heart rate starts to even out and my eyes start to feel hard to hold open, that's when Ty starts to move. Slow, directed thrusts that shake our heads just enough to keep our lips bumping together.

It's so different from how I imagined it would be the first time we went at each other, and yet, it's also so much better.

There's no outside noise rattling around in my brain, no obnoxiously fake sexy talk, no overbearing need to perform. It's all about feeling—and because of that, the sensation of every stroke is heightened.

In and out, Ty moves with infuriating precision, hitting all the right spots just enough to bring me to the brink and hold me there. Over and over and over, I throw my head back in eagerness of tumbling over the edge, only to come up just a fraction of an inch short.

"Ty," I whimper. "I don't know if I can…take…anymore."

He smiles against my lips, the sexy feel of the curve of his mouth pushing me just a hair closer to paradise.

"You can," he asserts, grabbing my ass tighter and bouncing me down on him to the hilt. "You're so fucking close, Rach. I can *feel* you. Getting wetter, getting hotter, getting tighter. I can't wait to feel you come."

"Ty," I cry on an exhale, losing complete control over petty things like the volume of my voice.

"Come on, Rachel. Let go. Stop thinking. Just feel."

I close my eyes then as his strokes get just the tiniest bit faster. Just one sweet, tiny change. But it's enough to send me careening over the edge into a bliss I've never experienced before.

Stars dance behind my eyes. Sound swells over and hums in my ears. And my whole body rolls into a wave of pleasure. It feels like every cell inside me is on pleasure overload and can't do anything besides shake and tremble. I can still feel Ty's breath on my neck, escalating, changing, getting harder and heavier, and I will myself to find a way to concentrate.

Ty Winslow isn't the kind of guy you have sex with, just to miss the big finale. I have to see his face when he comes. I have to hear the grit in his groan. I have to witness firsthand what hundreds and hundreds of other women go to bed at night fantasizing about.

Sweet Hamlet in movie form, this guy is the real deal. I watch avidly as he drives into me, harder, faster, steadier, striving for his own climax. His eyes are open but hooded, and his mouth is pulled into the sexiest fucking smirk to ever exist, I'm sure of it.

Finally, he exhales hard, groaning into the skin of my neck and sinking just the very tips of his teeth into my skin for a nip. It's incredibly erotic and intimate, and I know with pointed precision that I'll remember this moment for the rest of my life.

If the panties were my grand memory-making debut, this sex is Ty's main stage performance. *This guy has a doctorate in more than English Literature.*

Our breaths are fast and mingled, and Ty's jaw is misty with a thin layer of sweat. Still, though, he holds me in his arms as if I weigh nothing, even after all this time and exertion.

"You can put me down," I offer, but he shakes his head immediately.

"Are you kidding? I'm nowhere near ready to pull this pretty pussy off my dick."

I laugh a little, and he smiles against my mouth again, licking a line just deep enough to tickle my tongue.

We stay like that for nearly a minute, just barely touching and kissing, the strength in my limbs all but gone. When he finally pulls me off him, he lifts me with ease before setting me on my shaky feet and spinning around to deal with the condom.

I push my skirt down slowly, careful not to make the kinds of sudden movements I know would knock me right to the floor, and lean my weight into the door once more. It feels different this time, though, with the distance between us and Ty's back turned to me.

It doesn't mean anything; I know that. It just feels…weird.

Ty turns back around then, leaning in to place another soft kiss on my lips. He smells like us, and it's an immediate stimulus.

I've just had him, and yet…I can't wait to have him again. If he has any inkling of agreement, I feel so sorry for my vagina. The change in use is going to be unbelievably jarring.

But the thing is, I don't know what this means—what Ty wants. Ty's smile is the kind that you can get lost in for hours on end, but what it isn't is telling in any shape or form. I have no idea what he's thinking, and God, my brain is running a mile a minute.

"Ty… What… Where do we… What happens next?"

He leans in and puts one soft kiss to the underside of my jaw. "What comes next, is tomorrow."

"Right," I mumble, clueless as fuck as to what that's supposed to mean. Will tomorrow be like yesterday, or will it be like today? My brain can't process theoretical poetic bullshit right now.

Still, the last thing I'm going to do is let on that I want to know anything. Ty's been there and done that, and quite frankly, so have I. The Rachel

Rose of today isn't the kind of woman who begs anyone for anything, and she sure as hell doesn't wait on a man to decide. She takes what she wants, gives what she can, and lives in the moment.

And right now, I want to fucking kiss him.

I lean in, but before I can finish the motion, he's doing it for me. His lips brush mine, and the sight of his eyes up close is magic. They seem to go on forever, like vast oceans of iris.

"Oh yeah," Ty says then, confirming with absolute certainty that this won't be the last time we do this. "This is going to be fun."

TWENTY-ONE

Wednesday, February 13th

Ty

Rachel mewls as I grab a handful of her playfully curled hair and pull her head back to expose her throat. She's on her knees on the couch in my office, her hands gripping the back and her ass on display for my enjoyment. She's completely naked, and the lock on my office door has finally come in handy after I-don't-even-know-how-many years.

Feeling her now, I can't believe I managed to make it an entire twenty-four hours without fucking her, and I don't know if I'll be able to make it that long again.

I lean down and nip at her throat, and then I reach around to grab on to her heavy, perfect tits with my free hand. It feels so fucking good for both of us, I groan, and her ass pushes back harder into my crotch. "Put it in, Ty," she begs in a breathy, sensual voice born of arousal.

I let go of her hair and place a hard, sound smack to her ass that makes her throw her head back.

"What's the rush, baby? I promise you'll get my cock." She shoots a look of disgust over my shoulder, and I laugh. "Into spankings but not into nicknames, huh?"

"Spankings in the right moment are good, but nicknames seem like it'd make it a little too easy to forget my name."

I laugh again and drive my cock inside at the same time, taking her by surprise if her rolling moan is any indication. It's so out of the ordinary for me to be bantering during sex, but Rachel has something about her that makes fucking and joking at the same time feel right.

In fact, it feels wildly more intimate than all the fast, dirty fucks of the past. It feels…authentic.

"I couldn't forget your name if I tried."

Truth be told, *her name* is the only thing that kept us from doing this weeks ago. If she weren't who she is—and I weren't acutely aware of it—I never would have been able to hold back this long.

She reaches up behind the couch to steady herself, grabbing on to the front of a bookshelf I've filled over the years with rare editions of the classics. Brontë, Shakespeare, Paulo Coelho, Agatha Christie, Tolstoy—they're all getting a view today I bet they never dreamed of when they wrote these novels.

I start a smooth pace of long, detailed strokes that give my dick time to read the room. Is it firm or pliable? Wet or soaked? Each and every time I fuck, I do it to the best of my ability. But with Rachel, I want it to be an experience she'll never fucking forget. I want her to think about the feel of my cock when she's eating, when she's sleeping, when she's showering. I want her to think of it so often, in fact, that she comes after me looking for it.

I want to feel the power of her taking control—I want to feel what it's like when she's in charge. Weeks of playing our games have assured me that a Rachel-led encounter will be just as good if not better than the ones where I'm in the lead.

She's confident. She's unbelievably sexy. She's everything I love in a woman, plus a lot of things I never knew could exist.

She challenges me. And right now, I'm going to challenge her not to come within the next minute.

"Close your eyes," I tell her, grabbing her hair to pull her head back again. Her back is arched in the most glorious way, and I kiss one eyelid and then the other, and then I run my tongue across the crease of her lips. "I want you to feel each and every inch of my stroke, do you understand me,

Rachel? Nothing exists outside of this—" I grab her pussy from the front, my fingers wrapping around the base of my cock as it pumps inside. "Do you understand?"

She nods fervently.

"Good. I want you to do that, but I don't want you to come."

Her eyes fly open, and an almost-shriek falls from her lips. "What? What do you mean, *don't come?*"

"I mean don't come. Fight it. Challenge it. Make me work for it. Taunt me just like you did with the panties, and I promise, I'll make sure it's the best fucking fight you've ever had."

She nods in agreement then, turning back to face the shelves and bracing both hands on the wood in front of her this time. Her ass in my hands, I start my assault on her willpower.

One stroke followed by another, I move my hands all over her body. Her ass, her hips, her back and neck and shoulders, and then around to the front to hold her sweet tits in my hands and pull at her nipples. She moans and shifts her weight on her knees as her back arches and fights.

I skate my hands down the sides of her abdomen and around, grabbing on to the front inner part of her thighs. She gasps, and I slide them even farther up, to the point of transition from her legs to her pussy, rubbing at the sides with delicate fingers.

All the while, I maintain my grueling pace, even as a bead of sweat forms on my neck and rolls itself all the way to the base of my spine. The sensation almost makes me pull up short, the tingle mixed with the feel of Rachel's perfect cunt around me nearly too much to take.

Come on, you bastard. You can't tell her not to come and then come yourself. Sex is like walking through a door—the woman comes first, always.

I grit my teeth and bite down into my lip, doubling my efforts with my fingers skating across the sensitive lines where Rachel's panties would sit if she were wearing them.

"You feel so fucking good," I whisper into the shell of her ear, moving her hair out of the way with the surface of my lips. "So tight and wet and hot. I swear I could keep my dick inside you every hour of the day."

Rachel exhales, her legs starting to shake in their position in front of mine. I can feel her getting close, feel the desperation of every fiber of her body to stay on top of the cliff. She's a fighter, that's for damn sure. I thought I would have had her into euphoria by now, but the defiance feels insanely good.

It's driving me, pushing me to find the spots that turn her on the most. I move my lips down the line of her neck and rub at the sides of her pussy again, before shifting one hand around her hip and cracking her ass with just one more slap.

A red bloom flourishes on the affected skin, and my balls tighten into my body.

If you don't make her come soon, you're going to be in trouble.

Down between our bodies to the crack of her ass, I run just one finger along the line and pause over the bud. She arches her back into it, and after one smooth, soft circle with my finger, she comes—hard.

Her back arches farther, and her breath explodes in a cry of ecstasy.

The sound of her pleasure is enough to unleash mine, and I growl right into the space between her shoulder blades as I spend my load inside the condom.

I would give nearly fucking anything to put myself inside her bare. *Sweet Jesus, I know it would be heaven.*

But there's no way I'm putting her at that kind of risk without being absolutely fucking sure for the health and safety of both of us and making sure she's on an alternative birth control.

But I'm not going to pause and wait to make that happen either—I'm going to keep wearing condoms as long as it fucking takes. Because this is the kind of paradise you don't get lost in once in a while. It's the kind that you lose yourself in completely.

Both of us pause in our positions, almost as if we have a routine of giving the moment time to leave before separating ourselves. When I'm sure she's fully spent, I back myself off the couch and my cock out of her and stand, moving over to my desk to deal with the condom.

I pull it off quick, tie it in a knot, and toss it in the trash can, and then I use a tissue from my desk to wipe the rest of my come off my length.

I'm sensitive as hell, and just the feeling of the thin paper ghosting over me is almost enough to harden my dick all over again.

I can't fucking believe how much I want her. How completely I would abandon any and every other responsibility on my plate if it meant I could be inside Rachel for another hour.

When I turn back around to face the woman of the hour, she already has her slinky dress back over her head and is stepping into her high heels as she smiles up at me. "So, where are we having sex tomorrow, Professor?"

I bite my lip and shake my head on a chuckle at the formality of her address. "I can think of a place…or twenty."

She gets up from the sofa and approaches me, stopping just shy of touching her lips to mine. "Me too. How about you fuck me wherever you catch me?"

"Oh," I hum. "A game. I like it."

"Uh-huh," she nods. "Only with this game, if you do your job correctly, we both win."

"Oh really?" I scoff. "Do you think there's a chance I won't do my job?"

She winks. "Well, I only have two items of case study. Maybe a few more down the road, I'll feel more confident in making a statement of fact."

"You wound me, Ms. Rose."

She pushes her lips to mine and reaches around to grab my ass, shaking her head. "No, Professor. I *challenge* you."

Now that's a promise I hope she keeps.

TWENTY-TWO

Thursday, February 14th

Rachel

Waking up today—after two straight days of sex with Ty—feels different from every other day I've woken up in New York. My longing for something, my search for feeling at home, it's oddly…*missing.*

I'm not naïve enough to think Ty is the answer to everything I need in life, but whatever that restless thing inside me was—whatever was egging me on every time we engaged in a game of push and pull—it's quieted.

This morning, I can hear the birds. I can hear the city. And if I listen really closely, I can hear my mom.

Don't worry, I don't hear her, like, actually speaking to me from the dead—that would be a creepy sexual side effect—but I can feel her presence, here, with me.

I thought the fact that today is Valentine's Day might cause an awkward stir inside me, or maybe cause some discomfort in Ty, but with the way we left things last night, dirty texting well after midnight, I'd say we're both feeling pretty unfazed.

I grab my bag from the counter and head downstairs to the bakery to find Lydia and Lou having their morning coffee together at one of the tables now that the initial rush of the day is over.

They look at each other the way my mom always looked at my dad, and I couldn't be more thrilled for them that they were able to find the one person who puts them at ease.

I've never seen them have a real fight, and trust me, I would have if they were having them. Bakery weekends are just about the seventh portal of retail hell, and they both still do it, after this many years, with a smile on their faces.

It's impressive, really, and I can only dream of one day being that emotionally stable. I come by the craziness honestly, though—I've been this way my entire life.

Maybe it was being the youngest sibling, maybe it was losing my mom during some of my most crucial years, or maybe it's just the way I was made, but I'm not the kind of gal who knows she's doing the right or wrong thing right away. I'm the poor sap who has to find everything out the hard way.

I settle down in a chair at the table with Lydia and Lou and throw my brown leather gloves on the marble top. The two of them smile at me even with the screech of the chair legs caused by my abrupt movements, and I lean into my elbows on the table after I've taken a seat. "So, what time are we doing…you know…the thing?" I ask Lydia, knowing it's incredibly stupid that I still can't say the actual words *going to visit Mom's grave* after all these years.

She doesn't criticize, though, instead giving me the space I need and an answer too. "I think Dad said around two. It's supposed to sleet later or something, so he doesn't want to wait too late."

I'm supposed to be in class with Ty at two, but hell, maybe this is better. With what I have planned for the two of us today, it's better if we don't see each other beforehand.

I pull out my phone to text him about it, and then I think better of it when I see Lydia and Lou both watching me closely. I tuck my phone back into my pocket and state nonchalantly, "Okay. I'll have to let Professor Winslow know I won't be in class, but it shouldn't be a big deal. I can send him an email or something."

"Professor Winslow, huh?" Lou teases. "So, have we officially moved on from the panties?"

I nod, humming my answer instead of saying it for the purposes of plausible deniability. "Things are good."

I feel a little bad not giving them the whole rundown—I know they wouldn't be judgmental—but there's something about staying in a tiny little bubble with Ty and myself as the only inhabitants while we're messing around that seems like the best option. I mean, I don't know what this is or if it'll go past next Tuesday. I don't want to permanently tinge the way they look at him for no good reason if I don't have to. He comes in here every Sunday, for crying out loud.

"Good. Good is good," Lydia says before bugging her eyes out at Lou when she thinks I won't notice. I roll mine and stand up, sliding my gloves onto my hands and then interlacing my fingers to mold them into place.

"Okay, I have to go to class and do some research, but I'll see you at two, I guess."

Lydia nods. "I'll let you know if anything changes."

"Sounds good." I smile and wrap my scarf tight around my neck and head for the door.

It only takes me two seconds of being on the sidewalk, and away from Lou's and Lydia's eyes, before I'm taking one glove off and pulling my phone out of my pocket once again to text Ty that I'm going to miss his class later. He reacts as expected, telling me that's fine. It's only when his second text comes in, though, that I expand my smile.

Ty: I'm going to see you at some point today, though, yeah?

Me: Yes. In fact, I'll text you with instructions later.

Ty: Instructions?

Me: Yes, Professor, instructions. Do you think you can follow them?

Ty: Count on it. In fact, count on me following them a little too well.

I laugh aloud before tucking my phone into my pocket and heading on my way. Valentine's Day and love and shopping for flowers and chocolates may not be the reason, but today is going to be a busy, busy day.

Lydia and I stand off to the side, in a grove of trees, as our dad has a moment alone to place his flowers on our mom's grave. At this point in my life, she's been gone more years than she was here, but for my dad, she's still the singular love of his life. He spent more years with her in the first half of his life than he did without her, and I know he misses her every day.

I know we have our differences, but this is one area where I can genuinely say I empathize with him.

Lydia wraps her arm around my shoulders and pulls my body toward her in a big, dramatic swing. I wrap my arms tight in return, and the two of us share a moment of letting our mom's love wash over us on her favorite holiday.

She loved love, and she dedicated her life to writing about human nature, of which love is an amazingly large part. She didn't think this holiday was corny. She didn't think it was a marketing scheme. She thought it was a magical day to remind yourself what you were living for.

I, of course, try not to think too hard about any of that. I'm sure one day I'll be in the position to love and be loved and pass that on to kids and grandkids and beyond. But for right now, I'm a single, twenty-six-year-old grad student, fucking the professor she TAs for just for the fun of it.

It's not the kind of thing they put on Hallmark cards.

I hug my sister tighter. "I love you, Lydie."

"Love you too, Rae." She pulls back from the hug but holds me by the tops of my arms just far enough away that she can look me in the eyes. "You know you can always come to me, right? No matter what? I'll be there for you."

I don't know what she thinks is going on in my life that's that detrimental, but I don't read too much into it. Instead, I accept the kindness of her gesture and nod. "I know. You've always been the best big sister."

She leans forward and puts a kiss on my cheek just as our dad is joining us. I offer him a half smile before turning to walk to the car. I know it's a little childish given the circumstances, but I've had enough experience to know that nothing I say to him will end well.

We're like oil and water, and no effort to be thoughtful or kind ever helps that. One of us always manages to construe the other's words, and then we're off to the races fighting.

I really don't want that today. Not here, under these circumstances, and not at all, really. I just want to enjoy the plan I have in place with Ty and forget the rest of it. Period.

The first thing I do as I enter the old, multistoried building on Washington Square in Greenwich Village is look at the clock behind the desk to check the time. I have a little bit of scouting to do to pick the final location, but in the meantime, Ty's out of class, and it's time to start the clues.

I stop in the lobby and take a seat on one of the rounded black couches, unwrapping my scarf and pulling off my gloves first and tucking them into my bag.

Once I'm unbundled and my stuff is secure, I take my phone out of my pocket and pull up the notes app where I've been typing my ideas for clues all morning.

After double-checking them all, I copy number one from the top and then pull up my message thread with Ty. The last text from him last night sits at the top of the screen, in all its explicit glory.

Ty: I can't wait to fuck you until you're fuck-drunk tomorrow. You're going to feel me between your legs for days to come. How's that for sweet dreams?

A shiver runs down my spine, and I paste the clue into the message, proof-reading it one more time before hitting send.

Me: Finders keepers, losers weepers. Your first clue for finding me today is simple. One step, one step, one step, two, find your way to the floor with the doors that go outside of this building of NYU.

I wait not so patiently for a response as the bubbles wiggle to indicate he's typing a message, my foot bouncing on the tile floor all the while. It's not so much that I have an expectation of impressing him—it's more that the anticipation of what's to come when he finds me is almost overwhelming.

Ty: Okay, I've bitten, sweet little rosebud. Whatever am I to do now?

I toggle back to my notes and copy the next clue, sending it to him quickly.

Me: The first president's park, an arch at the edge, come to the building that houses Poe and Maugham and Ellison and many books with the word hedge.

I know that one wasn't the greatest, but after class and homework and visiting Mom's grave, I didn't have a ton of time to make these things happen.

Ty: Okay, please, please tell me we're playing naughty librarian.

Me: Just follow the clue.

Ty: Fine, fine, I'm on my way.

I get up from the couch and make my way to the ninth floor, where, from my research, I know the most obscure books can be found. Spanish lit, Ross's book on paleontology—you'll find them on this floor.

I step off the elevator and circle the floor, scouring the shelves for the darkest, most out of traffic corner, and place my belongings on the table by the window.

My heart rate escalates, the excitement of Ty's approach and the danger of possibly getting caught sending my blood pressure up a few notches.

Ironically, I thought I'd be nervous, but I'm not. I thought I'd be worried about the consequences or be trying to figure out a way to make sure we don't get caught by security, but now that I'm here, I find the only thing I'm worried about is finding a surface on which Ty can put his cock inside me.

My phone buzzes on the table, and I pick it up immediately.

Ty: I'm in the lobby, oh great clue-giver. Where do I go now?

Me: Up the elevator, and off to the right, don't stop walking until there's nowhere left to go in sight.

It's a bit of a maze to get back here, but I'm confident, driven by the reward of sex, Ty Winslow will find it. Plus, it's the kind of maze that you can't get lost in as long as you keep walking until the path ends.

I finish disrobing to an acceptable level by taking off my cardigan and slipping off my black tights from under my skirt, and then I lean against the bookshelf with my phone in my hand. My pulse thrums and my breathing is starting to sound like a pant, but I know it'll all be worth it in the end.

When Ty finally rounds the corner, he does it cautiously, slowly, seductively. His movements are completely in contrast to the state of his being, however, which looks hurried and frazzled, nearly manic.

He may seem calm now, but if I had to guess, I'd say Ty Winslow's been in a sprint since the moment he got that first text clue.

Everything inside me vibrates with power.

"Looks like I found you," he says smartly, a smirk crinkling the corners of his eyes. "Now what am I supposed to do?"

I shrug. "I told you we'd do it wherever you caught me. The rest is up to you."

His grin deepens so much that a little crescent dimples the flesh of his rosied cheek. "You didn't tell me there'd be clues."

I quirk a brow. "Are you complaining?"

His smiling face is suddenly serious. "Not in the fucking slightest."

I lean back against the library shelf of the kind of obscure literature that no one at even NYU touches and crook a finger toward him. "Well, get over here, then."

Ty's grin could illuminate even the darkest corner of this old building. I expect his immediate approach to follow, but he turns in the other direction, leaving our little alcove and disappearing out of sight.

What the hell? Where's he going? I spent at least two hours of time that I should have been using to work to come up with those clues, and he's just going to smile and walk away—

Ty rounds the corner and back into sight, effectively cutting off my mental rampage before it can get a good set of legs under it. He's walking a chair in front of him, and I lift my right eyebrow in curiosity.

"A chair?" I ask simply when he pushes it up against the bookshelf beside me and nods, satisfied with his positioning.

"Yep. You did a great job with the clues, but I have a picture in my mind I can't let go of."

"A picture in your mind? Of what? A new furniture design for the space?"

He chuckles at my sarcasm, leans down to place a kiss behind my ear, and then whispers warm air directly into it. "No. I have a vision of you riding me. And today, we're going to turn that vision into a memory."

"Is that right?"

Ty nods lasciviously. "I think I read somewhere that the only rule of doing what we're doing on a day like Valentine's Day is to keep it as sex-centered as possible."

Where the hell did he read that? Cosmo magazine?

"Yeah? And?"

"Well, the best way to center our sex is to sit you right in the middle of my lap. With my cock inside you, of course."

I nearly snort. "Of course."

"Take off your panties, Rach. Because if you don't, I'm going to rip them off you, and I don't know that I should be single-handedly responsible for running you out of underwear."

He doesn't have to ask me twice. I shimmy them down my legs and kick them to the side as he pulls the chair up to the shelf and sits down. I lean forward and unzip his pants.

It's eerily quiet in this obscure library space, and the only thing I can hear is the ragged exchange of oxygen into carbon dioxide for both of us.

I hike my skirt up to my hips and place one knee at the side of Ty's thigh before climbing up and doing the same with the other. I'm straddling his bare cock, and the feel of its warmth against me is enough to make me throw back my head and moan softly.

Ty grabs my chin and pulls my head forward, forcing my eyes to hold his. It's dominating and assuming—and it's fucking hot as hell.

Leaning forward, I seal my lips over his and arch my back as he puts both hands to my breasts. The silk fabric barrier feels like almost nothing, and yet it stimulates friction on my nipples at the same time. I'm so turned on, I can hardly keep my eyes open.

I thought this would go a little slower, but now I don't know. Now, all I can think about is him sticking his cock inside me as soon as physically possible.

He reaches into his pocket for a condom, and I grab him by the wrist before I even know what I'm doing. "I'm on birth control."

Ty's eyes brighten with both excitement and concern, and he digs a hand into the back of my hair to tilt my head back a little. "Are you sure? I just got tested, I'm clean, but I don't want to do anything you're not comfortable with. It's not worth it. We can just use the condom."

I shake my head. "I want to feel you skin-to-skin."

Convinced, he abandons the search in his pocket and brings his other hand to the back of my neck too. With control of my head in his hands, he tilts and turns me where he wants me, just right so that he can explore the vastness of my mouth with his tongue. It's sensual and incredibly intimate in a way that our sex hasn't felt yet.

I grab ahold of his cock in my hand and rise up higher on my knees to position him perfectly. Once I've pushed the head inside, I dispense with any and all caution and sink down completely. The two of us groan, and I lean forward to cover his mouth with my own.

Captured there, our sounds with nowhere to go but mingling with each other, I pull back up and then slide down again, slowly this time. Ty's moan vibrates in my throat, and I do it again, just to see if I can get the same reaction.

Over and over, he sounds off into my mouth, and I keep my pace steady. In and out with the kind of Kegel squeeze that will get his attention every single time.

His hands find my hips and his fingertips flex into my flesh, but as much as I know he'd like to try to take control of the pace, he doesn't. He lets me keep the time and rhythm, and he does it without endeavoring to convince me otherwise.

I chase my own orgasm, shifting to find the right angle, the right friction, the right ache. When I do, I don't stop. I don't stop to kiss or to talk or to muse over what we're doing or where we're doing it. I chase my pleasure with single-minded enthusiasm.

The bonus effect is a dogged, paced deterioration of Ty's control, one stroke at a time.

I'm not sure when I learned the secret—that going after your own pleasure is just as likely if not more to bring a man to orgasm as catering to them—but I've never forgotten it since.

Work for you, ladies, and the man will come. I promise you.

Ty's shoulders get tighter and tighter under my hands, and he finally has to pull back from my mouth. His whisper is one of desperation. "I'm close, Rach. So fucking close. You're so fucking incredible I don't know what to do with myself. Please come."

It's not just a suggestion; it's a plea. He's holding back—fighting. And if I don't come soon, it's going to be a big disappointment for everyone.

I deepen my grind at the base of my strokes and pull back to hold eye contact. I can feel a soft smile as it washes over my face. I'm floating right on the edge of euphoria, and in the land of pleasure, there are no hard lines.

My body feels pliable and languid, the only tension right at the apex of my thighs. It's hanging, bracing, waiting, and I know with just a few more strokes I'll be tumbling over the edge.

My eyes start to roll shut and my mouth curves into a full smile as the wave starts—rolling at first and then rushing, rushing, rushing to break at the peak. My head snaps back, and Ty buries his growling groan into my throat. There's no question, both from the swelling feeling inside me and the clutch of his fingertips, Ty's come too, in a stream of blinding glory inside me.

Holy sex and books, I can't believe how good that felt.

For the first time since our encounter started, I remember our surroundings and scan them. It's largely quiet, but I'll be honest, a herd of elephants could have come through here while I was in the throes of my orgasm, and I never would have known.

Once my breathing slows and my heart rate returns to normal, I climb off his lap, the sudden loss of his warmth inside me startling me more than I expected. Both of us find each other's eyes, almost as though he felt the same thing. I don't stay there in the moment, though. I can't. It's too scary, and I kind of have more urgent things to deal with—*a la cleaning myself up.*

By the time I put myself back together, he's standing at ease, his ankles crossed with his thumbs hooked into his pockets as he leans into the adjacent bookshelf.

He smirks when I look him in the eye. "What?" I ask.

"Nothing," he muses, biting at his lip and checking me out up and down. "This is just the best Valentine's Day on record for me."

I giggle a little, admitting, "Me too."

In the past, they've always been so fussy. So much pressure—not enough pleasure. I think this is going to be my tactic for the holiday from now on, to be honest.

He shoves off the shelf and walks toward me, placing a soft kiss on my lips that's completely unexpected. I search his blue eyes for some kind of reason, but all I can find in them is complete and utter satisfaction.

"Tomorrow?" I ask simply, hoping he doesn't make me tap-dance too hard to get a real answer out of him.

"We could go to dinner if you want? Have another round today?"

Out of nowhere, panic seizes my chest, and I have to look away to gather myself for a moment. I've settled into our routine of once a day easily enough, but ramping it up? I'm not sure if that's the right direction to go. If Ty notices, he doesn't mention it, and for that, I'm thankful.

I couldn't explain if I tried. But dinner sounds…serious…*scary*.

And I'm not ready for those things.

"Sorry, I have a paper due tomorrow that I have to put the finishing touches on," I offer and bump my hip playfully into his side. "If I stick around you any longer today, I'm afraid I'll never get it done."

"Some other time, then," he offers, and I turn to gather my belongings in an effort to deflect the emotions running rampant on my face.

"Yeah," I agree, looking directly at the carpeted floor and nowhere else. "Some other time."

He grabs me by the waist and spins me around before laying the kind of kiss on me that makes me forget everything else. It's expansive and mind-erasing, and before I know it, I'm leaning into it so hard his back bumps into the shelf behind him.

I might be scared at the idea of more, but there's no denying I'm one hundred percent on board with the sex. *That's for sure.*

"Tomorrow," Ty remarks at the shell of my ear, squeezes my ass, and then disappears into the maze of shelves again.

I take a moment to gather myself, sinking to the floor and pulling my panties and tights back on.

Fully dressed once more, I let my head fall back into the shelf behind me and free up my brain for a tiny sliver of a moment.

Lydia's words and my dad's voice and Ty's invitation all swirl into view and fight for dominance so quickly, I barely manage to shove them back behind the door to the hidden area of my brain and stand.

Nope. Those aren't the things to think about now.

Right now, all I want to think about is *tomorrow.*

TWENTY-THREE

Friday, February 15th

Ty

Justin, a kid who does very little talking in class, places his test facedown on my desk, and I make a show of kicking my feet up onto the surface and leaning back into my hands behind my head.

"That easy, huh?"

He shrugs one shoulder without saying anything, heads back to where his seat is, hikes his backpack up on his shoulder, and proceeds to exit the room.

I know teachers on exam day aren't exactly best-friend material, but I normally get at least an awkward smile.

Sliding my feet off the old, wooden surface and sitting straight up, I pick up his test as soon as he leaves the room and start flipping through it. It's all pretty normal-looking—not that I have the answer key on me to check how many he's gotten wrong—but the essay section is as bare as a newborn baby's ass.

Curious, I turn his test facedown in a second stack and pick up another from beneath it. My scan is short-lived and cloaked in the same results. Answered questions and then at the essay, nothing.

I move on to the final test in the pile from the early finishers, and when that one comes up the same way, I snatch my phone off the surface of the desk and start typing furiously.

This is strange. So much so, that I'm starting to wonder if I'm hallucinating.

Me: Rach, do me a favor and go double-check that people aren't leaving

the essay section blank. I've gotten three exams turned in with nothing. I'm starting to think I'm the only one who can see it. Like, WTF, did we use invisible ink?

I watch closely for the moment the text hits her phone, and she pulls it out from a spot tucked between her breasts. I shake my head like a wet dog. *Holy shit, I've got to be hallucinating.*

Rachel: I don't think those three people are the best test of diligence, given their track record on the first two exams, but I'll make a circle around the room and scope out the situation.

Me: Great. And then after that, you should take a trip to my dick and scope out that situation too. Did you really just pull that phone out from between your tits? Like, that happened, right? I didn't imagine it?

Rachel: Ty, we're in the middle of an exam.

Me: Yes. And then after that, we're going to be in the middle of fucking on my desk. What's your point? I need to know the ins and outs of the titty phone conference.

Rachel: There was a point, but I can see now that I'd forgotten who I was talking to. And this outfit doesn't have pockets. It's the only place to keep it.

Me: I also do not have a pocket to stay in. Please keep me there.

I watch her smother a smile with her hand from across the room.

Rachel: Ty, you shouldn't be talking about my boobs right now. Or sex on your desk, for cripes' sake.

Me: Are you really saying you're not picturing it right now? Your back on my desk with your tits in my hands and your perfect nipples in my mouth?

I hit send, then type out another, and hit send on that one too.

Me: What about how wet your pussy is going to be? You're telling me you can sit here, in this quiet room, without thinking about that?

When she doesn't respond, I keep going.

Me: How about the way you moan when you come? And how your eyes just barely flutter before you can't keep them open anymore? Or the way you bite into the sexy center of your bottom lip to keep from screaming? What about that? I, for one, am thinking about those things right now. I think about them all the time, actually.

I lean back in my chair again, empty essay sections of the exam forgotten. All I care about now is watching the way Rachel's breathing has seemed to shallow and the way that makes her heavy tits move.

She is truly, in my opinion, the perfect specimen of a woman. Round and lush and curvy. She has so much tits and ass, I could get lost in just those two things for at least a week.

Rachel: Ty, I don't think about any of that.

I raise a skeptical eyebrow in her direction and type two words into my phone.

Me: You don't?

Rachel: No.

What the fuck?

A frown settles into the corners of my mouth, and I put my fingers to the screen of my phone, eager to call her out on her bullshit. I stop and calm, though, when she leans into a spot against the back wall, her head tilted down and her fingers moving quickly. The bubbles on my screen confirm that she's typing, and for one of the first times in my nearly four decades on earth, I decide to wait it out—to think before I act.

Rachel: I think about the way you start to breathe heavier when you're getting close. And the way your voice turns gritty just before you come, as if your orgasm takes something from it. I think about the way you always know just the right pace and the right pressure, and how sexy your veins are in your forearms when you're looming over me. I think about the way your warm, hard body feels next to my soft and curvy one, and I think about how you always, without fail, make me feel like the most sensual woman in the world while we're having sex.

Well, fuck me. I stand corrected.

Me: Ah, I see. Yeah, I have to agree. I guess that stuff's good too.

I look up into the stairway on the left side of the classroom to watch her look at her phone and smile. Her eyes find mine, and that's all it takes to send my cock into a half-hard version of itself. I'm starting to think I don't want any of these fucking kids to find the essay portion of the exam, I want it to be over so bad. I mean, screw it, I can grade on a curve.

Rachel shakes her head as if she can read my mind and resumes the task of checking out papers and answering questions from any student who happens to raise their hand.

After this many years teaching, I'm always mystified by how many of them would rather wallow in the absolute dark than chancing asking a simple question and getting told they can't get an answer.

The psyche of humans, it seems, is a little too universal. The thought of rejection in any form often prevents trying. The truth is, the odds aren't all that bad when you ask people for stuff. Sure, they can say no, but there's also a chance they say yes.

And when you don't ask? The chance of a yes is *always* zero.

For the next half hour, students trickle down out of their seats to turn in their exams on my desk, and it's almost scary how perfect the arc of confidence is. Now that class is getting close to ending, we're in a violent downward swing into sheer panic. Hands scribble furiously, and Rachel can barely keep up with how many people she has to hop around to see.

I'm making a diligent effort not to take my eyes off her, but she's making it a little difficult by darting around the room at the speed of a rocket.

I pull out my phone and type one more innuendo-laden message.

Me: Save some energy for me.

She glances my direction and rolls her eyes, and I fight the urge to laugh.

I look up at the clock as the timer on my desk chimes. "Two-minute warning," I call out, my voice sticking in my throat just slightly after not using it for the entire hour.

Rachel's gaze jerks to mine as though I've done it on purpose. *Ah, that must be the gritty voice she referred to.*

I continue to try to watch her hips and ass sashay around my room and grow more turned on by the second. Normally, by now, I'd be over the idea of fucking the same woman. I'd be bored. She'd be clingy. And I'd move on to my next blink of a relationship.

But I'm still hungry for Rachel in that can't-eat, can't-sleep kind of way that's usually only there for a first encounter.

Maybe it's because she's so hard to read? Or because she likes to keep me on my toes? I'm not sure I understand the reason at all, but for now, with the idea of fucking her on the top of my desk within the next fifteen minutes playing the lead role on my priority list, I don't give one single shit.

My tongue runs over my lips as I watch her bend over slightly to help a student in the front row, and when another kid comes to turn in their test, I lean around them to keep my line of sight.

He follows it and then gives me the thumbs-up like only an eighteen-year-old, hormone-riddled dude can.

I shake my head at him and purse my eyebrows into a frown deep enough that my forehead wrinkles, and he just chuckles.

I shoo him out the door with a wave of my hand, but he looks back a time or two to check out the same thing I am.

Forcing myself to focus on the test stack is a challenge, but as the tide of students finally committing to their fate turns into a line in front of my desk, it gets a little easier.

The timer on my desk goes off with a buzz, and I call out into the largely emptied classroom for all the stragglers who are left. "Time's up. Pencils down. Come on up here and turn them in on the stack, please."

A few grumbles resonate in the echoey space, particularly from the last student that Rachel attempted to help, but slowly and surely, they get their asses out of their chairs and head in my direction.

A smile in place, I try to comfort them both as poignantly and as quickly as I can. I want my students to succeed—and chances are, ninety-five percent of the ones who care this much have—but I also want to see Rachel's legs up in the air and back on this desk more than I want my last breath.

Rachel lingers at the door, patting kids on the shoulders as they leave and gifting them with a genuine smile. When the last one exits, though, I look up to see her shutting the door and locking it, and a smile so sinister spreads across my face, I'm surprised I haven't already been cast as the villain in the next major superhero movie.

"I forgot that door even locked." The truth is, I've never had a reason to consider using it until now.

Rachel's answering smile is sexy and confident. "I scoped it out fifteen minutes ago."

"Fifteen minutes ago? Had I even texted you about desk sex by then? Or are you telepathic?"

"Telepathic, probably," she teases, her slow walk toward me feeling almost agonizing. "Or maybe I was just thinking about it first."

Sweet fuck, that's so hot.

"That's okay with me," I concede immediately. "I don't need to win. In fact, I might even prefer this."

She smiles, coming to a heart-throbbing stop in front of me, and the only thing I can see clearly are her bright green eyes through the flutter of her lashes. "Take off my clothes, Ty."

"Yes, ma'am," I drawl immediately, suddenly being overtaken by a Southern gentleman. Which isn't all that big of a surprise. If my metaphorical tail wags any harder, I'm going to turn into a puppy next.

Starting at the top and working my way down, I unbutton her silk blouse and slide it off the smooth skin of her shoulders, revealing a white lace bra and the prettiest pair of breasts I've ever laid witness to. In an ode to her phone pocket, I stoop low enough to kiss the skin right on top of her sternum, the plump flesh surrounding my cheeks as I do.

Her breathing changes, escalating in caliber but slowing in cadence. And I love it so much, I have to kiss my way up her throat and gulp a few of her exhales right into my mouth.

We kiss and grasp at each other, and I spin us around to put her back to the desk before pushing her down on top of it. Her tits bounce with the motion, I can feel it against my chest, and suddenly all I can think about is uncovering them until they're bare.

Rachel's eyes are fierce and fiery, and she must read my mind because it's not even a moment before she leans up enough to unclasp the back of her bra and pull it off the front, tossing it to the side.

I suck a nipple into my mouth and massage the other breast with my hand before swapping sides and doing the same. Rachel arches her back against the desk, her legs churning against my thighs to find purchase, and my dick jerks inside my pants.

I kiss my way down Rachel's stomach to the top of her skirt, my hand skating along her hip until I find the zipper at the side. With ease, I pull it down to loosen the waistband's hold and slide the skirt off her, slinking it all the way over her high-heeled feet.

The shoes are sexy as hell, but also obviously awkward while lying back on a desk, so I pull them off without hesitation and toss them to the side too.

With bare feet, she's able to find the front edge of the wood and push herself up and back, lifting her hips to ease my removal of her panties. They're white satin—fucking beautiful, just like the rest of her—but I don't pay them much mind. All I need right now is to feel Rachel around me.

And with one long, smooth stroke, I do.

And I'll be goddamned if it isn't even better than all the times before.

TWENTY-FOUR

Monday, February 18th

Rachel

I pull my coat tighter around myself, the tiny slip dress from under my work outfit the only thing underneath.

I've been waiting all weekend to feel Ty's hands on me, the two of us making some kind of unspoken sex hiatus agreement on Friday that I now can't understand for the life of me. I'm not sure how on earth it seemed like a good idea at the time. Maybe because doing it on the weekend would mean giving up the comfort of neutral ground?

I don't know, and the sex-crazed horndog inside me can't believe I agreed to it.

It did give me time, however, to masturbate like an addict and plan this whole little dog and pony show of the sexy slip and nothing else I'm wearing today. With a quick change in the bathroom and some time to let him get settled in his office after his last class, I'm ready to rock and roll.

I'm downright giddy over the idea of seeing his face when I open and show him my sexy gift-wrapping.

My heels click so loudly on the tile floor of the hallway, I half expect the sound to call in a herd of models from Fifth Avenue. I try to walk more quietly, but the anticipation of the moment turns my stride into that of a wounded-looking gazelle.

Just walk normally, Rachel.

Ty's office door is close by, and butterflies flutter in my stomach. It's not that I'm nervous—quite the opposite. I'm anticipatory. The kind of sex

Ty and I have been having for the last few days has been nothing short of extraordinary. Far and away the best of my life.

And it's almost as if we've created a game out of it, each time trying to see if we can make it better, hotter, *wilder*.

I stroll into Ty's office with a confident strut, shoving the door open and grabbing the edges of my coat in preparation for the big reveal.

My heart pounds in my chest and throat, and I pause for effect, hoping to get Ty's attention before making his jaw hit the floor.

But when his head comes up, I'm surprised to see that he has his cell phone pressed to his ear, and his face looks nearly ashen.

"Right now?" he asks, his voice brusque in a way I've never heard before. By and large, Ty Winslow is a playful, good-natured man. Even when he's been angry with me, he's been easy to talk to. But he looks nearly choked now, a heaviness seeping into his bones and trapping him under the weight of the world.

"No. I'm done with class for the day. I'm on my way." He frowns as he hangs up the phone, and the instinct to comfort him is immediate.

"What's wrong?" I ask, stepping up to his desk to put a hand to his rigid forearm.

I don't like seeing him like this—in turmoil.

He shakes his head without speaking and then grabs his coat from the hook in the corner. "Come on. We have to go."

"Go? Go where?" I question, but his hand is in mine and he is dragging me out the door long before the words have time to land. He's focused to the point of single-mindedness, and right now, it's not on me.

Normally, I would push. I would make him stop and explain. But I'll be honest, seeing him upset like this makes all my needs seem unimportant, and I don't even consider doing either of the two.

He drags me down the hall and out the main lecture door, sticking his fingers into his mouth and whistling for the first taxi he sees. It comes to a sliding stop in front of us and he opens the door, ushering me in straightaway.

I scuttle into the seat on the other side of the bench so he can get in, and I wait for him to tell the cabbie where we're going. At least I'll find out then.

"St. Luke's Hospital, please. As fast as you can go."

"The hospital?" I squeak. "Ty, what's going on? Are you okay?"

"I'm fine. It's my sister-in-law Daisy. She's having her twins today, but there's something going on. I didn't get the details, but Jude sounded freaked, and Jude doesn't get freaked."

"Jude?"

"My brother. I have three brothers, actually. And a sister, Winnie. I'm the proverbial middle child of all of us—or, you know, third oldest, as I like to call it."

"You…you have *four* siblings?"

"Yeah."

Suddenly it hits me that not only does Ty have four siblings, but seeing as we're on our way to the hospital for his sister-in-law's distressed labor, there's a pretty good chance I'm going to meet at least some of them. I don't know that that's a good idea.

My mind races with a bevy of insecurities I haven't heard from my inner voice since I was a kid. Worry about whether someone will like me, anxiety over how a situation might look, questions over if this is the kind of thing I can handle or not.

Pulling myself out of my own head and looking over at Ty is the only thing that makes the overwhelming internal noise grow quiet.

He's staring out the window, his mind clearly racing as we make our way across town. I want to speak up, to tell him I don't think I should be a part of this, but when he reaches out to my lap to slide his hand under mine and squeeze, I shut right the hell up.

His grip is tight, and his message is clear, even without words. I'm a comfort to him in this moment, whether I like it or understand it or not.

Fucking liar, my brain taunts. *You know you like it. The problem is that you like it too much.*

I shake off the noisy bitch and hold on tight for the rest of the ride. We sit in silence, and I don't try to change it. I know when I'm at my most distressed, the last thing I feel like doing is talking. My throat gets tight, and my eyes get overly watery. Even the slightest hint of conversation from someone and I'm likely to devolve into tears.

I don't know that that's what Ty is feeling, but it doesn't matter. I can respect his needs without knowing why.

When he doesn't let go of my hand upon arrival at the hospital, even digging in his pocket to get the money for the cabbie at a completely awkward angle with his free hand, I don't even bother begging off going upstairs like I planned in my head.

To be completely honest, something about the way he's holding my hand like a lifeline makes it impossible to use my vocal cords at all.

Ty pulls me into the front entrance of St. Luke's and heads straight for the front desk. I hold on to his hand in the background and listen intently as he does the talking.

"Maternity floor? Daisy Winslow?"

I swallow thickly at the sadness and worry in his voice and grip his hand reflexively. His tightens in return, and I lean into his shoulder with my cheek.

I don't know how I've ended up here—both at the hospital and feeling this emotionally invested in a man I absolutely *should* not—but I don't like to see him hurting. I don't like it at all. Zero out of ten, do not recommend.

"You're going to go straight down this hall, all the way to the end, and take the elevator to the fourth floor," the receptionist explains. "She already has several guests checked in, so you'll need to go directly to the waiting room, okay?"

Ty nods jerkily.

"I just need you both to sign in here and then wear these visitor badges on your shirts."

Ty grabs the pen quickly before scribbling down his name and handing it to me. Once again, the absolute insanity of it all hits me—along with the truly horrifying fact that I'm wearing very, *very* little under this coat—and for the first time, I timidly attempt to beg off.

"Ty, maybe I should just wait down here or—"

"No," he says immediately, his answer almost a bark.

I nod. I'm not going to argue anymore if he feels that strongly, even if the level of mortification in my body is rising so fast, I'm getting dangerously close to resembling an erupting volcano.

Taking the pen in my free hand, even though it's my left and not at all the one I'm used to writing with, I scribble my info in the open notebook on the surface of the desk as quickly as possible and collect my sticker from the receptionist. Ty has us in motion before I can even blink, and we're headed for the hall at a near run—at least, for me, anyway. His legs are much longer than my own.

He pushes the button for the elevator five times, and I just hold tight to his other hand and watch as the numbers count down at the top of the cart doors at a painfully slow pace.

My emotions are a mixed bag of wanting it to move faster along with wanting it never to come.

When it finally arrives with a ding, Ty barely lets the doors part before pulling us both inside and mashing the number four with the same manic intensity as before.

It's startling to me just how little it seems I know about him after this many months of working together and multiple days of sleeping together.

Sure, I knew he had a family and assumed that he was marginally close with them, but this isn't the behavior of a man who calls his mom once a month and sees his siblings at the holidays.

This is the behavior of a man who's involved. A man who *cares* about family.

An unexpected sting of tears rushes to my eyes as my mom's soothing voice plays through my ears. *I know you don't understand now, sweetie, but the love of the right man is like a warm blanket. It's not about small differences or political beliefs or the dramatic theater of the movies. It's about a man who cares. A man who you know would devote his life to family above all else. A man whose presence is all you need to feel complete.*

Those were the lessons, she said, I had to *learn ahead of my time.* The lessons she wanted to instill before she was gone.

On days like today, when I'm feeling as confused as I ever have, I miss her so much it feels like there's a permanent hole in my heart.

The elevator's journey to the fourth floor ends with a swoosh in both the cart and my belly, and I take a deep, deep breath to prepare.

Ty moves with ease down the halls, pulling me behind him until we find the room with the plaque outside that reads "Waiting Room."

We're inside before I can even do another breathing exercise, and the sheer number of people is immediately overwhelming. Rachel Green is no longer the only Rachel to find herself doing life in nothing more than an undergarment. I mean, thankfully I have a coat, but holy red velvet muffins in a handbasket, I hope like fuck no one offers to take it. This might just be one of the scariest moments of my life.

Buckle up, Rachel. Here we go.

TWENTY-FIVE

Rachel

All the heads in the waiting room whip in our direction and move almost comically—*and quickly*—from me to Ty and hold on him. I fight the urge to curl up in a ball behind his body and stay rooted to my spot beside him, forcing my shoulders down and away from my ears.

When no attention comes back to me, instead focusing on Ty alone, the hairs on the back of my neck stand on end, and I step a little closer to Ty without even thinking about it.

I suppose it makes sense that they'd be focused on him instead of me, but the potency of it feels…weird. I don't know, I can't explain it.

"Ty!" a large, similar-looking man shouts from the other side of the room, combing his way through the crowd and dragging a lithe, absolutely stunning brunette behind him. She's the beautiful model to his strikingly handsome and well-dressed demeanor, and I have an immediate sense that this must be one of Ty's brothers and his significant other.

Shoving through people when he has to—it's practically fucking standing room only in here—he finally makes it to us and slaps Ty on the shoulder. "Hey, man."

"Fuck hey. Do we know anything about Daisy yet?"

The tall dreamboat shakes his head, his mouth pulling down in a frown. I can tell by the way his skin stretches that being unhappy is a completely infrequent occurrence for him. *A lot like Ty.*

Maybe the happy-go-lucky thing runs in the family?

"Nothing. Flynn went back there over an hour ago for an emergency

C-section. The first baby was breech. And then the second started having issues with his heart rate. I guess the doctors were pretty firm about C-section being the only option. Daisy was upset."

My mind immediately rallies itself, searching for something to put all the scary words from Ty's brother to sleep. I don't know a lot of people with kids, but I've had two cousins both have C-sections within the last couple of years, one of them being emergent, and they both turned out fine. I know going this route is scary and major surgery, but I think C-sections are pretty standard practice these days. If you ask me, it's at least a modicum of comfort.

Still, I don't dare say anything—thanks to the overwhelming feeling that I probably shouldn't be here in the first place. If it were just Ty and me, I might mention it, but taking the audience with his brother and the woman I'm assuming is his significant other into account, things feel different. I'm an outsider. They're not looking for comfort from me. Especially since no one has said anything to me yet. I get the feeling they'd rather I say nothing at all, and it's starting to feel a little awkward.

I know they're all worried about Ty's sister-in-law, so I'm trying not to read too much into it, but I thought maybe I'd get a hello or a wave from the woman at Ty's brother's arm or something. Just like the essay section on the test last week, it's almost as if they can't see me.

The speaker crackles with a page for one of the doctors on the intercom, and everyone gets briefly quiet to listen. I think they're all well aware that they're not actually going to hear any news over that thing, but I know in times of distress, it can be hard to think rationally.

Scooting closer to Ty, I try not to notice the cloying, almost suffocating hospital smell. I know this isn't the hospital where my mom died, and that this doesn't even have anything to do with me, but the olfactory memory of watching her struggle in her final days is knocking a little too loudly on each and every one of my mind's doors.

"Paging Dr. Olsen to room 611. Paging Dr. Olsen." When the speaker quiets, the tension in the room seems to get even thicker. Ty, however, startles before pulling me nearly in front of him and waving a hand between his brother and me. "Rachel, this is my youngest brother, Jude. Jude, this is Rachel."

I hold out my free hand for an awkward shake and pull my mouth into a self-conscious grin. "Nice to meet you, but I'm really sorry for the circumstances."

"Rachel," Jude says, his eyes widening in a way I can't quite read before turning to the woman at his arm and smiling. "This is *Rachel*, Sophie." My eyebrows draw together at the odd emphasis on my name, and Sophie rolls her eyes before holding out a hand to me for another awkward lefty shake.

"Nice to meet you, Rachel. Ignore my husband, he's weird."

Her *husband*. So, this is Ty's sister-in-law.

"Hey," he snaps playfully, but all she has to do is give him a hard stare, and he's shrugging. "Yeah. She's right. Just ignore me."

Ty laughs at that, cracking the hard edge of his worry for the first time since I walked into his office and saw him on the phone.

At the sound of his laugh, several other people's heads come up and look over, and upon a narrowed-eyed survey of me, they also start to make their way toward us. Ty drops my hand briefly.

It's kind of a nightmare in the package of a dream, and I don't know what to do with my newly found freedom. I shove my hands into the pockets of my coat and clench at the inner fabric.

Ty frowns as he looks down and sees it, and he reaches into my pocket to once again retrieve the hand he'd been holding. Jude and Sophie share a look I can't put my finger on, just as a tall, dark-haired, nearly godlike man with piercing blue eyes approaches the group. He looks like he belongs, but the easygoing attitude of both Jude and Ty is pointedly missing.

"Oh hey, Remy," Jude says with a huge smile, glancing back at me. "This is *Rachel*."

Remy's reaction is normal, even in the face of Jude's exaggeration, and for the sake of my sanity, I decide to focus on that.

"Nice to meet you, Rachel," he remarks, thankfully forgoing the offering of a hand.

"You too," I say easily enough, glancing among the group of strangers and willing myself not to shrink. "I really hope there's news soon."

It's a genuine statement. But the depths of where it comes from are a touch more complicated. I'm looking for relief for Ty and his family—obviously—but I'm also hoping for some relief for the heavy feeling inside my pounding chest. I'm growing so uncomfortable, I might as well be the one in labor with twins.

"Me too," Remy says, his eyes both warm and watchful. A silence palls over the group after that, and I'm instantly sorry for saying it. They were just starting to get distracted, and I ruined it.

Sophie is the first to chime in, and much to my dismay, it's to direct a question right at me. "So…how do you and Ty know each other?"

"I…well, we…we're—"

I'm just about to get to the part where I start putting real words together when another tall, dark-haired, much more intense man bursts through the doors and throws his hands into the air. "She's good. The babies are here, and they're healthy. Everyone's doing really well."

A cheer takes over the room, and emotion overcomes who I know now must be Ty's fourth and final brother. "Thank fuck," he mutters and sinks to his knees.

A couple of women rush him immediately. One is young, possibly around Ty's age or a few years younger, and the other has a startling resemblance to all of them that makes it impossible to classify her as anything other than their mother.

My stomach flips over on itself at being witness to such a tender, intimate family moment, but Ty pulls me into his arms and into a hug before I can think about it too much.

All I can feel is the warmth of his long arms around me and the relief in his laugh at my neck. *Why does this have to feel so good?*

It's only when he pulls away that panic sets in again. Because he's pulling me out of the room and down the hall, right along with the rest of his family, headed to meet his freshly sliced sister-in-law and her adorable babies.

I don't know that we're ready for that. I don't know that it's appropriate.

Two months ago, I was at the beginning of a new start. I was proud, I was poised, I was ready.

Now, I'm so tangled up in a man, I don't know where the knot begins and ends.

How in the world have half a semester of fighting and a week of fucking landed me here?

TWENTY-SIX

Ty

The feeling of tightness in my chest has finally left and been replaced by the best news in the world. Daisy and the babies are happy and healthy, and I can go on knowing my brother Flynn will live to see another day without darkness.

It's strange to say—and even stranger to recognize—but Flynn's world starts and stops with Daisy Winslow née Diaz. Their relationship certainly moved at what felt a rapid-fire pace to me, but I'll be damned if my brother wasn't born the day he met her.

He's happier, healthier, chattier. I mean, don't get me wrong, he's still one of the most mysterious fucks on the planet, but I get more than a nod and a grunt these days. And that's a big change.

I watch and wait as Winnie, my mom, Remy, Jude, and Sophie file into the maternity room in front of us, a couple other people I don't know particularly well in front of them, and then pull Rachel's hand to follow. But I'm met with a resistance I'm not expecting.

I turn back to face Rachel, question on my face. "Rach?"

"I don't think I should… Ty, I think you should just go in yourself. You and your family. This is a personal moment."

I shake my head, trying to focus on what she's saying but just as eager to get into the room and see Daisy. "Come on, Rach, it's fine. I promise. I want you in there."

The truth is, I'm not sure I could let go of her hand if I tried.

I didn't get it at all—the marriage and the babies and the little white picket fence that's seemed to fascinate my brothers as of late. But hearing the news that all might not be well with the babies and Daisy and putting myself in Flynn's shoes shook me.

I know Flynn before Daisy, and I know him after Daisy. And now that he's with her, I can't picture them apart. She's the voice he never used and brings smiles to his face that were never there.

He's not terrified of having twins—he's thrilled. And the thought of something tainting that joy was almost too much to bear.

I pull Rachel through the door, her resistance finally giving in as we pass over the threshold, and jockey us around to a front position in the crowd. No offense to Daisy's friend Pam, but I'm not going to stand around in the back of the group. She can wait until the family's done.

Daisy's friend and boss, Damien, and the closest thing she has to a mother, Gwen, squeeze to the front on the other side of the bed, and we all marvel down at the sweet babies lying in Daisy's arms with googly eyes and glory.

And I'm certain Flynn's smile, as he looks down at his wife and newborn sons, is bigger than all of ours combined.

"They're absolutely perfect," I say aloud, glancing over to Rachel and angling her closer so she can get a better view.

She hesitates again, but I pull her to my front and wrap my arms around her waist. I'm sure it's overwhelming being in a room with this many people she doesn't know, but I want her close. I *want* her here.

Which, honestly, is no bigger surprise to anyone else than it is to me. But I've had more fun with her in the last month and a half than I can remember having in the last ten fucking years.

She's playful and strong and brilliant. And hell, sex with her is mind-blowing.

I watch her face as she looks at Daisy and the babies, and I tuck her body close to mine. "They're fucking perfect, Dais," I say, eliciting the wrath of my mother and the laughs of everyone else.

"Ty, for heaven's sake! Can you at least watch your mouth around newborns?"

"I'm sorry, Ma, but I can't," I say with a twinkle in my eye and a laugh in my throat. "They're too fucking cute."

"Fucking adorable," Jude chimes in, ever the shit-stirrer.

"Really fucking tiny," Remy adds in unexpectedly, making everyone dissolve into uproarious laughter once more.

"Beautiful fucking babies," even my baby sister Winnie continues.

"You're all fucking grounded," Mama Winslow finally announces, throwing her hands in the air and topping it all off.

"What are their names?" Lexi asks over our collective laughter, a subtle pulsing smile on her cute face. It takes a lot to light her up inside, but seeing her cousins this shortly after their arrival into the world has clearly done it.

"Ryder and Roman," Daisy answers, her voice a melody as she looks down at them. Lexi's smile stretches all the way to her eyes.

I've got to admit, I'm feeling the light too, Lexi.

I don't know the last time I've felt like this—like I have everything I've ever wanted right in front of me.

But today, Ty Winslow is on top of the world.

TWENTY-SEVEN

Rachel

Thirty minutes later, we're still in the room with Ty's family, they're still laughing, and he's still got me tucked as tight to the front of his body as he can manage.

I'm both uncomfortable and too comfortable at the same time, and the combination of the two makes me feel like I could walk myself right on over to the psych floor and declare myself as crazy, only to have them agree, admit me, and put me under close watch for seventy-two hours.

I glance up for the third time in the last minute to find Remy's eyes still on me, watching. I thought maybe he'd move on when I found a particularly interesting spot on the floor and the ceiling and the wall and then on Daisy's forehead. I can't believe how good she looks given what she's been through, but I can only stare at a woman in admiration for so long when I've just met her without people starting to think I'm strange.

Without even meaning to, the next time I catch Remy staring at me, I bug out my eyes, and he smiles in return. It's as if he knows my game and is already six moves ahead of me. As a woman who feeds on control sometimes, I find it wholly disconcerting.

The chatter dims as Flynn finally waves a hand in the air, and Daisy's eyes start to look heavy. I can only imagine the visiting has been nice, but she has to be exhausted at this point.

"Okay, guys. It's time to clear out. My wife needs to rest, and I have a couple of babies to take care of."

The sweet, protective edge of his words is enough to send a shiver down my spine and instill cooperation from everyone else. Ty moves me by the hips easily enough, shuffling me around and out the door, just like he's been hustling me everywhere else all day.

I wrap my arms around myself as he steps away briefly to peer down the hallway.

"You okay here for a second?" he asks, hooking a thumb over his shoulder. "I just want to run to the restroom, and then we can go."

I nod and smile, trying desperately not to show just how overstimulated I feel by this whole experience.

He's happy—blissful, really. And I don't want to spoil that in any way. With some time to collect myself and get back to normal life, I'll probably be fine. But I need the time to decompress. And it's coming…at some point. At least, that's what I tell myself to talk my feet off the proverbial ledge.

Ty disappears down the hall and into the bathroom, and I fight the urge to take off toward the exit. It's not that anyone's being rude to me—in fact, it's just the opposite. Since Ty introduced me, his family's been nothing short of magnanimous during a truly trying time for them.

I'm impressed by their ability to manage manners with emotions and wonder why my father and I never got that memo.

Still, everyone is outside Daisy's room now, busy chatting with one another and celebrating the growth of their obviously tight-knit family. And I'm just standing here, willowing in the wind.

I am a woman who doesn't really know what to do. I don't feel like I should be involving myself in their conversations, and truthfully, I don't think I could even manage that.

I discreetly take a few steps away from the little crowd, but I don't miss that Ty's eldest brother Remy is watching me again, stealing furtive glances in pauses in his conversation with Jude, and it's making me uneasy.

Don't get me wrong, it's not, like, creeper-type scary. It just feels like he knows. Like he knows what's going on with Ty and me and knows the inner workings of my soul.

And I feel entirely too bare under the scrutiny.

Just look away, Remy. You're dancing around a couple of things I'm not even talking to myself about right now, let alone a stranger.

I manage to avoid his eyes for another thirty seconds by spinning to admire a random piece of cheap art on the wall, but my avoidance is caught short when he touches me gently on the shoulder, letting me know the time of reckoning has arrived.

My spin is dramatic, but my smile is fake, so all in all, I'd say they balance each other out as I turn to face him—and the music.

"Hey, Rachel," he greets, a genuinely friendly smile making him look slightly less frightening—but only slightly. "Thanks for coming out to support Flynn and Daisy. Means a lot to all of us."

I nod, licking my lips. "Uh, sure." *I didn't exactly get much of a choice, but you don't need to know that.*

He holds out a business card between his ring and middle finger, and I blink down at it numbly.

"Here. I thought I'd take the opportunity to give you this, just in case you need to get in touch with me someday."

I shake my head as I read the fine print on the front. "Well, thanks. But I don't think I'll be in need of any help with day trading or investments anytime soon. I'm about as poor as it gets in the graduate student world. I know these shoes look fancy, but they're secondhand and a gift from my sister."

He shrugs curiously, chuckling a little—I think, to put me at ease. It doesn't work, of course, but I appreciate the effort. "That's okay. Take it anyway. Just in case."

My eyebrows pinch together in confusion, but I know to the depths of my being that taking the card and putting it in my bag, even if it'll never be seen again, is the easiest option here. I can't exactly make a scene in the middle of the maternity ward of St. Luke's Hospital, and even if I could, I wouldn't want to.

I may not be completely confident in what my role is here today, but it isn't to make Ty's life harder.

I reach out and slide the card out of his fingers, opening the main compartment of my purse and tossing it inside. He nods and smiles, stepping away just as Ty is returning from the bathroom, shaking his hands out in front of him with a giant goofy smile on his face.

"No paper towels," he remarks, flicking a water droplet onto Remy as he arrives just for the fun of it.

I purse my lips into a semi-smile and then cross my arms over my chest.

"You're lucky we just witnessed the miracle of life today, or I'd slap that grin right off your face," Remy fires back verbally, making Ty laugh even deeper and look to me conspiratorially.

"He's been threatening that for years." He puts his hands out wide to his sides and then waves them up and down. "Here I am. Still grinning."

I hate how much I like this version of Ty. The no-holds-barred, no-work, all-play, happy-to-exist man who has a whole lot of love to give.

He's fun and comforting, and if I let myself, I might just start to feel a little too much for him.

I take a deep breath and steady my voice to make it sound as friendly as possible when I request, "Can we get going soon? I don't want to rush you at all, but I… Well, I'm supposed to take the closing shift at the bakery tonight. I almost forgot."

The truth is, I'm not supposed to work at all. But a bunch of mindless hands-on activity is just what I need to alleviate some of my anxiety, and Lydia and Lou could definitely stand to have the night off. I'm sure as soon as I get there and offer, they'll jump at the chance to have a little time to themselves.

"What? Oh geez. That sucks," Ty says with a frown and then smiles when he gets an idea. "I know! I'll come with you."

I shake my head before he even finishes talking, and I ignore the weight of Remy's eyes as they watch me.

And boy, are they fucking heavy.

"No, that's okay. In fact, you should stay. Hang out with your family a little more. I'll see you tomorrow."

"Are you sure? At least let me come down and get you a cab."

"No," I refuse, leaning forward and placing a gentle kiss on Ty's cheek, even with the audience, even with the turmoil. At the end of the day, Ty hasn't done anything wrong, and I don't want him to think he has. When I back away, I pull from the dark depths of my being in order to give him a real, genuine smile. "That's okay, really. I'll see you tomorrow."

Ty nods then as I turn to Remy and offer him a hand. "It was really nice to meet you. Thanks for welcoming me during such a special family experience."

Remy holds my hand a little too long for my comfort, but his smile is gracious as he finally lets it go. His meaning when he speaks, though—well, it's doing double duty.

"Anytime, Rachel. *Anytime.*"

Anytime. Welcome to come around, welcome to use the card.

The Winslows are a friendly bunch, and I'm thankful for their welcome. But spending time with his family isn't taking me in the direction of no trouble—it's taking me to the direct opposite.

Come around or use the card? Rachel Rose is smart enough that she won't be doing either.

TWENTY-EIGHT

Ty

Now that I'm standing here, outside of the mostly dark bakery, I'm starting to question if it was a good idea to show up unannounced.

Not because I don't think it's the right thing to do—I *know* it is by the strange way Rachel was acting as she left the hospital this afternoon—but because I don't have a lot of experience being a woman alone, and yet, I have to imagine closing up at night by yourself only to be startled by someone standing outside would be terrifying.

Luckily, the lights in the cases are still on and the door's unlocked, so I pull it open and peek my head in, hoping to give her ample warning before she can get scared.

"Rachel? It's, uh…it's Ty. Is it okay if I come in?"

There's a bang in the back and a couple of mumbled curses and then a change in the light, shining through the cracks in the door that leads to the back.

Wide-eyed, flour-covered, and as beautiful as I've ever seen her, Rachel pushes through the swinging door from the kitchen and looks at me from head to toe without saying a word.

My mouth curves into a smile, feeling good about the surprise again now that I know I haven't scared her, and I step past the threshold and let the door fall closed behind me. I point back to it. "Do you want me to lock this?"

She nods, and my smile grows deeper.

"Are you regretting not having locked it sooner?"

That puts a crack in the resounding shock and emotional vagueness of her shell, and her face melts into a familiar grin. "I guess you could say I wasn't thinking about how just *anybody* could walk in." It's an innocent-enough statement if you don't know Rachel Rose like I've grown to. She's giving me shit, plain and simple.

I chuckle, and she comes forward more, rounding the counter and stopping just in front of it with a towel in her hands. The bakery cat I know as Matilda follows her, prancing all the way around the counter until she's tracing my legs with warm purrs.

"What are you doing here, Ty?"

Truthfully, there's a whole explanation I could go into about the way we left it at the hospital and how I wasn't comfortable not making sure she's okay, but I don't think that would set us off on the right foot.

And there's an equally truthful, much simpler answer too. I go with the latter. "I wanted to see you."

"You wanted to see me?" she asks, and I don't miss the hint of hope in her voice. As if that reality would make her happy versus upset.

Which only makes me more certain that coming here was the right thing to do.

"Doll, I don't know if you've noticed, but I always want to see you."

Rachel's face melts into total contentment, and before I know it, she's walking straight through the collection of tables and right into my arms. I lift her up, her feet coming off the floor as she wraps her arms around my shoulders, and I bury my face into her throat. Matilda scatters, and I officially lose track of her for the night. My attention, it seems, is elsewhere.

"I know today was a lot," I admit into the supple skin there. And I do. At the time, I couldn't see past the end of my own nose, but *now*, I get it. "And I'm sorry for the awkward position I likely put you in, but I'm still glad you were there."

She exhales a deep breath and then pulls back just enough to touch her mouth to mine. It's a soft, subtle kiss, so unlike everything we've shared before, and I drink it in languidly.

"I'm glad I left the door unlocked," she whispers against my lips. "But if you don't mind, I'd really like you to lock it now."

My laugh is loud in the otherwise empty space, and I set her back down on her feet. I turn around to lock the door, and she doesn't waste any time grabbing my hand and dragging me toward the back.

I go willingly, my long legs keeping up easily behind her much shorter ones.

"I've never been behind the counter before!" I remark excitedly as she takes me around one end and directly by the cabinet that I know houses my favorite cookies. Though, there are no cookies in sight, and I look at the empty space a little longingly.

"Don't worry, Ty." She reads me like a book and giggles. "I have some left-over chocolate chip almond in the back."

"Really?" I nearly cry, like a kid at Christmas.

She nods, reaching out to grab my hand with both of hers, and pulls me along with a sexy smile on her face. "Uh-huh. And that's not the only thing."

"*Ohh*, I like the sound of this." I waggle my eyebrows. "What else do you have back here?"

She pulls me around a shiny metal table that's five or six feet inside the door, and I follow dutifully until we stop on the other side.

"I guess you'll just have to wait and see," she replies with a smirk and gestures for me to sit down on a stool, conveniently located behind my legs. I do, and she proceeds to grab a cloth napkin and surprise me by wrapping it around my eyes.

"Blindfolding me?" I ask salaciously. "*Day-um*, Rach. I sure hope this goes where I think it's going."

"Before we get started, what would you say your pain tolerance is?" she asks, and my eyes grow wide beneath the napkin.

"Excuse me?"

"Your *pain tolerance?*" she repeats. "High or low? I'm just trying to get a gauge for how far I can take this."

"Uhhh…" I pause, and it only takes two seconds for her to cackle like an adorable crazy person.

She's totally fucking with me, and I have no qualms with playing along.

"Do you trust me, Ty?"

"Yes." I answer without hesitation.

She presses a playful kiss to my lips, and there's a snicker in her laugh that would probably make a normal guy's nuts crawl up inside him. Luckily, I'm not a normal guy. I love to play and tease, and I can handle just about anything she throws my way.

My only kryptonite, it seems, is a set of blue balls while she does it. And since we've opened the floodgates on sleeping with each other, I don't have to worry about that anymore.

"By the way," she adds and kisses me once more. "There's no pain involved, and this *is* going somewhere really good."

Rachel moves around in the kitchen a little, I can tell by the noises to my sides and off in the distance, and then calls out from the back. "I'll only be a minute. Don't move. Just need to grab something."

I like the sound of her needing to grab a surprise, so I offer a thumbs-up, a smile, and a promise. "I'll be right here."

The sound of her retreating footsteps fades away, and then I hear the soft thud of her padding around on the floor above me. When she returns, her breathing is slightly labored as though she's been running around, and I can't help but smile. "What's up there? A back, back room? A back attic? A back bakery?"

She laughs a little, surprise cutting the noise short and ending it in a near snort. "Oh. No. I guess I forgot you didn't know this already, but I live up there. That's my apartment."

My eyebrows rise, though I doubt she can see them under the napkin blindfold. *Now that is interesting.*

"That's cool. Convenient for work."

She laughs. "Yeah, and it's a good price too. My sister and her wife let me live there for free in exchange for part-time bakery work."

I smile. "I'm glad to see you have a tight-knit family too. I never knew my dad—he left when I was little—but the rest of us are about as tight as it gets."

"Yeah," she replies. "I noticed."

"This is actually fun. Not seeing you but *seeing* you."

"What do you mean?"

"I like finding things out about you. What else do I need to know? Tell me all about Rachel Rose and how she came to be here now."

She snorts. "Well, if you ask my father, it's been a long and winding, quite unnecessary road."

I save my comments for later, giving her the space to continue.

"I guess you could say I was a bit of a wanderer. I went to college on the West Coast, at Stanford, and then…just kind of stayed out there."

I hear her getting closer, opening something, and then rearranging the napkin to where it just covers my eyes. Next thing I know, something cold and a little tacky feeling is being spread all over my face.

And I don't say shit. Because she's talking and sharing and opening up, and I don't care what I have to sit through to facilitate its continuation.

I do flinch at the weird feeling, though, and her laugh is nearly evil. "What's wrong? Want me to stop?"

I shake my head just enough to get my point across without sending whatever she's painting on me all over my cheeks. "Nope. Keep talking, keep doing whatever it is you're doing."

She giggles again. "Okay, then." I feel some sort of a brush move over the ridge of my nose, and I wiggle it at the tickle.

"So, what did you do out there?"

"Where?"

"On the West Coast? After school? On the long and winding road."

She sighs, a laugh mixing in that makes me smile. "A bunch of stuff, really. For a while, I waitressed at a place on Pacific Coast Highway, and then I dabbled in working for some Hollywood insider parties. I was a huge nobody—a nobody to the nobodies, really, but it was fun for a while."

"And after that?"

She pauses briefly, both in her speech and the movement of her hand, and I hold my breath, willing her to continue. "Well, that's when all the social media influencer stuff really started to take off, so I got involved in that."

I chuckle. I don't want to ruin the mood, but hot damn, I know her father well enough to guess how that went over. "I bet Professor Rose loved that."

She snorts. Like, actual snot-bubble, saliva-trapped sounds coming from her snorts. "Oh yeah, it was his most cherished dream for his baby girl."

"Did you like it?"

"Actually? Yeah. For a while, anyway," she admits, a softness and truth in her voice. "I was good enough at it that it was viable, at least. My YouCam account had reached the point where it was easily paying the bills and just letting me do my thing, but even I knew it wasn't my long-term goal in life."

"What is your long-term goal in life, then?"

I can't actually see her shrug, but I can imagine it. I've been watching Rachel Rose avidly enough, for long enough, that I can just about visualize everything she does.

"To be happy, I suppose."

I smile. "That's a kick-ass goal."

"Thanks. I think so too. Nathaniel would prefer I homed in on something a little more *specific*."

"You'll know it when you see it, feel it, experience it. You'll know then."

She hums softly, and I wish I could pull off the blindfold, just to get a good look at her eyes. It seems like I could read them if I could see them—like they'd spill all her secrets for her. And damn, do I want to know her secrets.

"Sometimes, I think I'd like to write like my mom did…" She pauses, and the admission feels incredibly vulnerable. Like it's something she has a hard time admitting out loud.

"Really?"

"Yeah," she answers quietly and rubs something across my lips. "But that's also what my dad wants me to do, and there's a lot of…pressure."

I lift my shoulders and reach up to my face to still her hand for a minute, holding on to it. "So, don't do it for him. Do it for you, and do it your way. If it's what you really want, don't avoid it just for the sake of avoiding him."

"You don't understand what he can be like."

"You're right, I don't," I agree. "But you do, and much to his chagrin, you've managed to maintain your independence this long. Why can't you maintain it while you're doing what *you* want?"

She pulls my blindfold off then and leans in to place a gentle kiss to my lips. The taste is sweet and sugary, and for the first time since this little exercise began, I'm starting to wonder what she's been doing to me.

"Is that…is that strawberry?" I ask, licking my top lip as she pulls away.

She shrugs, and the cutest smile pinches up the bridge of her nose and settles all the way into her eyes. She reaches to the side easily, procuring a mirror I can only deduce she got upstairs and showing me her finished project—my face. Ivory skin, rosy cheeks, and equally pink lips, I've been transformed using what appear to be baking supplies.

From the nose down, I look like Little Bo Peep.

"Holy shit, Rachel." I chuckle, but I also grin like Little Bo Peep would if she found her fucking sheep.

Rachel's clearly talented, and I'm beyond impressed. I'm also wondering what she could do with real makeup and time. *Damn, what could she do with Halloween makeup for Jude's and my yearly group costume?*

"So…do you like it?" she asks, her voice high-pitched and fighting giggles at the same time.

"Rachel, Rachel, Rachel…" I shake my head and offer a quiet laugh. "I can't believe…"

She bites her bottom lip, visibly bracing herself, waiting for me to dive into some kind of rant or something, and a thrill runs down my spine at the opportunity to surprise her.

"…how talented you are."

She freezes, her face cutting back to serious like a tear in a roll of film. "What?"

"You're really good at makeup." I grab the mirror from her hand, admiring myself side to side and up and down. "I mean, look at me. I'm a total babe. And it's sick as hell that you managed this in five minutes. With fucking baking products. What else can you do? I'm dying to know."

She shakes her head at me, a mystified smile crinkling the sides of her eyes. "You're not mad?"

"About what? I look awesome."

She barks a startled giggle. "I-I… Well, I used to do makeup tutorials online. That was one of my main platforms when I was influencing."

I nod, admiring myself in the mirror some more. "I can see why."

"I was going to record this to post it as a joke…for the bakery's Instagram…" She points behind herself to her phone and the ring light I hadn't even noticed, and then she looks back to me. "But I wasn't expecting such good conversation while I was doing it." She purses her lips. "I think I'll keep it to myself."

I'm starting to think I might keep her forever.

TWENTY-NINE

Rachel

"Now, I'm ready for my dessert," Ty says with a mischievous grin.

Before I even know what's happening, Ty is off the stool and lowering me, back first, onto the metal prep table behind me, his hands at my ass.

My gasp is short-lived as he brings his lips to mine, licking a path to open them and then kissing me like anything but the character I've painted his face to look like.

I kiss at his lips at first, but then I make my way around his face, licking at the colored sugar paint I took out of the refrigerator supplies to erase my work. There's something nearly frenzying about the mix of sugar and Ty, and I work my tongue along the line of his jaw like a woman starved.

Ty groans when I flick my tongue at his ear and makes short work of pulling my leggings off. It occurs to me briefly that I'm going to have to sanitize this table *really* well when we're done, but it'll be worth it. Of that, I'm certain.

My rose-gold lace panties are next, and I catch only a glimpse of him tucking them into his pocket. "What happened to your concern for my underwear supply?" I tease.

"That only applies when they don't look like these," he answers too easily, making me laugh and then swallowing the sound in a kiss.

I've cleaned off most of his face, but a little icing is still lingering around the edges. I imagine I'm going to be finding it in places tonight that I never dreamed it would be.

"Oh, my sweet Rachel, I can't wait to taste you." Ty waggles his brows as he spreads my thighs and sinks to his knees on the hard, tile bakery floor.

A shiver runs through my entire body. Mostly due to the fact that we have to keep it pretty cold in here, just to keep the sugars pliable before they set. Evidently, the cold air is good for icing, but it's a little bit of a shock on girlie bits.

"Cold?" Ty asks, in tune with my body enough to notice even without my saying it.

"Uh… Yeah." I giggle through chattering teeth. "But I'm okay."

"Don't worry, I'm going to make you warm soon," he promises, closing his oh-so warm mouth over the sensitive flesh between my legs. The sensation of his tongue and the illicitness of what we're doing is unbelievably hot. So hot, I'm not thinking at all about the temperature of the room anymore.

The ceiling lights shine down on Ty's brown hair, and I reach out to grab a handful as he slowly runs his tongue against me. It's a tease and a pleasure, and I can't decide if I want him to get on with it right now or do this forever.

Luckily, he chooses for me, and I lose the ability to think altogether. His tongue is like magic, thrusting inside softly but firmly and then circling my clit with just the right amount of pressure. He's an expert with his mouth, that's for sure, and if I could magnanimously thank all the women who came before me who got him here, I'd do it.

I've never been one to get worked up about other people's past lovers. I'd be a hypocrite if I did. And while I'm sure he's responsible for some raw talent, this kind of precision could have come only at the instruction of a woman.

He flicks his tongue against my clit and slides a finger inside me. The combination is so perfect that my back arches and my breasts push up into the air.

I moan, and my body is at war between wanting to come like this or wanting to come with him inside me. Eventually, though, I know there's only one way that will leave me completely satisfied.

"Ty," I whimper and gently tug at the hair on his head. His head comes up in question, a shine on his lips that isn't a mystery. "I want you inside me," I admit freely, opening my legs wider and prompting him to step in between them. He leans down over me to put a kiss on my lips, and I taste the lingering evidence of myself on him. A heady mix of sex and sugar and us.

He keeps up his sweet assault on my mouth as he works at his zipper between us, and then he enters me with one smooth, clean stroke. It's not rough—it's precise and efficient. I gasp at the feeling of fullness, and he smiles against my lips. "You feel so good, Rach. Every fucking time."

I moan again, since that's the only reciprocation of the sentiment I'm currently capable of, and wrap my arms around his shoulders. For some reason, tonight, I want him close. I want to see his eyes while he moves inside me, see the way his neck crooks when he comes.

I don't need anything extra or fancy—I just need a front-row seat to him.

He sinks his head into my throat while his hips do all the work, and I hold on tight for dear life. The table shakes beneath us, and I'm hoping on a wing and prayer that it holds its ground through the onslaught.

Ragged breaths mingling, Ty thrusts and swirls his hips at the end and then repeats it over and over again. My skin is on fire now, the cold officially gone, and I can feel the tension of my pending orgasm all the way into the tips of my toes.

"God, Rachel." Ty finds my lips again, running his tongue along the surface with a reverence I'm not expecting. It's slow and poignant and feels like it *means* something. I just can't put my finger on what.

But my orgasm can't wait any longer, no matter how hard I try. Pleasure and hypersensitivity crash over me, tumbling me to the bottom of the ocean floor and repeatedly coming back for more. I'm caught in a tide, washing away anything and everything I've ever known other than this moment, for what feels like an eternity. I can't blink, can't speak—I can barely hear anything other than the roar of overwhelming fogginess in my ears.

This is, without a doubt, the most powerful orgasm I've ever had in my life—and with the way Ty and I have been for the last week, that's saying something.

It's so good, it hurts—and not just where it should.

My chest aches too, an overpowering feeling of something *more* nagging at my heart. Ty Winslow is so many more things than I knew.

And I'm beginning to think I might be becoming a fan of way too many of them.

THIRTY

Monday, February 25th

Rachel

The last student files out the door of Ty's lecture hall, and a sigh falls heavy from my lips. It's safe to say it's been a long Monday.

Another week of sex with Ty has been extraordinarily great for my vagina, but it's not doing a lot for my sleeping. Keeping up with our rendezvous and TA work and class and the bakery and everything else is a lot, and if I thought about it for even a second, the exhaustion would set in and put me into a two-day-long coma.

Not that I've taken any action whatsoever to stop it. In fact, I'm the one fanning the flames at least half of the time.

He's just *so* hard to resist. Always smiling and teasing and joking. I haven't had this good of a time with a guy in—well, forever.

I'm starting to gather my things from my seat at the front of the room when Ty slaps me on the ass and then takes off at a jog, yelling, "Tag, you're it!" over his shoulder.

I roll my eyes at first, but after another drive-by slap to the ass, I'm on the run. We round the desk and jump off the stage platform and up the stairs to the back wall. He climbs over chairs and across rows in a couple of moves that I'm entirely incapable of mimicking in my skirt.

Still, I'm a woman, so I was built to work smarter, not harder, and following his exact path isn't necessarily the shortest route between points A and B.

I book it down the stairs and catch him just as he's getting to his desk.

I slap at Ty's shoulder, and he lunges out and grabs me by the wrist. I wrestle free and jump around his desk, only to come to a stop on the other side, breathing hard. We're both on the cusp of laughing, smiles on our faces and fire in our eyes, when a throat clears from the door, catching both of our attention.

My father stands watching the two of us, his hands in his pockets as he leans into the jamb. "Well, I see the two of you are getting along," he remarks casually, pushing off from his relaxed position to come toward us.

I gulp down against a rough throat, and I don't dare look over in Ty's direction. Playing tag at the end of class is definitely not the kind of behavior Nathaniel Rose puts on his syllabus.

"Nathaniel," Ty finally manages, clearing his throat audibly before stepping over to shake my dad's hand. "What brings you to my classroom today?"

I look down to the desk and start gathering the papers long forgotten in favor of our tussling match, largely seeing myself right out of the conversation.

"I came to catch up. See how the semester's going. If I could be a resource to you or your classes." I nearly roll my eyes at the floor—*aka he wants to both have his moment and stay removed, typical Nathaniel Rose*—but he doesn't leave it at that, and he doesn't leave me out of it.

Quite the opposite, in fact. He drags me right back into the conversation, kicking and screaming.

"I'll admit, too, I also came to check up on Rachel. Make sure she's living up to the expectations of a tenured professor."

Making sure I'm living up to my potential, is what he means. If I've heard it once, I've heard it a million times. So much so that I can play the words over in my head exactly as he'd say them.

Ty glances between the two of us as my gaze shoots up and narrows, and I have to bite the inside of my cheek to stop myself from starting a scene right here. Fighting between my father and me is natural—ingrained by years of practice. I'd like to move on and grow out of it, but sometimes it's so instinctual.

"She's doing really well, actually. I've never had a TA this capable before," Ty proclaims, going to bat for me in a way I didn't expect. I mean, it's not that I thought he would bad-mouth me. It's just…he's never actually told me he thinks I'm doing a good job before. As far as I'm concerned, being the best he's ever had in an arena other than sex is news to me. "I haven't even touched a test question this semester on her drafts. She has great intuition as far as avoiding the obvious without relying on the obscure."

My dad's eyes light with a little bit of pride, and I'm ashamed of my stomach as it flips over itself. I've always known my worth on my own—I don't need to be validated by a man, even if I'm made from half of his DNA—but watching my father show me something other than distrust is… overwhelming.

"Well, I'm glad it's working out," my father eventually comments. Being sure to leave me completely out of it this time because, obviously, the last thing he wants to do is acknowledge I'm doing something right. "I wasn't quite sure what I was walking into."

Ty glances at me, I can feel his brief attention from my periphery, but I don't look in his direction. I don't fucking dare. Instead, I hold my dad's eyes in blatant challenge to his implications. He's butting in, like always, sticking his neck in a personal arena he has no business playing in. I won't play this game right now, especially not in front of my boss.

Sure, I'm also sleeping with him, but that doesn't demean the value of my work, goddammit.

I'm not a little girl anymore.

Nathaniel is as stalwart as ever, holding my eyes right back without even a crack in his façade. We consider each other for long moments before he finally turns his attention back to Ty.

"Ty, we're having a faculty gathering before the start of break next week if you want to stop by." Then he turns to me, unable to resist getting in one last dig. "Sorry, Rachel, but this one's for the grown-ups."

My eyes narrow as he offers a smile and a wave and exits the room the same way he came—quietly. I only wish he'd kept his mouth shut a little more while he was here. Or, you know, not come here at all.

I know Ty well enough to know he's not reading into my dad's words, but I'm not sure he knows me well enough to know I *am*. They're all I can hear—all I can fucking think about.

For as confident as I am, my dad knows just how to slap me with stuff that's too close to home. Calling Ty a grown-up and implying I'm not one wasn't without purpose. No, it was calculated.

Ty's nearly forty, and I'm only meandering through my late twenties. I wonder why I haven't paid more attention to that before now.

Embarrassment tinges my cheeks as I head for my bag again, the game of tag long forgotten—replaced by an onslaught of questions I'd do well to remember.

There's one question in particular that, no matter how many times I ask it, I never seem to come to an answer.

Where in the hell am I expecting all this to end up?

THIRTY-ONE

Ty

Rachel heads straight for her bag in the front row of seats as her dad leaves the room. She's not manic or hurried or anything, but it's more than clear at this point that she doesn't plan to stay in Dodge long before getting the fuck out of it.

In some ways, I can't blame her. It didn't feel good looking a guy I've respected for most of my adult life in the eye and lying by a big, honking piece of omission. But it didn't feel as *wrong* as I thought it would either. The thing is, I like what I'm doing with Rachel, and, I think, she likes what she's doing with me, too.

We're consenting adults with a grasp on reality, and we're both still dedicated and practiced at doing our jobs as we should. The education of my classes hasn't suffered this year; if anything, they've gained. The professor of one year ago didn't have this level of insight, and he certainly didn't have this many personal experiences that tied into literature that's largely based in romance.

Nate was a lot tougher on her than he was on me, however, and I can see why their relationship is strained. He doesn't see her, not really. And from a completely outside perspective, it doesn't even seem like he's trying to.

As a person whom he's always gone above and beyond to understand, even while others have criticized me, I find it a real fucking shock. And it makes me feel…confused by how, over the years, I've respected a man this much who is capable of treating his daughter like that.

"Rachel," I call, getting only a modicum of her attention at first. She glances over her shoulder but mostly keeps packing her bag.

"Rachel," I appeal again, this time a little firmer. "Look at me, please."

She stops what she's doing and turns then, her arms falling to her sides in the most hopeless position I've ever seen her in. She's normally confident—sassy, even. She's hands on hips and cocked legs. She's not meek. Not even close. But this version of her has just been run over by her father—and he did it with a witness.

"Are you okay?"

She sighs heavily and then crosses her arms over her chest. It's safe to say, every ounce of the playfulness before has long since left the building. "I'm fine. But Ty, maybe we need to cool it a little, you know? I'm really busy with classes and the bakery, and I know you're busy too. This is complicated—like, really complicated. And I don't know if it's the right time to be putting our energy into it."

An overwhelming wave of uneasiness washes over me and through my skin and muscle and all the way down to the bone. I don't think I'd like hearing this kind of talk from anyone—I don't think anyone likes to be on the losing end of rejection—but the nature of this feels sour in a different way. It feels forced. Unnatural. The kind of wrong that being together doesn't.

I know she's teetering on the edge, though, and convincing her to leap in with both feet isn't the kind of thing I see myself talking her into in the next thirty seconds. I'm a fast-talker, nevertheless, born from years of practice trying to get a word in edgewise with four siblings, and I'll be damned if I'm just going to let this go.

Not to mention, I'm not convinced that cooling it is what she actually wants. Especially since it's coming moments after I just watched her dad railroad her with words.

"You're right," I start, loosening her up with common ground. "It's getting a little intense here on campus, and I completely understand where you're coming from with the busy schedule." Her face melts in a combination of relief and a flash of disappointment, so I rush on to transition the thought with one very important word. "*But…*"

"But?" she asks cautiously when I don't continue. "But what?"

"But you heard the old man. Next week is spring break. We can get away from here. Spend a little time. Just be ourselves without thinking about all the complications."

A little bubble of hope creates a window of brightness in her pretty eyes. "You think?"

I nod fervently. "Absolutely. You won't have to worry about class, and I don't want to presume, but maybe you could take some time from the bakery too, and we could just have the week."

"Away from all of this," she says. It's a statement, not a question.

I nod zealously—perhaps a little *overzealously*, if I'm completely honest. I want this badly. Way more than I ever could have imagined I would want anything with anyone.

I don't want Rachel to run unless I'm running too—and a lion is chasing us or some shit.

"I could probably talk Lydia and Lou into the week off. I mean, I don't want to leave them in the lurch, but if it's okay with them, I guess I could…"

"Yeah?"

She shrugs then. "You're right. Being away from here…not thinking about this…it sounds nice."

A whole week with just Rachel and me and none of the complications? Fuck yes.

"It doesn't just sound nice," I argue with a smirk. "If you ask me, it sounds perfect."

"One week?"

"One week," I repeat. "Just you and me."

"And until then, we'll be good?"

"Perfect angels. Completely on the up-and-up. Like, the most boring set of people you've ever met."

"Promise?"

"I promise." The truth is, I'll do whatever it takes to get Rachel Rose all to myself for a week. *Whatever it takes.*

THIRTY-TWO

Thursday, February 28th

Ty

One day away from the end of the week might as well feel like a thousand when spring break is on the other side. Kids seem to think they're the only ones looking forward to a week without school, but I don't know a single adult who doesn't want a week off work.

And in this case, a week with Rachel all to myself.

About fifteen minutes before class ends, I'm not surprised when one particular student tries to question the deadline on their current essay assignment. I gird my loins against the unpredictable—God only knows what's going to come out of this kid's mouth.

"Prof, can I get an extension on my essay interpretation of Roaming Heights?" Landon, the roughest of all of my pupils this year, asks, waggling his eyebrows as if it'll somehow convince me.

"It's *Wuthering Heights*, bro," I correct him with an exhausted smile. "And there's no extension because you'll have tomorrow and *all* of next week to write it."

"Duuuude. I'm gonna be in Panama for spring break!"

"We're all aware it's spring break, Landon," I say with a companionable glance around the room. "But you've had this assignment for nearly a week. If you'd been proactive about all the beers and babes in Panama, you would have already gotten it done."

"Ugh, bro. You're cockblocking me so hard." Landon groans, sinking his scraggly head into his hands. The rest of the class laughs at his try at dramatic theater, and I wave my hands downward in a shushing motion to settle them down.

"Raise your hand if you think this paper is the reason Landon's cock is going to be blocked."

No one besides Landon raises their hand, and the class erupts into outrageous laughter.

Landon glances around at all his turncoat peers with a playful sneer. "Harsh, dudes. You're all harsh."

"All right," I say, hopping up to take a seat on my desk and crossing an arm over my knee. I look Landon directly in his sleepy, hazy eyes. "I'll make you a deal. If you can tell me the last name of just one of the families that are of prominence in the book, I'll give you an extension."

The whole class shifts in their seats as Landon considers the question. I'm not entirely confident he'll win this little game, given the fact that he didn't know the name of the book when we started this conversation, but if anything, I'm a man of honest chances. I won't call for Landon's failure before he seals it for himself. Innocent until proven guilty, if you will.

A few students cough behind their hands, trying to pass along the answer, and I hold up an open-palmed hand toward the room. "Ah, ah. No cheating, kids."

A hush finally falls over the crowd as they all wait for Landon's moment—will he be the hero or a pariah?

"Time's up, dude," I tell him bluntly. "What's your answer?"

He racks his brain—I can practically see the wheels turning in his sluggish mind through the fog in his eyes—and then finally surges to his feet. "Oh! I got it! Earnhardt!"

The class explodes in groans and shouts, and I have to smile at the pure confidence of his answer. "Sorry, Landon. The only thing the last name Earnhardt is prominent in is NASCAR."

The class whines and howls at large, and I hold up another hand to silence them. When the hand doesn't do it, I put my fingers to my mouth and let go with a piercing whistle.

"Yo! Everyone calm down. I'm not done." Those three words finally quiet them down enough to hear myself think, and I steal a quick glance at Rachel as the room settles. She's smiling widely, looking as beautiful and vibrant as I've ever seen her. I look back to the class. "Now, that wasn't the correct answer, Landon, but it was close enough that I'm starting to think you just might have gotten into NYU for some reason other than a rich uncle on the board."

Landon's eyebrows pull together as he asks, "You know my uncle?"

I shake my head. *No, Landon, no.*

He chuckles. "I didn't think so. He's not really a school kind of guy. My dad, though, my dad's way up NYU's ass. The great *Carl Conrad*," he expands in a mocking, annoyed voice. "Mr. Big Shot Manhattan Lawyer of the rich and famous."

I definitely know the name. Hell, most of New York has seen that name on billboards. But I don't give a shit about this kid's dad, big shot or not. All I care about is Landon.

"You're smart, Landon. You've got what it takes. You just need to apply yourself."

"But then I'd be doing exactly what my father wants me to do."

"Yeah, I know that feeling," Rachel mutters a little too loudly, and both Landon and I look over at her. Her gaze is still fixated on her laptop, but after a few seconds, she looks up and realizes the attention is on her.

She cringes. "I said that out loud, didn't I?"

"Yep." Landon nods with a big-ass smile. "You got daddy issues too?"

"Well…" Rachel sighs and takes off her blue light glasses. "This conversation isn't about me. I'm not important here."

When I realize how strongly she wishes she could burrow a hole straight to China, I smile and glance at my watch. It's time to dismiss class—and lucky for Rachel, that also means it's time to let her off the hook.

"Okay, guys. That's it for today."

Everyone jumps up out of their seats, but I raise my voice one more time to get their attention.

"Before you go, though… For another chance at that one-week essay extension…" Everyone quiets immediately. "Who else can tell me the last name I'm looking for?"

Dozens of hands shoot up like rockets, and I smile broadly. Young minds are shaping; lifelong readers are forming. Goddamn, I live for this shit.

"Okay, then, let's all say it together, shall we?"

I put up three fingers to count down, removing one at a time until none are left. When I get to the moment of truth, practically the whole class shouts, "Earnshaw!"

My grin is huge as I hop down from the top of my desk and pretend to swing an imaginary baseball bat. "Home runnnnn!" I call dramatically into the large space, starting up a run and high-fiving all the students in the front row. "Looks like you get an extension after all!" I shout, and they all erupt in happy cheers.

I stop in front of Rachel and yell once more. "Get out of here!"

Afraid, perhaps, that I'll change my mind, no one wastes any time before they bolt for the door.

Rachel smiles up at me over her laptop from her seat, and I'll be damned if I can turn away.

My eyes flit down her body, taking inventory of every beautiful aspect that is her. The way her shiny brown hair hangs down her shoulders, her parted lips, her elongated neck, her full breasts, and the way her legs peek out from beneath her skirt.

Well, *hell.*

Somehow, I've survived four days without touching Rachel, kissing Rachel, putting my mouth on Rachel's sweet, *sweet* pussy, but these last fifteen seconds feel like a lifetime.

This one week of being good is for the fucking birds. How the hell do I still have more than a day to go?

Fuck. I *have* to do something to relieve *some* of this pent-up frustration or else I fear I might explode.

She shuts her laptop and bends down to tuck it into her bag. The movement plumps her breasts, and they're practically spilling out of the neckline of her top.

That's the moment I decide to throw caution to the wind. So what if I break the rules? I've been going against the grain of authority my entire life.

Walking away from Rachel and over to the door, I wait until the last student leaves the class to shut the door and engage the lock.

Rachel is standing near my desk now, her messenger bag over her shoulder and her head tilted in curiosity. *Why in the hell are you trapping me in here, Ty?* her pretty, glittering eyes ask.

"Sit on my desk, Rachel," I instruct, stalking toward her.

Her eyes are wide and worried, but she's not following orders—and right now, that just won't do. "*Sit on my desk, Rachel,*" I repeat.

"W-what are you doing?" she asks—only while following orders, though.

Her eyes watch me as I round the desk and take a seat in my chair. She spins her body to follow, just as secretly eager and excited as I am. I can see it in the pounding of her chest and the light in her eyes.

Rachel Rose, whether she would admit it or not, has missed me just as much as I've missed her for the last four days.

She stares down at me from her perch, her long brown hair falling toward her face and her skirt edging up her thighs that are currently clamped closely together.

With one index finger, I reach out and just barely caress the spot where clothing meets skin.

Her body shivers, and ever so slightly, her hips fidget in a way that makes her thighs spread the teeniest amount.

"Ty," she warns, reaching desperately for the will to enforce our "be good for a week" agreement.

Her mind might be clinging to our arrangement, but her body is not. Her nipples are hard beneath her silk blouse, and her teeth have nearly created a permanent crease in the plump flesh of her bottom lip.

"I'm trying to be good," I tell her, smiling up at her through hooded eyes. It may not seem like it, but I'm telling the truth.

Every cell inside me wants to pull her onto my lap and show her just how fucking much I miss the feel of her skin against mine and how badly I want to fill her up and feel her tight cunt wrapped around my cock and how desperate I am to swallow her moans into my mouth as she comes, but what I'm doing now isn't about that.

What I'm doing now is about teasing. Taunting. *Making* her *come*.

I move my index finger to her other thigh, creating an invisible straight line from one side to the other, and only hovering for a moment when I reach the spot that's slightly open.

"You call this being good?" she questions, a knowing smile forming at the corner of her lush mouth.

"Yeah, Rach. I call this *really good*." I lean forward in my chair as I gently spread her thighs all the way apart. Her panties are visible now, and they're a delicate, sexy version of lace and silk that makes my cock do a double take.

"Ty…"

"Don't worry, I'm just looking. Not touching."

Her hips fidget again, spreading her legs even farther for me, and I glance up to see that a little pout has formed on her lips at the news of no touching.

Yeah, doll. I feel the same exact way.

I move my face closer to the apex of her thighs, so close that my mouth is just a brush away from her panties, and Rachel's breasts push out as she inhales a deep breath.

"How many more days?" I ask, staring desperately at her lace-covered pussy.

"Uh…technically, two," she breathes out. "But if we're saying spring break starts the moment our last classes end, then only one."

"So, we'll go with one, then."

She laughs, but when I blow on the overheated center of her, she chokes to an immediate stop, all humor strangled out by a moan. "Yeah, okay. Yes. It's *definitely* one day."

Her gorgeous hips squirm on my desk, and all of my patience flees. I can't wait any longer—I'll never survive it. "You know what I need?"

"What?" she whispers.

"I need to see you come. Right here. On my desk."

"But…"

"I locked the door. My next class isn't for another hour. And you still have forty minutes until yours."

"But we said we were going to be good."

"Oh, we're still going to stick to the rules," I tell her and reach up to grasp her hand in mine. I guide it to the apex of her thighs and use my other hand to slide her panties to the side so her fingers touch her clit. "Like I said, I won't touch. I'm only going to watch."

A little whimper leaves her lips, and I know she needs this just as much as I need to see her do it.

"Do it, Rachel. Show me how you pleasure yourself. But imagine it's my mouth and my tongue and my cock while you do it."

Slowly, hesitantly, she starts to rub her fingers against her clit, and the sight of it—the sight of her sitting on my desk with her legs spread and her hand between her thighs—is the hottest fucking thing I've ever witnessed in my life.

"Fuck, I'm jealous of those fingers," I whisper and brush my lips over the top of her still-moving hand.

She moans and cries out, but she doesn't stop. She keeps touching herself, picking up the pace, but at the same time, not going so fast that she can't savor the buildup.

Yes, the buildup. That sweet fucking buildup.

I reach up with gentle fingers, and without touching her directly, I undo the first four buttons of her silk blouse. Her shirt falls open just enough to reveal the matching silk and lace white bra to her panties.

But it's not enough.

I need more. I need her to *feel* the illicitness of this moment.

With a capped pen from my desk, I use it to slide the material of her bra down her breasts until both are visible for me. Her pink nipples are hard, and the movement of her now-erratic breaths pushes her chest closer to me.

"Damn, I want to suck on these," I whisper and stand up to hover my lips over each of her breasts. Still not touching, but close enough that she can feel the warmth of my mouth.

"Ty," she whimpers again, and I know she's close.

"Keep going, baby," I whisper in her ear, still making sure no part of my body touches hers. "Push yourself over the edge for me."

Her eyes fall closed and her head falls back, and her gorgeous brown locks are a wave of beauty over her shoulders. Her hand stays busy between her thighs, two fingers rubbing along her clit, and occasionally one finger finds itself inside her.

She is the most beautiful thing I've ever seen. Vulnerable but aroused. In control but pushing herself to lose control.

It is the best fantasy that I've never been creative enough to imagine on my own.

The moment her orgasm starts to consume her body, she leans forward and buries her face in my dress shirt, using my chest to muffle her moans.

It's only then that I let myself give in to the need to touch her. Arms around her back, I pull her body tight to mine and give her a few quiet moments to come down from the high.

Once her breaths are back to normal and I don't feel the pounding of her pulse at her neck, I lean back to slide her breasts back into her bra and button up her silk blouse. I even reach down and put her panties back in place.

She sits there as I work, half smiling but still a little dazed.

"What about you?" she asks and glances down to my pants, where my cock is raging.

"What about me?"

This isn't a tit-for-tat situation. This was air, water, and shelter. This was a thing I needed for life.

"I got exactly what I needed…for now."

Tomorrow is a whole different story.

I help her off my desk and not-so-discreetly squeeze her ass in the process. "So, what time do we officially get to stop being good? I want to make sure I enter it accurately into my calendar."

"You already know this." She giggles. "*After* our last classes."

"Are you sure it's not midnight tonight?"

Rachel rolls her pretty eyes. "Nope."

"One a.m., then?"

"No."

"Five a.m.?"

"Nice try," she says, trying to act annoyed but her smile showing her truth. "Anyway, I'll be busy then."

"Pulling a shift at the bakery?"

"Nope." A little sigh leaves her lips. "My sister is forcing me to go to some early morning dance class thing."

"Rachel Rose dances?"

"Sometimes." She stands on her tippy-toes and presses a barely there kiss to the corner of my mouth. "But I'm pretty sure you already knew that."

Yeah. I definitely did. All of this started with a dance nearly two months ago, and since then, she's been a stellar participant in the horizontal tango.

"Only twenty-four hours to go, *Professor*," she taunts with a little giggle as she heads for the door.

Yeah. I can't fucking wait.

THIRTY-THREE

Friday, March 1st

Rachel

The subway lights flicker, and I stare down at my favorite white Adidas with gold stripes before looking up at Lydia, who sits across the aisle with her head resting on Lou's shoulder.

"Tell me again why I had to wake up at five in the morning?"

"The class starts at six, Rae," Lydia says, acting like that's a real explanation. "Plus, exercise is healthy."

"But why *this* early?" I counter. "Isn't it possible to exercise at a more reasonable hour?"

"Because it's a great way to start your day."

"It's also the easiest time for us to sneak away from the bakery and let Maude run the ship," Lou adds, and I nod.

"Well, that makes way more sense than the whole bit about starting your day out right," I respond with a tired smile. "Because from where I stand, this is a terrible damn way to start the day."

Lydia snorts. "You're the worst in the morning."

"Yes. I am," I agree without shame. "Which is why you should have never attempted to drag me along to a dance class before the sun rises."

Lou grins, and Lydia sighs.

"Bitch and moan all you want, but when we're done, you're going to feel like a new woman."

I open my mouth to refute that ridiculous statement, likely with a colorful word or two or seven, but the feel of my phone vibrating in my purse grabs my attention and saves my sister from a verbal battle. With uncoordinated, five-in-the-morning hands, I pull it out of my purse, nearly dropping it to the dirty subway floor in the process.

When I finally have it secure, I open up my text inbox, where a new message sits unopened from the man I think about way more than I should. After receiving several sad-face picture messages at midnight telling me it was a bad decision to go against our ancestors' definition of time when determining the "being good" deadline from him, I never expected Ty would be up this early.

Ty: How are we this morning, Dancing Queen?

Me: She's tired. And grouchy. And not yet queen of any dance moves. And wondering why the hell you're awake right now.

Ty: Easy. I'm at the gym.

Me: WHAT? Why? What in the world does everyone have against the sun?

Ty: Sun is our enemy, not, but finite in time. Many rewards rendered, are found in the suffering. (Plus, I like the way you stare at my sexy muscles, so I'm trying to keep them.)

I roll my eyes, but I also laugh.

Me: I'm barely achieving basic function this morning, and you're spouting some sonnet bullshit. Ugh.

Ty: You really are a crabby patty in the morning, huh?

Me: Uh-huh.

Ty: Don't worry. I'll break you of that.

I nearly scoff aloud but just stop myself when I notice Lydia watching me. I look back down to my phone and type out a quick message.

Me: Oh yeah, how?

Ty: It's hard to hate anything when you've got a mouth on your pussy.

Sheesh. Is it getting a little hot in here? I have to admit, his reasoning is sound. A five-a.m. session of oral and I might just get over my snit.

Me: I guess we'll have to wait and see if that's true.

The truth is, the prequel he gave me in his lecture hall yesterday afternoon is the only thing I've been able to think about since. He won't have to work too hard to prove his point—I'm going to enjoy it; it's a biological certainty.

Ty: No worries, Rach. I have an entire week filled with lots of special plans to prove it to you.

Me: Special plans? Are you going to tell me what they are?

Ty: It's a surprise. ;)

Me: You're a tease.

Ty: Says the Queen of Teases.

Me: Excuse me?

Ty: The first night I met you, you put your panties in my hand and left without giving me your name or your number…

He has a point.

Me: In my defense, I was merely following through with a challenge.

Ty: What challenge?

Me: Ohhhh, looks like we both have secret information.

"Who are you texting with?" Lydia's voice grabs my attention, and I look up from the screen of my phone to see her staring at me with a curious smile.

When I don't answer, she asks me again. "Seriously, who are you texting with?"

"Um…" I pause and pop my lips together. "A professor?"

"A *professor* is texting you this early *and* has you smiling like a loon?" she questions and lifts her head off Lou's shoulder to look at me closer. "Holy shit! Are you talking to Ty Winslow?"

Bingo, sis. I bite my bottom lip and shrug, trying to look innocent but, I know, failing miserably. "Like I said, it's a professor."

"Oh, what the hell!" Lydia says through a laugh and points one index finger in my direction. "I can't believe you've been hiding this from me! Dish the dirt! Right now!"

"There's no dirt," I respond just as a message that's so full of filth, I might have to start going by Jimmy Hoffa rolls in.

Ty: *That's okay. In about twelve hours, your ass is mine, and I'll get to the bottom of ALL your secrets. Don't even bother coming to my class today. Just get ready. I'll be in touch again later.*

"Oh my God, you liar!" Lydia exclaims loudly as I feel a layer of heat bloom in my cheeks. "You're blushing!"

I shove my phone back into my purse and close my eyes to take a deep breath. When I open them again, Lydia and Lou are both staring at me weightily. There's no way I'm getting off this subway car without clueing them in.

And honestly, I'm not sure I want to. For as much fun as I've had with the professor, it's been a lonely and confusing road of push and pull that's just starting to get good.

My sister and Lou won't judge me—they never do. It'd probably do me some good to get it all out on the table.

"Okay, yes. You're right. There's dirt…so, so much dirtiness."

"Eeep!" Lydia shrieks, making Lou reach out and pat her knee to calm her down.

"Ty and I are…enjoying each other."

Lydia slaps a hand over her mouth and rolls the other one in front of her, begging me to proceed, and Lou rolls her eyes playfully.

"It was completely innocent for a long time…just a game, really, and I didn't think anything of it. But we've been sleeping together for several weeks now, and this coming week—you know, when I asked to be off from the bakery—we're going to spend it together."

I shrug, trying to ignore two sets of extremely wide eyes.

"Holy hell," Lydia mutters. "You're in a full-fledged affair with your professor."

I snort. "He's not *my* professor."

"You're right," Lydia agrees. "He's your boss."

"When you put it like that, it sounds terrible," I muse. "But it's not like that. I mean, I'm twenty-six, Lyd. A consenting adult. It's not like I'm an eighteen-year-old college student banging her actual professor."

She considers me for a long minute, chewing at her lips nervously. I can see the words she's not saying stark in her eyes. *But you are the daughter of the head of the English Department who is currently banging the professor her father arranged for her to be a teaching assistant to.*

"I'm guessing Nate doesn't know about any of this?" Lou asks into the silence.

I eye her sarcastically. "Oh yeah, Nate knows *all* about it. Ty even has an arrangement to put a sock on his office door whenever we're in there fucking so Dad doesn't walk in."

Lydia snorts. Lou grins.

"Yeah, okay, I'm done with this conversation."

"Yeah, if I were you, I would be too." Lydia laughs then, easing the blow by reaching out to grab my hand. "I hope it works out, babe, I really do. Only you can know how worthwhile it is—how you feel about him." She shrugs. "If I were you, and he were Lou, I'd risk it all."

They smile lovingly at each other, and my stomach clutches in longing. I don't give in to the temptation to assess how I feel or wallow in evaluating my choices. No, I choose the route of blissful ignorance.

Because if you gave it a moment of consideration, my mind whispers, *you'd have to admit you might be falling for him.*

Thankfully, Lou breaks the ice by announcing we've arrived at our stop, and I put my brain back to bed. It's *wayyy* too early to be dancing my way into thoughts like those, Dancing Queen or not.

All three of us file off the mostly empty train and head up the stairwell to the outside world.

The studio is evidently five blocks from the station—another fun little surprise—but Lydia at least does me the courtesy of not questioning me further. Instead, she lets go of my shoulders and walks ahead of Lou and me in silence for most of the five blocks.

"Are you ladies ready to get your dance on?" she exclaims when she finally does reboot the conversation, and I feign a dramatic groan.

"No. Not at all. Because it's too flipping early for anything but sleeping."

"Trust me, Rae. You're going to love it!" she whoops and skips ahead a few feet and comes to a stop in front of a building with a sign that reads **Groovin' Goddesses**. "Plus, the instructor for the morning class is a regular of ours."

Lydia holds the door open as Lou and I continue to walk toward her.

"This instructor enjoys baked goods?" I question, getting a little hope from that possibility. I mean, a workout instructor who eats cookies and cakes is someone I can stand behind.

"Well, baked goods that are vegan, gluten-free, and keto-friendly," Lou offers as we step out of the chilly morning air and into the warm entry of the studio's lobby.

Hope bubble officially popped.

No offense to people who follow a strict diet, but I'm more of an eat-it-all-in-moderation kind of gal. You won't find me skipping tacos and margaritas or beer and pizza in the name of my figure. Though, more power to the people who can. I applaud you!

But the music that's currently blasting through this place? I do *not* applaud. I swear, it feels like Kelly Clarkson is all hopped up on speed and singing along with techno-house music. Not to mention the neon lights that hang from the ceiling are so bright, if I took a selfie, I'd be able to see inside my pores.

A good time for a club, maybe, but it's a hell of a lot of sensory overload for six in the morning.

"Oh, this is going to be a real blast," I mutter.

"How about instead of being all grouchy, you focus on thinking about how good you're going to feel after we finish this class?" Lydia nudges me with her elbow and grins. "Exercise equals endorphins, Rae. And endorphins make people happy."

"Wow. Thank you, Elle Woods."

"Good morning, ladies!" a lady in pink leggings and a matching halter top chirps from behind a reception desk. She's dancing along to the music and smiling so big I can see her freaking molars. "You ready to get your groove on?"

I flash Lydia the side-eye, my expression mostly *Why the hell did you bring me here?*

But she ignores me. "Yep! We sure are!"

"And what class will you be groovin' in this morning?"

"Hip-Hop with Holly."

"Oh, that's a fabulous class!" Peppy responds. "Such a great workout and so much fun! Give me a minute, and I'll get your Groovin' Bands!"

I steal a quick glance at Lou, and from the firm placement of her lips, I get the feeling I'm not the only one who is a little underwhelmed about Hip-Hop with Holly.

"Blink three times if you want to escape from this endorphin cult," I whisper toward her, and a few unexpected laughs burst from her throat.

"Damn it, Rae. I'm trying to be a supportive wife," she murmurs back, and Lydia gives us a look over her shoulder while she waits for Peppy to get the groovy belts or badges or whatever the hell she called them.

"I can hear you guys," she whispers through what sounds like clenched teeth. "Knock it off."

"Personally, I don't know how anyone can hear anything over the *groovy music* that's pumping through this place."

Lou has to cover her mouth not to laugh.

"*Rae*," Lydia says through a tight jaw, her eyes damn near bugging out of her head as she looks at me again. "I swear on everything, you better put a smile on your face and be nice."

"Fine." I raise the white flag via both hands in the air. "I'll be on my best behavior. Promise."

Lydia exhales an annoyed breath and turns back to Peppy...I mean, the very nice lady in the pink tights. Once our arm bands are handed over, we are off to see the wonderful wizard of hip-hop.

Down a hall lit with more obtrusive lighting, I follow the leader until we step inside an open room with mirror-covered walls and pretty wooden floors.

It doesn't take a genius to figure out who Holly is.

A woman with an insanely white smile, a high ponytail, and dressed in black tights, a neon green sports bra, and a colorful sequined jacket with the words Hip-Hop Holly embroidered on the back is at the front, already starting to lead the class of all women into a warm-up stretch.

"*Shit*. We're late," Lydia mumbles and hurriedly rushes over to an open spot in the corner of the room.

Lou follows her without as much enthusiasm, and I try to act like I didn't see where they went. Like, maybe, they'll forget I'm here, and I can sneak out and ask Peppy if there are any Pop-Tarts in the lobby vending machine.

"Rae!" Lydia whisper-yells toward me, and when I don't respond—*and also pretend not to understand where the sound is coming from*—she decides to raise her voice loud enough that Hip-Hop Holly looks up from her toe-touching stretch and directly at me.

Busted.

"Hi. Sorry," I say and awkwardly shuffle over to where Lydia and Lou are located.

My sister-in-law gives me a look that says *nice try*, and all I can do is shrug.

Lydia is already getting her stretch on, and I do my best to follow Hip-Hop Holly's instructions as she guides us through all sorts of exercises that are thankfully pretty easy.

Some quad stretches. A few lunges. Several squats. A nice two-minute stretch that includes me sitting down and touching my toes.

Okay, maybe this isn't going to be so bad.

As soon as the peaceful thought enters my mind, Holly starts to get *real* hyped up. She jumps on the balls of her feet and claps her hands and starts shouting things like "Let's get this party started, ladies!"

It's that moment when she starts to lose me. And by the look on Lou's face, I know I'm not alone in my underwhelmed, not-amped-at-all state.

Lydia, though, well, she's following right along, jumping around and clapping her hands and shit. A whole lot of enthusiasm vibrates from her body.

When I see the rest of the class is loving what Holly is putting down, I make a concerted effort to make the best of it. To go with it. To search deep within myself and find some hippity-hoppity vibes.

But when Holly puts on a song called "Dirty Talk" and begins to show the class the dance we're supposed to learn, things really start to take a nose dive for me.

Holly is *all in* to her routine, rubbing her hands over her sports-bra-covered boobs as she mouths the lyrics about *not being an angel* and *whipped cream* and *dirty talk* and *going down* and all kinds of sexual shit with pouty lips and hips that won't quit.

She's up and she's down.

She's on the floor, rolling around, and then she's back up again, spreading her thighs like she's riding a dick and rubbing her hands seductively down her thighs.

She hip thrusts. She twerks. She even does the fucking splits.

At one point, she gets a chair and proceeds to do some sort of interpretative lap dance on it.

"Um…" I pause and look over at Lou. "Are we in the right class?"

"I'm afraid so."

"Why do I feel like I need to pay her when this dance is over?"

Lou bites her bottom lip, fighting the urge to laugh again. Lydia glares at me. "Stop it, Rae."

"Lydia, I love you, but, like, this is a lot for six in the morning."

When the music comes to a stop, everyone in the class starts cheering, and Hip-Hop Holly smiles and takes a little bow. "Aw, you guys are too much! Thank you! Thank you!"

Once the fanfare is done, she grabs a towel, dabs the sweat from her forehead, and announces, "Okay, ladies, who is ready to learn the dance?"

Ha-ha-ha. No. *It's too early for this shit.*

Self-preservation activated.

Hoots and hollers fill the room, and I proceed to utilize a dance move I like to call "getting the fuck out of here."

"*Rae*, where are you going?" Lydia whisper-yells to my exiting back, and I don't hesitate to point toward the door.

"I'll be out in the lobby with Peppy."

When I steal a glance over my shoulder, Lou is laughing her ass off, but Lydia is giving me the kind of stare that could melt skin off bones.

Sorry, sis.

I tried, but Hip-Hop Holly and the Groovin' Goddesses are a little too much for me at this hour of the morning. Maybe a night class would've been a better option.

Plus, now isn't the time for me to pull a muscle. I have a whole week of *not-being-good* ahead of me. Surely I'll catch up on the missed exercise *and* the endorphins then, *right?*

THIRTY-FOUR

Rachel

I stare down at my bed, clothes strewn all over the damn place, and try to decide what I should pack for a trip I know nothing about it. Frankly, I don't even know if it's a trip. For all I know, we're just going to hole up in his apartment and have sex for seven days straight, and to be completely honest, I wouldn't be mad about that.

I just wish I knew, one way or another, what I needed to bring with me to be equipped.

After a long day of classes, and skipping Ty's freshman lecture for the sake of my sanity and his, I'm ready to get out of here. The thing is, I need to know where I'm heading.

I grab my phone from the nightstand and type out a fevered text, frustration from being so in the dark starting to set in.

Me: What exactly am I packing for, here? Bikini weather? Parka weather? A sex dungeon of some sort? Please, I'm begging you, clue me in just a little.

Ty: I'm sorry, but I'm not at liberty to give you that information.

Me: Ty! The time is nearly upon us. I think you can give it up with the surprise at this point.

Ty: Okay, fine. I'll give you a teeny, tiny little hint…

I put my phone down to start sorting through more clothes when he seems to be taking forever to type, and then I nearly jump when the chime sound goes off. I'm already smiling as I pick it up to look at the screen, but my grin disappears immediately when the body of the message is not at all what I'm expecting.

Dad: Rachel, I have great news. The NYC Literary Conference is next week. This year, they've even added workshops that are writing- and publishing-focused. I reserved two tickets so we can attend. Can you be ready by 8 a.m. on Monday? I'll pick you up.

I stare down at the message, equal parts flabbergasted and annoyed. *He can't seriously think I'm just sitting around waiting to do as he decrees. That might be his MO, but this is taking it to a whole new level.*

I look up toward the ceiling of my bedroom to find the strength I need and then look back to my phone, type out a message, and hit send.

Me: Dad, I'm sorry, but I already have plans next week. I can't attend.

Dad: I'm sure Lydia will be fine with you skipping bakery shifts. This is far more important than any other plans you could have.

"Well, Dad, I'm going to spend the next week naked, fucking one of your department's professors," I mutter quietly, mocking myself and the entire conversation. "You know Ty, right? Yeah, he's the guy. What a small world, huh?"

Son of a bitch.

I waver on what to message him back, my emotions volleying between guilt and anger.

Eventually, though, I settle on being firm.

Me: I'm sorry you feel that way, but I don't agree. I've already made plans, and I intend to keep them.

Dad: Rachel, just because it's spring break doesn't mean you should stop focusing on your career. This type of conference would be a huge asset for you. I'll text you Monday morning, and I'm hoping you'll have come to your senses by then and realize this is far too important of an opportunity to pass up.

Oh, for the love of everything. Just back the fuck off.

I want so desperately to say that to him, but I know I won't, and barring that kind of bluntness, it feels useless texting him back again.

His mind is made up.

Too bad for him, so is mine.

When the damn thing chimes again, I scowl and pick it back up. Thankfully, with Ty back at the helm as my messaging partner, all the bad juju in the air melts away.

Ty: I'm going to pick you up from your apartment in 15 minutes.

Me: What? You said you were going to give me a hint, not a heart attack.

Ty: That is the hint. Be ready.

A giggle jumps from my throat, and I make a snap decision that instead of trying to be organized and pack specific outfits for specific days, I grab my biggest suitcase from my closet and just start tossing anything and everything inside.

It's not precise, but I'd say the odds are high I'm not going to be needing a whole lot in the clothing department anyway. By the time I'm zipping it up, my phone announces another text.

Ty: 5 minutes

Me: Are you texting and driving? That's very unsafe.

Ty: Only when I'm at a stop light. PS: 2 minutes.

Shit! I squeal and grip the handle of my suitcase, dragging it off my bed and down the hallway until I pull it to a stop beside the door.

With the time ticking down at a rapid-fire pace, I grab my purse, run into the bathroom, and quickly freshen myself up with some lipstick, blush, and mascara. By the time I finish up with my hair, my phone chimes again, and it's Ty letting me know he's here.

Ty: Let the week of being bad commence.

My mind fixates on two words—being bad.

Yes, please. After another push of my buttons from my dad, the rebellious side of Rachel Rose is *all in.*

Ty holds the door key above the sensor, and the light turns green while a little click notifies that the lock has disengaged. He pushes the door open and grins down at me as he steps out of the way for me to walk inside.

His big plans? A week at the famous Carlyle Hotel in Manhattan.

"Let me be the first to welcome you to our spring break," he says behind me, and I hear the wheels of my suitcase being dragged into the foyer area.

Yes, *foyer area.* Of a freaking hotel suite.

"This is quite the spring break, Professor," I say through a giggle and walk into the lavish space. Ty didn't just book a simple hotel room for our secret spring break getaway. No way. He booked a flipping *suite* at one of the most expensive hotels in New York.

And it does not disappoint.

There's a full kitchen with marble countertops and stainless-steel appliances. A living room has a plush sofa and a large flat-screen TV. The bedroom includes a king-sized bed and bedding that looks so luxurious it's probably been used for magazine photos.

And the bathroom? Well, it's highlighted by a massive, glass-encased walk-in shower *and* a white porcelain soaking tub.

This is the kind of hotel suite celebrities hide out in under aliases like Betty Boop.

"Can I interest you in a glass of champagne?" he calls from the kitchen, and a quiet laugh escapes my throat.

Damn, these plans of his are certainly something. I have to admit, when he avoided telling me them so much, I half expected him to find a crusty hotel on the side of the highway and call it a day.

I walk back out of the bedroom and find him standing at the marble island, expertly popping the cork from a bottle of champagne that I can only assume comes complimentary for fancy digs like this.

He pours the bubbly liquid into two flute stem glasses and holds one out toward me. It's then that I notice, on the center of the kitchen island, sits a charcuterie tray of cheeses and crackers and fruit and cured meats and nuts.

I reach out to grab a grape and pop it into my mouth before taking a long sip of my champagne.

"So," he says with a secret smile. "How did I do? Have I exceeded your expectations?"

I shrug one nonchalant shoulder. "That depends."

He quirks one curious brow. "On what, exactly?"

"On what you're going to do with me now that you have me here."

A devil-may-care smile kisses his mouth, and it reminds me so much of the man I met all those weeks ago at Orchid. The one who caught my eye. The one whom I picked for a very specific and temporary purpose but found it hard to stick with the plan. The one who nearly tempted me into forgetting what that challenge card said and seeing where the night took us.

"*Everything*," he says, and his voice has that raspy edge that I love so much.

"Everything?" I repeat with a little smile. "That sounds promising, but in order to achieve everything, you're going to have to catch me first."

"Catch you?" he questions and sets down his glass of champagne, but I don't give him a verbal response. Instead, a giggle escapes my throat as I make a beeline for the bedroom.

But by the time the bed is in my sights, Ty is right behind me and swooping me into his arms.

"Ah!" I squeal and he laughs, and before I know it, he's carrying me into the massive bathroom.

In an instant, I go from up in the air, secured against Ty's chest, to my favorite black flats being planted on the tile of the shower floor.

"What are you doing?!" I screech, and a melody of laughs leaves my lungs.

He just smirks, keeping eye contact with me the entire time, and reaches out to turn on the rain shower. Water pours from above our heads, and it is *ice-flipping-cold.*

"That's so cold!" I exclaim, and he just laughs, stepping forward to pull me tight against his body.

"Don't worry, doll, it'll heat up soon." His words are laced with silent and sexy promises that I don't have time to calculate because he presses his lips to mine. He takes my mouth in a hot, seductive kiss, dancing our lips and mingling our tongues, and his fingers thread through the strands of my now-wet hair at the base of my neck.

Holy hell, I needed this.

He growls as he deepens the kiss and reaches out to place his big hands on my ass. I'm back in the air again, my legs wrapped around his waist, and I can feel the hardness of his cock through our wet clothes, pressed directly against the apex of my thighs.

"Too many clothes," I whimper. "We have too many clothes."

He shows his agreement by setting me back on my feet and making quick work of our attire, each item hitting the tile floor with a wet plop.

Steam billows in the shower, the water is deliciously warm now, and Ty stands before me, completely bare. Droplets skate down the firm muscles of his chest and make their way over his rippled stomach and prominent V, until they showcase the way his hard cock juts out from his body.

He is the epitome of a perfect male specimen, and I am aroused to the point of insanity.

I want his mouth on me.

His hands on me.

His cock inside me.

I want him everywhere and all at once. It is an all-consuming feeling, and it's what spurs my body to crash into his.

"Fuck," he growls again, and his hands are all over me. His mouth is locked with mine again, teasing and feasting and sucking.

I moan and whimper, and I brace myself with my arms wrapped around his neck. And then I lift my legs again, wrapping them around his waist and opening my hips so that his cock is pressed right at my entrance.

It's the one place I need him the most. I'm downright desperate for it.

"Please," I whisper, and I should probably be embarrassed by how desperate I sound.

But fuck, I need this more than I need my next breath.

When he still hesitates, I take things into my own hands. I ease myself down onto him, his cock sliding past my entrance and just barely filling me.

But it's not enough. Not even close.

"Rachel," he breathes out my name again, but it's not out of questioning or concern. It's the same desperation that I'm feeling. That my voice and eyes have been showing. "I need you."

"I need you too."

On a groan, he grips my ass and pushes his cock inside me. He's deep, so deep, and tears prick my eyes. But it's not from intensity. It's from something else. Something intangible that I can understand. Something that feels a lot like relief. *And something that feels like you're falling.*

"One week was too long," he says, his mouth at my neck now, and his lips are kissing a path toward my ear. "I swear, I could spend the rest of my life inside you, and it wouldn't be enough."

Water blurs my vision, but I don't think it's from the shower.

"How do you always feel so good?" he questions and starts a rhythm that makes my breasts bounce against his chest. "Always so fucking good."

All I can do is bury my face in his shoulder, my hands still clutched around his neck, and synchronize my hips with his. And each time he fills me all the way up, incoherent moans spill from my lips.

How on earth does this feel so good?

Sex with Ty feels like a fever dream. Like I'm hallucinating. Like there's too much pleasure that my mind can't fully wrap itself around the reality.

And he doesn't stop.

He keeps sliding his cock in and out of me.

Keeps kissing me and touching me.

Keeps pushing me toward the edge.

"That's it," he whispers, and his voice is hoarse with pleasure. "Come on my cock, Rachel. Let me feel that sweet pussy of yours squeeze me tight."

I am a genie, and his words are my command. I come *hard*, so hard that every inch of my body, my legs, my belly, my arms, my breasts, *shake* in response.

And moments later, he comes too. With his cock deep inside me.

Holy Flipping A.

Did you just have the best sex of your entire life?

I can't be sure, but yeah, I think I just did.

THIRTY-FIVE

Ty

The sounds of the television fill my ears as I grab a clean *and* dry pair of boxer briefs from my leather overnight bag and slide them on.

When I turn around, I smile at the sight of Rachel perched on the king-sized hotel bed. She's still completely naked, her hair still slightly damp from our shower-sex rendezvous, and her eyes are fixated on the flat-screen on the opposite wall as she scrolls through channels. She's lying on her belly, her legs curled up over her gloriously bare ass, and her heels are crossed in the most adorable way.

Fuck, she's beautiful.

Unbidden, a thought pops into my mind, an unanswered question that I'm ready for her to answer.

"All right, I have to know. What was the challenge?"

Rachel pulls her eyes away from the television and tilts her head to the side. "What challenge?"

"The *challenge*," I repeat. "The night we met."

"Um…" A cute-as-fuck but mischievous smile kisses her full lips. "I don't remember."

"Bullshit!" I exclaim and dive headfirst onto the bed. My body bounces on the mattress, and I wrap my hands around Rachel's waist and flip her onto her back. She giggles and squeals as I tickle my fingers into her belly and ribs.

"Ah! Stop it!"

"I'll stop once you fess up, missy."

More giggles.

"*Rachel*, what was the challenge?" I ask, staring down at her and raising my brow as if to say, *I won't stop until you admit the truth.*

"I think I was mistaken," she says, and I start to tickle her ribs some more. She tries to squirm out of my grip, but it's useless. "Ah! Okay! Fine! I'll tell you! Just stop doing that!"

On a smile, I stop, but when she isn't quick to respond, I flash a pointed stare in her direction and start to gently dig my fingers into her belly again.

"Ty! Okay! Okay!" she shouts, raising the white flag. "I will tell you. Promise! Promise! Just stop tickling me!"

"Deal." I release her from my hold and gesture with one hand in the air. "Please proceed."

She rolls her pretty green eyes but does, in fact, proceed. "The challenge was based on some kind of promotional card for The Secret Club. It was the brand that was throwing the party that night at Orchid."

"I'm aware," I answer with a shrug. "I mean, it was my brother Jude and sister-in-law Sophie who threw the shindig."

"Holy hell. I literally just now put that together. I thought they looked kind of familiar at the hospital, but—" She shakes her head. "Man, sometimes, it really is a small world. Anyway, both Lydia and I grabbed one of these challenge cards they had set out for people to take. And the challenge on my card is what led me to the dance floor where you just so happened to be."

"Wait… The challenge card instructed you to give a random stranger your panties?"

"Well, no, not exactly."

"Then, what did it say?"

"I don't know," she says and turns on her side to bury her face into one of the cushy pillows. "*Some bout hotnessth eye duh might forget they sight.*" Her muffled voice and garbled response make me laugh.

"What?" I question and flip her back around toward me. "Repeat that one more time."

This time, she covers her face with both hands. "The card said to make the hottest guy in the room remember you for the rest of his life," she rambles in a rush and then proceeds to bury her face in one of the pillows again.

"Hold up…" I pause with what I assume is the biggest smile in existence. "The challenge was to find the hottest guy at Orchid? And you chose me?"

Oh, hell motherfucking yes.

"Don't get too cocky," she retorts and sits back up to meet my eyes. "I mean, I didn't take that much time to find a hot guy. So, it's not like I scoured the place or anything."

She's so full of shit, and I love it.

"Let me ask you this," I continue on, my smile a permanent fixture now. I could die, and they'd still have to bury me like this. "Did you decide to give your panties away before or after you decided that I was the hottest guy at Orchid?"

"Why would that matter?"

"Oh, trust me, it matters. A lot."

"I don't know," she responds and rolls her eyes. "I can't remember the order."

"You are so full of shit," I tease her and proceed to pull her onto my lap. I adjust her body so that her legs are straddling my hips and she can't avoid eye contact. "Admit it, Rachel. You didn't want to give just anyone your panties that night. You wanted to give them to *me.*"

She eyes me with annoyance. "I take it that version of the story is making you feel really good about yourself, huh?"

"Yeah." I press a kiss to her mouth and nip at her bottom lip. "But I also know that's not a *version* of the story. It's the *truth*."

"Whatever you say, Ty."

"Admit it," I whisper into her ear and use one hand to brush her hair off her shoulder. "You wanted to give me your panties." My lips are at her neck, and I don't hesitate to reach my tongue out and taste her sweet skin. "Damn, Rachel, I thought that night was hot to begin with, but this new information, well, it takes it up one thousand fucking notches."

"What?" She leans back to look into my eyes. "Seriously?"

"*Seriously.*" I take one of her pert nipples into my mouth and suck. "And now, because of all that, it's time for round two."

"Round two?"

"Yeah, doll. Round two." I punctuate that statement by pressing my hard cock against her. "I need to be inside you. Again. *Right now.*"

Rachel doesn't balk at my demand.

Not my sweet Rachel. She's always game.

"Ohhhh, *round two*," she muses and flutters her eyelashes dramatically before tossing herself back onto the bed and throwing her hands out beside her. "Fuck me like I'm one of your French girls, Jack!"

Titanic. She just quoted *Titanic.* Well, almost. *Fucking hell, how can one woman be sexy and adorable at the same time?*

"Uhh…" I pause on a laugh as I remove my boxer briefs and toss them to the floor. "I'm pretty sure that's not how that went, but I'll work with it, Rose."

She giggles, grins, and then, she surprises the fuck out of me by placing her hands on my shoulders, climbing back onto my lap, and slowly easing herself onto my cock. Inch by inch, she takes *all* of me inside her. And fuck if I don't feel equal parts proud and in awe of her.

No other woman on the planet compares.

"You're the best," I say and grip her gorgeous hips, guiding her movements with mine. "*The fucking best.*"

I swear, if I end up fucking us to death tonight, I'll die a happy man.

We've only been in our hotel suite for four or so hours, and I'm realizing that orgasms make Rachel sleepy.

After we fucked ourselves senseless, I made a quick phone call to room service, and despite how badly I wanted to wake Rachel up for round number four—*or is it five?*—I let her sleep and busied myself with the task of a hot shower.

Shower number two, mind you, but one that was horribly boring in comparison to the first one that occurred inside this hotel bathroom.

I take my time, knowing that room service won't be here for at least another forty minutes, and by the time I'm clean, dry, and dressed enough to answer the door, I step back out of the bathroom.

Though, I'm shocked to find that sleeping beauty is no longer sleeping.

Still completely naked, but with a pen in her hand, she has a furrowed brow as she writes something on the flesh of her right thigh. She's completely engrossed in whatever she's doing and not the least bit aware of my presence in the bedroom.

"Hey there," I greet, my voice quiet so I don't startle. But when she doesn't respond, doesn't look up, I try again. "Rachel?"

Green eyes wide, she jolts her gaze upward until it meets mine.

"What are you doing?"

"Uh…" She pauses and glances down at her naked body for a brief moment before meeting my curious gaze again. "I'm sure this looks strange, huh?"

"Not strange," I correct her. "More like, *interesting.*"

"Well…" A self-deprecating laugh leaves her lips. "I'm…writing?"

"On your skin?"

"Yeah?" she answers, though it's more of a question than a statement.

"So…pen and skin is your preferred method?" I smile as I walk over toward the bed and sit down on the edge of the mattress that's closest to her. "I wouldn't say it's the most efficient method, but definitely the most fascinating one I've seen." With one index finger, I reach out and gently trace the words she's etched on her thigh.

In a garden of weeds

beneath ash and dust and dirt

and not a flower in sight

hope bloomed.

"Hi, my name is Rachel Rose, and I'm a weirdo," she whispers quietly through an embarrassed giggle. When I look up to meet her eyes, she cringes. Though, I don't know why she's cringing. This is the most adorable, intriguing fucking thing I've ever seen in my life.

"Do you do this often?"

"When I was a kid? Yes," she answers with a little shrug of her bare shoulder. "But for the past several years? No. Not at all."

I stare down at her skin again, tracing the words again with my finger, and smile. "This is beautiful."

"You think so?" Her voice is so quiet I almost don't hear it.

"I know so," I respond and mean every word. And I can't stop myself from wondering what these words mean to her.

What inspired her to write them? What hope has bloomed? And do I have anything to do with it?

"Can I tell you a secret?" she asks, and her voice is still so quiet, so vulnerable, that I give her my full attention without even thinking about it.

"Always."

"I love the idea of writing a novel, but if I had a choice, I would write poetry."

"And who says you don't have a choice?"

She shrugs. "The great Nadine Rose didn't write poetry."

"Yeah, but I didn't ask about Nadine Rose," I respond and reach out to brush a piece of hair out of her face. "I asked about the great Rachel Rose."

She rolls her eyes and snorts. Like my saying the great Rachel Rose doesn't apply. Doesn't mean anything.

"I already knew your words were powerful," I tell her. "I've seen it in the notes you write on my students' essays. I've also caught a few glimpses of some of your grad school papers that you maybe didn't want me to read, but I accidentally read them."

"*What?*" she questions on a shocked laugh. "When have you been reading my papers?"

"Don't be mad, but you've been saving them in my Drive, and I just couldn't help myself."

"Ty!" she exclaims and smacks a playful hand to my chest. "You little sneak!"

"I'm sorry?" I respond, though, I'm not sorry at all. Rachel's mind intrigues me endlessly.

"You don't sound very sorry," she chastises, though her smiling mouth is the opposite of her words.

"Well, I am. To a point. I mean, it's not my fault you're really fucking intriguing. And brilliant."

Her gaze turns so soft it makes a little ache form inside my chest. "You think I'm brilliant?"

"Yes. Of course I do." I rub my thumb across the words she drew on her skin. "And these words right here are proof that I'm right."

She just stares down at where my hand meets her thigh.

"You should write more, Rachel," I whisper toward her and press a soft kiss to her forehead. "Not because I think you should live up to some kind of expectations, but because I think you're really talented."

She starts to open her mouth but quickly closes it.

And I decide not to push the conversation further.

I said what I needed to say. I said what I think she deserved to hear.

"By the way, I hope you're hungry," I add, purposely changing the subject as I get off the bed. "Because I ordered just about everything off the room service menu. They should be here shortly."

She snorts. "You're all about the everything this week, aren't you?"

"Oh, doll, you have no idea," I answer and walk back over toward her to bury my face between her bare breasts. I lick and suck at her nipples until she's squealing uncontrollably.

And I don't pull away until I hear three knocks sound from the door.

"Room service!" a male voice calls from the hallway.

"First, we eat," I call over my shoulder as I head out of the bedroom. "And then, I dine!"

Her responding laughter follows me all the way to the door.

I'm starting to think it might be the best thing I've ever heard.

THIRTY-SIX

Monday, March 4th

Rachel

Sunlight peeks in through the windows of our hotel room, and I blink my eyes open. When I reach out to feel the spot beside mine, the one where Ty should be, I realize he's already out of bed.

What time is it? I wonder and turn on my side to grab my phone off the nightstand.

7:30 a.m. glares back at me.

Ugh. Too early.

I squint, and when I spot two missed text message notifications on the screen, I open my inbox and realize they're from my father. The first came in about thirty minutes ago.

Dad: There's still time for me to swing by and pick you up on my way to the conference. Call me.

And the second one was delivered about ten minutes ago.

Dad: Rachel, sweetheart, I can't deny this is highly disappointing. I thought you were realizing what it means to be focused on your career.

Why does he always have to make things so damn difficult?

I throw my head back onto the pillows and sigh. When that doesn't ease the annoyance, I turn onto my belly and silently scream into the cushy fabric. And once I finish with my tiny hissy fit, I decide on two things—I'm not going to text him back, and I'm not going to feel guilty about it.

I already told him that I was busy this week.

Sure, I'm busy spending the week with someone he explicitly told me not to, but I don't care. It's no one's business but mine. And Ty's. We are both grown-ass adults who are capable of making their own decisions.

Officially talked off the guilt-ledge, I slide out of bed, my mind focused on enjoying the day.

After a quick pit stop in the bathroom to pee and brush my teeth, I head out into the main area of our suite to see where the sexy man with the talented mouth and big cock is hiding.

It doesn't take long before I spot the sight of his tight ass in a pair of boxer briefs.

"Good morning," I croak out as I shuffle from the small hallway of our suite into the kitchen, where Ty is currently pouring coffee into not one but two mugs. "I really hope one of those is for me."

"Of course." He grins, and I don't miss the fact that he adds two scoops of sugar and a little bit of whole milk to one mug—*my exact coffee preference*—and hands that mug to me. I also know that he won't add anything to the other cup, which he doesn't, because Ty prefers his coffee black.

I have no idea when we got to the point where we know how each other likes our coffee, but apparently, that's exactly where we're at.

It's probably because things are starting to feel serious…

I force myself to take a drink from the mug, and Ty hitches one boxer-brief-covered hip against the counter.

"How'd you sleep?"

"Like I have the past two nights." I smile at him over my coffee. "Like a damn baby because I'm pretty sure this hotel's mattress and bedding are produced in actual heaven."

"Same." He chuckles and reaches out to playfully tug on the belt of the white hotel robe that's currently covering my body. "By the way, I ordered us a room service breakfast. Should be here in about twenty minutes."

"If you tell me there are going to be waffles again, I will kiss you right now."

For the past two mornings of our not-being-good week together, I've had the Carlyle's room service waffles. And let me tell you, they are the best damn waffles that have ever existed. It's as if they ship them in from Belgium every morning.

His responding smile is as wide as Texas, and he taps his mouth with one index finger. "Go ahead and pay up, Rach."

"You're my hero!" I cheer and stand up on my tippy-toes to softly plant my lips against his. "Thank you."

"If that's the response I'll get every time I get you waffles for breakfast, I swear, I'll keep you stocked in them for a lifetime," he teases, but his words aren't lost on me.

For a lifetime. As in, we're going to be together for that long?

A little zing of something shoots inside my chest, and I have to clear my throat to quell the sensation. "So…uh…what's on the agenda today?"

"Considering we've spent the past forty-eight hours holed up in this suite, fucking each other's brains out, I figured we'd get out for a bit. Get some fresh air. Pretend to be New York tourists for the day."

He's not wrong. Ever since he checked us in to our room, it's been a certified naked sex-fest. In the shower. On the bed. On the couch. On the kitchen island. We've christened just about every surface of this suite. So much so that I now walk around with a constant, delicious ache of a reminder that proves just how many times Ty has been inside me.

But even though I think his plan of spending the day in the city is absolutely grand, I can't stop myself from toying with him a little.

"Wait…" I pause and feign a pout. "Are you saying you're done fucking my brains out?"

"No." A laugh jumps from his lips as he sets his mug down on the counter. "That's not what I'm saying at all."

"Are you sure?" I put a hand to my hip. "Because it really seemed like you were saying you're done with all the hot fucking and you just want to do touristy stuff."

"Oh, my sweet, clever Rachel," he muses and steps toward me. A moment later, my coffee mug is out of my hands and set on the counter beside his. "I love how you love to challenge me. It's like you can't stop yourself from it."

"Challenge you?" I ask with an innocent little tilt of my head. "I'm not challenging you."

He smirks like the devil and lifts me up by the ass to set me down on the counter. "Oh yes, you are, but like I said, I fucking love it."

"So…is this a change of plans?" I ask hopefully, and he smirks like his head is full of dirty, bad things that I'm certain I'd love to hear about.

"First, I'm going to eat *my* breakfast," he explains, pushing my legs apart and shoving my robe up my thighs until I'm completely bare from the waist down. "Then, room service should be here with your waffles."

"And what's your breakfast?" *Please say me. Please say me.*

"I love when you act all innocent, even though you and I both know that you're silently hoping I'm going to put my mouth on you." He slides one finger inside me, and it feels so good that my head falls back against the overhead cabinet door behind me. "That's what you want, isn't it, Rachel? You want to come on my tongue."

Call it a coincidence, but that just so happens to be *exactly* what I want.

"Show me how much you want it," he demands, and I can't hide my truth.

Though, I don't give him actual words. I only give *action*. I dig my teeth into my bottom lip, spread my thighs as far as they can go, and lift up my legs so that my heels dig into the counter beneath me.

He nods, surveying my exposed position. "That's what I thought."

And then he buries his face between my thighs and doesn't come up for air until I'm doing exactly what he said—*coming on his tongue.* Just as he promised he would, he's changed the way I look at early mornings forever.

Hot damn, what is this man doing to me?

Like he said, everything.

For the past three hours, we've engaged in all things touristy. Things I have honestly never done, even though I've lived in New York for most of my life.

After a stroll through Central Park, we headed to Times Square, where Ty made me take a million selfies with him while crowds of people got annoyed at us for standing in their way.

We walked into the M&M'S store and bought about three pounds too many of colored chocolate candies. Ty took a picture with Pikachu. And Spider-Man. And Batman. All of them costing ten bucks a pop.

And we bought every piece of *I heart New York* merchandise that we could find in a little mom-and-pop shop. Hats, sweatshirts, magnets, coffee cups, you name it, and we now own it.

For an early March day, it is unseasonably warm, and the sun is shining as we stroll through a little part of the city better known as Greenwich Village.

Ty comes to a stop in front of a store, and I look up to read the sign above the door—**NYC Vintage Books.**

"You want to give it a look?"

"Are you kidding me?" I whoop and nod three times too many. "Vintage books are my jam."

"Well then, after you, milady." He smiles down at me as he holds open the door.

A little bell chimes as we step inside, and instantly, I'm hit with the most wonderful smell in the whole wide world—*old books*. And right before my very eyes sit shelves and shelves and shelves of literature.

Oh man. This is a booklover's dream.

"It's go time, Rach." Ty turns his I heart NYC ball cap around, and his eyes turn all business. "You can't bring an English professor into a vintage bookstore and not expect him to go HAM."

I laugh. "You're insane."

But he ignores me completely, spinning on his heel and heading toward the back of the store.

"The best shit is always hidden in the back!"

An older man with white hair and spectacle glasses looks up from his spot behind the register and glares at me.

"Please excuse him," I apologize on Ty's behalf. "He gets really excited about books."

"Because I fucking love books, Rachel!" Ty's voice bounces off the walls. "Tell him how much I fucking love books!"

"Again, I'm very sorry," I whisper toward the man even though it's taking everything inside me not to laugh. "He doesn't get out much."

The man just huffs out an exasperated sigh, going back to reading the newspaper that sits in his lap, and I proceed to put as much distance between Mr. Annoyed and me as I can.

But once my eyes catch sight of a giant glass case with a sign that reads **First Editions**, I take a sharp right to check it out.

"Damn," I mutter to myself once the display stands before me like a literary beacon.

Truly, it's one heck of a collection. Austen and Whitman and Woolf and Fitzgerald and Lee, all the greats are inside. I gently run my fingers along the glass as I move down the cabinet, taking in every name, every title, every cover. And when I reach the middle point of the shelf, I realize this cabinet is unlocked.

As in, I can peek inside.

As in, I can carefully touch the books of my heroes.

I probably shouldn't…

Or should I?

When I make a silent promise to be gentle with the books, I quietly slide open one of the glass doors and ease the fingers of my right hand inside. Once they make contact with vintage spines, I peek over my shoulder to see if the man at the front is about to call the cops.

But when I see that he's still staring down at his newspaper, I decide I have the green light to touch the books a little longer. The realization makes me giddy, and a barely there squeal jumps from my throat. I know, to most people, I probably sound ridiculous, but…vintage books. *First edition* vintage books at that.

It's almost better than sex. *Almost.*

I am smiling like the sun as I move down the row of books, my fingers still touching every single spine with the most delicate touch. But my smile turns to something else when I pause at a title, *a name*, that steals the breath from my lungs.

Nadine Rose. ***I am in all things.***

My mother's book, her *only* book, and I can't remember the last time I saw it.

Or *read* it.

It's probably been years.

This book, right here, is the novel that made Nadine Rose a name. It's the book that allowed the world to see she was a writer. A *real* and worthy writer.

A reviewer in the *New York Times* called her book "a literary gem that would live on for generations to come."

This book kept her on every best-seller list in existence for months. It landed her interviews in magazines and appearances on talk shows and book signings that drew insane crowds.

I was just a kid, but I remember all of it.

I remember her dancing and screaming in the kitchen when my father showed her she'd made her first best-seller list. And I remember sitting inside a studio green room with Lydia while our mom was being interviewed by a celebrity journalist.

It was one of the most exciting times in my life. An absolute whirlwind. But in hindsight, I realize that it was actually the calm before the storm. It was the short span of time when everything felt exciting and vibrant and wonderful before it turned into one of the hardest times of my family's life.

When I look down, I realize the book is now in my hands. I have no idea when I pulled it from the shelf, but it's there, gripped between my fingers. I stare down at the cover. At her name etched at the bottom. At the title.

I flip it over to read the back and fondly remember the novel itself. A tragic story about grief and loss and love, successful Marcus loses his wife and child and spirals into a black hole. And it takes a therapist by the name of Cecilia to pull him out of it.

It's one of those books that carves a hole in your heart, but somehow, once you finish it, you're thankful for that hole. Because it's a reminder. An imprint. A core memory of something you never want to forget.

I open the book and run my fingers over the pages, and I don't stop until I find the one page that holds my favorite passage. I stare down at the words in awe. *My mother, she was talented beyond belief.*

"What are you looking at?"

I startle at the sound of Ty's voice and nearly drop my mother's book in the process.

"Shit," I mutter and gently grip the novel back to my chest. "You scared me."

"Sorry, doll," he says, his voice all laid-back and relaxed. Before I know it, he's standing beside me with his arm around my shoulders. "What book is—?" he starts to ask but stops himself when his eyes take in the title. "Wow."

"Yeah." I nod, and all of a sudden, I have the strangest urge to cry in the middle of this bookstore. I swallow hard around the ball in my throat, forcing the tears to go back to wherever they came from.

"This is one of my favorite books," Ty says quietly, and I look up to meet his eyes. "I'm serious," he adds, as if my face is calling him out. "It's one of the best novels I've ever read."

All I can do is look back down at the book in my hands, the pages still open to my favorite passage.

"It's my favorite book," I say, but my voice sounds so quiet. "Though, I guess you could say I'm biased."

"*Love is in all things,*" Ty reads the exact words I've been staring at for the past however many minutes, and it makes my heart feel all weird inside my chest. "*Love was in your child's eyes. It was in your wife's kiss. And it is in the tears of your grief. The cracks of your heart. And each painful breath you take. Love is the reason for everything. Without love, we are nothing. Mean nothing. Want nothing. Need nothing.*"

Once he finishes, he doesn't say anything. He simply presses a kiss to my forehead and just stands there with me, his arm tenderly wrapped around my shoulders, and both of us staring down at my mother's book.

And I'm overwhelmed again, but this time, it's because I feel like I need to admit something.

Something that feels like a dark secret.

"You know, I don't even have a copy of her book."

"Why not?" he asks, but there's no judgment or assumption in his voice.

"I did, but then, I didn't." I shrug, and even I can't explain why.

Because it made me miss her? Because seeing her words made me feel as if it was impossible for me to live up to my father's expectations?

A combination of both?

Anyone's guess is as good as mine.

"And just think, you could get this very copy for only twelve hundred dollars," Ty teases, and oddly enough, it's exactly what I need.

A soft laugh jumps from my chest. "Nadine would lose her shit if she knew her first editions were going for that much."

Ty squeezes my shoulder on a chuckle, and eventually, I slide my mother's book back onto the shelf and pull the glass door closed.

"Did you find anything good?" I ask him, and he shakes his head.

"I think it's a sign I have too many books."

"Too many books?" I question on a theatrical gasp. "That's blasphemous, Ty. Take those words back right now."

"Relax, little bookworm," he says with a chuckle and squeezes my ass. "I'm just kidding."

"Thank goodness," I say and brush my hand over my forehead. "Otherwise, we couldn't be friends anymore."

"Friends?" he questions with a waggle of his brows. "Rach, my cock has been inside you too many times for us to be just friends."

I giggle at that. "Yeah, you're probably right."

"Damn straight," he volleys back. "Now, are you ready to get out of here and do something...unexpected?"

"Unexpected?" I nod. "Hm. Yeah. Okay. You have my attention."

"So, I know you already found the hottest guy in the world, but are you up for another challenge?"

"Hottest guy in the room," I correct him on a laugh, but he ignores me completely.

"I know it's no easy feat finding the hottest guy in the universe, but this challenge is doable. Fun, even."

"Oh, so you're the hottest guy in the universe now?"

He waggles his brows again. "It's a tough job, baby, but somehow, I manage."

"Did anyone ever tell you that you're a little bit full of yourself?"

"Hottest guy in existence? Yes, I've been told. But full of myself?" He taps his chin like he's actually thinking about it. "Nah. I don't recall that one."

I playfully shove at his chest. "What's the big challenge?"

"Now, don't get excited. I know when I say big, you're automatically thinking about my cock," he whispers into my ear. "Which, I get. I do have a big cock."

I roll my eyes even though I can't deny the facts—Ty is big. Like, the biggest I've ever been with. Though, I'm keeping that information to myself for obvious reasons.

"Are you ever going to get to the point?" I question with a defiant hand to my hip. "Or are we just going to stand inside this bookstore while you wax poetic about yourself?"

"C'mon, bossy." He wraps his arm around my shoulders and guides me out of the bookstore and toward the nearest crosswalk. "It's challenge time."

As we cross the street, I realize I'm smiling so big it's starting to hurt my cheeks. Which then makes me roll my eyes and laugh silently. This man, I swear. How does he always manage to put me in a good mood?

Because he's the one...

I pause, chastising my own thought, and then finish it in a way that makes me feel at least a modicum better.

Because he's the one chasing your happiness.

THIRTY-SEVEN

Ty

I grab Rachel's hand and lead her to a shop I spotted right before we walked into the bookstore. Originally, I didn't even consider it as something we needed to check out, but after I found her standing in the aisle with her mother's book in her hands and her eyes glazed over with emotion, it became imperative.

But it's not for the reasons most people would think. It's a hell of a lot more complex and solely based on intuition.

When we come to a halt in front of the entrance, Rachel stares up at the sign that hangs above the door and contains only two words—**Secret Pleasures**.

"You brought me to a sex toy shop?" she asks and glances between me and the sign.

"I sure did." I grin at her and step forward to open the door. "Just…trust me, okay?"

"Why do those feel like famous last words?" she retorts back, and I chuckle.

"Just get your sexy ass inside so I can tell you the challenge."

She stares at me for a long moment before huffing out a melodramatic sigh and stepping over the threshold.

"Welcome to the best sex toys that New York can offer," I announce and gesture toward the inside of the store with an accommodating hand. "This store is legendary. Anyone who is anyone has been inside these four walls. Marilyn Monroe. Frank Sinatra. Three of the Kardashians. Rumor has it that Jack Nicholson buys all his favorite ladies a special gift from this very place."

"Jack Nicholson?" She stares forward, her eyes taking in the discreet shop that is filled with just about every kind of sex-related toy, lube, lingerie, dildo, game that you can imagine. "Are you serious?"

"Not at all," I answer with a wink. "But I'm sure you'll be able to find what you're looking for."

"Oh my God, I should've known!" Rachel's responding giggles make my heart feel like it's about to burst through my damn rib cage. "You're insane."

"When you say insane, I'm pretty sure you mean awesome and handsome and really fucking fun."

She snorts. "Oh yeah, that's exactly what I mean."

"Now, Rach, are you ready for your challenge?"

"If you're going to tell me we're fucking in the dildo aisle, I'm leaving."

I laugh. Outright. "That is not the challenge. Though, you pose an interesting premise."

"Ty."

"Fine. Okay." I hold up both hands. "Your challenge… Walk around this store and look at all the inventory until you find one thing, one special, exciting, wild thing that you want to try but have never done."

"Try? As in, this week? With you?"

"It is our week of not-being-good, right?"

"Right." She grins, and I can't stop myself from stepping forward to press a kiss to her lips.

"Let the challenge begin."

She turns on her heel, but a second later, she turns back around and meets my eyes. "Wait… Are there any restrictions?"

I shake my head. "The only rule is that you have to pick something that makes you excited to try."

She taps her chin and squints toward me. "And if I want to try putting nipple clamps on you? That counts?"

"If it makes you excited to think about, yes."

"Damn, you didn't even blink before you answered," she muses on a laugh. "You'd actually let me put nipple clamps on you?"

"Doll, if it's something that will give you pleasure, I'm open to it. Always."

Truthfully, this challenge isn't really about sex or pleasure. Though, it's certainly a bonus. It's about Rachel getting to make a choice. For herself and only herself.

Why do I think she needs this? I don't really know; it's just something I felt when we were standing inside the bookstore. She's a woman who is carrying the weight of the world in expectations. Some are self-inflicted, but a lot are not ones she's chosen.

And right now, she needs to feel in control. Empowered to make her own decision without my or anyone else's involvement.

She searches my eyes for a long moment, for what, I'm not sure, but eventually, she turns on her heel again. Only this time, she starts her perusal of the store.

Obviously, I'm silently hoping she doesn't decide on a pair of goddamn nipple clamps for me, but yeah, I don't get a say in the matter.

And if she *does* come back with nipple clamps for my chest? Well then, looks like I might need to buy a little Vaseline on our way back to the hotel.

Rachel spent an hour inside Secret Pleasures, searching through the shelves of all things sex-focused. And I gave her the time and space to make her choice. Instead of following behind her, I simply handed the nice young lady at the register my credit card and let her know I'd be outside and to use that to pay for whatever Rachel chose.

By the time she made her way out into the sun, a discreet, little black bag was clutched between her fingers and a contagious smile was on her lips.

"So, when do I get to show you what I bought?" she asks when we're about three blocks away from the hotel.

I wink at her. "When I tell you it's time."

"So, like, when we get back to the hotel?" she questions, swinging the black bag at her hip and leaning forward to meet my eyes as our feet move down the sidewalk and take a right onto the street that leads to the Carlyle.

I shrug. "Not necessarily."

"Is this happening this week?"

"Yes." I wrap my arm around her shoulders, tucking her close to my side, and carefully move her out of the way of a man walking a mile a minute and staring down at his feet.

"Today?"

I shrug again. "Maybe?"

"Tomorrow?"

"Maybe?"

"What the hell?" she blurts out on an exasperated laugh.

I love that she's excited to use whatever is inside that bag, but I also know that when you have to wait, when you have to let that excitement grow, it makes it even better.

"It's all about anticipation, doll."

I can't say when we're going to open that bag, but I know, when the moment is there, Rachel is going to experience something she's never done before.

I can't fucking wait.

THIRTY-EIGHT

Friday, March 8th

Rachel

I step off the elevator with fresh coffee and bagels from a little shop up the street from the Carlyle and head down the carpeted hallway toward our hotel suite.

Once I'm inside, I can hear the faint sounds of a news station playing on the television. And when I make my way into the main room, I find Ty sitting on the couch, his fingers tapping across the screen of his phone.

"Well, good morning," I greet him and carry our breakfast over to the marble coffee table.

He meets my eyes and smiles a sleepy, sexy smile. "I was wondering where you went."

"I figured we'd go for a lighter breakfast this morning."

He chuckles at that. "I was wondering when you'd get worn out on waffles."

"Don't be ridiculous." I roll my eyes and hand him his black coffee. "I will never get tired of this hotel's waffles."

Well, I am *temporarily* tired of them after having them every morning for six days straight, but I'll die before admitting that. The waffles would hear me, and I'm not willing to tarnish the one good, steady relationship in my life that easily. Food and I, we're ride or die.

"Whatever you say," he responds and takes a hesitant sip from his coffee. "*Mmm.* Americano. Just like I like it." But when he opens his mouth to say something else, his phone chimes from his lap. He picks it up and reads the screen, a laugh and a sigh leaving his throat at the same time. "I should've known this day would come."

"What day?" I question. Ty holds up his phone toward me, and my eyes scan the text messages that are front and center on his screen.

Mama Winslow: Ty, he is a very nice man. His name is Howard Sulken.

Ty: How did you meet this guy?

Mama Winslow: TapNext. We've been chatting over the past few weeks, but this will be the first time we see each other in person. I'm a little nervous, honestly.

I meet his gaze over the screen of his phone. "Your mom online dates?"

He rolls his eyes and shakes his head at the same time. "It's something new she's doing."

"Well, that's not a bad thing, right? Everyone deserves someone if that's what brings them happiness. I mean, I wish my father would date. Maybe he'd forget to ride my ass if a woman kept him busy."

Ty smiles brightly and without judgment, despite the petty sound of my gripe. "He's never dated?"

"C'mon." I snort. "You know him. Have you ever seen him doing anything besides work?"

"No, I haven't." Ty smirks. "Honestly, it took several years of knowing him for me to know anything about his personal life. He always kept it about literature and my career. Though, I think I needed that more than he did. If he'd made it about himself, I think personal conversations would have been way more frequent. He needed a friend after losing Nadine, but he knew I needed a mentor more."

For some reason, the information is a shock to my system. Maybe because it feels like Ty's revealing something about himself and my father at the same time.

"What do you mean?"

"Your dad is one of the reasons I managed to get my shit together," he explains. "I was kind of a lost cause back in the day. I was wild—uncontrollable almost—but Nate was patient enough with me to see beyond that. He saw potential in my personality and found a way to focus it."

"*Potential*," I gripe. "That's practically a dirty word as far as I'm concerned. All I've ever been told is that I'm not living up to it."

He shakes his head. "Rachel, he doesn't say those things because he thinks you're a lost cause. He says it because he thinks you're brilliant. Hell, when he asked me if you could be my TA, that's the word he used to describe you. Someone thinking the world of you isn't a bad place to start. You just have to find a way to common ground."

I don't know what to make of his words, so I just leave them be and turn the conversation back to his mother.

"And when is your mom going on this date of hers?"

He studies me closely for long moments and then gives me my peace, moving on as well. He slides his finger across the screen, scrolling to the bottom of the text chat, and then types out a message, turning the phone to show me after he hits send.

Ty: The nerves are nothing to take seriously, Ma. Everyone feels that way on a first date. But one thing you should take seriously is date SAFETY. Name the time and place, and I'll be there.

Mama Winslow: How chivalrous, darling. But there's no way in hell I'm telling you where my date is tonight.

I laugh so hard I snort, turning the phone back to him.

"She knows you well, huh?"

Ty's fingers move furiously over the screen after he gets a load of her response, and I can't help but giggle as I watch him. Watching his mom make him squirm might be even more fun than doing it myself.

Ty: It's tonight??? What the F, Ma???

Mama Winslow: Goodbye, Ty. Enjoy your secret spring break week with Rachel.

He told his mom about our week? That's…surprising.

"I wanted us to go chaperone, but she refuses to tell me where in the hell they're going."

"Ty!" I exclaim on a giggle. "You can't chaperone your mom's date."

"Why the fuck not?" he questions and sets his phone down on the coffee table. "What if this Howard is a lunatic?"

"Don't be dramatic. *Howard* screams bingo, not psycho. Your mom deserves to be able to go on a date without one of her sons spying on her."

"I wouldn't be spying. Just *observing*. To make sure she's safe."

"You'd be spying, and you know it." I flash a knowing grin at him, and he pulls me into his lap on a groan.

"Fine. I'd be spying. But it'd be for good reason. I should be able to make sure this old fuck keeps his hands to himself."

"Wait a minute…" I pause and search his eyes. "Are you worried about something happening, or are you jealous that your mom is going on a date night that doesn't include you?"

The other evening, when we were chatting about our families over dinner at an Italian restaurant and I was telling him about my relationship with Lydia and Lou, he mentioned that he takes his mom out on monthly date nights.

And you thought it was really fucking cute.

"A little bit of both?" he retorts on a quiet chuckle. "But mostly, I'm worried. She's my mom, and she met some random idiot on TapNext. Pretty sure I have a right to be concerned."

"That's valid," I tell him and tap his nose with my index finger. "But you need to give her space on this. She deserves it."

"Yeah, yeah," he mutters and slides his hands under my ass to give it a squeeze. "I'll give her space. But you bet your ass I'll be texting her tonight to make sure she got home okay."

"How about you text her that?" I suggest. "Just tell her to have fun, but that you would appreciate it if she let you know when she makes it home safely."

He sighs. Searches my eyes. And then adjusts me on his lap so he can reach down and grab his phone again. His fingers fly across the screen, and I watch as he types out a message.

Ty: Three more things, Ma. #1: Have fun tonight. #2: Text me when you get home, so I know you're safe. #3: Let that clown know if he does anything stupid, I'll break his fucking fingers off.

"How's that?"

"Uh…" I laugh and press a kiss to his lips before climbing out of his lap and onto my feet. "A little aggressive, but a lot better than you trying to go on her date with her."

"Where are you going?"

"I have to pee!" I call over my shoulder.

"Grab the black bag when you come back."

I skid to a stop in the middle of the hallway. "I'm sorry, did you say *black bag?*"

"I did."

Oh boy. *The black bag.* The one that's been sitting on Ty's nightstand since Monday afternoon. A nondescript little bag that holds the item I picked out from the sex store.

Instantly, a rush of excitement sets up shop between my thighs, and I make quick work of the bathroom. Two minutes later, I have the bag in my hands and I'm handing it over to him.

"I can't fucking wait to see what you chose." He grins up at me and his fingers gently pry open the bag, but he doesn't pull out my selection right away.

Instead, he just stares down at it, and all of a sudden, my excitement and anticipation start to mix with awkwardness.

I've been waiting for what feels forever for this moment. Almost the entire week, in fact. But now that it's here, I don't know what to do with myself. Or my hands. I am Rachel Rose playing Will Ferrell playing Ricky Bobby, and my hands are up and they're down. They're at my sides. They're all over the damn place.

"You're nervous," Ty states, his eyes raking over my now-jumpy state.

"I…*yeah*. A little."

"Why?"

"I don't know." I shrug and fidget my hands together. "I guess because I don't know what you're going to think?"

"Come here." He shifts the bag and gestures for me to sit down in his lap. "Let's look at it together."

Oh boy. I don't know why that shoots a thrill up my spine, but it does.

Once I'm back on his lap, he wraps his arms around me and slides my selection out of the bag right in front of both of us. His fingers make quick work of the small box, and then, it's there, the item I chose.

A small, glass anal plug.

It feels like it takes him three lifetimes to say something, but I know that's just the anxiety talking. Time whooshes in my ears, and dust floats in front of me. It's not him going slow—it's me having an out-of-body experience.

"Why did you choose this?" he asks me, putting me out of my uncertain misery.

I turn my head to explore his face for criticism or judgment or question, but his eyes are relaxed, and the hint of a smile sits at the corners of his mouth. It's comforting. "Because you said it should be something a little wild, something I've never tried."

"And because the idea of trying it excites you?"

I nod, though if I trusted myself to speak, there'd be more to the story. The idea of trying it *with him* excites me. I've never really been the type of girl who was into anything like this, but for some reason, with Ty, the idea is thrilling.

"Any other reason?"

"Because I want to feel full. *Back there.* While you're inside me." *And because when you said my ass was yours, it made me feel crazy. But in the best way.*

He presses a soft kiss to my lips. "Then that's exactly what we'll do."

"Yeah?" My heart starts up one hell of a pounding rhythm inside my chest. "Like, right now?"

"Yes." One word and I feel like I might start panting like a dog.

Oh, holy moly! It's happening! Everyone calm down! It's happening! My insides are a Michael Scott GIF come to life.

"Hold this." He sets the plug in my hands, and it's cold and smooth and only making me more excited about what he's going to do with it.

And then he's up from the couch, with me still in his arms, and carrying us into the bedroom.

Once he's standing beside the bed, he lowers me to my feet and takes the plug from my hands. He sets it down on the bed and then removes my shirt, my jeans, my panties, and he doesn't stop until I'm standing before him, completely naked.

"Get on the bed. On all fours. With that glorious ass of yours pointed toward me."

I swallow but follow his command. At the end of the day, I know Ty Winslow is a safe space, no matter what we're trying. I climb onto the bed, and once I'm in the position, I wait for his next move.

He doesn't do anything right away. Instead, I can just feel him behind me, watching me, taking me in, and a rush of arousal makes itself known between my legs.

"Fuck, you're beautiful," he whispers, closer now. And then his warm hands are on me, touching me. They start a path from my shoulders and skate down my back, over my ass, and behind my thighs, until they move right back to my ass and squeeze.

My head falls forward on its own, and a silent moan opens my mouth.

He slides one of his fingers to the one spot the plug is supposed to go and delicately circles the area in such a way that my hips squirm against the foreign sensation.

I've never done anything like this, never had anyone touch me there besides him when we had sex on the couch in his office. But here I am, wanting this—wanting to take it further—with Ty.

That devious finger of his makes a path toward the front of my thighs. It rubs along my clit, and then it's inside me, where his cock has been what feels like a million times, but also, not enough times.

I moan and writhe, and I can feel myself getting wetter as he slides his finger in and out of me.

When he pulls that finger away, I whimper.

And I almost ask him to go back to what he was doing, but his finger is back at my ass, and then slowly, gently, it makes its way inside me. *Inside my ass.* The intensity and tremors of pleasure are unexpected. It feels bad and forbidden, but fuck, I think that's what's making it feel so good.

I chose this. *Me.* No one else. *I* chose it because *I* wanted it, and the thrill of all of that coming to fruition is downright exhilarating.

My hips shift back and forth, almost as if I'm trying to push his finger deeper inside me, and Ty growls out his approval. "That's a good girl."

Damn. Why does this feel so good?

Because it's with him.

With his other hand, he glides his fingers between my thighs, across my clit, and then pushes one inside me there too. "You're so wet," he whispers. "So wet and so ready."

My breaths come out in tiny pants when he pulls both of his fingers out of me and picks up the plug from the mattress. But he doesn't put it inside me. *No.* Instead, he steps to my right and holds it toward my mouth.

"Suck," he says, his voice all raspy yet stern. "Make it wet so I can stick it in your ass."

Holy moly.

I don't hesitate to follow his command, sucking the glass plug into my mouth.

"That fucking mouth of yours," he whispers, and with his free hand, he rubs two fingers over my lips that are now wrapped around the base of the plug. "I think I'm going to need them on my cock soon."

My body jolts at his words. A moan pushes past my throat, and it is muffled by only the plug that's in my mouth. And all I can do is suck it harder, letting my tongue slide around the now warm and smooth surface.

It's like the harder I suck, the more aroused I get.

But then, Ty is telling me it's time, and he's gently tugging the plug out of my mouth with a soft pop. I want to protest. I want to tell him to give it back. Or replace it with his cock. But I also want to know what it feels like to have the plug inside me.

His hands move to my ass again, and I moan. And then, the plug is right there, the tip just barely inside me, and slowly, *oh-so fucking slowly*, he starts to push it inside.

My body stretches around it as the plug slides farther into my ass. It's a delicious, intense kind of ache and like nothing I've ever felt before. I feel *full*—and yet, empty at the same time. I want his cock inside me so badly I shake.

I am aching, and I can feel my arousal dripping down my thighs.

Fuck, this is intense. And good. And amazing. And all the fucking things.

"Yeah, you made a good choice, doll," Ty says and runs both hands over my ass. "Now, it's time for you to get on your knees."

It's as if my body is at his mercy. I don't even think twice. I am off the bed and kneeling in front of him without a second thought. Each movement only making the plug shift and move inside me in ways that just make me ache more.

Ty is naked, his cock hard and jutting out from his body. He grips himself at the base and feeds his length into my mouth.

Goodness, this might be the hottest thing I've ever experienced.

I am downright panting, shaking, trembling for more of whatever he has to give, and I don't hesitate to suck him deep. He is firm and hard yet velvet and silk at the same time.

"Fuck." He groans when I alternate between sucking him toward the back of my throat and sliding my tongue along the tip and length of him. His hands are in my hair, tenderly gripping the strands as I lose myself to the pleasure and power of making him feel this good.

I am a feather and a rock at once. Both acutely aware and dazed at the same time.

And I feel like I could do this forever. But Ty doesn't give me that option.

Between one mewling breath and the next, I go from on my knees to back on the bed and my body adjusted on to all fours by Ty's expert hands.

Ty poises himself behind me, and without pause, his big, hard cock is inside me.

My head falls back, my breath gets all tangled up in my lungs, and the strangest sounds fall from my lips.

This is pleasure personified. It's the most intense thing I've ever experienced.

"Come for me, Rachel," Ty demands, and his voice is hoarse and raspy, and it sounds like he's holding himself back. He needs to come—I can hear it—but he's waiting for me.

All that power pushes me over the edge, right over the cliff and into an abyss of ecstasy I didn't even know was possible. And at the peak of my climax, Ty twists the plug at my ass and buries himself as deep as he possibly can.

You're everything, my mind hears. I can't distinguish if the words came from his lips or my imagination, but they're there…willing my heart to explode.

THIRTY-NINE

Monday, March 11th

Rachel

I step out of the small, intimate space where my nine a.m. Thesis Workshop is located and make a mental note to stop at the library before I leave for the day. Lord knows after Dr. Fink's lecture this morning, I'm going to need to do a little more research before I can really finalize my thesis for his class.

Ugh. Take me back to spring break.

I pull my cell out of the front pocket of my messenger bag to check the time. I see it's only five past eleven, plenty of time to grab a sandwich, but I also find a missed text message from earlier that makes me smile.

Ty: *I want another week of being bad with you.*

It's been less than twenty-four hours since we checked out of the Carlyle, and apparently, I'm not the only one missing the bubble of sex and fun and mischief we created there.

Me: *Ditto. So much ditto.*

I start to put my phone back into my messenger bag, but it alerts with another text, and I quickly hold up the screen with my smile still intact.

And then it's gone in one fell swoop.

Dad: *Come to my office. We need to talk.*

The bubble is officially popped and then some. Not only is it not the man I'm expecting, but it's also ominous.

The realization of the reality I've been avoiding so pointedly slaps me right in the face.

I spent the last week not thinking about my father or his expectations or school or the fact that what Ty and I are doing has consequences that reach beyond the two of us.

I don't know the official university policy, but I do know my dad's stance on the matter—he made that clear. And as the head of the department, what he says goes.

God, I hope I haven't been a party to jeopardizing Ty's career.

Relax, Rachel. You don't know that's what this is. You don't know what he wants to talk about.

My pep talk is swift and strong and filled with effort. The problem is, even if this isn't the time of reckoning now, one day, it's going to come.

I inhale a big breath, forcing myself to text my father back.

Me: What time?

Dad: Now, please.

Ready or not, time to face the music.

Roiling in my gut makes the walk up the two flights of stairs that lead to the faculty offices feel like a climb to the top of the Empire State Building. Trudging down the hall, I work diligently to calm the racing speed of my heart.

It's time to get prepared—prepared to go to war for myself if I have to. The best way to do that is by removing the element of surprise.

I can do this. I'm ready.

His door is partially closed when I arrive at the end of the hall, so I push it open with a soft knock—only to nearly fall on my ass.

Fuck prepared; I'm blindsided.

Because not only is my father in his seat behind his massive desk, but Ty is sitting down in one of the leather chairs on the front side. This isn't a meeting with me—it's a meeting with *we*.

Desperation makes me cling to another possibility, though, and I volley a polite offer to do this another time. "Oh, uh…do you need me to come back?"

"No, actually, we've been waiting for you," my dad says and gestures toward the only empty chair across from his desk. "Take a seat."

Waiting for me? Like, together? What in the hell is going on here?

I wish I could get a read on the room, but I can't. The only option I'm left with is to take a seat beside Ty and wait for the onslaught. So, that's what I do.

My dad stands up from his chair and paces the spot to the right of his desk. Both Ty and I follow his movements, and I find myself looking at Ty again, trying to figure out what's going on.

But his blue eyes give nothing away. Chillingly, they don't even glance in my direction.

"Is everything okay?" I eventually ask, and my dad turns on his heel to face me, the expression on his face cutting me all the way to the bone.

"No, Rachel. Everything is not okay. We need to discuss what's going on."

"What's going on with what, Nate?" Ty questions, and if my father's mouth was firm before, it's downright acidic now.

"I know what you two are doing."

Oh no. The time of reckoning really has come.

I almost open my mouth to deny it, but I stop myself before following through. It's not the time for excuses. Not anymore.

"I saw you. Both of you. Together," he expands. "Last week, near the Carlyle."

Ty's gaze falls to his lap briefly and then lifts again, meeting my father's judgment head on.

"You were both very...*involved* with each other." He pauses briefly to take his glasses off his nose and rub at the space between his eyes harshly. I watch silently, as does Ty. The irrational urge to reach out and take his hand in mine is both overwhelming and insane. Touching him right now would *not* be in our best interest.

"The conference I asked you to attend, Rachel, just so happened to be a block up the street from the hotel you two were apparently staying in together," he continues. "I know this because I was blessed with the visual of one of my professors getting far too close with my daughter." He turns his glare to Ty. "I had a feeling something was up between you two, and I was right. And I think it goes without saying that your being involved with your TA goes against university policy, Ty."

This is not good.

"But perhaps less explicitly outlined by HR, it goes against everything I ever taught you to be. You two are putting both of your careers on the line," my father continues, his voice rising in irritation. "You're putting everything in jeopardy. And for what? Some kind of game or thrill? *These are your lives.*"

I start to open my mouth with a rebuttal, but Ty's voice is louder than mine.

"It's not a game, Nate," he says, and his voice is laced with a serious edge that I've never heard before. "It might've started out that way, but it's not anymore."

"What the fuck is that supposed to mean?" my father shouts, losing his cool and using the f-bomb for the first time in my life. Even when Nathaniel Rose is mad, he's dignified.

Evidently, finding out your daughter is sleeping with one of your star professors is the point at which poise breaks.

"This goes beyond putting your own career at risk by being childish, Rachel," he continues, his eyes meeting mine. "But you're putting Ty's at risk too." He tosses both hands out toward his sides erratically. "Am I losing my fucking mind?'

Oh, I see. This is all *my* fault. I should've known. Everything is Rachel's fault in Nathaniel Rose's eyes.

I bark out a sharp laugh, and my father's attention is back on me.

"You think this is funny?"

"Yeah, Dad. I think it's pretty freaking funny that at the end of the day, even someone else's actions are my responsibility. Not only do I have to *Be serious, Rachel* and *Take your career in your hands, Rachel*, and *Do as I say, Rachel*, but now I also have to worry about keeping up with someone else?" I shake my head. "I don't think so, Dad. You can count me out."

I shake my head and start to open my mouth again, a lashing the likes of a sadist coming, but Ty's voice is there again, carrying over me.

"This isn't a game, Nate," he says and stands up from his chair.

"This isn't a game?" my dad retorts, his voice harsh. "Well, then what the hell is it? Some kind of sick joke?"

"I'm in love with your daughter!" Ty shouts, the sound echoing even within the cozy, overcrowded, book-filled space. It feels like his words repeat a hundred times.

I'm sorry, what?

Did he just tell my father he's in love with me before he actually told me?

My skin tingles and my tongue feels thick, and if I don't get out of here soon, I'm going to black out. After all these years, after all this time, after all that I've fought to change, I now find myself in a room with *two* men who are happy to speak for me.

"You're in love with my daughter?" my father questions, outraged at Ty. "What do you know about love? Do you even realize the consequences that this type of relationship could have on your future? *On her future?* She is finally back in New York. She is finally back to focusing on the important things instead of flitting about with no plan. You are nothing more than a distraction."

"With all due respect, Nate, you're wrong," Ty continues and steps closer to my father, neither one even sparing a glance in my direction. "You are right about a lot of things, but this is one thing you're wrong about. *I am in love with your daughter.* And that means I'm the man who wants to support her, encourage her, and be what she needs."

What I *need* is to be an active participant in my own life. To make my own decisions, be my own woman, pick my own destiny. No one gets to tell me what my future holds but me. *No one.*

"Ty, you don't know what's best for her," my father refutes, firing the gunshot that triggers my fight-or-flight response.

I feel out of control. I feel violated. And I feel like if I sit here for even a second longer, my heart will shatter into a million tiny pieces.

"No," I say so forcefully as I stand from my seat that both of them have no other option but to look me in the face.

"Rachel—" my father starts to interject, but I hold one hand up in the air.

"I've had enough." I grab my messenger bag from the floor and sling it over my shoulder. "I'm a grown woman, and I *will not* sit here any longer while the two of you discuss my life as if I don't exist."

"Rachel—" Ty tries, reaching out his hand to grasp my arm, to stop my momentum, but I yank it away without a second thought.

"No. You two can stay here and fight it out for as long as you want. I'm done."

Out the door of my father's office, I stride as quickly as my legs will take me. And I don't stop on my way down the stairwell and out of the English building. And I don't stop on my way off campus. And I don't stop then either.

I need away from my father. Away from Ty. Away from all this fucking bullshit.

To a place where I'm in control for good.

FORTY

Ty

Every cell inside my body wants to run after Rachel, but I don't. Instead, I stay here, where I know the buck starts and stops.

Rachel is right to be upset with me. She's right to feel disrespected by my timing in telling her that I love her, and she's right to feel like a third wheel in a very important conversation.

But Nate Rose's influence on the way she views how to love and be loved is invasive. It claws at the shell of her heart and sits like lead at the bottom of her stomach. Without a change in her relationship with Nate, she'll never be ready for something else—for the amazing thing we've managed to find within each other.

For the love I swore I'd never experience.

If I don't make myself clear here, I'll never be able to build what I want to with her—*never*.

Nate *glares* at me, his nostrils flaring with every sharp inhale of breath he takes. "I demand that you stop this relationship between the two of you right now. I'll not stand by and watch my daughter throw her life away."

Frankly, I'm flabbergasted. I'm shocked that he can't realize that by continually attempting to insert himself into Rachel's life, to control her life, he is pushing her away.

"Nate, look around you," I state quietly. "There are only two people left in this room. You and me. Don't you see an issue with that?"

He just stares at me.

"Your daughter is an adult woman, and you just treated her like a child," I tell him the truth. "You treated her like she can't handle her own life. Like she can't make decisions for herself. Like she doesn't know what's best for herself."

"Because she doesn't!" he shouts, surprising me. For a man as intelligent as I know he is, he's missing the mark by a mile.

"You are so wrong on this, it's not even funny," I retort without guilt. He needs to hear this. He needs to understand what he's doing and the consequences it's going to have. "When are you going to realize that you are pushing her away with all this? When are you going to realize that she deserves space and respect from you? When are you going to realize that if you continue on this path, one day, Rachel will cut ties with you completely?"

"That's bullshit."

"But is it?" I question. "Because she just ran out of your office. As far away as she could possibly get from the both of us. I'm willing to change—to put my heart and soul on the line, to go to the ends of the earth, to understand her on an intrinsic level. Because of all that, I *know* I'll get her back, Nate. Can you really hear yourself right now and say the same?"

I shake my head. He can't.

"Ty, you don't know my daughter like I do. You don't know how brilliant she is and how much her mind has to give to the world. The only other time I've seen her kind of brilliance was from her mother. And—"

"But she's not her mother," I cut him off. "She's not Nadine Rose, Nate, no matter the shared DNA. She's Rachel."

"She could be just like her mother."

"But what if she doesn't want to be? What if she wants to be Rachel?"

He starts to open his mouth, but then he shuts it. He does that again three more times before clamping his jaw tight and looking out the window of his office.

At his core, I know Nate loves his daughter. And I even think he truly wants the best for her. But somewhere along the line, he's lost sight of what's important. He's been too busy putting expectations on her, too busy asking her to be someone she's not, that he's suffocating her.

"Look, I respect you a lot," I eventually say, my voice the only thing breaking the silence. "Hell, I'll forever feel indebted to you for your guidance. You turned me into the man I am, and that includes the man who's standing in your office right now saying all this to you. But when it comes to Rachel and me, I don't care what you think."

"Excuse me?"

"I'm in love with your daughter, sir. And that means I *only* care what she thinks."

Rachel is my priority. I hope, if she's willing to forgive me, she'll be my priority forever.

I could give two shits if he digs his toes into the sand and tries to find a way to fire me, even though I'm tenured. I didn't murder anyone, but I imagine, for a father, someone sleeping with his daughter is just about the same thing. But it doesn't matter—none of it does. None of it matters but her.

As I move to leave, I pose him with one more morsel of food for thought. "Would Nadine want your relationship with Rachel to be like this?" I question. "Would she be pushing for Rachel to follow in her footsteps? Or would she give Rachel the space to spread her wings and fly on her own?"

I don't wait for his answers because, honestly, I don't expect that he has them. Nate needs time to think.

As for me? The only thing I need is to get my girl back. As soon as fucking possible.

FORTY-ONE

Rachel

I don't know where I'm going.

I just know I need to get away. From my father. From Ty. From every-fucking-one.

My heels clap across the pavement of the sidewalk, and even though my thigh muscles are burning something fierce from a lengthy run I absolutely haven't trained for, I pick up the pace. It's like, if I could only go faster, then I would somehow find relief from this gnawing pressure inside my chest.

My phone vibrates from my bag, but I ignore it.

I don't want to talk to anyone right now.

I *can't* talk to anyone right now.

I just need to be alone. I am literally the only company I can tolerate, and even that's pushing it.

By the time I make it to Nolita, a line of sweat discolors the front of my blouse, my breathing is ragged, and tears are streaming down my cheeks. I can't feel myself crying—my body is numb—but the evidence is plain to see.

Upon arrival at the bakery—and seeing Lydia and Lou at the front, chatting and laughing with a customer—I realize my plan to run until I couldn't anymore has still landed me somewhere it shouldn't. This may be my home, but it's their *life*.

There is no way I can walk into their bakery looking like this. I won't do it to them and their unflagging sympathies, and I won't do it to their business.

Bringing that kind of pain and stress to their doorstep and leaving it there would be my undoing.

I round the block to the rear of the building and sneak in through the back doors, and I somehow manage to slide underneath Maude's attention while she stays focused on piping white icing onto a tray of cupcakes. She's got earbuds in or something, and for that, I'm thankful.

Bathed in the safety of my apartment at last, I lock myself inside.

But the relief I thought I'd feel by separating myself from everyone, from the outside world, doesn't come. If anything, I feel more anxious. Like a caged animal in a zoo that just wants to return to its home in the wild.

The silence of my apartment is so thick it makes my ears ring. Mindless, I reach for my phone and look at the screen—the absolute stupidest thing I could do.

10 missed calls Ty Winslow.

6 text message notifications Ty Winslow.

The pressure comes rushing back into my chest like a freight train, but I can't stop myself from reading the texts inside.

Ty: Where are you?

Ty: Call me back, please.

Ty: Look, I know I said something back there that probably was a lot to comprehend, and I absolutely didn't do it the right way, but…just…call me back. Please.

I lock the screen of my phone before I can read the rest and toss it back into my bag.

I feel frazzled. Shaken. Confused to my very core. I don't know how I want to feel or why I'm feeling the way I am. All I know is that I can't stay here. I can't stay like this, or it'll kill me.

I shouldn't have come back to New York.

My phone rings from inside my bag, and I don't have to look to know who it is. I can't face him—not right now. The undeniable urge for space roots deep in my chest and sprouts itself into something I can't deny. It's pervasive—*debilitating*.

Without even thinking, I head to my bedroom and start slamming shirts and shoes and random toiletries into my favorite messenger bag, my eyesight blurred heavily by uninvited tears.

I know my sister's in the middle of the afternoon bakery rush, and I know she'll be too busy to check her phone. And that's why I have to handle it like this.

Me: I'm going somewhere. I will call you when I get there and explain everything.

I hate leaving Lydia and Lou high and dry when it comes to bakery shifts I've already agreed to for the foreseeable future, but I can't stay here. I can't wait to explain.

I have to go, and I have to do it now. Once and for all, I have to take back control.

FORTY-TWO

Ty

Texting, calling, scouring the campus, and even climbing the fire escape at the back of Rachel's apartment like a fucking stalker have all turned up empty in my search for her.

I held class in the hopes that she'd show, but when she didn't, I told all the students to go home. It was unprofessional and a direct violation of my rule to never let my personal life affect my job, but this is different—this is the kind of thing that I would go to the ends of the earth for if I had to.

This is the woman of my dreams.

There's only one more place to go for answers—a place where I doubt I'll find Rachel, but may just find the clues that will lead me to her.

Her sister's bakery and the enabler of my cookie addiction—Little Rose Bakeshop.

I swing open the door and step inside, and the bell chimes above my head. Lydia is busy at the front, switching cupcakes from a tray onto the glass shelf underneath the register.

I move quickly toward her without delay or any regard for the tables in my way, bumping into a couple of them clumsily. Still, it takes me standing in front of her and clearing my throat for her to look up and meet my eyes. I'm fairly certain, just because of that, she already knows it's me and not another customer.

"Where's Rachel?" I ask without preamble. After this many hours looking for her, I'm past the point of pleasantries and small talk. I'm edging on desperation.

"Oh hey, Ty," she says, quickly setting the now-empty tray on a shelf behind her and rubbing her hands down the front of her white apron. She never answers my question, and I have a pretty strong feeling the avoidance is on purpose.

"Lydia, please," I implore, hoping the earnestness in my voice will compel her to dispense with all the older-sister protectiveness. "Do you know where Rachel is?"

The back door swings open and startles Lydia, and now Lou, her wife, is at the front, glancing between the two of us curiously. "What's going on?" she asks perceptively. Evidently, neither Lydia nor I is doing a good job of hiding our emotions.

"I'm looking for Rachel," I tell her openly. "And Lydia was just about to tell me where she is."

Lou looks at me and then back at her wife. "Lyd, what's going on? Where's Rae?"

Lydia glances between Lou and me and then finally admits, "She left." Her answer is sullen and resigned, and I don't like the feeling it gives me at all. It seems too permanent—irreversible.

"Left where?" Lou questions, upset now too. I'm not surprised. That's the effect Rachel has on your life when she's in it—you want her to stay there.

Lydia shakes her head apologetically. "I'm sorry, but I don't know where. At least, not yet. She just said she was going somewhere and she'd call me when she got there." She looks me in the eye and lifts a gentle hand up over the counter to squeeze my shoulder. "No offense, but I had a feeling the reason had to do with you."

I close my eyes and will myself to stay calm. To keep trying, to keep searching, no matter how long it takes. I will find her eventually, and when I do, I'm going to make things right.

"What happened?" Lydia asks, her scrutinizing eyes examining mine. "Why did she hit the eject button?"

"Your father called us into a meeting this morning," I explain. "He found out about us."

Lydia takes a deep breath and nods, sagely aware that this day was coming. Obviously, she knows her sister well enough and cares about her enough, though, to let it run its course. She and Lou exchange a look, and Lydia reaches into the case and pulls out one of my favorite cookies while Lou fills a couple of coffees at the back of the counter.

"I knew it would eventually come to this. I wish she would have come to me." She shakes her head to clear it and then puts the cookie on a plate, handing it over to me. "Come on. Let's have a seat and talk."

I shake my head quickly. "Thank you, but no. I need to find Rachel. I don't have time to sit and chat."

"Sit, Ty," Lou commands then, handing me the cup of coffee. "If you want to find Rachel, you'll listen to what we have to say." Lou's eyes turn sad. "Rachel is known for running when her father is involved. There's a long and sordid history there, and it'll do you good to let us fill you in on the gaps."

Known for running, known for running, known for running. Lou's words play over and over in my mind, and a deep pit forms in my stomach. I feel sick over the possibility that's forming in my mind.

"There's no way she went back to…" I can't even finish the sentence.

"Back to LA?" Lydia's face is gentle—sympathetic. And I hate it. "Ty…"

"Fuck." The one word is a tortured whisper, dredged from the bottom of my gut. "I have to do something. I have to stop her."

They share another look that makes my stomach churn. One that says stopping Rachel in the throes of this decision is about as likely as finding a time machine to go back and fix it.

"I love her, Lyd. I'm *in* love with her. I won't stop until I find her."

Lydia nods, a small smile playing at her lips. "Good. Don't give up on her. She's worth it, I promise."

"I know that."

"I figured you did," she agrees then, a maternal tone to her love for her sister. I suppose after their mother died, it was a natural transition to the role of caregiver and protector. "Now…what can we do to help?"

I take the cookie and coffee and head to the table behind me, determined to use the resources before me to find a place to start.

FORTY-THREE

Rachel

"Hi," I say quietly to a gentleman in a suit and tie who is currently staring down at his phone. I nod toward the empty seat—my window seat—beside him. "Mind if I squeeze in there?"

"Certainly," he says and quickly stands up to allow me to ease past him.

Once I sit down, I shove my messenger bag—the only bag I brought with me—under the seat in front of mine. Two flight attendants assist passengers with their carry-ons, alternating between shoving the luggage in the overhead bins and shutting the doors once they're full.

"You heading home or leaving home?" the man beside me asks, and I look up to meet his eyes.

"Excuse me?"

"Heading home or leaving home?"

"Uh…" I pause, unsure of what to answer, and an overwhelming feeling of sadness overcomes me. Before I know it, my vision is blurred with tears, and I'm sitting there, moments away from falling apart and unable to speak words.

Am I coming or going? Truthfully, respectfully, sir, I don't fucking know.

Home feels like an intangible—like it simply doesn't exist. There is no place of comfort, no support to turn to. I am, once again, on my own and bumbling.

My vision blurs even more. Tears fall past my lids, stream down my cheeks, and show my truth.

"I'm sorry," the man apologizes, completely caught off guard by my manic emotions. "I didn't mean to—"

Didn't mean to open the biggest can of worms to hit American Airlines this century? Yeah, me neither.

"No," I mutter, shaking my head and holding up a hand to hide my face. "It's not you. Things are just…not the greatest."

He doesn't know what to say to that—I can only imagine the helplessness a man feels when faced with a woman he doesn't even know dissolving into tears—and I certainly don't know what to say either, so we just kind of sit there, him now avoiding looking in my direction and me trying like hell to stop crying.

But it's no use. The dam has been broken. The floodwaters charge.

I don't like how I feel, and I really don't like that I'm this much to blame for feeling it.

My father inserts himself into my life, and what? I don't know how to do anything but run?

I am such a coward.

Admitting it is the first step. The second is finding a way to stop, my mind coaxes me gently. *Come on, Rachel, take control of your life—for real this time.*

"Good evening, everyone. This is your pilot speaking. I apologize for the short delay, but we had a minor issue with ticketing at the gate. If you'll just bear with us, once we get that situated, we'll be ready to get you on your way to LAX."

Why am I going to LA? Why do I think that's the answer?

Easy, my mind taunts. *Because it's just about as far away as you can get from here—as far away as you can get from dealing with things head on.*

God. This has to be the most impulsive, stupidest thing I've ever done. The *stupidest* fucking lie I've ever told myself.

New York is *my home.*

It's the place of my birth and the memories of my mother and laughter and love with Lydia and Lou. It's late nights at the bakery and early mornings at stupid dance classes. It's poor choices and life-changing excitement.

The road isn't smooth, but fuck, what did I expect? New York traffic is always a nightmare.

And I can't imagine being anywhere else in the world when I write my first poetry book.

Because that's what *I* want to do. It's my passion, my purpose, my solace.

And the man who helped me figure all of this out is here too.

I…I think I love Ty. Think I could build a life with him—if he'll give me the time I need to sort the rest of my shit out first.

He *did* say he loves me.

Which is why you better get your ass off this fucking plane, sister.

In an instant, I'm on my feet and scrambling to climb over my seatmate in a rush. "I'm sorry," I mutter and jockey myself over his legs before I can even give him a chance to move. "I have to go."

Once I'm in the aisle, I realize my messenger bag is still under the seat, and I just lean right over him to grab it. "Shit. Sorry. I have to get off this plane."

"Miss?" a flight attendant asks, walking down the aisle toward me. "You need to be seated."

"No." I shake my head and lift the strap of my bag over my shoulders. "I need to go."

"No, actually, you need to sit down."

Geez-us, lady, I'm trying to have an epiphany here!

I feel manic. Crazy. Like if I don't get off this plane right now, I'm going to pass out.

"Miss, you need to sit back down," she repeats and points toward my vacated seat.

"No, you don't understand. I have to go. I can't be on this flight. I don't belong in LA."

"We are about to take off," she states firmly, and her brown eyes grow stern. "You need to sit down."

"I'm sorry." I look around to the now-confused passengers on the plane. "I'm so sorry, but I have to go. I can't go to LA. I don't belong in LA. I belong here."

I push past the flight attendant, and another one steps up to stop me. "Miss, you need to take a seat."

"I don't think you understand. I'm not staying on this plane. So, you need to let me off."

"We can't—"

"I have to go!" I shout and push past the second flight attendant and head toward the galley area where the exit door is located. "Keep that open!" I shout as I see two airport staff in neon vests beginning to close it. "I have to get out! I can't be on this plane!"

"Miss, sit down right now!" the lead flight attendant yells. I'm pretty sure I'm officially a security threat, but there's no turning back now. I am once again Rachel Green, and *I have to get off this plane!*

"I'm sorry!" I shout over my shoulder. "I know this is crazy, but I can't be here! I made a mistake, but now I'm fixing it, and I don't have the ten hours it'll take me to fly there and back to waste!" The cords of my throat strain, and tears sting my eyes. My voice sounds hoarse even to my own ears, and I know why. My adrenaline is preparing to crash—right into reality.

Surprisingly, the passengers take up in my favor, siding with me and appealing to the attendants.

"Just let her off!"

"Yeah! Just let her off the plane! It's fine!"

"She's obviously upset!"

"Everyone needs to calm down and stay seated." The flight attendant tries to calm the crowd.

"Just let her off!" more people start to shout.

"She's crying! Let the poor girl off the plane!"

I reach up to my face to feel that, yes, indeed, tears are streaming unchecked down the surface of my skin.

"Please, please," I plead with the staff from my spot in the galley. "Just open it a little bit and let me out."

"We need security! Call for security!"

"Yes! Yes! Get security!" I agree. "They need to escort me off this plane."

At this point, I don't care if I'm blacklisted from flying. One way or another, I have to get off this fucking plane.

FORTY-FOUR

Ty

"What do you mean, you can't tell me who's on the flight? This is a case of love or death," I beg the woman holding court at the gate for American Airlines, the sponsor of JFK's last and only flight to LAX for the evening.

When I left Rachel's sister's bakery, I drove to JFK as fast as I could. There's a small chance I'm at the wrong airport altogether, but based on years and years of knowing her sister, Lydia was fairly confident this was the way to go. My brothers and sister and I have the same kind of intuition about one another; I've experienced it many times. I'd bet a whole lot of important shit on the sibling relationship—and frankly, knowing that finding Rachel or not will change the course of my life forever…I have.

I still have no idea if Rachel is on this plane, but fuck, I'm here because I have this unshakable feeling that I'm right. I can't give up now; I can't just walk away.

"Sir, I have to maintain the privacy of my passengers."

"You don't understand. I don't need to know anything—anything—other than if Rachel Rose is on that plane or not. You don't even have to tell me if you can't…I don't know, just blink twice if you see her name or something. Anything—"

"I know you're upset, sir, and I'm really, truly sorry," she consoles, looking at me with an unbelievable amount of humanity. If I were on the other end of this exchange, I'm not sure I'd be able to do the same. "But I can't give you that information. It's strictly prohibited by both FAA regulations and the law."

Fuck!

I turn away from the counter brusquely and pace outside of the ropes that lead to the counter, unsure of what to do. I've called and texted Rachel no fewer than a hundred times, but it's no use. She's radio silent, not taking my calls, not answering, not even letting me know if she's okay, and it's fucking killing me.

I need to see her, to talk to her—to make this right however I can.

If I can't stop her before she goes, I'm going to have to go to LA myself and find her there.

Newly determined, I charge back up to the counter to beg, steal, and barter my way onto a flight to LA tomorrow morning if I have to, when the radio sitting on the counter next to the attendant squawks loudly with a call for security. Two people in uniforms come running past us, straight for the door that leads to this jetway.

What the hell?

At first, I'm just confused, but then, panic starts to slowly seep into my pores.

What if something has happened to Rachel? What if she's really on that flight and something is wrong?

My feet are moving before I even tell them to, back to the agent, to ask her more questions that she's probably going to try not to answer. "What's going on? Is everything okay?"

She sighs. "Sir, I already told you, since you don't have a ticket, I can't give you any info about this flight."

I tried to get a fucking ticket for this flight—it would have made all of this a lot easier—but the damn thing was booked solid. So, I ended up buying a ticket to Des Moines fucking Iowa, because it was the closest flight leaving out of the same terminal as this LA flight.

"I'm fine!" A familiar voice fills my ears, and I look toward the door that's now closed, the one the security guard just ran through moments ago. "You can let me go! I wanted off that flight anyway!"

In a rush, the door bursts open just as Rachel yanks her arm away from the security guard. "Like I said, it's fine! I just had to get off the plane!"

He looks at the gate agent, his face morphing into an exhausted expression.

"I promise, I'm leaving," Rachel reassures them, and it's then that I realize her face is red with fresh tears. "I'm not trying to cause trouble. I just have an emergency."

"Rachel?" I call for her, and the gate agent's attention comes back to me.

"Well, that makes sense," she mutters before turning to me with a small smile and a shrug. "I guess you got lucky." She chats briefly with the security guard holding Rachel, jerking her chin toward me, and the guy rolls his eyes heavenward. Still, I'm pretty sure that at this stage in the chaotic game, that security agent is supposed to take Rachel to some back room where they'll interrogate her with questions and search her bag for bombs. But instead, the man lets her go and walks away, leaving Rachel and me standing there.

Evidently, the gate agent with all the rules was looking out for me after all.

"Ty?" Rachel questions, her whole face nearly dissolving into the scrunched result of overwhelming emotion.

I close the distance between us hesitantly, trying not to scare her.

"I've… Well, I've been looking for you a lot today. Seems as though I finally found you."

"You came here? For me?"

All I can do is nod. The truth is, I would have gone anywhere. JFK, LA, the moon. Whatever it took.

I stop about a foot away from her, and her big green eyes search mine.

"Rachel, I have been scouring the city looking for you," I admit and run a hand through my hair. "You wouldn't answer my calls. You wouldn't text me back. I was so worried. I had no idea where you went. I…I…" I shrug, unable to put it in any other words than the ones at the tip of my tongue. "I don't want you to run."

"I know," she whispers and digs her teeth into her bottom lip. "I shouldn't have. I should have stayed. I should have faced you directly. You deserve that, Ty, and I'm really sorry."

"I love you," I tell her candidly, knowing this is the way I should have told her the first time. Face-to-face, heart-to-heart, without the audience of her father. "I'm sorry for the way you heard it the first time, but I'm not sorry for the way I feel." I shrug. "It's your fault, really, picking me as the guy to make me remember you forever," I tease. "It really fucking worked."

Her face melts into a soft, sad, emotional smile. "I have feelings for you too, Ty," she says, reaching out to take my hands in hers and rubbing at the backs of them with her thumbs. "Big, at times overwhelming, feelings. But…I also have a lot of shit I need to figure out. And I have to do that for myself before I can do anything for anyone else."

My throat feels clogged and my stomach leaden, but I can tell by the earnestness in her eyes that there's not going to be any changing her mind.

I nod then, licking my lips to keep the tears in my eyes from escaping. "What does that mean? What do you want from me?"

"It means…I don't know?" Her eyes meet mine, but her shoulders sag forward. "I don't know, Ty. I just need some space. To figure things out—to make the decisions I need to and to mend the things that are broken inside me. You deserve a woman who's whole. Who's ready to go all in with you."

"All of that's great, Rach. But I just want you."

"I want you too, Ty. But this…this is what I *need*."

My ears ring, and my chest feels like it could crack in half. "So…that's it?" I whisper. "Space?"

"I'm sorry," she whispers, and her voice shakes with emotion. "I just need time, Ty."

"Okay," I say and slide my hands into the pockets of my jeans. "If that's what you need, that's what I'll give you."

"Ty, I'm so—" she whispers, but I shake my head and hold out a hand.

"Rachel, you don't owe me an apology. You don't owe me anything, actually."

"Don't hate me."

"I could never hate you," I tell her, and it's the truth. Rachel Rose taught me how to love. I place one last soft kiss to the apple of her cheek, and then…I walk away.

Back to my car and back to the city, back into the nothingness of life without her.

Everyone acts like love is such a great fucking thing, but they never want to talk about what happens when love isn't returned. What happens when you want to give someone your heart, your everything, and they don't want it?

What happens then, huh? *Fucking misery. That's what happens.*

Ty Winslow doesn't get the girl in the end. Cleo was wrong, and the fortune dog is officially dead.

FORTY-FIVE

Tuesday, March 12th

Rachel

I should be in class, but I can't bring myself to step foot on campus. At least, not today.

Not after my near cross-country escape, buckets of tears, and breaking the heart of the one guy I didn't want to break.

I did manage to send my two professors an email, letting them know that I wouldn't be in attendance today, and while it's not good to miss out on any class when you're at the graduate level, I needed a mental health day.

Surely anyone would understand yesterday's whirlwind was too much to process in a single night.

I clear my throat, push myself out of my thoughts with a little shake of my head, and make myself concentrate on taking a few photos for Little Rose Bakeshop's Instagram page.

A simple request from my sister, and one that normally wouldn't be that big of a deal but feels difficult as hell.

I spent several years taking photos like this and getting paid for it. Yet here I am, a woman who apparently can't stage a fucking Instagram photo because she's an utter mess.

Get it together, my mind whispers, and this time, I actually listen.

I arrange several of Lou's famous lemon meringue cupcakes on a cheery yellow plate and snap some pics. Every few shots, I adjust the lighting and the angle, until I eventually capture the kinds of images that would make any cupcake lover salivate.

But before I can load the new photos on to my laptop for a quick edit, my sister's voice fills my ears, coming from somewhere in the front of the bakery.

"Rachel!"

"What?"

"Delivery!"

I walk toward the doors behind me, the ones that lead to the dock where all the truckers drop off ingredients and supplies, but when I swing them open, there's nothing. *No one.* Not a truck or a delivery in sight.

"There's no delivery!" I yell over my shoulder, and she's quick to respond.

"Yes, there is, and it's for you!"

What is she talking about?

Instead of continuing our shouting match through the bakery, I walk toward the front, swinging open the divider door with a hard push. It crashes against the wall, and Lydia glares at me from her perch behind the register.

"Easy on the muscles, John Cena."

I put a hand to my hip. "There's no delivery at the back."

"I know," she answers and grabs a brown-paper-wrapped box from the shelf beneath the register. "This is the delivery I was talking about."

I take it from her hands and stare down at it with a furrow of my brow. "What's this?"

"I don't know."

"Okay…?" I look up to meet her eyes. "But where did it come from?"

"A messenger dropped it off this morning." She shrugs, slides open the glass cabinet, and starts to move sugar cookies from a tray to the inside display.

"They dropped it off this morning, and you're just telling me now?"

"It's been a busy morning, Rach," she explains, her voice tinged with frustration, and keeps focused on her cookie task. "Did you get the photos done?"

Apparently, I'm not the only one on edge today.

"Just need to make a few edits, but yes, boss."

"Okay. Can you email those to me? I'd like to post one later this evening."

"Yeah. No problem," I answer, waiting for further instruction. When none comes, I prompt her myself. "Do you…uh…need anything else?"

"Nope!" she calls over her shoulder. "It's all good in the bakery hood!"

Is it just me, or is she acting really flipping weird? Whatever. I don't have the time or the emotional capacity right now.

I spin on my heel and head toward the back, the package still clutched between my fingers. I *almost* get back to photo edits, but my curiosity over the mystery box wins out.

I set the package on the stainless-steel countertop and snag an unused knife from one of the kitchen drawers. One delicate slice through the line of tape at the center, and two of the cardboard flaps pop open.

Holy shit—*my mother's book.*

As I pull it out of the box, a small note slips out of the pages, and the scrawl is so familiar that I know who the writer is before I see his signature at the bottom—**Love, Ty.**

Tears prick behind my eyes, and I have to set the note and the book back down inside the box just to gather myself. I haven't even read the damn thing, and my face is already a soupy mess.

"Rachel, you need to read it," my sister says unexpectedly, wrapping two arms around my shoulders and pulling me into a tight hug from behind.

"I don't think I can," I whisper to Lydia and the kitchen and to anyone else in the mystical mix of sugar and sweets that could be listening. At this point, I don't think I could blink without the safety pins that are holding me together ripping open.

"Yes, you can," she says and tenderly runs her hand down my hair. "You both deserve for you to read it."

"I take it the messenger told you who it was from, huh?"

Her quiet laugh fills my ears.

Once I get my tears under control, I step away from her embrace and dry my face with a proffered tissue that comes from her hand.

"Would you like me to read it to you?" Lydia asks, and I'm nodding before I even process her question. "Are you sure, Rae?"

This time, though, I mull it over and realize my gut instinct was right. "Yes, please."

"Okay." She takes the note from the counter, clears her throat, and then starts to read. And I step beside her so I can silently follow along.

Rachel,

Don't be mad, but after we left the bookstore, I couldn't stop myself from going back and getting this book. It belongs with you.

I didn't know your mother, but I know, with absolute certainty, she would be proud of you. You are a strong, brilliant, amazing, awe-inspiring woman, and I know this because I know you.

One day, I hope the world gets to read a poetry book by the great Rachel Rose, and something tells me that your mother would've been the first one in line to buy a copy. Not because she wants you to live up to what she achieved during her life, but because she wants you to live up to what you can achieve in your life.

At your core, in your soul, you're a writer, Rachel. A poet whose words hold undeniable power. Never forget that.

And I know you wanted space, and I'm willing to give it. But I couldn't keep this book away from its rightful owner any longer.

When I said I love you. I meant it. I'll always mean it.

Love, Ty

"Wow," my sister whispers.

My vision is blurred again, but when I glance away from the note and meet Lydia's eyes, I see that I'm not the only one who was affected by his gift. By his words.

"He spent twelve hundred dollars on this book," I tell her bluntly, and her eyes widen.

"Holy shit." She sniffles and rubs at her eyes. "Mom's books are worth that much?"

I snort. "Apparently, her first editions are."

"Goodness," she says, and a nostalgic smile slides across her lips. "I don't know why, but that makes me happy."

"Me too."

We stand there for a long moment, comfortable silence stretching between us while Lydia flips through our mother's book and I reread Ty's words.

"You know what I think?" she eventually asks, and I lift my gaze to hers. "I think you love him, too. I think you already know this. And I also think, even though it scares you and you think you need to have your life in some kind of perfect order before you can be in a relationship, you need him. He's the man who should be by your side. The one person who should navigate life *with* you. He's the reason you got off the plane."

One lone tear falls down my cheek, and she reaches out to hold my hand.

"Don't avoid this, Rachel. Face it head on, okay? It would break my heart to see you walk away from this. From a man who loves you and so obviously would do anything for you," she says, squeezes my hand, and then lets it go. "Okay, I've officially said my piece, and I'm done. Promise." Her smile is a little self-deprecating. "Now, I'm going to give you some space and head back to the front."

And then she's gone, leaving me standing there, my eyes reading the note again.

The whole time, though, my mind fixates on her words—*give you some space.*

The exact thing I told Ty I wanted, even though the reality of space from him makes me feel more miserable than I've ever felt in my whole life.

Because you love him.

"What in the hell am I doing?" I mutter to myself. "I shouldn't be standing around here waiting for shit to solve itself."

Exactly. Get your ass moving, sister!

I snag my purse off the counter, and with a shove, I push through the swinging divider door so hard it startles a customer Lydia is helping by the register. But I don't have time to apologize. I have shit I need to do.

"I'm sorry, Lyd! But I have to go!" I announce as I stride toward the exit door.

"I had a feeling you'd say that!" Lydia answers, and when I steal one final glance at her over my shoulder, all I see is a bright smile. "I'm proud of you! It's about darn time Rachel starts doing things for Rachel!"

Yeah, sis. It really is.

It takes me twenty minutes to get to NYU's campus and another ten to make it to the second floor of the English building, but once my destination is in sight, I don't stop until I get there.

The plaque outside the closed door reads loud and clear: **Professor Nathaniel Rose.** The man at the root of all the noise inside me that I've never been able to mute.

I force myself to lift my hand and rap my knuckles against the wood.

"Come in!" he calls out.

I falter, for just a moment, the panic of a lifetime of resentment temporarily seizing my body, but then I wrap my fingers around the doorknob and push into his office. He sits behind his desk, his reading glasses resting on the tip of his nose, and it takes him a whole ten seconds before he lifts his gaze to me.

"Rachel," he greets, surprise to see me evident in both his eyes and the timbre of his voice.

"Uh, hi," I say, more out of awkwardness than anything else. Everything inside me feels like a ten-year-old girl getting ready to ask her father something important. Something she knows he's going to say no to.

But you're not a child anymore.

I steel myself and straighten my backbone. I may be his daughter, but I'm an adult.

"We need to talk," I tell him, and I will my feet to move my body toward one of the leather chairs across from his desk to stand in front of it. What I need to say to him, what he needs to hear, should come from a place of confidence, not self-doubt. Keeping my feet will remind me.

"Rachel." He slides his glasses off his face. "I want to—"

"No." I hold up a hand. "You're going to hear what I want to say first, and you're going to listen to every word without interrupting me."

He pauses, then nods. A first for my dad in the entire twenty-six years I've known him.

I take a deep, cavernous breath and then let it fly. "You have to stop trying to dictate my life and my career. You are ruining our relationship by placing expectations on me that I don't want. They're draining me dry, Dad, and taking the love I know I have for you away with them. If you don't stop, it's going to create a wound between us that runs so deep, I'm not sure we'll ever come back from it."

I'm surprised again when he nods, but I keep going. I have a million practiced things to say, and if I stop to think before I get them all out, I'll never get it all off my chest.

"I can understand that my relationship with Ty came as a shock to you, but I want you to understand that it came as a shock to me too," I continue and begin to pace the space in front of his desk. "We didn't plan it. It just happened. Truthfully, we were both helpless to stop it. And while I understand your position as head of the department, I want you to consider how you felt when you were in love."

His eyes widen slightly, and I look away, back to the surface of his desk. "I've never asked you to bail me out of anything ever, and I'm not starting now. If you have to exert some disciplinary action, I understand, and I'm willing to face the consequences. Sometimes you have to break the rules a little bit to end up where you're supposed to be. I know that now for a fact." I turn to face him again and place both of my hands on his desk so that there is no refuting my words. "But you have to let me live my life, even when it goes a little off the path you'd like. That's the journey. That's the experience. That's the point. I deserve that from you. My father."

"I know, Rachel." He pauses briefly, his eyes closing and his voice breaking just slightly, and then he repeats, "I know." The easy admission and unheard-of display of emotion are such a shock to my system that I have to take a step back. Never have I *ever* seen Nathaniel Rose back down this easily.

"W-what?"

"Rachel, I'm sorry." He says words I never thought would ever come from his mouth. "I have been pushing you to do the things that I want for you, but I've lost sight of what you want. And I'm sorry. I'm really sorry." A sheen of emotion envelops his normally matte brown eyes. "I hope you can forgive me."

"Y-you mean that?" I ask, and my breath hitches in my throat, every fiber of tension I've ever held in my being snapping in an instant.

"Yes," he answers. He stands up from his big chair, and then hesitantly, he walks around his desk until he's standing in front of me. The urge to look at my shoes is so fucking strong it might as well be the Hulk, but I fight it. I might not get the chance to see this version of my father ever again, and I need to soak it all in.

"I love you, Rachel. I'm proud of you. And I'll always be here for you. I hope you'll find it within yourself to forgive your old man for being…what does Lydia say…an asshat?"

A quiet laugh jumps from my throat, and then I wrap my arms around my father's waist and hug him for the first time in what feels like decades. "I forgive you, Dad. I can be a real asshat too."

He embraces me tightly, a chuckle rumbling in his chest, like only a father who loves his daughter would, and I savor the smell of his familiar aftershave that reminds me of my childhood.

When our hug ends, he smiles down at me, his eyes only soft and pure. "You know, I've always been in awe of how strong you are. Your mother was proud of that, too." I smile a real smile, and he smooths a hand over my hair. "It just took me a little longer to understand than it did for her."

I swallow hard. "What's going to happen with Ty and me?" It's a hard question to ask, but one that isn't doing any good in the dark. I have to know where to go from here. What the next move is and how to make things right.

"What do you mean?"

"I mean," I say, taking a deep breath and pulling away enough to shift to a spot behind the back of one of his chairs. "Did you fire him? Am I getting kicked out of the program?"

He shakes his head, a genuinely caring smile curving out the corners of his normally serious lips. "No. I don't think that'd be a very good start to this new dimension of our relationship, do you?"

"New dimension?"

He shrugs. "You're in love with each other, are you not?"

I open my mouth and gulp like a fish before finally admitting it on a nod. *Yes, I am one hundred percent, unequivocally in love with Ty Winslow.*

"I don't want the possibility of having fired my future son-in-law on my conscience."

Future son-in-law? Ho-ly shit. My breath catches in my lungs.

"Plus, I don't think anything I could have done to him would have mattered since he told me to shove it." My eyes widen as he continues. "Actually, I'm pretty sure his exact words were, *I'm in love with your daughter, sir. And that means I only care what she thinks.*"

"He said that?"

My dad nods, considering me for a moment. "I know you probably don't want my opinion, but in this case, I feel I need to give it," he adds and reaches out to pat my shoulder. "Yesterday, what I saw was a man who stood before me with only one intention—to stand up for and support the woman he loves."

I shut my eyes, and tears start to sting my nose.

Through all the panty games and push and pull and teasing and taunting and jokes, I never saw it coming. I fell in love with the ultimate player—and he fell in love with me.

"Dad, I have to go," is all I have the power to say.

"I was wondering when you were going to get out of here," he muses and pats my shoulder again before walking back to his desk chair. "Love you, sweetheart."

"Love you too," I say, and I spin on my heel to run out of his office and down to the opposite end of the hall. But when I reach the office that reads **Professor Ty Winslow** on the side, the door is shut and the lights are off.

Shit.

I scramble to get my phone out of my purse, but right before I hit the call button below his name, I stop myself.

No, not like this, Rachel. He deserves more than a hurried phone call and empty apologies.

A memory strikes me—one I was absolutely certain at the time would never equate to anything. But when it does, I can't help but smile at the familial foresight. Damn, those Winslow siblings are good.

Searching and scraping through my bag, I finally close my fingers around the card-stock rectangle I'm looking for.

Pulling it out quickly, I plug the numbers into my phone and hit the button to call.

FORTY-SIX

Ty

I stare at my television screen, mindlessly scrolling through channels and wondering when in the fuck my life turned to such shit.

When you fell in love, bro.

Oh, right. When I decided to fall in fucking love. That's when it all went to hell.

My phone vibrates from the couch cushion beside me, and I hate how my pathetic heart kicks up ten notches. But the hopeful bastard goes back to his slow and steady rhythm when my eyes meet the screen and find a text from my brother Remy instead of any godforsaken salvation.

Remy: Last-minute family dinner tonight. Meet at Winnie's house.

I roll my eyes and look up at the ceiling of my living room. *Yeah, no. Fuck no.*

But then my phone vibrates three more times with texts from my siblings.

Jude: Soph and I will be there.

Flynn: Count us in for four.

Winnie: Dinner will be ready at 8.

Once I read everyone else's messages, I shoot a quick text letting them know I'll be MIA.

Ty: Can't come. Busy.

I toss the phone back down on the couch beside me, but it doesn't even wait ten seconds before annoying me with the most annoyingly upbeat cocksucking ringtone in the universe—Pharrell's "Happy."

When in the hell did I think that fun-loving, Pollyanna, unicorn shit was a good idea? I mean, no offense, Pharrell, but I'm kind of in the middle of being depressed here.

I tilt the screen toward myself with a tiny fraction of hope, and then I curse and send it to voice mail when I see *Incoming Call Remy* flash across the screen.

Fuck that, bro.

It's only after being subjected to the fucking shitdicked ringtone five more demon-dial times that I decide to answer and let Remy deal with the consequences. "What do you want?"

"Cancel your plans," he says. "Be at Winnie's by eight."

"I said I was busy."

"I don't care," he retorts. "Your ass better be there."

"Well, you'd better start molding a fucking replica, because Rem, I'm not coming."

"Mom wants to introduce us to some dude named Howard."

"What?" I sit up then. "Seriously? She's still dating that clown?"

"Just be at Winnie's by eight." He punctuates his words by ending the call with a click.

Dickhead.

I check the time on my phone, and when I see it's already six, I huff out a sigh.

"Can't these assholes understand I don't feel like being around people right now? I don't want to meet Howard. I don't want to meet anyone." *Fuck. It's like love works out for everyone but me.*

When the only answer is my own quiet misery, I decide to get my ass off the couch and hop in the shower.

If I don't get some sort of control over my emotions soon, family dinner and the newly introduced *Howard* are about to get one hell of a show.

⁓

At a little after eight, I walk into Winnie's brownstone. Normally, I love the sounds of chatter and laughter on family dinner nights, but tonight's familiar sounds only spur annoyance.

I would rather be anywhere but here.

I walk into the kitchen and search the room for the one unfamiliar face that's supposed to be here, but I only spot Jude and Flynn chatting at the island, each one holding a swaddled baby in his arms.

Winnie, Sophie, Daisy, Aunt Paula, Lexi, and my mom are busy with the food. Each one engrossed in whatever task they've been assigned.

Wes and my uncle Brad are on the back terrace, Uncle Brad mostly just watching Wes handle whatever meat he has on the grill.

No one notices my presence.

"Glad you made it." Rem claps a hand onto my back. Apparently, he's the only one who sees me.

"Yeah," I mutter. "I mean, you didn't give me much choice, Stalin."

He grins, unfazed by my characterization of him as a dictator. It annoys me that it rolls off his back so easily. It makes me push the limits even more.

"Where's the old geezer I'm supposed to meet? Is he here, or did you run him off like you did Charlotte?"

It's cutting—ruthless, even—I know. But the pain inside me is so all-consuming, and growing by the second, the only thing to do with it is to lash out.

His eyes narrow, and I brace myself for the fist to my face I know has to be coming. I'm not scared, though. Quite frankly, a little time unconscious sounds like a relief.

Rem laughs, the sound downright evil around the edges. "I'm going let that shit slide…*once*. And it's only because I know you're in a fuck-awful place—a place I've been before."

How the fuck would he know what's going on with me? I haven't told any-one, and I'm not going to. I don't need to drag myself through the mud of all those emotions again. No fucking thank you.

"Howard," I remind him with a grind of my jaw, unable to apologize and unable to explain.

Face hard, he points toward the closed dining room doors. "He's in the dining room."

The fuck?

"He's sitting in the dining room by himself?" I question. "And you don't find this a little weird?"

He slaps a hand against my back, the force of it pushing me forward on my feet. "Just go say hi. And be nice, for fuck's sake."

"You know what?" I toss out and plant myself on one of the barstools. "Never mind. I'll chill here."

I'm not in the mood to meet new people. Hell, I'm not even in the mood to see the people I know.

"Get off your ass and go say hi to Mom's boyfriend." Rem grabs me by the back of the shirt and yanks me off the chair.

"What is your fucking deal, man?" I practically shout, but when I look be-hind me in preparation for my mother's disapproval, she doesn't even look up from the pan of asparagus she's shaking salt onto.

Am I invisible?

My outburst doesn't deter my eldest brother, though. With a hand to my back, he pushes me toward the dining room until I skid to a stop in front of the doors.

I look back at him. "Has everyone in this family lost their minds?"

Fucking hell.

I guess I might as well get this shit over with sooner rather than later and then get the fuck out of the Winslow Family Twilight Zone.

I push through the dining room doors and freeze.

Holy fuck does Howard look an awful lot like someone else.

FORTY-SEVEN

Rachel

"Rachel?" Ty questions, his eyes both wide and confused. He looks like hell—rougher than I've ever seen him—and I immediately suck in my gut as it bloats with guilt. "*Rachel?*" He says my name again, as if I'm a mirage in the desert and he just can't believe I exist.

"Hi, Ty." It's such a woefully pathetic greeting given the circumstances, but in my grand effort to be less critical of myself when I'm trying, I classify it amicably in the *at least it's a start* column.

"So," I continue, clearing my throat. "I know this is a surprise, seeing me here tonight, but what I have to say is too important for a phone call and would be outright criminal in a text."

When he doesn't say anything, I take a step toward him.

"I know things have been a mess—that *I've* been a mess—and I'm sorry," I tell him and take three more steps toward him. "I…um… I had a conversation with my father today. It was a good conversation. A great one, actually."

"Yeah?" It's the first word to leave his lips, and even in its barren simplicity, it makes me want to burst into tears.

"Yeah." I nod and take two more steps toward him. "I think our relationship will be much healthier moving forward."

"I'm glad to hear that, Rachel," he says, his voice soft but sad, like it's causing him physical pain to be in my presence. It's the worst scenario I can imagine—hurting Ty more than I already have—so I rush on to the good part and silently pray and wish and hope he'll be in a place to receive it.

"I love you, Ty!" I shout so loud, I swear it could've shattered glass, the words are so eager to exit my body.

His chest heaves and his fists come to his hips, and I can't help but say it over and over again.

"I love you," I whisper this time, tears falling down my cheeks unchecked. "I do, Ty. I love you. I'm *in* love with you."

"Thank fuck. It's about time," he mutters, and then he's on the move, his legs closing the distance between us in three long strides.

Within seconds, I'm in his arms and he's kissing me and I'm kissing him and his fingers are in my hair and my hands are gripping the material of his shirt.

Which only makes me cry harder.

"I love you," I whisper against his mouth, and I can taste my own tears on his lips.

"I love you too, Rachel," he says against my lips. "I didn't have a childhood fantasy of making the perfect family of my own…but these last twenty-four hours have been fucking misery without you. I want it all now. A life, a family, kids—the whole nine yards—and I want it with you."

Sounds like a dream. And I want it too.

I kiss him harder. His hands are on my ass, forcing my body to get as close to his as physically possible without climbing inside each other.

I don't know how long we stay like that, kissing and touching and just desperately holding each other, but at a certain point, the background noise gets so loud, it's impossible to continue pretending we're the only ones in the room.

Like, there are a *lot* of other people, and they're cheering and clapping their hands and saying things like, "*Hell yeah!*" and "*Get a room!*"

Ty breaks the kiss on a laugh, and I blink past the remnants of tears in my eyes. The entire Winslow gang is here, celebrating for us.

"It's about fucking time!" Ty's brother Jude shouts, and his mother reaches out to smack him across the back of the head.

"Language!" Wendy snaps as Winnie and Wes and Lexi all file in to take seats.

"I just read a Colleen Hoover book where they acknowledge that language is nothing more than a construct placed on us by society, Grandma. Fuck doesn't actually mean anything. It's just a fucking word," Lexi advises, rendering Ty's mom speechless and spreading another smile across both Ty's face and mine.

"Let's eat!" Ty's uncle Brad shouts, pushing past us and settling into a chair at the other end of the table.

By the looks of things, our moment is over and family dinner is in session, but Ty doesn't put me down. Instead, he kisses me again.

"Paula, pass me the potatoes," Brad requests in the background, and I pull away from Ty's mouth on a giggle.

An insult flies in one direction and a laugh in another, the chaos around us making me smile.

When Ty sees mine, his grows even deeper. "You ready for this to be our future?"

I pretend to consider it seriously for five seconds, but I already know my answer. "Only if you promise it'll last forever."

Ty shakes his head. "Dinner won't. But we will."

"I love you, Ty."

"Me too, Rach. Me too." He kisses me again, but then he sets me back on my feet.

I glance around the room at the love all around us. "You think we should, uh, maybe sit down and eat?"

"You'd rather sit down and eat?"

"As opposed to what?"

"As opposed to getting the fuck out of here so I can keep telling you I love you," he whispers quietly into my ear. "But only, naked and with my cock buried in you."

I blush. But also, I smile. "That sounds promising."

"Oh, Rach. This is just the beginning."

EPILOGUE

Over five months later…

Saturday, July 20th

Ty

"You ready for lunchtime, Tilly?" I grin down at Matilda, and she purrs her approval. Once I set down a bowl of tuna on the kitchen floor, I rub my fingers through the soft fur at her back. "Here you go."

She purrs again, rubbing her side against my leg, but only dallies about ten more seconds before getting down to chow-time business.

Miss Matilda used to be the official cat of Little Rose Bakeshop, but about a month ago, after Rachel and I moved in to this Greenwich Village apartment together, my girl missed her feline friend too much to leave her behind.

Though it did take an undercover, secret-agent mission of us sneaking into the bakery after hours when Lydia and Lou weren't there to successfully get Matilda to our apartment, we eventually managed to move her in.

Rachel's sister wasn't that thrilled—pretty pissed, actually—but she got over it when Rachel gifted her with a new "service animal" bakery cat. A boy this time, that Lydia and Lou named Heathcliff.

Personally, I'm a fan of the *Wuthering Heights* reference, even if that wasn't the intent.

My phone vibrates from the kitchen counter, and I snag it off the marble surface to find a text from my eldest brother.

Remy: I'm on my way.

Fucking finally. I'm not sure when his plane from LAX landed, but it feels like he should've been on his way over an hour ago.

Me: You got the goods?

Remy: No, Ty. I'm just coming over to have afternoon tea.

Smartass.

Me: At least tell me this, you bastard, are said goods being carefully handled and protected during transport?

Remy: Yes.

Me: By yes, do you mean that you are guaranteeing that you are not going to lose, drop, or ruin the very expensive goods on your way here?

Remy: For fuck's sake, Ty. Relax. I'll be there soon.

Relax? *Pfft.* It's hard for a man to relax when he's relying on his brother to deliver the most important thing he's ever purchased.

What am I talking about? Well…the answer to that question would be… *an engagement ring.*

Rachel's engagement ring, in fact.

The ring I've been searching for ever since she told me she loved me at my sister's house, in the middle of a Winslow family dinner. A dinner that was planned under the false pretenses of us meeting our mom's main squeeze, Howard, but I later found out was planned by Remy *for* Rachel. I didn't end up meeting Howard—who is actually a pretty nice guy—until a few weeks later when my mom found the courage to drag him into the viper's den that is her four protective, asshole sons and nosy-as-hell daughter.

But that dinner where Rachel ambushed me in Winnie's dining room? Well, it changed my life. It sent me from rock-bottom misery to a man on top of the fucking world. A man who can officially say: love isn't bullshit. It's *everything.*

Yeah. I know. Pretty damn crazy, huh?

I, Ty Winslow, have found the one woman who makes me the kind of man I used to make fun of Flynn and Jude for being. And even though I hate to say that ol' Crazy Cleo was right, the quack *was* right—fate led me to finding the one woman I want to spend forever with.

And after Remy drops off the ring he picked up for me from an expensive LA boutique while he was in town meeting with some rich hedge fund investors, I plan to get down on one knee and ask Rachel to marry me.

The whole idea makes me smile so big it should be embarrassing, but fuck, I'm a man in love, and I don't care who knows it.

"It's all happening, Tilly!" I announce as I shove my phone into my pocket and walk out of the kitchen, heading into the living room to plop my ass on the couch and watch a little ESPN until Rem gets here. But my plans are jolted when I hear the familiar sounds of keys jingling against the front door.

What the…?

I walk toward the foyer just as Rachel bursts inside our apartment.

"Holy hot tamales!" she exclaims, swiping beads of sweat off her forehead with one hand as she juggles her purse and messenger bag with the other. She kicks the door shut with her foot and drops everything in her hands unceremoniously to the floor. "Why is it so flipping hot outside?"

Oh no. Oh no, no, no. This is not part of the plan!

"W-what are you doing home?" I ask, anxiety clutching at my chest. Remy is on his way, *with her freaking engagement ring,* and while I love her with every piece of my being, she is *not* supposed to be here right now.

"The AC was out in class," she says on a dramatic sigh, fanning herself with both hands. "It was absolute misery. Everyone was sweating, and eventually, the professor just gave up and let us go home."

"Oh…" *Fuck.*

Every Saturday for the past few weeks, Rachel has been taking a summer writing workshop with a professor who focuses solely on poetry. It's something she's doing for herself, outside of her grad school classes, and I couldn't be any prouder of her.

But again, she's *not supposed to be here.*

"It's so freaking hot outside, Ty," she comments and slips off her sandals before heading straight to the kitchen, and all I can do is follow her like a confused fucking puppy.

With a swing of her arm, she opens the fridge door and grabs a bottle of water. And it feels like she has half the thing chugged down before I can blink or, you know, figure out what in the hell I'm going to do.

"So…uh…class was canceled?"

"Yeah." Rachel looks at me with a tilt of her head. "Like I said before, the AC was out, and we were all sweating like fools. It was either cancel class or call ten ambulances for heatstroke victims."

"So, no writing workshop today, then…" I pause and scrub a hand down my face.

Shit. Shit. *Shit.* I had a whole thing planned. A sexy dinner and a dessert that revolved around me eating whipped cream off Rachel's glorious pussy until she was all lax with pleasure and in the perfect mind-set for me to get down on one knee and propose.

"Ty? Are you okay?"

"Of course." I clear my throat and meet her eyes again. "Why?"

Her grin is equal parts amused and suspicious. "Because you're acting weird."

"Me? Weird?" I shake my head. "No way."

"Okay, weirdo." Rachel just laughs and walks out of the kitchen and down the hallway that leads to our bedroom.

"Where are you going?"

"I'm going to go take a shower," she calls over her shoulder, and I don't miss the hilarity in her voice. "Are you sure you're okay, weirdo?"

Get it together, man. If this was a game of poker, you'd be showing all your fucking cards to the table.

I scrub a hand down my face again and try to pull myself together.

This doesn't have to ruin my plans. Surely I can make up some excuse why Remy is going to stop by? Or hell, maybe I can just tell her I need to run an errand and meet him downstairs in the lobby?

Yeah. That could work.

I pull my cell out of my pocket and shoot Rem a quick text.

Me: *What's your ETA?*

When no response comes in, I head into our bedroom to give Rachel some excuse about needing to run to my office so I can just wait for Rem downstairs, but I find my beautiful, sexy woman standing there, removing all her clothes. First her shirt, then her bra, then her shorts and panties, and before I know it, I'm one-hundred-percent invested in the show.

And it's as if my body has a mind of its own, my feet moving of their own accord, and one hand dropping my phone onto the nightstand before it joins the other one in reaching out to grab Rachel's perfect tits.

"Ty!" she exclaims on a giggle. "Stop! I'm all sweaty and gross!"

"I don't care." I pull her into my arms after that, my hands still running up and down her body. "I love you clean. I love you sweaty. I love you dirty. I love you every-fucking-way, Rach," I whisper before pressing my mouth to hers.

She tastes like salt and the citrus-flavored gum she always chews, and it's not long before she's melting into me, her body bowing toward mine and her hands reaching up to wrap around my neck.

I move us to the bed then, our mouths basically fused together, and my cock is already standing at attention, a sex-soldier ready to conquer her perfect cunt.

Nothing else but getting inside her matters right now.

Fuck, my woman is a goddamn goddess, I think to myself when I take in her gorgeous curves and naked body beneath mine. I want to suck and eat and feast on every inch of her. I want to make her come on my mouth and my cock. I want to do it all, and I want to do it for hours.

And I am going to do just that. Right the fuck now.

"I'm glad you came home early," I growl out and kiss her harder. "I missed you."

She giggles against my persistent mouth. "You just saw me two hours ago."

"Doesn't matter. I never don't want to see you. I think I'll start coming to all your classes. Anywhere you go, I go."

"You sound like a psychopath." She giggles again, but then she says, "But I love you."

When moans start to spur from her lips and her hips start to fidget beneath me, I pull away to remove my clothes as quickly as humanly possible. And Rachel grins at me the entire time, her lips curving up into amusement as she watches me nearly fall on my fucking face as I kick my boxer briefs off and dive back onto the bed.

"You're a lunatic!" she squeals when I bury my face into her breasts and spend some time sucking and licking at her nipples.

"It's all your fault, doll. It's all your fucking fault."

"I love…" she starts to say but pauses and sits up on her elbows. "Wait, Ty," she says and taps my shoulder. "Did the power just go out?"

"Just ignore it," I answer as I move my mouth down her body.

And she does just that, lying back on the bed, *until* in the far-off distance, the sounds of a ringing phone start to echo from the nightstand.

"Babe. Someone is calling you."

"Again, ignore it."

"It's Remy."

Shit! He's probably here! I roll over onto my side and snag my phone from the nightstand. "Hey, what's up?"

"What's up?" he asks on a harsh laugh. "Well, I'm stuck in your building's fucking elevator."

Uh-oh.

"Okay. I'll call Lloyd."

"And Lloyd would be…?"

"Maintenance," I tell him and hang up the phone. But when I turn around and see Rachel on the bed, those tempting fucking curves of hers displayed like my own personal buffet, I can't stop myself from pulling her into my arms again and kissing her.

"Everything okay?" she asks around my persistent mouth.

"Remy's stuck in our elevator."

"*What?*" she asks. "What elevator?"

"Our elevator."

"Ty?! Are you serious!?" she exclaims and shoves me off her. "We have to call Lloyd, you lunatic! And the fire department too! Oh shit! And the power *is* out!"

I know she's right, that I should be a little more, you know, *urgent* in calling Lloyd and helping out Rem. It's my cock that didn't quite get the memo.

She's off the bed between one breath and the next, tossing my phone at me and sprinting out into the hallway.

"Ty! This is not good!" Her voice bounces off the hallway walls. "You call Lloyd! I'm calling the fire department."

Well, damn. This day certainly isn't going as planned.

Rachel

Today, because the New York weather was hotter than the freaking sun, a thirty-minute blackout occurred, shutting off all the power in several boroughs, including Greenwich Village, where our apartment building is located.

Normally, it wouldn't have been that dramatic of an experience, but because Ty's brother Remy was on his way over to drop something off, he ended up stuck inside our building's elevator.

Yeah. Literally stuck inside the cart smack-dab in between the fourth and fifth floors.

Two hours later, and with the help of New York's finest, I watch as two burly firefighters pry open the elevator doors, and the breath I didn't even realize I was holding releases from my lungs.

Thank goodness.

I look up at Ty, and the lines of worry that have been a permanent fixture on his face ever since I had to shake him out of his horny stupor slowly start to disappear. He squeezes my shoulders, and we both look back toward the doors, waiting to see Rem's face come into view.

But the first face I see isn't Rem's. It's a strikingly beautiful female one with big brown eyes and dark hair and a pregnant belly.

She's glowing—and though it's probably because of sweat—she's seriously one of the most gorgeous women I've ever seen.

Thankfully, mere seconds later, Remy *does* step out, his face much more relaxed than I would've expected for a man who was just stuck inside an elevator for the past two hours.

"Holy shit, Maria?" Ty questions, his attention on the woman, and the warm tone in his voice makes it apparent he knows her.

How, I'm not sure, but he grabs my hand and walks us over to where she stands beside Remy.

"You guys okay?" one of the firefighters asks, and Remy claps him gratefully on the back.

"Yeah, man. Thanks for saving our asses."

"Hi, Ty," the woman, whose name is apparently Maria, answers with a friendly smile.

Ty looks at his brother, who has now joined our small circle out of the way of the firefighters who are still working to get the elevator operational, and chuckles. "Talk about a small world, bro."

Rem just smirks. "Tell me about it."

"Rachel, this is Maria. Maria, this is my Rachel," Ty introduces us, and she holds out her hand toward me, and I take it without a second thought.

"Nice to meet you."

"I'm an old friend of this guy right here," she explains and nudges Remy's side playfully. "From way back in our high school days. Though, it's been quite a few years since we've seen each other."

"Wow." I blink in surprise. "And you just so happened to get stuck in an elevator together?"

She laughs. Outright. "Yeah. What are the odds, huh?"

"It's good to see you." Ty steps forward to give Maria a hug and then turns to face Remy directly. "So?" he asks, but I can't see Remy's face for his re-action. Ty's head is blocking my view.

"Thanks, man," Ty says quietly and proceeds to shove something into his pocket.

What the hell?

"What is that?" I ask him, and he just grins and shakes his head.

"I'll show you in a bit."

I tilt my head to the side, curious as hell, but Ty just wraps his arm around my shoulders and pulls me close to his chest.

"Okay. Well, then. It was good to see you two. Glad you're both okay. And now, if you don't mind, Rachel and I have something we need to attend to."

"Ty!" I slap at his chest.

"What?"

"Your brother and Maria were just stuck in an elevator for two freaking hours," I comment on an exhausted laugh. "Don't you think we should invite them up for a bit?" I look toward both of them. "Come upstairs so we can get you some water and food and whatever else you need."

"No, it's okay," Rem answers with a gentle smile. "We're going to head out, actually."

We're going to head out. Interesting.

"That's great!" Ty exclaims, and before I know it, the crazy bastard leans down and proceeds to toss me over his shoulder.

"Ty!"

"Bye, guys!" He just laughs, ignoring me completely and turning on his heel toward the stairwell doors.

"I'm so sorry he's a rude idiot!" I call toward Remy and Maria. "And it was really nice meeting you, Maria!"

They both just grin and wave, and as Ty carries me away, I don't miss the way she looks up at Remy. Or the way he looks at her as they laugh and chat about something that I can't hear.

But Ty, on the other hand, well, he's a man on a damn mission, pushing through the stairwell doors and taking the steps two at a time. By the time he reaches our apartment, he has the door unlocked and opened in ten seconds flat.

"What has gotten into you?" I ask, finally on my feet again, but the sexy bastard just grins at me.

"Nothing, doll."

I roll my eyes, but I also laugh. And while Ty slips his shoes off at the doorway, I find myself wondering about what I saw back there. With Remy.

"Was Maria someone important in Remy's life?"

"Huh?" Ty asks and leans down to take off my sandals for me.

"Maria?" I ask. "Who is she to Remy?"

"An old high school girlfriend," he answers, and he all but drags me to our bedroom.

"Do you think there's something between them?"

"I don't know…" He pauses and searches my eyes, but it's not even like he's searching for answers from me. More like, he's searching for answers from himself. "Oh *shit*." He laughs, but then he doesn't say anything else and proceeds to remove my clothes.

"Wait… What did that mean?"

"What did what mean?"

"That look that was just on your face."

"Tomorrow, remind me to tell you about a fortune-teller named Cleo."

"Tomorrow? Why tomorrow?"

"Because we're going to be too busy tonight," he says and tugs at the only article of clothing that's left on my body. "Are you attached to these panties?"

"What?"

"These panties," he says and tugs at them again. But he doesn't give me any time to answer. Instead, he just up and tears them off my body.

Holy fucking shit.

"Ty! What the heck?"

His clothing is gone in record time.

"Rachel, I love you, but I have to be inside you."

Okay, yeah, that's hot.

All I can do is nod my agreement. *Yes, let's do that. We'll reconvene this conversation tomorrow.*

He doesn't waste any time, pulling us both onto the bed and lifting me up so that my thighs are spread across his bare waist and we're face-to-face.

"Fuck yes," he says through a groan as I lower myself onto him. "I needed this. I needed you."

"You feel so good," I whisper and press my mouth to his, threading my fingers into his hair at the back of his neck. "Even though you're completely insane, I love you. So much."

"I love you too," he whispers back, and he moves his hips in a way that makes me feel even fuller. "Fuck, Rachel, I want to do this forever with you."

I moan. "Ditto."

"Then let's do that," he says and leans back to meet my eyes. "Marry me. Be my wife. Let me be your forever."

Time. My heart. Everything just up and stops. Wait... *What?*

"Did you just...?"

"Yes, I did."

"You just proposed to me while your dick is inside me?"

"Uh-huh." He's grinning now, and still, he's moving his hips and making it impossible for me not to moan. "Will you marry me, Rachel Nadine Rose?"

Even though this is the craziest flipping proposal that has probably ever occurred in humanity's existence, I can't find any other answer besides one.

"Yes," I respond without a second thought. "Yes. Yes. Yes."

"Thank fuck." He kisses me hard and buries himself deeper. "I love you."

"I love you too," I say through a half giggle and half whimper. Because again, he's inside me, and it feels *oh-so good*. "But also, you're fucking crazy."

"For you? Always." He thrusts again. "And don't worry, I have a ring."

"You do?"

"Oh yeah," he says with a little smirk and grabs both of my hips to speed up our rhythm. "But you need to come first before you get it."

Ty Winslow is certainly one crazy motherfucker.

But he's *my* crazy motherfucker.

Forever and ever and ever. Till death do us part.

THE END

Love Ty, Rachel, and the rest of the Winslow crew and want to read MORE Winslow Brothers?

Well, we have *great* news!

You can cure your Winslow Brothers' cravings right now and find out what really happened during Remy's bachelor party in this FREE novella!

GOTTA HAVE FATE!

https://dl.bookfunnel.com/1dvqktv6el

It's completely FREE and not-to-be missed!

AND

You can preorder the next book in the *Winslow Brothers Collection* today!

The Winslow brother we've all been waiting for, Remy Winslow, is next.

And holy moly, we can't wait!!!!

The Redo is coming soon!

Completely new to the Winslow Brothers?
Grab *The Bet* to read all about how Jude and Sophie fell madly in love.
Trust us, you won't regret it.

BEEN THERE, DONE THAT TO ALL OF THE ABOVE?
Never fear, we have a list of nearly FORTY other titles to keep you busy for as long as your little reading heart desires! Check them out at our website: ***www.authormaxmonroe.com***

COMPLETELY NEW TO MAX MONROE AND DON'T KNOW WHERE TO START?
Check out our Suggested Reading Order on our website!
www.authormaxmonroe.com/max-monroe-suggested-reading-order

WHAT'S NEXT FROM MAX MONROE?

Stay up-to-date with our characters and our upcoming releases by signing up for our newsletter on our website: *www.authormaxmonroe.com/newsletter!*

You may live to regret much, but we promise it won't be subscribing to our newsletter.

Seriously, we make it fun! Character conversations about royal babies, parenting woes, embarrassing moments, and shitty horoscopes are just the beginning! If you're already signed up, consider sending us a message to tell us how much you love us. We really like that. ;)

Follow us online:

Facebook: www.facebook.com/authormaxmonroe

Reader Group: www.facebook.comgroups/1561640154166388

Twitter: www.twitter.com/authormaxmonroe

Instagram: www.instagram.com/authormaxmonroe

TikTok: vm.tiktok.com/ZMe1jv5kQ

Goodreads: https://goo.gl/8VUIz2

ACKNOWLEDGMENTS

First of all, THANK YOU for reading. That goes for anyone who has bought a copy, read an ARC, helped us beta, edited, or found time in their busy schedule just to make sure we stayed on track. Thank you for supporting us, for talking about our books, and for just being so unbelievably loving and supportive of our characters. You've made this our MOST favorite adventure thus far.

THANK YOU to each other. Max is thanking Monroe. Monroe is thanking Max. Yes. We know. But this is what we do. For every book. *Can't Stop, Won't Stop.*

THANK YOU, Lisa, for being an editing goddess whom we can't live without. We love you forever and ever and ever.

THANK YOU, Stacey, for making the insides of our books always look so pretty! We adore you!

THANK YOU, Peter (aka Banana), for rocking our covers and making Ty Winslow look like the sexy, irresistible, charmer that he is.

THANK YOU, John, for rolling with the punches we're constantly throwing your way!

THANK YOU to every blogger and influencer who has read, reviewed, posted, shared, and supported us. Your enthusiasm, support, and hard work do not go unnoticed. We love youuuuuuuuuuuuu!

THANK YOU to the people who love us—our family. You are our biggest supporters and motivators. We couldn't do this without you. Although, it should be noted, sometimes you guys are hella distracting. But the ones who are the most distracting are under the age of eleven, so we're not going to hold that against you. HA-HA.

THANK YOU to our Awesome ARC-ers. We love and appreciate you guys so much.

THANK YOU to our Camp Love Yourself friends! We love you. You always find a way to make us smile and laugh every single freaking day. You're the best.

As always, all our love.

XOXO,

Max & Monroe